1

THE
VERSIPELLIS
MYSTERIES

A PORTRAIT
OF DEATH

RHEN GARLAND

Published in Great Britain 2021
by Amethyst and Greenstone

Copyright © 2021 by Rhen Garland
Illustrations by Adam Garland

ISBN 978-1-8384604-0-2 (Paperback)
ISBN 978-1-8384604-1-9 (eBook)

First Published 2018
This Second Edition 2021

For my wonderful Mum
who has always supported and encouraged me.
And for my beautiful man... Always.

DRAMATIS PERSONAE

Detective Chief Inspector Elliott Caine	Investigating Officer
Detective Sergeant Abernathy Thorne	Investigating Officer
Constable Thom Greyling	Local Police Officer
Lord Vyvian Lapotaire	Government Minister
Mlle Giselle Du Lac	Opera singer
Lady Bunny Ellerbeck	Socialite
Lord Foster Marmis	Government Minister
Lady Rebecca Marmis	Society Hostess
Sir Hubert Kingston-Folly	Government Minister
Lord Titus Coalford	Government Minister
Mr Weatherly Draycott	Society Nerve Specialist
Lord Bartholomew Scott-Brewer	A Lord
Lady Rowan Scott-Brewer	A Lady
Gregory Hardcastle	The Butler
Mrs Valerie Higginson	The Housekeeper
Colin Greyling	The Head Footman
Valentine Carstairs	A Concerned Nephew
Versipellis	A Secret Agent

With a supporting cast of maids,
valets, footmen, and others.

Marmis Hall

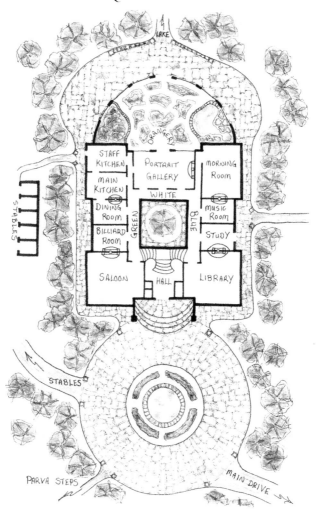

LAKE

STABLES

ORANGERY

STAFF KITCHEN

MAIN KITCHEN

DINING ROOM

BILLIARD ROOM

SALOON

PORTRAIT GALLERY

WHITE

GREEN

BLUE

HALL

MORNING ROOM

MUSIC ROOM

STUDY

LIBRARY

STABLES

PARVA STEPS

MAIN DRIVE

The horse drawn hansom cab slowly made its way along the city crescent, the cab's curtained windows the passenger's only protection from the worst of the New York weather. The fog's oily thickness dulling all sound of the vehicle's traces as its icy fingers plucked at the exposed neck of the shivering cabby.

There was a sharp thump from inside the cab as the fare indicated their desire to stop. The cab slowed to a halt and a dark figure wrapped in an Ulster, and carrying a Gladstone bag alighted and paid the driver. As the cabby touched his hat and left, their fare paused to look up at the small, well-lit airship passing overhead, the fog muffling the amplified message about the efficacious properties of Wolverstone's Miracle Liver Pills. The figure pulled their black felt hat down over their eyes and turned their attention to one house in particular before quietly making their way down the narrow alley that ran to the back of the building; there were many things they had to arrange for the evening ahead, it simply wouldn't do to have the lady of the house know they were there just yet!

Within the house, and unaware of the approaching figure, Carrie Lynn Cater sat at her desk and finished her tallies. She finally closed the household accounts book and pushed it back into its nook on the writing desk with a contented sigh. Everything had been accounted for, including that dratted butcher's bill. Father would be pleased indeed.

She glanced at the clock on the mantle; ten past seven.

Heavens, she was late! Carrie Lynn moved swiftly to the windows in the sitting room and pushed aside the heavy curtains; glancing out into the private crescent beyond, she could see no sign of her guest. She twitched the curtains back into position and moved through the rest of the large brownstone, methodically checking all the windows and doors, ensuring all was locked and safe.

As she shuttered the windows and pulled the heavy red drapes in the dining room, she thought about the evening ahead. Was everything ready? Her father would be spending his evening dealing with yet another urgent business meeting to deal with a problem that had materialised earlier in the day. Despite her pleadings he had left without dinner; instead, he had promised to have a late supper at his club. The cook was visiting family, and their manservant, Clay, and both the maids had been given the evening off, so she and her guest should have enough privacy.

Carrie Lynn paused as the peal of the front doorbell broke the silence. Glancing at the ornate little clock on the mantelpiece she frowned: quarter past seven. If her guest had arrived, they were indeed early; half past seven was the agreed time.

Pausing to check her appearance in the hallway mirror, she studied the reflection that gazed back: smooth chestnut-brown hair, neatly pinned; wide hazel eyes set in a still-young but slightly worried face; a slender figure modestly covered with a simple yet becoming blue evening gown unadorned with the usual trappings.

Yes, her appearance was quite acceptable, except for one little detail. Carrie Lynn carefully pinched her pale cheeks and looked critically at the resulting light blush. Yes, now she would do. She walked down the thickly carpeted hall, and pulling back the catch, opened one of the double doors, a tentative smile of welcome on her face.

house again, even for a private meeting. Indeed, if her father or Clay had been there, or even if her guest had been on time, she would have had someone to help her deal with this new and worrying situation. As it was, it fell to her to resolve the dilemma she found herself in.

Carrie Lynn's curiosity and determination won over her fear, but she could feel her heart pounding in her throat as she crept down the hallway towards the closed door. With trembling hands she reached towards the kitchen door and slowly pushed it ajar.

A high-pitched mewling cry suddenly pierced the silence of the old house. Carrie Lynn froze: that was no child! As she stood paralysed in horror, a heavy force struck the other side of the kitchen door, throwing her off her feet as it smashed open. As she fell backwards, the back of her head struck the handle of the door to the under-stairs cupboard with a sickening thud. Carrie Lynn tried to get to her feet but the effort made her head swim, and her vision faded as she sank into unconsciousness.

A few moments later, a shadowy figure appeared from the kitchen and advanced towards her. It stood over Carrie Lynn's unmoving body, watching with interest as the blood from her head wound pooled around her still form. Walking to the front door and ensuring it was locked, the intruder began to search each room in the house; pulling out drawers, opening cupboards and ripping upholstery, before returning empty-handed to the entry hall. With a snarl of anger they smashing a gloved hand into the ornate mirror. As sparkling shards of glass rained down on the unconscious Carrie Lynn, the attacker's face split into a grotesque smile; they started to giggle as they slowly walked towards her and began to remove their gloves.

○

11:10pm

Warrick Clay made his way back to his master's brownstone in a state of jubilation. Not only had he beaten Big Henry at poker and won a tidy sum, but he'd also spent the better part of the evening with his beautiful wife, Violet, and shared a fine dinner with her at The Fandango Club. Yes indeed, a wonderful evening.

Violet had returned to the small house they shared with their little girl and Violet's elderly mother. Warrick had promised to go to the Cater house to see to his duties, then return home so that he and his wife would have the rest of the evening to themselves. He hadn't stayed out too late, and he hadn't got so drunk that he didn't know where he was heading or what he was doing.

A tall, well-proportioned man in his mid-thirties, Warrick Obadiah Clay had been born a slave, and as a child had been gifted to the Cater family in lieu of a gambling debt. It had been a double-edged payment; the man who owned him knew old Quincy Cater disapproved of slavery, but also knew he would accept the offer in order to give the boy his freedom. That meant he wouldn't have to waste any money paying off his debt.

Warrick Clay had been barely nine years old when he arrived at the Cater family home from his old master's plantation in Georgia. As slavery had been abolished in the state of New York many years earlier, Quincy Cater's acceptance of the boy as payment had granted Warrick his freedom, but Cater had also offered him paid work in the house, and so Warrick had been taken on as a boot boy. Now, almost thirty years later, he was the Cater family butler.

Humming under his breath, and looking forward to spending some more quality time with his wife, Warrick picked his way through the thick yellow fog that billowed down the crescent where his master's house was situated. He approached the front of the well-tended brownstone and was about to walk down the narrow alleyway that led to the servants' entrance when he noticed the front door standing ajar.

He stopped. Miss Carrie Lynn was very keen on locking up the house, especially if her father and the servants were out. A feeling of foreboding slithered up Warrick's spine as he stared at the doorway. He walked to the end of the crescent, stood under one of the gaslights, and placing his fingers in his mouth, let out a piercing whistle. From the next block came an answering whistle, and Police Officer O'Malley made his way down the foggy street towards the worried manservant.

"Clay," O'Malley said, with a quizzical expression. "You look worried, man. What's wrong?"

Warrick nodded at the officer, turned and pointed at the open front door. "You know how Miss Cater is about locking up the house, her father being who he is."

O'Malley nodded. "Aye." He sniffed the air around Warrick. "But then I'm also knowin' what you're like, my friend. How much have you had?"

Warrick glared at the policeman and moving close, he snapped, "Not enough to fuddle me so bad that I can't see trouble when it's looking me in the face!"

O'Malley put his hands up. "All right, man, all right. Let's go and check on the lady."

The two men started to walk towards the Cater house, and O'Malley cleared his throat. "Out of interest, how did you do tonight?"

Warrick darted a sharp look at the policeman and

decided honesty would be the best policy. "I took Big Henry for two hundred!"

O'Malley whistled. "Well now! I take it you're sensible enough not to go back there any time soon. That really would be bad for your health, if you take my meanin'!"

Warrick stopped by the ornate wrought-iron gate and pointed towards the front door. "That's how I found it."

Officer O'Malley looked at the open door and nodded slowly, his eyes raking over the house, taking in the unbroken windows and the lack of damage to the front door. He addressed Warrick without taking his eyes from the house. "Well now, I think the two of us can go in, but you'd better stay behind me. And you can be the one to apologise to the good lady if we're wrong, and scare her to death, eh?"

As he spoke, O'Malley reached into his belt and removed his heavy wooden nightstick. Warrick looked at the weapon, then reaching into his pocket, he pulled out the brass knuckle duster he always carried; as a free black man in New York, it made sense to keep something in reserve. His knuckles cracked unpleasantly as he gripped it tightly.

The two men approached the front of the brownstone and slowly mounted the steps. As O'Malley was about to step through the door, a raw, visceral scream suddenly erupted from the house and ripped through the chill New York night, making the hairs on the back of the men's necks stand up.

O'Malley's face turned pale. "Jesus Christ!" His hands trembled as he shoved his whistle between his lips. Three piercing blasts cut through the air, almost as loud as the appalling sound that had just issued from the brownstone. O'Malley took a deep breath and leapt through the doorway brandishing his nightstick. Warrick followed and the two men entered the gaslit hallway.

The first door on their right was open. The red-wallpapered sitting room, with its stiff-backed chairs, aspidistras and heavy dark green jardinières flanking the fireplace, was empty but in total disarray; broken ceramics, shredded paperwork, and earth from the smashed aspidistra planters lay scattered around the once neat room, while the remains of a box of chocolates were perched incongruously on the side of an overturned and ripped armchair. O'Malley looked cautiously up to the landing but could see no movement. As he turned away from the stairs, he caught sight of a wet patch on the handrail. He reached out and touched the patch with his finger; it came away red. The flickering gaslight caught what appeared to be several similar patches further up the rail. As he walked past the stairs, he saw the outlines of damp footprints on the richly carpeted floor, coming from the kitchen and continuing up the stairs.

O'Malley narrowed his eyes. Moving slowly down the hallway, he felt a sudden change in the carpet beneath his feet. Bending, he dug his forefinger into the stained carpet pile; it was sodden with blood. He turned and showed his hand to Warrick. The muscles of his jaw clenched in Warrick's dark, set face as O'Malley gestured towards the ruins of the kitchen door.

There was total silence as the two men took in the wrecked door at the end of the hall. The massive oak door hung within a heavily reinforced frame, the ruins of which now hung in splintered strips on either side of the doorway. The men could only guess at the hideous amount of force required to nearly rip such a door from its hinges. As they gazed at the damaged frame they both caught a sudden movement, a shadow of feet moving beyond the broken door.

O'Malley mouthed, "Ready?"

Warrick nodded.

O'Malley squared his shoulders, and gripping his night-stick, he strode towards the door. Warrick, squeezing his knuckle duster-clad fist, was just behind him. As they reached the door, O'Malley took a deep breath. With a sudden burst of force he shouldered the remains of the door and shouted, "Police! Don't nobody move!"

The door tilted on its one good hinge, then fell with an almighty crash as the two men rushed into the room and stopped dead.

Officer Joseph O'Malley, pride of the NYPD force for over twenty-five years, turned to the wall and retched.

Warrick gazed in horror at what had once been the domain of the family cook, Mrs Havers. No amount of scrubbing would ever cleanse the kitchen of the horror and death that now permeated it. That atmosphere would linger in the entire house long after the master closed it down.

Warrick passed his hand over his face, trying not to gag as he took in the gore-spattered room. Bloodied knives and other tools lay on the floor next to the torn, stained blue dress that his mistress had been wearing when he left the house. On the far side of the room, the wide-open back door led out into the foggy New York night.

O'Malley straightened up, gazing in disbelief at the mess and ruin. "Clay," he whispered. "All the blood...she's got to be here. Where is she?"

In the sudden, dead silence of the cold white room, the little brass alarm clock shrilled from its place above the gas stove. O'Malley jumped and turned to Warrick. The butler looked at the little clock. "Mrs Havers uses it to time the—"

The two men looked at each other.

O'Malley reached out an imploring hand. "Don't open it, Clay. For the love of God, man, don't!"

Ignoring O'Malley, and with a feeling of sick certainty churning in his stomach, Warrick made his way across the kitchen, taking care not to tread on the bloody streaks and puddles that dotted the black and white tiled floor. As he approached the stove he smelt burning, and gagged. Closing his eyes, he took a deep breath through his mouth, willing himself not to be sick as he turned off the gas and picked up the oven gloves.

He opened the oven door and, reaching in, removed one of several large pie dishes placed inside. As he turned, holding the dish, both Warrick and O'Malley realised what had happened to Carrie Lynn's beautiful hands.

By the time the officers on patrol in the surrounding area finally responded to Officer O'Malley's alarm, he had begun to vomit blood.

○

Constantinople
Thursday 12th February 1891

The tall, strongly built figure stood over the corpse of their most recent victim and cast a cynical eye over the remains. The body looked so much smaller in death than the person had in life, but their killer knew that people always looked small without their souls.

The murderer paused, surveying the scene of the crime; a narrow alleyway ending at a small door of plain design, far enough off the beaten track to ensure privacy for the next step.

Without effort, they lifted their victim and went through the door, closing and barring it behind them. Beyond the door lay a tiny courtyard, leading to three small rooms and the stairs to the second floor.

They would miss this place. It had served them well for many years, but now it was time to bring their carefully crafted plans to fruition. Entering the left-hand room, the figure paused in front of a large, ornate iron-bound chest, covered with carvings of Ouroboros; snakes eating their own tails…the symbol of eternity. Lifting the lid with one powerful arm, the figure carefully placed the corpse into the lead-lined cavity. Taking a deep breath, the killer caressed the dead face: stroking the curve of the jaw, the shape of the nose and ears, smoothing the hair…

Then the killer rose, and began to smooth their own face in the same manner. Slowly, almost imperceptibly, their face was replaced by that of their victim.

The killer groaned as their body adjusted to the height and weight of the corpse in the chest, their spine cracking and shortening as they changed to resemble the object of their many months of study.

The transformation complete, the figure stood in the centre of the little room. Their clothes, now far too big for their new form, slipped to the floor as they looked in the polished brass mirror to judge their final appearance. An exact replica of the shell in the chest looked back. The physical change was always swift, but the memories of their victim would take a little longer to appear in their mind.

They were now perfectly placed for their plans to succeed!

Very little could stop them now—except, perhaps, *him*!

South-West England
8:10pm, Friday 15th September, 1899

The shabbily dressed man walked along the moonlit lane. The chill fog that rose through the trees made a mockery of his cheap overcoat, but he ignored the discomfort. Not far to go now—but perhaps further than he had ever been.

Shivering in the cold night air, he considered that perhaps he should have accepted the kind offer of money to pay for his airship fair to Benchester...but he couldn't bring himself to accept charity, even under such circumstances.

A dark shape loomed out of the shadows on his left; he slowed as he approached the massive wrought-iron gates, which barred the entrance to Marmis Hall.

Ornate leaves, vines, and fauna twined black metallic pathways between the intricately carved gateposts. In the warmth of a sunlit day the patterns were beautiful, artistic and reassuring, but now, in the chill moonlight, they appeared almost nightmarish, the cold, twisted metal accentuating the leers on the faces of the satyrs and nymphs as they hunted their prey, forever suspended between this world and the next.

As he stared at the suddenly unfamiliar gateway he felt a momentary qualm. Did the family know? Were they aware?

He slid his right hand into his breast pocket and fingered the contents. Gaining strength from what was within, he walked towards the gate, and reached out with a calloused and trembling hand to trace the patterns of the trailing vines. He gazed past the opulent metalwork to the small gothic gatehouse with its crenulated lines. Beyond, the tree-lined driveway disappeared into an inky blackness which even the bright moonlight could not penetrate.

At the heart of that darkness was his destination. Marmis Hall was just out of view, built into a dip on the other side of the trees, but he remembered exactly how it looked. A massive white granite pile in the most cheerfully vulgar style of the Gothic revival, Marmis Hall, in its current form, had been the ancestral home of the Marmis family for nearly one hundred and fifty years, and she was a testimony to the eccentric English family that had built her and survived with her. Built on the foundations of the previous family pile, which had dated back to William the Conqueror and which had been romantically ruined by the back-handed lightning bolt of some humourless deity, she had been designed by an ancestor with a liking for the Gothic tales so popular in the mid-eighteenth century.

She had supported the family through wars, scandals and intrigue as an almost omniscient member of the clan. Her four towers, glass-roofed Great Hall and three-storey orangery, complete with waterfall and pond, had nearly bankrupted the eighth Lord Marmis, whose financial standing was saved only by the money his new wife brought to the family coffers. Luckily for the eighth Lord, his marriage was not only a business proposition but a love match, as his new bride shared not only his dedication to the family estate and good works, but also his somewhat questionable taste in literature.

After his death, she had designed the enormous stained-glass panels set in the gallery as a memorial to her husband. The fact that she then left the hall to spend her last few years living in a palazzo on the banks of Lake Garda was not lost on their heirs.

A smile touched the man's worn face as he remembered the last time he had seen the stained glass in the gallery. It had been only two years ago, but those two years seemed as several lifetimes. He was about to try the gate when he heard the sound of horses approaching. Moving quickly, he pushed through the bracken that grew around the gateposts and crouched in the shallow ditch that ran along the wooded lane.

A smart carriage drew up pulled by two glossy black mares, their polished harness fixings glinting in the cold moonlight. The carriage door was almost totally covered by a crest bearing a stylised, gilded G. The driver was heavily muffled against the damp weather, while the occupants were hidden behind drawn blinds. The driver brought the horses to a halt, and stepping down, he approached the gate and tugged at the bell pull. The familiar tone of the bells caused the shabby man's eyes to sting. He squeezed his eyes shut as he listened to the sound he had not heard for so long.

As the echo of the bells faded an old man's scratchy voice, as familiar as the bells, called out from behind the gates.

"Yes? State your business here."

The shabby man opened his eyes and peered out from the undergrowth. The driver was talking to a dim figure on the other side of the gate. The two men spoke quietly through the bars for a few moments, then the driver climbed back up to his seat as the gatekeeper undid the bolts and swung the huge, counterweighted gates open on their well-oiled hinges. The ornate carriage swept in, moving past the gatekeeper and up the lengthy white gravel driveway.

As the carriage was swallowed by the trees, the shabby

man climbed painfully out of the damp bracken and approached the aged gatekeeper.

The old man turned at the sound of steps on the gravel behind him. "What do you want?" he asked gruffly, the sudden appearance of a man on foot taking him by surprise.

The shabby man stopped a few feet away from him. "Don't you remember me, Morris?" The voice was low and husky, as though it had not been used for a long time, but it was undeniably the voice of a young man, and a man Morris recognised.

○

8:25pm

On the other side of the gate, the carriage containing the star guest of the weekend was making its way briskly up the half-mile-long, tree-lined drive towards the brightly lit turning circle in front of Marmis Hall. Huge fire pits threw their barbaric orange light across the grand entrance, while the interior of the house joined in the spectacle with a more civilised showing of gas lamps in every room, as Lord and Lady Marmis treated a selection of friends and society to a weekend house party.

The event had been arranged as a stylish soirée for a select group of people with similar tastes, and so far, the weekend had been a success.

Lady Rebecca Marmis stood in the library doorway and breathed a sigh of relief. She felt satisfaction that the party was a success, but also worry for her husband and his work as she watched three tables of guests enjoying spirited pre-dinner games of Bridge and Backgammon.

It was always so difficult, she mused silently, to mix day guests and weekenders. Making sure one had just the right mix of friends, well-connected old families and a light smattering of the new was all part of the game, and winning that game was the only possible outcome for a successful society hostess.

Realising that it was time for her to mingle once more, Lady Marmis moved into the library. As she walked between the green baize-covered tables that had been set out in the large, lavishly decorated room, several men paused in their play to admire her. A graceful woman of thirty, Lady Marmis' mane of jet-black hair was artfully pinned up with a golden comb studded with garnets and topped with a red ostrich plume. Her neck, graced by the Marmis family rubies in a rich gold setting, gleamed like ivory in the gas lights while her rustling, low-cut crimson silk evening gown with matching elbow gloves and fan, was the very height of fashion and a perfect foil for her full-lipped, heavy-lidded beauty. Attractive as she was, however, none of the men tried to catch her eye. Her reputation was that of a devoted wife and mother, in spite of the dress.

Lady Marmis paused by a card table in front of the massive window overlooking the turning circle, and watched with a slight smile as the society nerve specialist Weatherly Draycott nudged his flushed and flustered partner Lady Ellerbeck into a winning overcall, much to the dismay of their competition, Lord and Lady Scott-Brewer.

Yes, a very successful weekend indeed.

The ornate door linking the library with the Great Hall opened quietly as the butler Hardcastle entered. A thickset man of early middle age, Gregory Hardcastle had been their butler for just over two years, all trace of his original accent veneered with deferential, manicured middle-class English.

Lady Marmis turned as he approached her. "Yes, Hardcastle?"

"Excuse me, your ladyship, but you asked to be informed when a certain guest had arrived."

Lady Marmis smiled with genuine pleasure. "Oh yes?"

"That guest has now arrived, my lady. I took the liberty of having Smith escort her to the suite that you requested."

"Thank you, Hardcastle."

Lady Marmis gave the guests a quick glance, her practiced eye hovering for a moment on one of the ladies.

"Will you see to it that everyone has what they need, please?" she murmured. "Perhaps, in the case of Lady Ellerbeck, no more than she has already had. I must go and greet my dear friend."

The manservant bowed from the neck as Lady Marmis swept out of the library. Hardcastle glided to the bar that had been set up in a corner of the library and gave the contents a swift glance. There were enough clean glasses, but was there still enough ice?

Hardcastle lifted the dainty silver and crystal ice pick from the tray and placed it back in its holder on the side of the ice bucket. He checked the contents and nodded in satisfaction: more than enough for the next few hours. He replaced the lid and left the room to continue his duties.

8:30pm

Lord Foster Marmis and his fellow cabinet minister, Sir Hubert Kingston-Folly, stood together in the leather and tobacco-scented study, poring over the pile of documents, maps and scribbled notes scattered across the knee-hole desk facing the French window.

Both young men were considered to be among the guiding lights of their country's government. Exceptionally young for ministers, with a combined age of only seventy, they were highly intelligent, disarmingly charming and very, very dangerous on the floor of the Commons, as several members of the opposition and not a few members of their own party had found to their cost. They had met at prep school and spent their formative years enduring the scholastic torture inflicted on those boys whom Dame Nature had endowed with intellectual gifts but not sporting prowess.

Their tutors and elders had felt that the boys were too clever by half, and that they must therefore be subjected to the most painful of privations in the name of controlling their innate ability to express themselves better than their masters.

In the case of both Lord Foster Marmis and Sir Hubert Kingston-Folly, their tutors had failed spectacularly.

Lord Marmis was the younger of the two, but only by a few months; tall and slim, with dark hair neatly clipped well above his collar and slicked back with pomade, he carried the 'elegant in evening wear' look to perfection. His open, friendly face suggested an easy-going nature, but friends and members of the opposition knew his genial expression would change quickly if someone tried to take advantage of him.

Sir Hubert, or 'Bertie' as he was known within his circle, was physically the opposite of his friend: almost a foot shorter and several pounds heavier. His fluffy blond hair stubbornly disobeyed hair pomade, starting to curl as soon as his comb was returned to the dressing table. His style of evening wear could be politely described as comfortable, and impolitely as scruffy, but only a fool would read his untidy appearance as a sign of an untidy mind.

Sir Hubert Kingston-Folly was, at the tender age of thirty-five, the government's chief advisor on warfare. His remit covered troops, armaments, and the latest training and tactics to ensure the British armed forces remained the greatest on earth, and Sir Hubert was very good at his job.

The comfortable, well-appointed room which the men were using for their meeting had been furnished by a distant ancestor in the late eighteenth century, and had changed very little since. The solid mahogany bookshelves groaned with political tomes, while any blank wall space had been filled with family portraits, landscapes, and unusually, neatly framed children's finger-daubs. In pride of place over the fireplace, hanging in a heavy gilt frame, was a life-size portrait of the eighth Lord Marmis' wife, Lady Marianna. A strong-minded and fearless woman, she had been responsible for many of the works within the hall and not a few good works beyond it. She wore a gown of deepest green, her vibrant young face surrounded by a mass of glowing auburn hair that brought out the deep blue of her sparkling eyes.

Muffled sounds of card play and laughter occasionally passed through the locked door that linked their room with the library. Sir Hubert raised his eyes from the document in his hand and looked at his friend. "I say, old chap, is it safe to do this with all the ballyhoo going on in there?"

Lord Marmis smiled. "Safety in numbers and all that, Bertie, but if you think that's a ballyhoo, just you wait until the main act. When the second half of the weekend starts, we may have to retire to another floor to hear ourselves think, although we may not want to." He paused. "Rebecca has asked Giselle Du Lac to sing for us tomorrow night."

Sir Hubert's jaw dropped. "How the deuce did you manage to get Giselle to sing at a house party?" he blurted out. Realising that what he said could be taken as a slight, he coughed. "I mean to say, Giselle!"

Lord Marmis grinned at his friend's faux pas and

straightened up. Walking over to the fire crackling and snapping in the green marble fireplace, he sank into the chestnut leather wing-back chair placed in front of it, and picked up his glass of whisky. He gestured to the chair's twin on the other side of the fire. Sir Hubert walked towards the proffered armchair and the glass of whisky on the table next to it, tripped over his open Gladstone bag and landed with unbecoming speed in a sprawl across the chair. Straightening himself with a faintly embarrassed expression, he settled into the wing-back and coddled his glass of whisky and water between his hands.

Lord Marmis smiled. "In answer to your question, Bertie, Rebecca and Giselle knew each other in finishing school. They kept in touch, just like us." Lord Marmis grinned at his friend over the top of his glass. "Giselle sang at our wedding eight years ago, but you were away with Lord Lapotaire on that business in The Ottoman Empire, remember?" He paused. "Whatever happened to the chap you were after?"

Sir Hubert looked uncomfortable. "Blighter escaped and he stayed escaped," he said shortly. "He got to America and simply disappeared." He shifted in his chair. "Back to business, Foss; how are we going to thrash this deal out? Being honest, I really don't think it's a good idea to have a dozen people a few doors away while we're trying to fix the South African problem. Even with Giselle's voice soaring over us, someone might be curious." He thought for a moment. "What is she singing, by the way?"

Lord Marmis smiled. "Sibelius. Some of his new works, I believe, including one called Souda, Souda...something or other."

Sir Hubert smiled back. "Sometimes, Foss I think you've got the soul of a brick!"

Lord Marmis nodded ruefully. "You wouldn't be the first to say it, Bertie. Now, to business! Our colleagues should be arriving within the next hour or so. They will have tonight to refresh, then our meeting will be tomorrow evening. I think you're right; we should be professional and withdraw, but where?" He gazed thoughtfully into the fireplace, his expressive face flickering in the light as he discarded various options. "There is an empty classroom in the nursery. It's out of the way so no one could 'accidentally' trip over us, and the sweet voice of our resident nightingale shouldn't disturb us. What do you think?"

Sir Hubert looked worried. "Umm, won't Nanny be there?"

Lord Marmis laughed. "Bertie, the nursery covers most of the third floor. Nanny Parker, the boys, and Evie are all in the south wing overlooking the orangery, and the room I'm thinking of is in the north wing overlooking the driveway. Nanny is run ragged looking after our wonderful offspring. Believe me, the orangery could collapse into the wine cellars and Nanny wouldn't hear it over the cacophony in the children's playroom. Yes, it's perfect. I'll tell Hardcastle to see to it."

Lord Marmis put his glass down, walked over to the bell pull and gave it a tug.

A few moments later, the door swung inwards as the butler entered.

"You rang, my lord?" Hardcastle's voice was smooth and low, with just the right amount of deference, but Lord Marmis again felt the inexplicable loathing he always did when he looked at his butler.

"Hardcastle, this room is inadequate for our needs. See to it that the schoolroom on the north side of the nursery is cleaned and readied for our use. It must be done immediately."

Hardcastle bowed his head. "Yes, my lord. Would you like her ladyship to be informed, my lord?"

Lord Marmis looked at his butler coldly. "No, Hardcastle, I shall inform my wife. That is all."

Hardcastle again bowed his head. "Yes, my lord." He silently left the room.

Sir Hubert looked at his friend with concern. "Foss, is there a problem with Hardcastle?"

Lord Marmis was still staring at the door; he turned to look at his friend. "It's nothing I can put my finger on, Bertie, just a feeling of acute dislike." He walked back to his desk and staring at the documents scattered across the leather surface, he sighed. "It's got nothing to do with his ability to give satisfaction. Indeed, he came with very good references – Lord Carter-Browne, Admiral Bellford, and the nephew of Lady Carstairs – but something about him makes me uncomfortable—"

A soft knock sounded at the door. Lord Marmis pulled it open, and his face relaxed into a gentle smile as his wife entered the room.

Sir Hubert jumped to his feet at the presence of a lady, felt dizzy, and sat down again with a bump.

Lady Marmis turned a concerned face to her husband's oldest friend. "My dear Bertie, are you all right?"

Sir Hubert flushed brick red as he struggled to get up from his chair. "Yes indeed, quite all right, I assure you." He managed to get to his feet, remembered at the last minute to put his tumbler down, and approached Lady Marmis with his right hand outstretched. She took his hand in hers and smiled as he gallantly kissed it.

As he released her hand, Lady Marmis turned to her husband. "I'm not interrupting anything important, am I?"

Lord Marmis took his wife's hand and squeezed it. "Not at all, my love. Bertie and I have decided to move our meeting to the spare room in the nursery; I was just about to come and tell you."

Lady Marmis smiled. "How opportune. I came to tell you that Giselle has arrived, and Smith has taken her to the Red Suite."

"Excellent. Are you going to see her now?"

"Yes. It has been quite a while since we saw each other – at least two years – so it will be nice to have a private talk."

"Very well, my darling." He kissed his wife's hand. "At what time will Giselle sing tomorrow?"

Lady Marmis smiled. "She has agreed to a quarter past eight, but given the necessary fifteen minutes polite lateness, I think she will start at half past."

Her husband nodded. "Very well. I've told Hardcastle to ready the spare room for our meeting tomorrow, if our discussion begins at eight o'clock, there should be enough entertainments and noise on this floor to keep everyone occupied. Do you agree, Bertie?"

His friend nodded enthusiastically. "Absolutely, old chap. Um, a complete change of subject and not wishing to be rude and all that, but we are eating this evening, aren't we?"

Lord Marmis turned back to his wife with a grin. "My love, shall we be starving our guests?"

Lady Marmis laughed. "Mrs Higginson assures me that Cook has outdone herself this evening." She turned to Sir Hubert. "A buffet supper for our official guests, my dear Bertie, and a very late private supper for you and your guests." She looked at her husband, one eyebrow raised. "As your guests are arriving later and cannot be seen to mingle."

Lord Marmis squeezed his wife's hand again. "This weekend has taken a lot of planning, my dear, for both of us. But you look a trifle concerned, is something troubling you?"

Lady Marmis frowned slightly; her full lips pursed in an adorable moue that made her husband suddenly wish his old friend were somewhere else. "No, not really."

Lord Marmis' eyebrows met. "You seem uncertain, my love."

His wife heaved an exasperated sigh. "Mr Draycott mixed Lady Ellerbeck a drink, but it was far too strong. The poor little thing is quite unused to alcohol and so she couldn't concentrate on her cards...I told Hardcastle not to serve her any more alcohol."

"Anything else?"

Lady Marmis shook her head, the rubies at her throat flashing in the light from the gas lamps. "No, my dear, nothing that I can think of." She glanced at the grandfather clock, then smiled at Sir Hubert. "Now if you gentlemen will excuse me, I must go and see how my dear friend is settling in." She dimpled at her husband, who gave her hand a final squeeze as he walked her to the door. As he placed his hand on the door handle she turned to him. "When are your other guests arriving?"

"Lord Coalford and Lord Lapotaire should be here within the hour."

Lady Marmis nodded thoughtfully. "Very well, gentlemen, I shall leave you to your meeting."

As she entered the corridor, she turned to face her husband, gripped his lapels with her fine, well-manicured hands, and purred, "And I shall see you later!"

Her husband grinned and looked up and down the blue corridor before kissing his wife on the lips. With an answering smile, Lady Marmis sashayed down the corridor and into the Great Hall.

Lord Marmis re-entered the study with a smile on his face. Sir Hubert was hovering over the paperwork on the desk, his face slightly pink as he turned over page after page of information on the South African situation. "Foss, what were you saying about your butler?"

"How do you mean?"

Sir Hubert threw himself back into his chair and picked up his drink. "It's just...one of the names you mentioned from his references sounded familiar."

Lord Marmis screwed up his face. "Let me see...Lord Carter-Browne, Admiral Bellford, Lady Carstairs's nephew—"

Sir Hubert sat up straight. "That's it! Old Emily Carstairs...that was a dashed bad show; the old girl was quite a shocker in her day. Did you hear of the time she and Lady Valier turned the Grande Hotel Triomphe into a casino, under the nose of the Prefecture of Police? Mind you, he was entertaining a lady guest in the hotel at the time." He grinned. "I doubt he wanted to be interrupted."

Lord Marmis laughed. "Bertie, you gossip like an old woman. But now that you mention it, I do remember the case. Did they ever reach a verdict on her death?"

Sir Hubert nodded. "Suicide: apparently she had been seeing that society chap Draycott for her nerves. She thought there was something wrong, he said she was fine, and the next thing you know the poor old fruit's dead in her bed from an overdose of chloral hydrate and you end up with her butler." He looked up at the ceiling as he swirled his whisky round the tumbler. "As I recall, her nephew was terribly upset about the whole thing. He said his aunt would never have harmed herself, and he was quite insistent about foul play until Draycott's solicitor informed him of our slander and libel laws. It was quite a while ago now; at least two years, because it was just before Frederick...oh gods, Foss, I'm sorry." Sir Hubert winced at the expression of pain on his friend's face. "I'm sorry, old man, I didn't think..."

Lord Marmis shook his head, a pinched expression on his face. "It's all right, Bertie; it was a long time ago. This business tonight with Lord Coalford was bound to bring it all back, anyway." He took a deep breath and steadied himself.

"Yes, it was about two years ago—" He paused and cleared his throat.

Sir Hubert silently cursed his thoughtlessness as his friend composed himself. Lord Marmis turned to face the French window, and tugged at his collar.

"Would you mind if I opened the windows, Bertie? It's a little warm in here," he asked huskily.

Sir Hubert coughed self-consciously. "Whatever makes you comfortable, old thing." He gave a tentative smile and waved his tumbler. "How about a top-up?"

Lord Marmis smiled at his friend, who sat hunched in his chair. "You know where the decanter is, Bertie, and where my glass is. If you don't mind, I think I shall open that window." He pulled back the thick red velvet curtains, and as he did so, came face to face with the shabbily dressed man.

Lord Marmis stared at the broad, tanned face that gazed back at him. His jaw worked convulsively as he gazed in utter disbelief at a man he had thought long dead. He tried to speak, but could only mouth a name.

"Frederick!"

○

8:40pm

Lady Marmis walked along the corridor and into the Great Hall, pausing to give instructions to a footman carrying a tray of dirty glasses to the kitchen. She gathered the folds of her elegant evening gown in her left hand, and carefully mounted the massive oak staircase that dominated the entrance to Marmis Hall.

As she reached the top, Lady Marmis heard the front bell ring. Her right hand resting on the polished oak banister, she paused to watch Hardcastle cross the hall and admit the last two guests of the evening.

○

8:40pm

In the library, things had gone from bad to worse for Lady Ellerbeck. The drink that Mr Draycott had mixed for her had been a teensy bit strong – perhaps having that on top of the sherry had been a little silly – and now she could remember neither her partner's hand nor her own, even though she was looking at it!

She had caught Lady Marmis' remark to Hardcastle even though it had been murmured sotto voce, and was still pink from both alcohol and embarrassment. Her partner Mr Draycott had also heard, and was trying to hide his embarrassment and guilt, since he knew full well that his drinks were fine for the gentlemen but a little too heavy for the ladies.

Lady Bunny Ellerbeck sighed as she looked again at her cards. She couldn't even blame anyone else for her bad hand, as she herself had dealt it. It really was quite pathetic, she thought. Bridge was so fashionable these days, but it was so terribly difficult to remember the rules; her American mother had drilled Russian Whist into her from a young age as a suitable card game for a lady, but because of its similarity to Bridge, she repeatedly mixed the two up...and the alcohol was not helping!

Bunny looked across the table at her partner. Her request for help was clearly written in her large blue eyes, but her partner did not notice.

Mr Weatherly Draycott kept his pale eyes on his own cards and smoothed his sleek dark head with his hand;

unlike Sir Hubert's hair, his did exactly what it was told. A suave, dapper, rather fussy-looking man in his late forties, Weatherly Draycott had been at the pinnacle of his profession for nearly two decades, and was very much in demand for seminars on both sides of the Atlantic. He was seen as highly sympathetic and helpful to those ladies whose nerves were strung like piano wires. Draycott understood this, and had cultivated a charming, encouraging manner which his patients found most calming, and which their husbands found most expensive.

Draycott was still oblivious to his partner's disquiet; his overriding desire was to go to the saloon for a glass of something warming and then outside for a spot of fresh air and a small cigar. Satisfied that the game was proceeding according to his plans, Draycott glanced at his table companions and placed his cards on the table. In his most charming manner, he turned to his partner and in his beautifully modulated voice said, "It looks like I'm dummy. I'm terribly sorry, Lady Ellerbeck, but I'm afraid I must leave you." He produced his most charming smile, encompassing not just his partner, who was looking at him rather as a rabbit looks at a weasel, but also the tight-lipped, rigidly corseted mature blonde on his right, who had taken him for over twelve pounds on the last occasion they had played Bridge.

Lady Rowan Scott-Brewer had a permanent expression of disapproval stamped on her finely drawn and rather bitter features, while her husband, Lord Bartholomew Scott-Brewer, a short, bland, grey little man a good fifteen years older than his wife, blinked quietly behind his monocle as he split his myopic gaze between his cards, his wife, and Draycott.

Lord Scott-Brewer, though insipid in appearance, was known in most of the grand houses in the county for his moonlight flits into the servants' quarters. Indeed, his reputation was such that Mrs Higginson, the Marmis family's housekeeper, had been notified by Lord Scott-Brewer's own housekeeper, and was ready to lock the connecting door to the servants' quarters at midnight on the dot. Any requests for below-stairs assistance after that time would go through Mrs Higginson, with a chaperone on call.

Draycott again smoothed his gleaming hair. He knew the Scott-Brewers were snobbish enough to resent Lady Ellerbeck's genealogy. Her father's family were highly titled with no money, while her mother's clan were untitled but brought a great deal of trade wealth from New World timber and fur...amongst other things. Draycott therefore took great delight in addressing Lady Ellerbeck by her full, higher-ranking title.

"Lady Ellerbeck, please excuse me. Lady Scott-Brewer, Lord Scott-Brewer, I shall leave you in the capable hands of my partner, in the firm belief that she will, in the words of our American cousins, wipe the floor with you."

As Lord Scott-Brewer's monocle fell out, Draycott smiled at Lady Ellerbeck and left her to her fate as declarer. Smiling serenely at the distaste on Lady Scott-Brewers' face, and congratulating himself on a job well done, Draycott walked out of the library, across the Great Hall, and into the saloon.

○

8:40pm

Hardcastle heard the peal of the front-door bell as he was on his way from his master's study to the kitchen. He consulted his pocket watch and frowned; he hadn't been informed of any more guests. He turned and walked into the Great Hall. As he crossed the highly polished parquet floor, he caught a flash of crimson as his mistress made her way upstairs.

Before reaching the door, Hardcastle paused to adjust his attire. Satisfied that his appearance was suitable, he reached for the door as the bell rang again. He pulled the door open and glared down his nose at the two men on the doorstep. "Yes?" he enquired, in his most officious tone.

The younger of the two swept sharp, intelligent brown eyes over him and addressed him in a dismissive, leisurely drawl. "Lord Lapotaire and Lord Coalford: we have been invited by Lord Marmis. My man has our luggage; see to it."

Hardcastle's eyes flashed but he bowed his head as the men entered. He ran through the guest list in his mind; there had been no mention of either man. Hardcastle knew who they were, of course, but he should have been informed of their invitation. Irritated by this slight, the stony-faced butler closed the door and turned to relieve the guests of their coats. Before he could open his mouth, Lord Coalford removed his black silk topper and snapped in a thin, reedy voice, "We do not have time to observe the customary pleasantries; take us to his lordship immediately."

His irritation rapidly becoming anger, Hardcastle again bowed his head and led the two men towards the blue corridor. He noted that Lord Lapotaire, the younger of the two men, had followed behind Lord Coalford. Hardcastle decided that what he had heard of this languid young popinjay's political status was exaggerated. He was nothing to worry about, a mere second fiddle to the more experienced older man.

Hardcastle halted at the study door and knocked. As he waited, the door was flung open by a pale Sir Hubert, who moved to block Hardcastle's view into the room and barked, "What?"

Hardcastle jumped in spite of himself; he was not used to being shouted at by Sir Hubert. He gathered himself and murmured, "Lord Coalford and Lord Lapotaire, for Lord Marmis, sir."

Sir Hubert glared at Hardcastle. "I didn't think they'd be for me!" he snapped. He looked past the butler and nodded graciously, "My lords, do please come in." He moved aside for Lord Coalford and Lord Lapotaire to enter. As he did so, Hardcastle caught sight of Lord Marmis standing with his back to the fire, and another man sitting with his back to the door. He fumed to himself; another guest he had not been informed of, and this one hadn't even arrived by the front door!

Once the two lords had entered, Sir Hubert again blocked the door. "Thank you, Hardcastle. See to their lordships' luggage. That will be all." And he slammed the door in the butler's face.

○

8:45pm

As her partner left, Bunny experienced an attack of fuzzy panic which brought both irritation and sudden sobriety. Seriously miffed with Mr Draycott for abandoning her to her fate at the hands of the awful Scott-Brewers, she determined to beat them, plead a sick headache and take herself off to bed. Perhaps not quite the done thing when one has been invited to a weekend party, but Bunny realised that she had lost her temper not just with Mr Draycott and the Scott-Brewers, but also with herself.

Why on earth had she accepted the invite? What had she been thinking? Two whole days stuck with at least two of the sort of people Mama and Papa had warned her about: those who looked down on people who had made their fortune and not inherited it. Even though her father's family had a very grand and impressive title, her mother's low birth was enough to condemn her in their eyes.

Bunny fumed; sitting at the table with two of the vilest, most insulting brutes on the guest list, she longed to tell them that they had only been invited to fill a last-minute gap. But that would never do; her family had suffered far, far worse than this and survived. For Bunny, it was a matter of pride.

Suddenly both sober and determined, Bunny started to lay out her cards.

○

8:45pm

Still seething, his anger twisting in his gut like a knife, Hardcastle marched down the blue corridor. As he passed the music room he looked in and saw the housemaid, Florence Smith, tidying a vase of flowers that one of the clumsier guests had knocked over earlier.

A predatory expression crossed the butler's face and he walked quietly into the room. Florence, her back to him, continued with her duties, carefully placing the hothouse blooms back in the exquisite hand-blown glass vase. As he crept towards the maid, Hardcastle felt that he was back in control. He grabbed Florence by the wrist, swung her round to face him and gripped her throat, but his grin of anticipation faded as he felt the sharp point of the flower scissors through the soft material of his trousers.

The pinched little face in front of him looked up with an almost quizzical expression in the large brown eyes, and Florence's soft, clear voice piped up, "That's the thing about glass vases, Mr Hardcastle; you get a lovely shine on them, almost like a mirror. Did you want anything else?"

He let go of her and stepped backwards, and in a low, hoarse voice he muttered, "Two extra guests have arrived. Go and help with their bags."

Florence rubbed her neck as she moved away from him. "Yes, Mr Hardcastle."

Hardcastle put his hand on the front of his trousers to check nothing had been damaged, while the housemaid stared at him, expressionless. Then he remembered Lord Marmis' order about the nursery. "And tell the Spence boys to tidy the empty schoolroom in the nursery for his lordship. Go!"

"Yes, Mr Hardcastle." Putting the scissors ostentatiously into her apron pocket, Florence walked out of the room.

Avoiding the Great Hall, she instead followed the blue corridor around the central courtyard garden and into the white corridor that ran almost the full length of the south side of the house, encompassing the three entrances to the portrait gallery on one side and the large arched windows and doorway to the courtyard garden on the other. At the far end of the white corridor was a narrow passage leading to the kitchens and the servants' quarters. Florence dodged down this little alley and entered the main kitchen which was full of noise, smells and movement as the kitchen staff prepared the exquisite buffet supper that had taken Lady Marmis, Mrs Higginson and Cook weeks to plan.

As she entered the room, Florence saw David and Harry Spence, two of the younger footmen, sitting by the small pot-bellied stove. She approached them and said quietly, "Hardcastle gave me a message."

David looked at the weals on her neck. "It looks like he did."

Florence rubbed her neck self-consciously. "He wants you to tidy up the empty schoolroom in the nursery; he wants it done now."

The lads looked at each other, then back to the little fire burning cosily in its cast-iron grate. "Oh well," David said philosophically, "we can get it done and get back before the fire burns down too much."

Harry nodded. "Aye, let's get it over with."

They eased themselves out of their chairs and crossed the room to the servants' spiral staircase, neatly hidden behind thick, heavy orange curtains.

As the two footmen disappeared upstairs Mrs Higginson, the housekeeper, approached Florence. "What happened?" She gently placed her hands on Florence's shoulders and turned her to the light, peering at the marks. The housekeeper's usually gentle face was grim. "Did Hardcastle do this?"

Florence didn't answer.

Mrs Higginson gave an exasperated sigh. "I can't do anything if you don't tell me."

Florence's lip trembled suddenly, and she gave an almost imperceptible nod as she whispered, "It's not the worst he's done."

Mrs Higginson's face changed and she wrapped her arms around the young housemaid. "I will talk with his lordship tonight. This will be Hardcastle's last night in Marmis Hall, Smith, I promise."

○

8:50pm

William Case, the head groom at Marmis Hall, climbed into the driver's seat of Lord Coalford's carriage. He was about to take it round to the stables when a white-blond head suddenly appeared through the hatch behind him, and a male voice with a clipped accent inquired, "May you tell me please where the servants' entrance is?"

William nearly fell out of the driver's seat. "Bloody hell, mate, I didn't know there was anyone left in it!" Taking a steadying breath, he indicated the path to the left of the turning circle. "Go around the back; you'll know the kitchen door when you see it. The housekeeper's name is Mrs Higginson."

The blond head nodded. "Thank you."

There was a sudden motion within the vehicle as the young man extricated himself and a valise from the small space where his master and his travelling companion had been sitting. William stared as the man straightened up: he was huge!

"A damn sight taller even than Blacksmith Joe, and he's six foot six!" he was later heard to say to one of the chamber-maids, who promptly passed the information round to all the other single girls on the staff, and more than a few of the married ones too.

The tall young man turned to the groom. "The Lord Coalford, he did not travel with a valet. I shall leave his valise in the carriage, yes?"

"I would," said William. "Hardcastle will probably send Florence to take his gear in." He added bitterly, "Bastard always does choose Flo."

As he said this, Florence ran down the path and stopped by the carriage, breathing heavily.

"You all right, love?" William asked. "You look done in." He caught sight of the marks around her neck and his face darkened. "What's that bastard done to you now?" he growled.

Florence touched the young groom's arm. "Nothing I couldn't handle." She smoothed her uniform. "He tried to sneak up on me in the music room while I was fixing the flowers, but I saw him in the vase and I had these." She reached into her pocket and showed the flower scissors. "So he had to let me go. It's all right, love, I told Mrs Higginson. She said she would talk with the master and this is Hardcastle's last night here. His last night," she whispered, eyes flashing. "Mrs Higginson said so." She gazed at the young groom. "Don't worry about him anymore, love, he'll be gone." Then she noticed the young man sitting on the footplate of the carriage, still holding the valise. "And who might you be?" she asked sharply.

The large young man bowed slightly. "I am Lord Lapotaire's valet, Kimi Vanamoinen."

Florence raised her eyebrows. "Kimmy how much?"

He put the valise down on the gravel. "Va-na-moy-nen. It is a Finnish name."

The housemaid nodded slowly. "So you're Finnish?" She smiled. "I don't even know where that is. You'd better come with me; his high-and-mighty-lordship Hardcastle will have a fit if you're not in and briefed before your lord is shown to his suite."

"Careful, Flo," said William quietly. "If he hears you you'll get in trouble, and if this is his last night he'll want to do some damage before he goes. You know what the old bastard's capable of, better than any of us."

Flo nodded slowly. "Aye, but not as much as Edith."

Vanamoinen took in this allusion to previous events, but said nothing.

Florence looked at him. "Well come on then, chop-chop. Is that valise all your lord brought? Or are you holding on to it for a bet?"

Vanamoinen looked at her with a serious expression. "There is also the trunk." He placed the valise on the gravel, and climbing up to the driver's seat of the carriage, leant over the roof and lifted a large trunk from its resting place. Twisting round, he stepped off the carriage, and without any apparent effort swung the trunk onto his right shoulder. He addressed William, who was staring at him. "Would you please pass me the valise?"

William picked up the valise and nearly fell over when he felt its weight. "What the hell you got in here, then?" he grunted as he passed the bag to Vanamoinen, who handled it as though it were air.

He smiled at William. "That I am not permitted to say."

Florence pursed her lips; she had never been impressed with displays of physical strength. "Finished, are we? Come on then."

She led the valet across the turning circle to the pathway that wrapped itself around the entire hall. William watched them until they disappeared, then walked slowly back to the carriage.

The light from the saloon and dining room lit the smooth, paved path, but Florence and Vanamoinen could not see inside the house. The path, Florence informed him, had been deliberately lowered by Lord Marmis' grandfather so that he would not have to see the servants as they worked around the hall. As they approached a large door, Vanamoinen stopped and lowered the trunk. "Are there any secret passageways?" he asked.

Florence paused, her hand on the door, and looked at him thoughtfully for a moment. "There must be, in an old place like this." She smiled. "But I can't say as I know where they are."

Through the kitchen door, they heard raised voices. "Oh, Christ, what now?" Florence muttered as she pushed the door open.

8:50pm

Hardcastle stomped into the servants' kitchen and flung his silver tray at the scrubbed oak table. "Bloody rude bastard!" he spat.

Mrs Higginson, sitting at the table, glared at him. "I will not tolerate that sort of language in my kitchen, Mr Hardcastle. Kindly compose yourself."

As Hardcastle turned from his surly contemplation of what had just happened in the study and faced the housekeeper, the look of extreme anger on his face changed as he caught sight of the young woman next to her.

The servants' kitchen was almost deserted, as all hands were needed in the main kitchen to deal with the buffet supper that would soon be laid out; almost empty, save for the housekeeper and a young woman who sat at the table, studying a map of the house. Hardcastle cast an appraising and predator eye over her; young, with dark-red hair neatly pinned under a crisp white cap. She had looked up at his entrance, then returned to her quiet contemplation of the drawing.

Mrs Higginson caught the look on Hardcastle's face and placed a protective hand on the young girl's shoulder. "This is Giselle Du Lac's maid, Lilith Tournay. I will not stand for any nonsense, Hardcastle, and neither will this young woman's mistress."

Hardcastle ignored the housekeeper as he eyed the demure young girl in front of him. She was just his sort: quiet and timid, the type who wouldn't cause a fuss afterwards. Not like that little bitch Edith, or Florence.

The young woman looked up straight into Hardcastle's eyes, and his plans for an entertaining evening faltered. The grey eyes that stared into his were determined and cold: the eyes of an experienced fighter.

"How do you do, Monsieur?" she murmured. Her voice was low and musical, with a faint hint of a French accent.

Mrs Higginson turned her back on Hardcastle and addressed Tournay. "The light supper tray you requested for your mistress will be made and sent up shortly. You should be on your way."

Lilith nodded and stood up, her long slim limbs neatly covered by her well-starched black and white uniform. "May I also take the map with me, please?"

Mrs Higginson nodded. "Yes dear, of course you can. Marmis Hall is an old place and quite large; keep the map so you don't get lost. Servants' stairs are here; you can go to any floor this way without being seen, and the stairs will be locked tonight at midnight." As Mrs Higginson said this she propelled the girl towards the archway. Tugging aside the thick curtains, she revealed the narrow spiral staircase which wound its way from the wine cellars two floors below to the nursery on the third floor. She gave the young girl a gentle push. "On your way now, dear."

Lilith smiled at Mrs Higginson and, ignoring Hardcastle, went upstairs.

Mrs Higginson let the curtains fall back into place, then glared at Hardcastle. In an even, icy tone she snapped, "I will no longer tolerate your behaviour towards the female staff, Hardcastle. The girls have had enough, and so have I. Lord Marmis will be made aware of your behaviour tonight."

Hardcastle stared at the housekeeper in disbelief, then spat, "And who do you think he will believe? A cheap tart of a maid, or an old bitch who claims to be married but was never wed? Do you think his lordship would like to know your little secret?" He moved around the table until he loomed over her. "We've all got our little secrets, *Miss*

Higginson. You try to tell him about me, and I will tell him all about you!"

Mrs Higginson looked at Hardcastle in disgust; the man was actually foaming at the mouth. But something piqued her curiosity; and not only his seeming ignorance of a common convention in domestic circles. As Hardcastle had lost his temper, his accent had changed. She couldn't quite place it, but it certainly wasn't the accent of the place he claimed to come from.

Realising that he too had a secret, she smiled grimly. "You do that, Mr Hardcastle. I have nothing to fear from the master, unlike you."

Hardcastle sneered. "I don't know what you're talking about."

Mrs Higginson spoke clearly and slowly, as if talking to a person of limited understanding; the explosive expression on Hardcastle's face showed that he felt this. "Don't give me that, Gregory Hardcastle. Anyone with experience of serving in a fine house knows full well that the housekeeper is always referred to as Mrs: it is a courtesy title. Your ignorance has betrayed you, and your accent has exposed another little secret. So where do you come from, Hardcastle? Since you are certainly not a trained butler nor indeed a man of Kent!"

Her satisfaction in scoring a point over Hardcastle faltered as he lunged at her. She sprang up and moved around the table, putting space between them.

"Don't you come an inch closer! This is your last night in Marmis Hall, and by the time I've finished you won't be able to get a butler's job anywhere in the country! You'll probably end up in a mud hut somewhere in the Dominions!"

Hardcastle gaped at the housekeeper like a gaffed fish, then responded in a voice thick with his unidentified accent. "How dare you presume to speak to me in such a way?" he roared; his face now purple with fury. "Treated like a damn footman by Coalford and Lapotaire...two guests Marmis doesn't even bother to tell me about, threatened by a whore of a maid, slammed out of the study by that bastard Kingston-Folly, and to cap it all..." He banged his fist on the oak table. "To cap it all, that bitch Ellerbeck brings a Kaffir into the house! It's bloody infamous what I have to put up with!"

As Mrs Higginson stared in shocked silence at the apoplectic butler, Florence and Vanamoinen entered the room. Vanamoinen lowered his master's trunk and stood to his full, not inconsiderable height as Florence inquired in a tight voice, "Is everything all right, Mrs Higginson?"

Hardcastle glared at Florence with an expression of utter hatred. Of all his conquests, she was the greatest danger to his position. If only he had shut her up permanently. Backing away from Mrs Higginson, he snapped, "Mind your own bloody business, girl." Then he drew himself up and glared at Vanamoinen. "Who the hell are you, then?"

Vanamoinen looked at Hardcastle without answering, making the butler even more uncomfortable and oddly out of his depth.

"Name yourself or get out of my kitchen," Hardcastle roared, slamming his hands down on the table.

Mrs Higginson's face darkened. "How dare you," she hissed. "This is my kitchen, not yours! And the safety of the maids is my responsibility...I have warned you, Hardcastle, after I speak with Lord Marmis tonight I can guarantee you will be dismissed with no references. Now get out of my sight!"

Hardcastle's face turned an even deeper shade of purple as he realised he had just been dismissed for the fourth time in fifteen minutes. He made a movement towards the house-keeper, and the large young man calmly moved in front of her. Hardcastle knew he was too big to attack singlehanded, and with an impotent snarl of fury he stalked into the main kitchen and then the white corridor. As he strode down the empty hallway, he looked at the doors leading into the portrait gallery. If he was to be thrown out of his living, at least one thing could not go wrong for him tonight; it would appear that he had timed his little appointment well.

○

8:55pm

Vanamoinen looked at the housekeeper. "Are you all right, ma'am?"

Mrs Higginson nodded. "Yes, thank you young man. I am most decidedly better now that he has gone."

Florence looked at her, concerned. "Would you like a cup of tea, Mrs Higginson?"

The housekeeper gave her a slightly shaky smile. "That would be lovely, Smith, thank you."

As Florence bustled over to the sink with the kettle, the door to the main kitchen burst open and the head footman, Colin Greyling, strode into the room with a face like thunder. He stopped when he saw Florence and Vanamoinen and turned to the housekeeper. "Are you all right, Valerie? We heard a row," He looked at her closely, noticing how pale she was. "It sounded like Hardcastle was up to his tricks again. Is everything all right?"

Mrs Higginson smoothed her hair carefully, looked into Colin's dark eyes, and smiled. "I'm quite all right, my dear, though I must tell you that I will be informing his lordship of Hardcastle's behaviour this evening."

Colin looked at Florence, who lifted her chin and glared back at him. He nodded approvingly. "Good for you, girl."

Florence's shoulders relaxed, and she moved to the range

to make tea. A silent conversation seemed to pass between Colin and Mrs Higginson, and as Colin sat down next to her, she turned to the young valet. "Well, we now know there are two more guests for this weekend. Lord Coalford has visited before and we know he doesn't travel with a valet. So you must be in Lord Lapotaire's employ." She looked at him expectantly. "Am I correct?"

He nodded. "Yes, I am Kimi Vanamoinen."

Mrs Higginson gave him a little smile. "I'm so glad you said it. How does one pronounce it again?"

The young man smiled back, displaying even, white teeth. He again enunciated carefully. "Kim-ee Va-na-moy-nen. I am, as you have said, Lord Lapotaire's valet."

Mrs Higginson looked at Colin. "I don't believe that Hardcastle has given instructions for the opening of two more suites…"

Colin shook his head. "He hasn't given the order, but I can deal with that." Mrs Higginson nodded thoughtfully as she turned to Vanamoinen. "Very well. Lord Coalford may have his usual suite, and I think your master shall have the Lilac Suite in the south wing. I trust this will be satisfactory?"

Vanamoinen nodded. "As long as my lord can see trees from his window, it will be suitable."

The housekeeper smiled. "Oh yes, there are beautiful views across Cuckoo Woods and down to the lake."

Florence came over and handed a steaming cup of tea to Mrs Higginson. "There you go: milk and three sugars."

The housekeeper accepted the cup gratefully and answered Florence's look. "Thank you, my dear; I think perhaps we will all feel better now."

Florence flashed a glance at Colin. "Well, if you're sure, I'll show Vanamoinen where his master's suite is, and then I'll see how the Spence boys are getting on with the schoolroom." She gestured to Vanamoinen. "Come on, it's the next floor up."

As Vanamoinen moved towards the trunk, Colin called over, "Do you need any help with that case, lad?"

The young valet swung the large case onto his back and shook his blond head. "No, but thank you." He turned back to the housekeeper. "Have I missed the evening meal?"

Mrs Higginson shook her head. "No, our evening meal will be late; I think we will probably sit down shortly before midnight."

Vanamoinen bowed slightly. "Until then."

Florence held the curtains open for him to pass onto the spiral staircase. She looked at the trunk, then the stairs. "I think I had better go in front, just in case." She waved at the housekeeper and the head footman and let the curtains drop.

After a few moments, Colin approached the stairs and looked up in time to see Vanamoinen pass onto the first floor. He turned back to Mrs Higginson and murmured, "It's all right, love, they've gone."

Mrs Higginson buried her face in her hands and started to weep. Colin swiftly crossed the room and wrapped his arms around her, cradling her gently as he kissed her hair. He whispered, "Everything will be all right, my love, I promise."

○

9:00pm

Weatherly Draycott stood by the large open fireplace in the luxurious saloon and sipped his whisky. Built as a mirror image to the library on the other side of the Great Hall, the saloon was sumptuously and somewhat colourfully appointed with gold wallpaper, purple velvet couches and green leather chairs facing a massive black marble fireplace, while a huge mahogany bar ran almost the full length of the north wall. The floor was covered with an almost obscenely thick black carpet.

The door from the Great Hall opened and Bunny entered. She paused when she saw Draycott, but continued into the room, being careful to leave the door open to indicate no ulterior motive.

He smiled at her and raised his glass. "Would you like another drink, my dear Lady Ellerbeck?"

Bunny shuddered and pulled her wrap around her shoulders. "No thank you, Mr Draycott. One of your concoctions is quite enough to last the entire weekend."

He waved his hand in a polite gesture of acceptance. "As you wish, my dear. I hope you don't mind if I have another?" He walked over to the bar and reached for a clean glass.

"Not at all." She turned to look at a landscape on the wall behind her. "I am quite sure you know all the remedies for the morning after!"

Draycott laughed as he mixed his drink. "If you won't join me in an alcoholic beverage, may I offer you a cordial, or perhaps soda water?"

Bunny hesitated. "An elderflower cordial would be most pleasant, thank you."

Draycott carefully poured out a measure of elderflower and looked over at Bunny, who was staring at the painting with a great deal of interest. As he paused in his bartending duties, he looked at her with a slightly pained expression.

"Lady Ellerbeck, I am sorry about earlier. Please forgive me, I tend to forget that my drinks can be a touch strong."

Bunny turned to look at the suddenly sheepish specialist. "I accept your apology, Mr Draycott," she murmured graciously. "But you will forgive me if, besides cordials, I do not accept any other drinks from you this weekend?"

"Of course."

Draycott smiled, placed a tall glass on the highly polished mahogany bar, and declared, "One elderflower cordial, my dear Lady Ellerbeck, absolutely free of the demon alcohol!"

Bunny laughed, sipped the drink and smiled her approval, taking a seat on a purple velvet chaise in front of the fire. Draycott was feeling in his breast pocket for his cigar case when Bunny called out, "Lady Marmis does not approve of smoking indoors, Mr Draycott." She gave him a sweet smile. "I'm afraid you will have to go outside if you wish to smoke."

Draycott pulled a rueful face. "It was ever thus." He drained his glass with a flourish and placed it on the bar. Reaching into his breast pocket, he removed his cigar case and solemnly checked the contents. "Dear Lady Ellerbeck, I'm afraid I must leave your delightful company, at least until it is time for our much-anticipated supper." He tucked the case back into his pocket, took Bunny's hand, and bowed over it with a smile. As he closed the door behind him, a puzzled frown suddenly appeared on Bunny's face.

Outside the saloon, Draycott rang the bell pull. Moments later, a surly Hardcastle appeared. "You rang, sir?"

The specialist gazed at the ill-tempered the butler with his pale eyes. "Yes, I did. I need to pop out for some fresh air, but I'm not sure when supper starts and I don't want to cause an incident by being late. Would you give me a bit of a warning when it's about to start, hmm?" He smiled to himself as a dark look flashed across the butler's face.

"The buffet supper will be served at half past the hour, sir, and I cannot leave my post."

Mr Draycott consulted his pocket watch. "Half past, eh? That gives me more than enough time." He waved his hand in a gesture that Hardcastle interpreted as a dismissal, then wandered towards the front door and turned back to the butler. "Well?"

Grinding his teeth in utter fury, Hardcastle opened the door and bowed as Draycott passed through, whistling under his breath. As the door closed behind him, none too quietly, Draycott smiled and walked down the front steps, reaching into his pocket for his cigar case. A few moments later, a thin plume of aromatic smoke drifted up as he contemplated the foggy scene

○

9:05pm

Bunny sipped her drink quietly in the saloon, a puzzled frown on her beautiful young face. It had been so familiar... but it was gone again! She sighed and pounded the armrest in exasperation; her memory really was quite dreadful.

She squeezed her eyes shut in an attempt to remember, and in so doing did not see the face that pressed for just a second or two against the saloon window.

○

9:05pm

As Colin and Mrs Higginson sat talking together in the kitchen, the door opened and Sir Hubert entered. Colin jumped to his feet, and the housekeeper stood up more slowly.

"Ah, Mrs Higginson, would you come to the study, please? His lordship would like a word." The two servants looked at each other nervously. "Oh, no, there's nothing wrong: quite the opposite. It's just that he needs you in the, um, study."

"Very well, sir." She looked at Colin, "I will be back to help with the supper in a moment." Colin nodded; his face inscrutable as he watched her leave the room.

Sir Hubert silently escorted Mrs Higginson to the study. While he had been gone, Lord Lapotaire had decamped to the music room and Lord Coalford to his suite. As Sir Hubert opened the door he patted the housekeeper's hand and gestured for her enter without him; this was to be a family-only affair.

Pausing by the now closed door, Sir Hubert turned and walked back down the blue corridor with a thoughtful expression, as he headed towards the doors that led to the music room and the gallery.

○

9:05pm

Lady Marmis walked out of the Red Suite and back down the corridor. It was so nice to see her oldest friend again, after so many years. They had attended the same highly advanced finishing school, they had endured the same French, music, and singing instructors but their lives had taken totally different routes. She was the Chatelaine of Marmis Hall and a mother of three, and her friend Giselle enjoyed an incomparable voice, an exquisite face and a highly scandalous and unconventional private life. She had travelled the known world, singing in such far-flung places as New York, Paris, Berlin, and Constantinople, or whatever they were calling the place this week…Istanbul possibly.

But Lady Marmis had travelled, too; when her husband had taken up a position in the Indian office, they had lived in a distant part of the Empire for two years before her father-in-law, Lord Josua, died and they had returned to take over the Estate.

Lady Marmis examined her feelings. Was she jealous of her friend's free and easy lifestyle? Candidly, she had to admit to herself that she was, just a little.

As she had entered her friend's room and been greeted by an operatic shriek of welcome, the years had disappeared. They had talked a great deal about the old days, and laughed like the schoolgirls they had once been. Not Lady Marmis, but Rebecca, and not Giselle Du Lac, as she was known to her adoring public, but Penelope Lake.

A smile of happiness curved her lips as she descended to the Great Hall. It vanished as she saw Hardcastle, his back towards her, kneeling in the cloakroom, rummaging through the pockets of the guests' outer garments. She frowned. "Hardcastle?"

The butler quickly straightened up from the heap of furs, cloaks and toppers on the floor and assumed an expression of total blankness. "Yes, my lady?"

"Did you receive my husband's instructions with regard to the spare room in the nursery?"

Hardcastle nodded. "Yes, my lady. I instructed the Spence boys to see to the room. It will be ready for his lordship when he needs it, my lady."

"Thank you, Hardcastle." She paused. "Are the last two guests settled in now?"

Hardcastle gritted his teeth. "I believe so, my lady."

"Very well." She paused. "Hardcastle?"

"Yes, my lady?"

"What are you doing?"

"Mr Draycott wished to go outside, my lady, and I'm afraid he closed the door somewhat harder than necessary. The bar that holds the hooks could not quite take the force, my lady."

Lady Marmis looked at the butler sharply; the wall and the bar were quite robust enough to suffer even the most violent of slamming. She was well aware of her husband's feelings towards their butler, she herself had similar qualms but she had no desire to bring things to a head while there were guests in the house. She smiled smoothly. "Ah yes, the well-known brisk manner of the doctor. Even when one becomes a specialist it lingers still. Make sure the bar is dealt with, Hardcastle." She turned away and walked towards the arch that would lead her to the blue corridor and her husband's study.

Hardcastle watched her until she was out of sight, then with a quick glance around him, finished his meticulous search through the guests' pockets. Nothing of much value, just a few coins; no paper money or interesting documents.

As Hardcastle stood up he looked at his pocket watch. Ten past nine now: perfect timing. He closed the ante-room door and silently followed his master's wife. Pausing at the arch, he heard her knock on the study door; as the door opened he peeped round the corner and saw her enter. As the study door closed, Hardcastle seized his chance and ran swiftly down the corridor. At the end he stopped, and listening carefully, assured himself that no one else was about.

Breathing heavily, he walked purposefully towards one of the interior doors on the south side of the house. Checking around him once more, he entered the portrait gallery and closed the door carefully behind him, making sure the latch clicked as he was enveloped by the dim, strangely warm room.

○

9:10pm

Lord and Lady Scott-Brewer sat in the library, partaking of one of their favourite pastimes; namely the character assassination of anyone they perceived as their social inferior. On this occasion it was of course Lady Ellerbeck who bore the brunt of the onslaught, although "that jumped-up opium-pusher Draycott" came a pretty close second.

Lady Scott-Brewer was bemoaning the loss of three pounds and ten shillings to "that wretched American gel", regardless of the fact that Lady Ellerbeck had actually been born in Surrey. While she complained, her husband fiddled with his amethyst cufflinks and looked at the door that led to the Great Hall, trying to work out where the entrance to the servants' quarters might be.

Lady Scott-Brewer, through some sixth sense brought on by many years of dealing with her husband's little peccadilloes, snapped sharply, "None of your nonsense tonight, Barty!"

Lord Scott-Brewer visibly jumped. "My dear Rowan, I don't know what—"

"Don't lie to me, Barty, I know you!"

Her husband, catching the hard gleam in her eye, turned his gaze on the floor. "I'm sorry, my dear, I – I can't explain why—"

"I know why," Lady Scott-Brewer snapped bitterly. "The familial habits of a lifetime!"

She stood up and her corsetry creaked alarmingly as she towered over her thin little husband. He jumped to his feet, looking at her with something approaching terror. "My dear, are you all right?"

Lady Rowan sniffed with displeasure. "I am retiring to our suite."

Lord Scott-Brewer looked flustered. "But my dear, the supper! It would be unpardonable to retire now!"

Lady Scott-Brewer glared at her husband of nearly thirty years with a look which combined dislike, distaste and disgust. Many people in their inner circle would have dismissed it as her usual expression when observing her husband. "I find the offerings of this weekend both dull and unappealing! Why Lady Marmis invited us to endure hideous modern caterwauling is beyond me. Opera at a weekend house party!" Her strident voice made her husband cringe but she ignored him. Indeed, she continued robustly in the same vein. "I will not tolerate the alleged musicality of that person Sibelius, nor the pagan mewling of that modern creature Giselle! Kindly inform anyone who asks that I am retiring for the evening."

With this complete denunciation of the weekend's enter-tainment, Lady Scott-Brewer swept to the door. As she reached the threshold, she turned and again addressed her husband. "And you know how I feel about alcohol, Barty. Not one drop!" With this final thrust, Lady Scott-Brewer and her formidable bust glided from the room.

As her husband sat alone at the green baize table, he was reminded that he and his wife were not been the only people in the library. Two tables of guests had eavesdropped from a distance, and had decided almost as one that it would be seemly to retire to the saloon to await the supper gong.

As the eight lords, ladies, clerical personages, and assorted others rose from their seats and made their way out of the library, they did not look at Lord Scott-Brewer. It would not have done to acknowledge his presence after observing such a public set-to with his wife.

As the day guests disappeared, Lord Scott-Brewer sat in

thought, staring at his short, stubby fingers. After a few moments had passed and all sound of his fellow-guests had faded, he lifted his head. Anyone who knew him would have been shocked at the change. The timid, henpecked little husband had disappeared, replaced by a sly, cunning man.

He got to his feet and walked towards the bar. With a mutinous expression, he picked up a tumbler and poured a generous double from a cut-glass crystal decanter. Replacing the stopper, he lifted the lid of the ice bucket and used the sharp ice pick to tap off some slivers of ice for his drink. He swallowed a large mouthful of whisky, and as he looked down at the large silver tray with its matching ice bucket and glittering ice pick, a thought slithered snakelike into his mind. Putting down his drink, a smile twisted his face as he lifted the ornate, vicious implement and turned it in his hands to catch the light. Perfect.

○

9:10pm

Lady Rebecca Marmis gazed at the shabby young man in front of her. With a trembling hand she reached out to touch her brother-in-law's tanned, battered face, and tears filled her eyes as she saw his expression.

"Dear Frederick," she whispered, "you have come home to us."

○

9:10pm

Hardcastle turned up one of the gas lamps, carefully choosing one a good distance from the door. Then he waited silently, blood pulsing in his ears in the stillness of the portrait gallery.

The huge, rectangular room was nearly empty; most of the larger pieces of furniture had been covered with dust sheets and pushed against the inner walls to keep them dry over winter. The musty smell of disuse made the large room feel even more uninviting.

As Hardcastle stood, he became aware of the snap and hiss of a fire burning merrily behind an ornate wrought-iron fire screen at the far right end of the gallery. A fire he had not ordered, he gritted his teeth; yet another complaint to add to the long list of insults and put-downs he had had to bear over the last two years.

Faces of the Marmis family past and present looked down at Hardcastle from three of the walls, while the fourth was an impressive, ornate creation made of huge panels of stained glass, separating the gallery from the orangery. Hardcastle stood in the midst of one of the most beautiful houses in England and sneered at the opulence and history of the paintings, the house and the family who lived there. Hatred for the people he had been forced to serve in order to achieve his ends swelled within him. As his anger again threatened to overtake him, Hardcastle forced himself to calm down. Not long now, just a little more time. Just one last job to complete and then he could finally return home, with enough money to buy his way into a society that mattered. Soon, oh yes, very soon...

Hardcastle grinned as he considered his future. He stood with his back to the orangery windows, gazing into the flickering fire. So occupied was he with thoughts of revenge and the money that would soon be his that he did not hear the soft slither of the dust cover on the piano, or see the long arm that crept out from beneath it.

As the soft noises behind him suddenly registered, Hardcastle realised that he was not alone. The person he awaited was already there, waiting for him. He turned, the insulting phrases he had practised for days dancing on the tip of his tongue as he smirked at the shadowy figure walking towards him.

His smirk twisted into a sneer as he recognised the dimly lit face before him and realised he had been fobbed off again. "You!" he snarled. "What the hell are you doing here?"

As he glared at his silent contact, Hardcastle suddenly realised that the form before him was naked.

The figure did not respond, but continued to walk towards him. It raised its hand, the fingers gripping something Hardcastle could not quite make out in the room's soft light. His eyes widened in fear at the figure only a few feet before him. He opened his mouth and took a step back as he realised what was held in the clenched fist. It flashed in the firelight as it plunged into the butler's neck.

○

9:20pm

The bloodied figure opened one of the connecting doors between the gallery and the orangery and walked into the beautifully tended indoor garden, pausing by a window to survey the foggy, moonlit gardens beyond.

Turning back to the indoor jungle, the figure approached the large pond and stepped into the cool water, thoroughly rinsing the thick blood from their body as they bathed amongst the waterlilies. Taking great care to make sure their hair was free of any residue, they stepped out and carefully dried their body with a dust sheet from the gallery. Moving quickly, the figure pulled their clothes from under a white-painted wrought-iron table, sneering at its quaintness as they dressed themselves.

The shadowy figure picked up a pouch they had left on the table and removed a small pot. As they unscrewed the lid to remove some of the contents, the air in the orangery filled with the scent of lilies. After a few moments the pot was replaced, and the killer checked the room was clear before returning to the gallery.

High above, in the nursery, a frightened little face turned away from the window. Clutching a much-loved stuffed bear, the child ran back to bed and hid under the covers.

○

9:30pm

Outside the library, Lord Scott-Brewer stopped to decide on the best course of action. The servants' quarters were on the east side of the house, which meant he would have to walk past at least two occupied rooms.

He looked down the blue corridor. The study door was shut, but the door of the music room was ajar. Blast! He had no choice; the only other route passed the dining room, where most of the servants would be setting out the supper, and he didn't want to spoil the surprise. Taking a deep breath, he sneaked past the study, hearing a muffled conversation as he passed the closed door. At least that one had been easy!

Getting past the music room, however, would be more of a challenge. Stealthily he approached the double doors, which had been pushed to, but not quite closed. He tried to look inside, but couldn't see anything but light; the gap was far too small.

As Lord Scott-Brewer hovered outside, he realised he

could hear music. Someone had put on the phonograph: perfect! Gleefully he crept past the door, hunching so that the servants in the dining room could not see him through the courtyard windows.

He paused at the corner, there were so many of them now, all using the little alleyway between the dining room and the white corridor, that he would never get a chance to sneak in.

Lord Scott-Brewer's lower lip pushed out in an ugly parody of a child's sulk as he thought. Servants' quarters were always off the kitchen, so if the kitchen was *there*, and the corridor into the kitchen was *there*, then there must also be a connecting door through *there*. As Lord Scott-Brewer looked at the door to the portrait gallery, he heard a noise rather like something being dragged across the floor. He listened more carefully. Ha! It must have come from the dining room.

Fingering the ice pick in his pocket, he smiled.

9:30pm

As the killer paused to admire their handiwork, a sudden noise came from the door to the white corridor. The figure hurriedly threw a dust sheet over the new piece of art in the middle of the room and turned down the lone gaslight, taking care not to turn it off.

The figure hid behind the door, waiting as it slowly opened and Lord Scott-Brewer entered.

The lecherous old lord didn't pause to wonder why a fire had been lit in a disused room, or why a gaslight was on; all his attention was focused on the possibility of a doorway on the far left-hand side of the room. He was not only oblivious to the dust-sheeted display nearby, but he was also without knowledge of the figure silently following him as he crossed the room.

Lord Scott-Brewer continued his single-minded trek to the east wall of the gallery; so focused on his plans, he was unaware that he had trodden in something unspeakable, and was now leaving rank, bloody footprints on the polished wooden floor.

Reaching into his pocket, Lord Scott-Brewer removed the ice pick and approached a large tapestry of the grail quest that partially hid the connecting door to the kitchens. The figure following him gave a strange little shudder as the foggy moonlight shone through the glass panels of the orangery and the ice pick twinkled in a sudden flash of coloured light.

Lord Scott-Brewer pushed the tapestry to one side and tried the door, it was locked. He knelt with a groan, his knee joints complaining, and lifted the ice pick to apply it to the door lock.

The figure behind him moved with shocking speed. Snatching the ice pick from the startled lord's hand, they grasped him by the chin and stabbed him in the neck.

○

9:30pm

Millie Jenkins carefully lifted the large silver platter, crowned with a beautifully presented and very expensive lobster, and walked through the connecting corridor into the dining room, where several of her fellow servants were laying out the main buffet table.

As she entered the room, Colin turned to look at her. "Have you seen Hardcastle, lass? That bastard should be in charge of this; he should have announced supper five minutes ago!"

Millie shook her head as she positioned the plate on the already heaving table. "No, I haven't seen him." She paused. "Come to think of it, I haven't seen Smith neither; not since we saw what he did to her earlier." An expression of worry crossed her face. "Oh God, he's not gone for her again, has he?"

Colin shook his head. "I wouldn't have thought so. Last I heard she went upstairs to see if the old schoolroom was set up for his lordship." He turned and barked at a footman. "Jones, have you seen Florence Smith?"

The young lad, who had only started at the hall three weeks earlier, jumped and shook his head. "No, sir, I haven't." He stood up from a table of glasses by the fireplace. "But I did see Mr Hardcastle going into the gallery a while ago, sneaky like."

"What do you mean, sneaky like?" Millie asked sharply.

Peter blushed, and his carefully cultivated accent disappeared almost as swiftly as Hardcastle's. "Well, he was lookin' round, checkin' the blue and white corridors before goin' in—"

Colin frowned. "If he was looking and he didn't see you, where exactly were you, lad?"

Peter stammered. "I-I was in the green corridor, just standin' quiet like, lookin' through the windows in the courtyard. He didn't look that way so he didn't see me, but I saw 'im, goin' through the door at the far end."

Colin and Millie looked at each other. "Right," said Colin firmly, "Jones, go to the kitchen and see if you can find Smith. If she isn't there, ask the others if they've seen her." He turned to Millie. "You come with me, lass; I might need you if he's got her."

Millie nodded, her pale face set. "I'll come; God knows I've dealt with this sort of thing before!"

Peter headed down to the kitchen as Colin and Millie made their way to the portrait gallery. As Colin paused before the gallery door, he heard a door open, and saw Lord Marmis, Sir Hubert and Lord Lapotaire coming out of the study. Lord Marmis placed a finger to his lips and beckoned the two servants.

Colin slowed down as he approached Lord Marmis; he had never seen such a look on his master's face before, and hoped he would never have to see it again. Colin bowed and inquired in a low voice, "My lord, is there anything wrong?"

A muscle beneath Lord Marmis' eye twitched as he looked at Colin. The thin sheaf of papers in his hand trembled slightly, but his voice was smooth and controlled.

"Yes, Greyling, something is wrong. Do you know where Hardcastle is?"

Millie, almost hidden behind Colin, winced. Sir Hubert noticed and addressed her gently. "Miss, do you know where he is?"

"My lord," said Colin, "has Mrs Higginson informed you about what happened earlier this evening?"

Lord Marmis looked at the footman. "No, Mrs Higginson has been busy with other things. Perhaps you will enlighten me?"

Millie and Colin exchanged worried looks, then Millie whispered, "My lord, we think Hardcastle is in the portrait gallery. We think he's got one of the maids in there...against her will, my lord."

Lord Marmis face wore an expression of disgust, mingled with another emotion that Colin could not quite define. He realised that they had to wash their hands of Hardcastle, for good. "He's done it before, my lord. Several times. That was what Mrs Higginson was going to tell you tonight. He attacked one of the maids earlier today, and Mrs Higginson informed Hardcastle that she would tell you this evening."

Sir Hubert and Lord Lapotaire both swore under their breath, as Lord Marmis blinked at Colin. "How long has this been going on?"

"My lord, as soon as Hardcastle arrived here the attacks began."

Lord Marmis looked sick. "Why was I not informed?"

Colin looked his master in the eye. "It was a servants' matter, my lord. Once she realised what he was doing, Mrs Higginson put all of us men on watch, keeping an eye out for the girls, and it worked until today. Hardcastle attacked Smith in the music room, but she managed to get away. I need to tell Mrs Higginson that Smith is missing, my lord; is she still in the study?"

Lord Marmis nodded. "Mrs Higginson is in the study with my wife. And my brother."

Colin's dark face lit up as he looked at Lord Marmis. "Master Frederick, my lord? He's...he's home?"

Lord Marmis nodded tiredly. "Please keep your voice down, Greyling. Yes, my brother has come home. Now, you say that you believe Hardcastle to be in the Portrait gallery?"

Colin was silent, watching Lord Lapotaire, who had pulled out a pearl-handled revolver and was quietly checking the bullets. He turned back to look at Lord Marmis. "Yes, sir...I mean, my lord."

"Thank you, Greyling. Please take Jenkins back to the kitchen."

Millie moved round Colin and looked at her master. "No, my lord, I'll not go," she said firmly.

Lord Marmis frowned. "I beg your pardon?"

Millie took a deep breath, not quite believing her nerve. "If Smith is in there, my lord, she'll need me. She won't like to be approached by men." She drew herself up to her full height and looked Lord Marmis in the eye. "I'm coming with you, my lord."

Lord Marmis looked at her with an inscrutable expression. "You have experience of dealing with this, Jenkins?"

She stared back at him. "Too much, my lord."

Lord Marmis closed his eyes and put a hand to his temple, he looked grim. "Very well, but if Smith is not in there with him, you will both leave at once. And you will pay no attention to anything said by us or Hardcastle that does not concern his behaviour with the maids. There is far more to his misconduct than the abuse of young women."

Colin and Millie nodded, bemused, and moved aside as Lord Marmis and Lord Lapotaire approached the gallery door. Sir Hubert fell in behind them, and Colin and Millie brought up the rear.

Lord Marmis wrapped his fingers around the brass doorknob. He turned to look at Sir Hubert and Lord Lapotaire, who nodded as he held up three fingers and muttered. "Three...two...one..."

Lord Marmis threw the full force of his weight against the door, which crashed against the wall.

Every gas lamp in the room burned at full strength as Lord Marmis and the others entered. Lord Marmis and Lord Lapotaire turned around quickly to check that the room was empty. The brilliant gaslights lit up every corner of the gallery, making it very easy to see what was standing in pride of place in the middle of the room.

Lord Marmis paled to the colour of chalk as he stared in utter horror. "Oh my God!"

Millie, still outside and fearing the worst, pushed past Colin and Sir Hubert. A strange feeling of detachment came over her as she gazed at the wooden easel that had been dragged into the centre of the room, and which now supported its revolting exhibit, standing in a spreading, viscous red pool that surrounded it like a moat.

As they took in the appalling display, Colin swallowed hard and looked at his master. "I...I think it's Hardcastle, my lord."

Millie looked at the mortal remains of the man who had ruled the servants of Marmis Hall with utter ruthlessness, causing untold pain to many of the girls and their sweethearts, and could not feel sorrow at his passing. Nor could she feel revulsion at what had been done to him. The only thought in her mind was that she sincerely hoped it had hurt.

Sir Hubert, still standing by the door, looked pale. In his position as War Advisor he was used to seeing photographs from the front, and had seen many corpses through his career, but actually seeing a dead body so hideously dispatched, and in the flesh as it were, was something else entirely. He covered his mouth and blinked rapidly.

Lord Lapotaire walked past Lord Marmis, and with a jaundiced eye and a handkerchief over his mouth and nose, studied the bound remains.

Millie looked away from the revolting thing before her, and saw a crumpled black shape lying against the wall at the far end of the gallery. "There's someone else over there, my lord."

Lord Lapotaire looked up from his study of the knots that bound what remained of Hardcastle's arms and legs, and headed with Lord Marmis to where Millie was pointing. They stared down at a body drenched in blood, but in far better condition than Hardcastle's.

The corpse was a thin little man in evening dress, huddled on his side in a bloody pool against the wall. Avoiding the red soaked material around the man's throat, Lord Marmis carefully turned the body over and looked into a dead face that still bore an expression of shock. A silver ice pick had been left behind, buried deep in the man's neck.

Lord Marmis looked up at Lord Lapotaire. "It's Scott-Brewer! What in God's name was the old fool doing in here?"

Millie spoke in a tight voice. "He was another one who liked to go raiding the servants' quarters at night, my lord. Looks like he got a bit more than he bargained for!" She pointed at the partially hidden door. "That's the old entry between the gallery and the kitchens. It hasn't been used for a long time; it's kept locked."

Shuddering, Lord Marmis moved the body back into its original position. Then, frowning, he examined the old peer's sleeves. He sat back on his heels and looked up at Lord Lapotaire. "How strange: he isn't wearing any cufflinks! What do you make of all this, Lord Lapotaire?"

Lord Lapotaire looked at him, his brown eyes thoughtful, then nodded towards Hardcastle's remains. "Based on the evidence to hand it is my humble opinion that a professional committed both killings; this was certainly done by someone who doesn't mind causing pain. Given the amount of blood, I rather fear that most of the injuries took place while your butler was still very much alive."

Lord Marmis winced. Sir Hubert swallowed hard and leant against the tapestry while Millie stood next to Colin, a faint smile on her lips.

Lord Lapotaire looked at the display on the easel and frowned. "I find it difficult to believe that no one heard anything; if you inflict that level of pain on someone you would expect them to scream. And yet no one heard a thing!" He looked at Lord Marmis. "I think we should get a professional opinion about the possible cause and time of death. Who is the chief coroner in this district?"

Lord Marmis was silent. Sir Hubert looked at his old friend and answered for him in a sombre tone. "Dr Peeves, but he's on holiday in Penzance and it would take him at least a day to return." Sir Hubert's face brightened. "We do, however, have a doctor of sorts here. He's one of the guests: a Mr Weatherly Draycott."

"The nerve specialist?" Lord Lapotaire asked sharply.

"Yes."

Lord Lapotaire nodded. "He'll do. I'll see if I can find him."

"You won't be able to miss him," Sir Hubert assured the lord. "The chap's wearing a purple silk cummerbund, matching Ascot, and enough Macassar oil to sink an ironclad!"

Lord Marmis pushed himself away from the wall and glared at Lord Scott-Brewer's body. "If it had just been Hard-castle we could have dealt with it ourselves, but because of this bloody old fool we will have to inform the police."

Lord Lapotaire looked at Marmis. "Yes, we must – but let's at least find a man we can work with, hmm?"

Sir Hubert looked at him hopefully. "Do you have someone in mind?"

Lord Lapotaire looked amused. "As a matter of fact, I have. I'll need to make a telephone call. You do have a tele-phone in the house, don't you?"

"Yes, we had it installed a few months ago. It's in the booth opposite the cloakroom in the Great Hall."

"Very well, then I shall place a call to Whitehall and ask them to send a certain someone. In the meantime, we should lock this room and prevent anyone else from entering until the police get here." He paused. "We should also inform the staff; they will need to know what is going on. Now, if you will excuse me, I'll go and telephone Whitehall, and then I think we had better inform Lord Coalford."

Lord Marmis winced again, but nodded. Turning to Colin, he murmured, "Take Jenkins back to the kitchen, please, Greyling. Perhaps it would also be a good idea if you informed the other servants of what has occurred, emphasising the need for discretion with the guests."

"Of course, my lord."

Lord Marmis studied the head footman. "Greyling, I know that now is not the best time, but we need to ensure the smooth running of the house. Would you take on the position of butler? Perhaps I should have asked you a long time ago."

Colin closed his eyes briefly, then looked at his master. "Yes, my lord, I will."

Lord Marmis smiled. "Thank you Greyling. Now, in spite of the turn the evening has taken, I would like us to keep as close as we can to the original schedule. Supper was set for half past the hour. Please inform the guests that supper will be at ten o'clock, and escort everyone into the dining room accordingly."

"Of course, my lord."

Lord Lapotaire opened the door and checked the corridor: no one was there. He gestured to the others and they quietly filed out of the gallery. Then Lord Lapotaire had a sudden thought. "Greyling."

The former footman turned. "Yes, my lord?"

"By all means inform everyone of what has happened, but do not tell them about the ice pick. That goes for you too, Jenkins."

Lord Marmis and Sir Hubert looked at him. "What are you thinking?" asked Sir Hubert.

Lord Lapotaire smiled. "Hold back a little piece of information, and the murderer may give themselves away with their knowledge."

Sir Hubert looked sceptical. "You mean the person who did that" – he pointed towards the gallery – "would want others to know of their crime?"

Lord Lapotaire looked Sir Hubert in the eye. "Hardcastle was mutilated and put on display. The person who did that would almost certainly wish to brag about their achievements, one way or another. If you will excuse me."

As Sir Hubert and a by-now thoroughly nauseated Lord Marmis left for the study, Greyling locked the gallery door. He and Millie hurried towards the kitchen as Lord Lapotaire made his way to the Great Hall and entered the little telephone booth. Closing the door tightly behind him, he lifted the receiver and after a few seconds a tinny voice arrived on the other end of the line, he breathed a sigh of relief; excellent, a human operator. He disliked dealing with telephonic automatons, they nearly always got the numbers wrong and this was not the time to be shouting confidential government contact details down an open line. Lord Lapotaire spoke into the telephone.

"Operator? I need to place an emergency call to Whitehall. I'll wait."

○

9:40pm

In the saloon, Bunny was still seated on the plush, rather garish purple chaise, gazing into the fire. In spite of the genial chatter from the day guests who were busily discussing the latest fashions in airship travel and the possible ramifications of such vehicles enabling a journey around the world in substantially less than eighty days, Bunny felt rather discombobulated. She still couldn't place what she had seen, but she somehow knew it was important.

With an exasperated sigh she stood and walked over to the bar. Putting her glass down on the little silver tray that already contained Draycott's empty tumbler, and pulling her yellow wrap tightly about her, she left the room and the day guests to their in depth discussion.

As she walked into the Great Hall, Bunny heard both the sudden ringing of the front door bell and a man's voice coming from the telephone booth. "Yes, sir, I can appreciate it is rather difficult. No, sir, he was killed before we could question him. Yes, sir, young Marmis brought back some very useful information. Yes, sir, still viable. Some very familiar names, though the fourth name in particular was rather a surprise. Yes, sir, I also doubt its authenticity…it was written in a different ink from the rest of the document. Very well, sir, and you will call the Commissioner? Yes, sir, thank you. Good evening, sir."

Bunny hurried across the hall and entered the library, leaving the door open just a crack.

The booth door opened and a tall, dark young man she did not recognise stepped out and closed the door behind him. As he walked towards the library he paused and turned as a series of impatient knocks sounded at the front door. The door opened suddenly and a dapper figure entered the Great Hall and looked at Lord Lapotaire with an air of aggrieved exasperation.

"It would appear that one must inure oneself to performing the work of a servant more and more these days! I've been waiting for someone to let me in for the last five minutes!"

Lord Lapotaire took in the bright Ascot and slick hair. "Ah, Mr Draycott? I don't believe we have been introduced: Lord Vyvian Lapotaire, of the Foreign Office."

Mr Draycott gripped Lord Lapotaire's hand firmly and shook it. "A pleasure, my lord. Someone must have advised you of my name, and perhaps also my profession."

Lord Lapotaire decided to employ some judicious flan-nelling, and shook his head. "Not by anyone this evening, sir:

the name of Mr Weatherly Draycott, and his reputation, are renowned. Right now, though, we are in need of your services as a plain medical man. I'm afraid there has been an...incident."

Mr Draycott preened slightly. "Has someone been taken ill?"

"Something rather more permanent than that, I'm afraid, Mr Draycott. Murder!"

Mr Draycott's immaculately plucked eyebrows shot into his hairline. "Good God! Though if this person is already dead I am not sure how I can help you."

Lord Lapotaire held out his hands. "It's more for information purposes: an approximation of the time and possibly the cause of death. In one of the cases it's a little difficult." He shuddered slightly.

Draycott frowned. "You said, 'in one of the cases'. Am I to take it there is more than one victim?"

"I'm afraid there are two. The injuries sustained by one victim are so many, so varied, and so utterly appalling that only a medical man could possibly distinguish between them."

Draycott's face became still. "My God," he murmured. He smoothed his hair and looked at Lord Lapotaire. "Very well, I will need my bag from my room. Has Lord Marmis been informed?"

"Yes: he was one of the people who discovered the bodies."

"Are you permitted to tell me who the victims are?"

"Lord Scott-Brewer and the family butler, Hardcastle."

Draycott's face blanched. "Scott-Brewer? I was playing bridge with the man less than an hour ago, and the butler let me out of the house not forty minutes ago! Good God! No wonder no one answered the bell."

Lord Lapotaire smiled grimly. "Thank you, Mr Draycott:

that gives us an approximate time of death for the butler. Please get your bag, go to Lord Marmis' study, and tell him I sent you; he will tell you what we need in greater detail."

"Very well." Draycott smiled wanly. "I warn you, I haven't been in general practice for quite some time, so I could be a trifle rusty. These things are sent to try us when we least expect it, I suppose. If you will excuse me, I shall collect my bag." He nodded at Lord Lapotaire and headed for the stairs.

Lord Lapotaire paused by the telephone booth, then re-entered it and placed another call to the same number. The man on the other end picked up after the second ring. Lord Lapotaire pulled the door to and hunched over the receiver.

Crouching in her hiding place behind the library door, Bunny muttered a very unladylike word under her breath. Now she couldn't hear anything. How very inconsiderate of him to close the door completely!

She straightened up, and thought about what she had just heard. She knew about the seedier side of society life – or some of it, at any rate. Her maid had informed her of both Lord Scott-Brewer's nocturnal wanderings and Hardcastle's brutish habits several months ago, so she was not particularly surprised that something nasty had happened to either of them. She just wished it hadn't happened while she was in the house. Why couldn't the killer have waited until she had gone home?

A sudden noise from the hall startled her. Bending to peer through the gap, she saw the dark young man close the telephone-booth door and walk towards the library. Bunny ran to an armchair by the fireplace, and with a lack of grace that would have given her mother a fit, assumed a sleeping position, her yellow chiffon wrap artfully thrown around her shoulders.

Lord Lapotaire entered the room and took in the human contents with one glance; a rather attractive young woman asleep in the armchair furthest from the door. How very odd! With an amused expression, Lord Lapotaire walked over to the recumbent young woman and looked down at her. A slight little thing with golden hair and pale, almost translucent skin, he could see now that she was a little older than he had first thought.

With a smile, Lord Lapotaire placed a hand on the young woman's warm arm and gently shook her. He had to commend her acting ability; she did indeed look as if she was just waking up.

Bunny opened her eyes and gazed up at the dark young man before her, his brown eyes crinkled in a smile. "Having a nice sleep, were we?" he inquired.

She glared up at him. "Yes, I was, until you woke me!" she snapped. She struggled into an embarrassing half-up half-down position on her chair, and scowled at the attractive man in front of her. "Would you mind moving so that I may stand?"

Lord Lapotaire looked at her expectantly.

"Please," Bunny muttered, pink and flustered; the slightly husky twang in her voice intensified as her predicament worsened.

Lord Lapotaire took pity on her, and with a gentlemanly bow moved towards the small bar in the corner. "May I get you a drink, Miss...?"

Bunny stood up, tugged her wrap around her shoulders, and turned to the elegant young man. "Ellerbeck, Lady Ellerbeck if you please, and no, I do not desire a drink, Mr...?"

Lord Lapotaire smiled and bowed: touché. "Lord Vyvian Lapotaire at your service. As you wish, my lady."

Bunny realised she was staring and turned away, her face a deeper shade of pink. Now thoroughly flustered, she made a show of looking at the clock on the mantle. "Oh good grief, is that the time?" she gasped. "I'm late for supper!" She headed towards the door but Lord Lapotaire got there before her, and as she reached out to grasp the handle, his hand closed over hers.

"I'm afraid supper has been put back until ten o'clock, Lady Ellerbeck. There has been an incident, but I'm sure you heard everything you needed to know through the door."

Bunny stared up into his warm brown eyes; he was close enough for her to see the little flecks of green and gold around his pupils, and she was suddenly very aware of his hand pressing hers. Lord Lapotaire felt his cheeks warming as he gazed at Bunny; he too was aware of their closeness.

There was a sudden knock on the door. The spell broken; Bunny pulled her hand from under Lord Lapotaire's. She hurried to the fireplace, trembling and confused.

His face still flushed, Lord Lapotaire opened the door and glared at a terrified young footman. "What?" he barked.

Young Peter had often thought about how he would react to an angry lord, and had come up with a few suitable ideas, but now all he could do was swallow hard. "Sorry, my lord, is Mrs Higginson in here?"

"The housekeeper? No, but she was in the study ten minutes ago." Lord Lapotaire paused. "Why do you ask?"

Peter drew himself up, and with a little more confidence, replied. "Well, my lord, um...we couldn't find Mrs Higginson or the maid, Smith, so I was sent to look for them, my lord."

"Yes, of course. You thought Hardcastle had taken Smith into one of the rooms. Have you found her?"

Peter, relieved that he had managed to find the right lord to talk to, nodded. "Yes, my lord, I found Smith upstairs. She was helping to tidy the old schoolroom, my lord, and if Mrs Higginson is in the study as you say, that's all right too, but I still don't know where Hardcastle is."

"I shouldn't worry about that," Lord Lapotaire muttered

as he glanced at Bunny, who was sitting on one of the armchairs in front of the fire and gazing at the flames.

Peter looked at him with a puzzled expression. "My lord?"

Lord Lapotaire sighed. "Do you know where the other guests are?"

"Yes, my lord. They're all in the saloon, except for Lord and Lady Scott-Brewer."

Lord Lapotaire's head snapped back from his contemplation of Bunny and he stared at the young footman. "If Lady Scott-Brewer is not in the saloon, then where is she?"

Peter swallowed. "I saw her when I was making my way to the nursery, my lord; I believe she was returning to their suite."

Lord Lapotaire's eyes narrowed. "What time was that?"

"Um, about twenty past nine, my lord, or maybe a little later."

Bunny stared intently at the fire while this exchange went on behind her. She couldn't believe she had been caught out. Being of a curious nature, she had perfected the art of lady-like eavesdropping, knowing full well that very few people ever told a young woman anything interesting for fear of harming her sensibilities.

She turned to Lord Lapotaire and attempted a detached manner, but her voice sounded a little breathless. "Has something happened, Lord Lapotaire?"

He faced her, and the distant, polite words he had hoped to use caught in his throat. His first priority was to secure the scene and wait for the necessary people to arrive. Not to inform the guests – that was Lord Marmis' responsibility as host – but Lord Lapotaire felt a sudden need to talk with the young woman sitting by the fireplace. While he wished to keep Hardcastle and his foul behaviour far away from her, he felt he ought to share his knowledge of the evening's events.

He turned back to the young footman. "What's your name, boy?"

"Jones, my lord."

"Well, Jones, don't worry about looking for Hardcastle; he has been found."

Peter became very still. "My lord?"

"He is in the portrait gallery and he is very, very dead. Murdered, in fact."

Peter was silent for several seconds, then nodded. "I'm not surprised," he muttered. He looked up at Lord Lapotaire. "It was just a matter of time, my lord: he wasn't liked."

"What about Lord Scott-Brewer: was he liked?"

Peter looked at Lord Lapotaire blankly. "Lord Scott-Brewer, my lord? I don't understand. You said Hardcastle—"

"And Lord Scott-Brewer. Both are dead: one quite brutally stabbed, the other torn to pieces and put on an easel as a public display!"

Over by the fireplace, Bunny gulped; perhaps this amount of information *was* damaging to a lady's sensibilities. She stood. "Lord Lapotaire, I feel I really must—" She put her hand to her forehead as she swayed.

Lord Lapotaire swore, and crossing the room he caught Bunny as she fell and carried her to the chaise, where he laid her down and rubbed her hands. He called out to Peter. "A glass of whisky, quickly, the decanter is over there."

Peter ran to the table and carefully poured a generous measure of whisky. But when he looked at the tray, an expression of concern crossed his face.

Lord Lapotaire saw him. "What is it?"

"I was going to put some ice in the drink, my lord, but..."

"But?"

He turned to look at Lord Lapotaire. "The ice pick is missing, my lord."

Lord Lapotaire stood motionless. "Is it now" he mused

softly; his eyes thoughtful. He looked at the perplexed footman. "It will be quite acceptable without the ice, Jones. Quickly now."

Peter handed the tumbler to Lord Lapotaire, who gently pressed the glass against Bunny's lips. "Take a sip, Lady Ellerbeck, it will help."

Bunny obediently opened her mouth and took rather more than a sip; she swallowed and coughed as the single malt whisky immediately spread its warmth through her stomach. She pushed the glass away and struggled into a sitting position, then looked up at Lord Lapotaire and murmured, in a slightly strained voice, "I think it would be best if I retired to my room."

Lord Lapotaire looked at Peter. "Where is Lady Ellerbeck's maid?"

"I-I think Alisha is in the kitchen, my lord, I'll go and get her." Peter turned at the door. "My lord?"

"Yes, Jones?"

Peter blinked. "Was his death...did Hardcastle's death hurt him, my lord?"

Lord Lapotaire looked at him with a steady expression. "Yes, Jones, I think it must have."

Peter thought for a moment and nodded. "Good!"

He left the room, leaving Lord Lapotaire staring after him.

○

9:48pm

Peter's pace became faster and faster until by the time he got to the servants' kitchen, he was running. He burst into the room. "Hardcastle's dead!"

Mrs Higginson looked up from where she was putting together a tray of tea. Colin spoke, "Aye lad, we know."

Peter drooped slightly. "Oh, right then." He saw Alisha and Florence and walked over to them. "You all right, Flo?" he asked anxiously.

Florence, her face pale, was about to answer when the back door was suddenly flung open and William ran in with a wild expression on his face. He stopped when he saw Florence, and walking over to her, he knelt and took both her hands in his. "I just heard," he whispered. "Are you all right, love?"

Her eyes filled with tears as she nodded, and William enveloped her in a crushing embrace as she finally wept. The other servants watched in silence as William gently guided his sweetheart to the worn settee by the pot-bellied stove, where they sat in silence, holding hands.

Peter turned back to Alisha, who looked up questioningly. In her soft American accent the young woman asked, "Well?"

Peter blushed. "Lady Ellerbeck needs you in the library; she heard what happened and felt unwell. Lord Lapotaire asked for you to go to her."

Alisha grabbed the little bag lying by her feet and hurriedly left the kitchen.

Peter turned to Colin. "Do the other guests know, sir?"

Colin shook his head as he measured some tea leaves into two large teapots on the table. "Not yet. Lord Marmis wants to inform Lady Scott-Brewer first." Colin consulted his watch. "I did inform the guests that supper would be served in about twelve minutes, so perhaps after we've had our tea we should head for the dining room, eh? I'm looking forward to using the beater on that gong!" He turned back to the stove as the kettle started to whistle.

Mrs Higginson frowned. "Surely someone should inform the guests."

Colin shook his head. "We should wait for Lord Marmis to do that, love, but he'd better make it quick; the guests might realise someone's missing."

The young footman sat at the table with a confused expression. "Lord Lapotaire asked about Lady Scott-Brewer. When I told him I'd seen her going upstairs earlier, he seemed interested."

Colin poured boiling water into the teapots. "Lord Lapotaire probably wants to ask her ladyship some questions." He paused and in a low voice added, "I expect this means the police!"

Mrs Higginson looked up at Colin. "Will we have to tell them about us, do you think?"

"I'm afraid we may have to, love."

Mrs Higginson sighed as she placed one of the hot teapots, a bowl of sugar and a milk jug on the tray. "That will make things difficult."

She cast an eye over the tray.

"I'd better get this up to his room…"

She caught Colin's eye as an expression of happiness appeared on her face. She smiled as he lifted the tray and nodded at her with a gentle expression.

"I'll carry it upstairs for you, love."

She looked at Peter and pointed to the teapot on the table. "Get a cup of tea, lad. We'll be back soon enough."

10:00pm

As Greyling struck the gong, the smooth even tone spread through the hall announcing supper. The guests, not yet aware of the loss of one of their number, obediently walked, sashayed, swept, and in the case of the Reverend Beardsley, toddled into the dining room, where they were met by the massed ranks of Marmis Hall staff. The guests were guided to their seats at the various small tables, the places unmarked by name cards, as the staff unveiled a mouth-watering meal memorable for all the right reasons, unlike the necessary after-dinner talk, which would be memorable for all the wrong reasons.

Aside from Lord Scott-Brewer and Hardcastle, three others were also missing; Lady Ellerbeck, who had taken to her room with her maid and a tray, Giselle Du Lac, who on being informed of the evening's events by Lady Marmis had also taken to her room with her maid, several trays, two bottles of champagne and a do-not-disturb sign on her bolted door, and Lady Scott-Brewer who was also in her room with her maid, but without a tray, though they would not be alone for long.

Lord Marmis walked up the great staircase. Pausing at the central landing, he turned right and walked past several doors before stopping in front of one that bore the title 'The Blue Suite'. He was in the act of lifting his hand to knock when his wife appeared at the end of the corridor and joined him, Lord Marmis whispered, "My love, I don't want you here; this will be painful enough for Lady Scott-Brewer and—"

"Indeed! And when a woman is in pain, she needs the support of others of her own sex. You are the man I love, Foster, but you can be blunt towards those you have no liking for. I will sit with Lady Scott-Brewer if she asks me to."

Lord Marmis gazed at his wife, who lifted her chin. Recognising the signs he sighed and knocked firmly on the door. There was a moment's silence, then the door was opened abruptly by Lady Scott-Brewer's maid, Philips. The thin, middle-aged woman glared at Lord and Lady Marmis with suspicion. "Yes?"

"We need to speak with your mistress; it is a matter of some urgency."

The maid looked at him with a sharp expression, then stepped out into the hall, pulled the door to behind her, and hissed, "He's not gone and done it again, has he? Our housekeeper warned yours about him and his ways, so you can't say you weren't told!"

Lord Marmis gathered himself. "No, no, your master has not attacked anyone; he himself has been attacked."

The maid straightened suddenly, her eyes sharp. "Is he dead?" she asked bluntly.

Lord Marmis, looking slightly flustered, nodded. "Yes, yes he is. I need to explain the circumstances of his death to your mistress. Take us to her, please."

She stared at him, then reopened the door, standing back to allow them in. She closed the door behind them and gestured to a chaise by the fireplace.

"Wait here. I'll see if my mistress will agree to see you." She walked to a closed door on the right of the sitting room and knocked. A voice sounded from within, and she disappeared inside.

Lady Marmis sat gracefully on the royal-blue chaise and arranged her skirts. Lord Marmis stood next to her, his hand resting on the pale blue marble mantelpiece his great-uncle had brought back from one of his jaunts to Italy, and thought over what he should say to the new widow. Bearing down on the opposition at the dispatch box had taught him a great deal about oratory, but damn all about how to explain to a wife that her husband had been done to death…and with an ice pick, of all things!

There was a sudden rustling behind him. Lord and Lady Marmis turned as Lady Rowan Scott-Brewer appeared from her bedchamber, her rigid carriage modestly covered with a surprisingly feminine peach coloured wrapper. Lord Marmis bowed from the neck as she approached.

Lady Scott-Brewer stopped before the fire, and in an icy tone acknowledged them both. "Lord Marmis, Lady Marmis. My maid informs me that something has happened to my husband. Tell me what has occurred, please…spare me nothing."

Lord Marmis took a deep breath. "Lady Scott-Brewer, I'm afraid it is the worst of news. It grieves me to inform you that your husband, Lord Scott-Brewer, is dead. Please accept our deepest sympathies."

Lady Scott-Brewer stood in complete silence, staring at Lord Marmis, her face expressionless. After some time Lord Marmis looked at his wife. Lady Marmis made a tentative gesture with her hand. "Lady Scott-Brewer, are you alright?"

She blinked, seeming to realise that they were still there. In a low voice containing none of her previous imperiousness, she whispered, "How did he die?"

Lord Marmis felt a sudden compassion for the woman before him, and turned to his wife with a helpless expression. Lady Marmis looked at her husband steadily before turning to Lady Scott-Brewer. In a soft voice she murmured, "Lady Scott-Brewer, your husband's body was discovered in the portrait gallery. I'm afraid he was murdered. I am so sorry."

Lady Scott-Brewer stared at Lady Rebecca for several moments, then in a quiet monotone murmured, "If you will excuse me, there are things that I must attend to. Good evening." She swept towards her bedroom door and entered, closing the door firmly behind her.

The maid turned away from the door and looked at Lord Marmis. "You'd better go; it'll hit her in a while and it won't be pretty."

Lady Marmis nodded. "The loss?"

Philips looked at her with a sneer. "The relief! Nearly thirty years of living with a man who thought he had the right to grope his way through the servants' quarters because his father and grandfather got away with it! Twenty-nine years of suffering in silence. She had to become a hard woman to protect herself from him. He may have been high-born, but he was a low bastard!"

Lord Marmis touched his shocked wife's shoulder. "Come, my dear, I don't think we are needed here." He looked at the maid. "Will your mistress be alright?"

The elderly servant's face softened slightly. "She'll be fine in a while; when she realises she's free, she'll be right as rain." She walked to the door and held it open. "Now if you please, leave us. I'll look after her...like I always have." Dismissed thus, Lord and Lady Marmis found themselves out in the corridor.

Lady Marmis put her hands to her cheeks, a look of shock and sadness on her face. "I knew of his reputation – every house in the county did – but to have lived with it for all that time! Oh, Foster, that poor woman, to have been married to such an appalling, selfish man...all those terrible, wasted years!"

Lord Marmis placed his arm around his wife's pale, bare shoulders and held her close as they walked towards the stairs.

PART
II

10:30pm Friday, London

In a quiet office buried in the heart of London's Scotland Yard a telephone started to ring. It rang for some time before a tenor voice called from an antechamber, "For the love of all the Gods, Goddesses and little imps combined; Thorne! Would you please answer that blasted device before the telephonic automaton takes a message and complains to head office about us again?"

Presently the outer office door opened and a tall, elegantly dressed man of approximately forty entered the room. From the neatly combed crop of dark-blond hair and the equally neatly trimmed moustache and Vandyke, to the shine on his purple patent-leather shoes by way of his soft grey, three-piece suit and rather hideous chartreuse and lilac Paisley Ascot, Detective Sergeant Abernathy Thorne in his after work finery was a sight to behold when sober, never mind when drunk.

Carefully picking his way through the now-closed Klaivaris case files, which were stacked around the little room awaiting collection, he eventually reached the desk. Using both manicured hands with their unusually long fingernails, he scrabbled through the piles of paperwork that spilled across the desk's surface, located the telephone that had only been installed a few weeks earlier, and lifted the receiver. In a rich, educated, and slightly fruity voice completely suited to his appearance he intoned, "Detective Chief Inspector Caine's office, Detective Sergeant Thorne speaking."

A voice spoke through what Caine insisted on referring to as the 'infernal device'. As Thorne listened his eyes widened, and after a few moments he murmured, "Yes of course, sir...I shall endeavour to find him for you."

Placing the receiver on an overflowing case file, Thorne walked over to the little antechamber that served as an occasional bedroom and knocked sharply on the closed door. It opened a crack and a low voice hissed, "I don't want to talk to him! If I do he'll send us to the far Antipodes to dig up Jack the Ripper! Tell him I've already gone home!"

As the door was pushed to it bounced off Thorne's immaculately shod foot, which he'd had the foresight to jam between the door and the frame. A moment later the voice inquired plaintively, "Thorne, am I being politely informed that I have no choice?"

Thorne smiled. "Yes, Elliott, you are. Shall I tell the Commissioner you'll come to the telephone?"

The voice sighed. "Don't bother, old chap. I'll come and talk to the blasted man myself." The door opened and Detective Chief Inspector Elliott Caine walked warily into his own office. Above medium height and broad in the shoulders, with a short dark beard and moustache and dark wavy hair far longer than the fashion of the day dictated, he resembled more a poet of the late romantic period than a police officer.

His face was gentle, with an almost sleepy expression. Under pressure, however, this was replaced by an unnerving intensity which, coupled with overlong canines that had caused him no end of trouble since the publication of Bram Stoker's novel some two years earlier, gave him a slightly concerning look, almost as though he were about to bite. Generally, he resembled a dreamy, somewhat languorous young man of the Lord Byron school of manners. He affected the use of a ruby-red Malacca cane that those in the know were wary of, as within that innocent looking sheath was a vicious blade that he had used to good effect over the years. But the less the authorities knew about that, the better!

Elliott V Caine was exceptionally young for a CID officer of his position. His file listed his age as just thirty-nine, but his track record was that of a much older and far more experienced man. Since ostensibly joining the force from the Civil Service some eighteen months earlier, he had shot up the ladder at a speed that had come as a shock to those under him, but not to those above, although this had led to some uncharitable remarks about his knowing the right kind of people...or, rather that he knew the right kind of information about the right kind of people!

Those who spoke in his defence argued that his abilities and successes on the job were justification enough for his repeated and swift promotions, while those who disapproved cited his maverick behaviour, his refusal to follow the necessary protocol, his insistence on accepting Thorne's habit of addressing him by his Christian name instead of 'sir', and his unnerving habit of breaking even the most hardened criminal down to dust: in some cases, literally.

He had originally been placed on cases with officers such as Detective Inspector Walter Dew and Chief Inspector Donald Swanson, but more often than not worked under his own steam with the invaluable assistance of Detective Sergeant Thorne, who had joined the force at the same time as Elliott and who was, oddly enough, promoted on the exact same occasions as his unusual colleague...

Elliott's ability to outthink intelligent villains was matched by his ability to take down the more common brutish type who was invariably the educated ringleader's weapon on the street. Indeed, in spite of Elliott's appearance he was more than capable of holding his own in a scrum, as one or two constables had discovered when they tried a jovial 'welcome to the force' scuffle in an alley behind the Yard.

Always dapper, today he was attired in the immaculately styled, pale blue three-piece suit he had picked up that morning from his tailor in Bond Street. In his debonair ensemble, finished with an Ascot in a suitably subtle shade of dove grey silk, he was the epitome of a city gentleman. Carrying his matching topper before him like a shield, he approached the telephone and lifted the receiver, holding it a few inches from his ear as though afraid it would bite him. He was obliged to raise his voice to be understood by the man on the other end of the line.

"Hello, Commissioner. No, I haven't left the Yard yet." He turned and rolled his eyes at a smiling Thorne. "What? But we've only just finished the Klaivaris case! You agreed to two weeks' holiday for both of us. Thorne's planning a much-needed trip to the Lake District with Veronique and a fishing rod!"

Elliott's voice matched his appearance: smooth and light, the voice of a trained orator. In his distant youth he had dabbled in theatre, and he was quite prepared to prove to his superior officer just how far he could project! But now he listened with a scowl on his face as the Commissioner rattled off several reasons why he had to obey orders.

Screwing up his features and holding the receiver at arm's length, Elliott blew a silent raspberry at Commissioner Bolton. Thorne, who was standing silently by the door, sighed philosophically as Elliott suggested the Commissioner send someone else; a new team would be fresh.

The Commissioner countered with Caine and Thorne's

track record of successes, citing the Polfaxen murder case; even when they had been exhausted from tracking down the killer they had still managed to crack the Grimpen Gang without a break.

Elliott argued back, pointing out that the Polfaxen Killer had been a member of the Grimpen Gang, and as the other members were intent on continuing where he had left off, they had no choice but to see it through.

In his office two floors up, and several wage slips to the north of Elliott and Thorne, Commissioner Bolton sighed and held the receiver away from his ear as Elliott ranted. Finally Bolton managed to break in. "I understand, Caine! But this doesn't come from me; you were asked for by name."

Elliott paused in the middle of a well-thought-out insult. "By whom?" he asked.

"Lord Vyvian Lapotaire of the Foreign Office." He paused with a slight frown. "He used a strange turn of phrase…he said that he knows you from a previous existence. I'm not quite sure what he meant."

There was a deathly silence on the other end of the device.

Bolton took a deep breath and hurriedly continued. "If I could do something about this, I would, but it is out of my hands. Your presence has been formally requested by a highly placed government official. It is not a request, Caine; it is an order."

The silence continued for several seconds. Bolton was about to speak when Elliott's voice, strangely subdued, asked, "What is the case?"

Bolton relaxed slightly in his chair and read from a sheaf of papers on his desk. "In as few words as possible, Lord and Lady Marmis were hosting a house party at Marmis Hall near Benchester when their butler was found quite spectacu-larly murdered! I have to say that this one is not for the faint of heart, Caine! Not far from the butler's remains was the corpse of a peer, Lord Bartholomew Scott-Brewer, who had apparently been skewered through the neck with some sort of sharp implement. As I understand, and this is not to go any further, Lord Coalford and Lord Lapotaire had been invited for a sub rosa government discussion, hidden under the auspices of a frivolous weekend party. The other important piece of information is that at some time during the evening Lord Marmis' brother Frederick returned home; he has apparently spent the last two years as a prisoner of the Boers in Southern Africa. There you have the makings of a rather intriguing case." Bolton paused before playing his trump card. "Did I also mention that Giselle Du Lac is one of the guests?"

A sharp intake of breath was clearly audible down the line. The Commissioner smiled. "If you take this case, Caine, I promise both you and Thorne an entire month of holiday. That should give your man enough time to take his Labrador and his fishing rod all over the Lake District. What say you?"

The silence on the line continued for some time, then, "Marmis Hall. The family name is Marmis, you say?"

"Yes, Lord and Lady Marmis. He is the—"

"The twelfth Lord Marmis of Westrenshire."

Commissioner Bolton frowned down the receiver. "Yes, he is as it happens. So, what do you think?"

Elliott stared down at the desk, his eyes blind to the piles of unfixed documents. Marmis! Ye Gods, he hadn't heard that name for years. Of course that didn't mean he hadn't thought about...after all, she might be long gone but the house was still there, and with Giselle in the same place...

Commissioner Bolton was about to break the silence when Elliott cried, "Thorne! Check the BAC for airship times to Benchester!"

Bolton exhaled in relief. "We've put together a file on the

known guests: rather an interesting group. I'll send the information down to the front desk, and you can collect it on your way out." Now for something a little more worrying, he gripped the receiver and cleared his throat. "On a different note, someone has again tried to access your personal files."

Elliott gripped the phone; the flickering gaslight seemed to catch a green light deep within his dark-brown eyes. "Did they get anything?"

"No, luckily a clerk entered the office before anything could be taken. But unluckily for the clerk, the intruder attacked him and knocked him unconscious, poor devil."

Elliott frowned. "Is he all right?"

"Dr Daniels believes so. A bit of a headache, but nothing worse."

"Did the intruder escape?"

"Unfortunately, yes. I fear they only needed to get out of that particular office to be hidden in plain sight, as it were."

There was a pause. "You believe it was another officer?"

Bolton sighed. "Look at the evidence, Caine. This is Scotland Yard. Could you see someone breaking in and strolling through corridors full of policemen to get to a windowless room in the attics? Who else would know where we keep our officer's personal files? It must be another officer. There were many questions about both your sudden appearance and the speed with which both you and Thorne achieved promotion. Especially given your refusal to divulge any personal information about yourself. There was bound to be talk, and occasionally, more aggressive action."

Elliott rubbed his temples. "You're absolutely sure they were after our files?"

"From what I can gather the cabinet that contains the files for A through to D was open when the clerk entered, and yours was the only file that had been removed. As the intruder fled, he ran into the clerk and dropped the file he had taken; the clerk was pushed aside and hit his head on a cabinet. The intruder then ran down the stairs into the building and towards the officers...towards the officers, Caine, not away from them."

"What about Thorne's file?"

"His file was located on the other side of the room, and judging by the amount of dust on it, that cabinet hasn't been opened for several months. However, just in case, I took both files and put them in the locked filing cabinet in my office."

Elliott frowned, his dark eyebrows jutting over his eyes. "Is that safe?"

"Well, somewhat safer – if not for you, then certainly for the poor bloody clerks! It isn't their job to deal with this sort of thing; they are just there to look after the paperwork."

"Which clerk was injured?"

"Isaiah Davidson. Why?"

"Just to know. Commissioner, did Davidson give a description of his attacker?"

"No. He said that the room was dark and the only reason he went up there was to investigate a noise." Commissioner Bolton sighed. "He obviously didn't read about curiosity and the cat."

Elliott nodded thoughtfully. "He nearly got himself killed. But if the room was dark enough to prevent Davidson from seeing the intruder, how could the intruder see what he was after?"

Bolton leafed through the report on his desk. "It says here that Davidson saw a light under the door and as he entered the room the light went out. When he didn't return to his desk, the clerk who sits opposite went to look for him and found him on the steps leading to the top floor."

"Why didn't this friend go with him in the first place?"

"Apparently he thought it was just vermin. We do have a bit of a rat problem, you know."

Elliott smiled grimly and looked at Thorne. "Apparently not just the four-legged variety. When did this happen?"

Bolton winced; he had hoped Caine wouldn't ask that question. "Two weeks ago."

"What?"

Bolton held the receiver further away from his ear. "Be reasonable, Caine, you and Thorne were finishing the Klaivaris case. I felt it better that I deal with the...the intruder situation while you wound up the case. You do understand, don't you?" Bolton's voice was almost pleading.

Elliott ground his teeth. He understood exactly what the Commissioner was saying, and he would have done the same. Indeed, he had withheld information on many separate occasions, and from many different superiors.

He took a deep breath and straightened his shoulders. "Yes, Commissioner, I understand. If any information on this intruder comes up, Thorne and I will be at Marmis Hall." Elliott paused. "And Commissioner, please be assured that I will find out if it does." And with that, Elliott hung up.

As the line clicked, Commissioner Bolton breathed a trembling sigh of relief; a job well done. Now, where was that bottle of whisky?

Back in Elliott's office, Thorne glanced up from his timetable and looked at Elliott with a hard expression. "I heard most of it, Elliott. Do you think he's lying? *Has* someone seen our files?"

Elliott shook his head. "He isn't lying. Nothing in his voice suggested untruth, just concern. And there isn't much in our files, anyway. We made sure of that!" He ran his hands through his unruly brown hair and snarled. "Gods, there are times when I really despise this job, Thorne. Another murder to deal with, and an intrusion into our past, straight after dealing with the damn Klaivaris case!"

Thorne looked at his old friend with a rueful expression.

"Veronique had her heart set on us going on holiday soon, Elliott. When she's asleep I'm sure she dreams of taking a dip in Windermere. But don't let it worry you; I'll talk with her and with some luck she won't hold it against you too much!"

Elliott smiled. "Bearing in mind what she left in my shoe the last time I crossed her, I should hope not! And on that happy note, let's get started, shall we? In the midst of that little exchange, the Commissioner offered us four weeks' holiday if we take on this case. Are there any airships heading for Benchester, or if my memory serves me right, Marmis Parva?"

Thorne looked at Elliott with narrowed eyes. "You despise travelling by airship...what aren't you telling me?"

Elliott shrugged in a slightly self-conscious manner. "There have been two murders in the home of a government minister, time is of the essence and airship is the fastest way to travel...beggars can't be choosers, that's all. Are we in luck?"

Thorne consulted the British Airship Company's timetable and shook his head. "The last airship for Pelloe-haven left over an hour ago. However..." Thorne rummaged through the piles of paperwork on his desk, found the train timetable and waived it triumphantly before thumbing through to the right page. "There is the sleeper train to Penzance, it leaves Paddington at midnight. That should get us into Benchester at about half past two, give or take. As I recall, Marmis Parva is a few miles further on and not served by a halt."

Elliott nodded, "Excellent." He opened the desk drawer, and removed an empty leather holster which he glared at. He rifled through the contents of the overflowing desk, then looked at Thorne, exasperated. "Put me out of my misery, Thorne, where is it?"

Thorne walked over to the filing cabinet and opened the

drawer labelled 'O to S'. Reaching in, he pulled out a smart non-government-issue revolver with an ivory and mother-of-pearl inlay and handed it to Elliott.

Elliott placed the gun in the holster, shrugged off his smart blue jacket, and strapped on the holster. Pulling his jacket back on, he smoothed the line of the material. "What do you think; can you see it through the material?"

Thorne stared at the jacket and slowly shook his head. "No, and with an Ulster over the top..." He didn't need to finish the sentence; an elephant could safely be hidden within the copious folds of an Ulster.

Elliott looked satisfied. "We need to pack for a few days, and we will both need evening dress." He looked at Thorne nervously. "Giselle Du Lac is one of the guests."

Thorne's eyebrows shot up and a smile appeared on his face. He nodded thoughtfully. "That's why you thought of the airship...we would have arrived far sooner; Marmis Hall and Giselle, eh? Well, that's somewhat better than having to chase her around the world again, isn't it? And if we can solve this case within the week, we might both get what we want."

He looked meaningfully at his friend, who flushed but laughed good-naturedly, his dark eyes again sparkling with that green light. "Get on with you, you old goat. Let's pack, shall we? And before we leave we both need to apologise to Veronique."

Thorne frowned. "And ask our dear landlady Mrs Hard-court if she will play canine Nanny for a few days!"

Marmis Hall
11:00pm

The guests stood in silence in the saloon, listening in horror and not a little ghoulish enjoyment to what Lord Marmis had to say.

Several day guests were wondering how best to claim a subsequent family emergency and leave, while others, almost against their will, were interested in hearing all about the murders of a peer of the realm and a butler. Certain of the guests, who numbered less than ten, and who could all account for their movements with friends who would vouch for them, were informed that it would be best if they returned to their homes and awaited any further instruction from the authorities; not a few breathed a fervent sigh of relief.

The chosen ones decamped to the turning circle as swiftly as good manners would allow, climbing into their elegant carriages and returning to the safety of their homes. While the few guests left to rue the day they had accepted their invitations to stay at the hall for the weekend were encouraged to retire to their suites and bolt their doors until morning.

Saturday
01:30am

A dark figure appeared at the head of the ornate staircase that led down into the Great Hall, and paused before descending. Looking around the dimly lit hall with a sharpness and ease that spoke of ample experience in such things, the figure walked silently through the long shadows the moonlight and marble columns threw across the polished floor as they made their way to the foot of the stairs.

Looking around again and seeing nothing that could threaten, they entered the long corridor leading past the study and the music room. Ignoring the little hallway on the right that led to the morning room, the figure paused at the first door to the gallery. With a furtive glance about them, they listened for signs of company. Hearing nothing, the figure reached within their voluminous blue robe and took out a small canvas pouch. Opening it, they removed two thin pieces of metal that Elliott and Thorne would have been very interested in, and carefully twisting them together, inserted them into the lock.

The moonlight that flooded the corridor by way of the courtyard afforded them ample light for their work. After a few moments there was a sharp click, and the figure again glanced around. As the swaying ivy that clung to the courtyard walls cast writhing shadows that rippled across the gallery door, the figure scowled and shook their head. *That* really didn't help.

The silence seemed to soothe them as they carefully removed the two metal pins from the lock. The figure placed one hand on the door handle and paused; from information gleaned from various sources, they had an idea of what lay behind the door and truly didn't wish to enter, but they had an obligation to their employer. The figure turned the handle and the well-oiled hinges swung silently as the figure entered the room, pushing the door shut behind them.

There was a pause as they turned up the gaslight nearest the door. On Lord Marmis' orders, the lights had been left on; partly from respect for the dead, but also for the more prosaic reason of not running the risk of stepping in something foul.

A few moments later the gaslight was turned back down, the door opened again and the figure reappeared, breathing heavily and swallowing hard as they leant against the now-closed door and shuddered. It had been worse than they had feared! Relieved that they had avoided the urge to vomit - that really would have announced their presence - the metal picks were again used to lock the door, and turning, the swaddled figure advanced towards the Great Hall.

Outside the study, the figure had a sudden thought and tried the door. With a soft click the door swung open, the figure walked inside and closed the door behind them.

The dying embers in the fireplace gave just enough light to see by as the robed figure hurried to the desk and rummaged in the pile of documents left on top. Nothing of interest! Damn! Were any of the drawers open? The intruder pulled at the drawers, but as they tried the last, there was a sudden noise in the blue corridor and the study door slowly swung open.

Moving quickly, the robed figure squeezed into the knee-hole under the desk and held their breath as a shadowy pair of legs clad in tartan pyjamas and a dark dressing gown walked into the middle of the room.

The figure under the desk prayed that the room was dark enough for them to go unseen. If they were discovered in their current, rather embarrassing position it would take quite a bit of explaining and ruin their opportunity to find the information they needed.

Another pair of legs, this time draped in a diaphanous red material, appeared in the doorway, and a soft female voice called out. "Beloved, there is no one here. Come back to bed."

The legs clad in tartan turned back to the door. "I know,

my dear, I just needed to check one more time." The legs disappeared as the door closed behind them.

With a sigh of relief, the figure unwound themselves from their cramped hiding place and staggered over to one of the fireside chairs, on which they leaned, waiting for their rapidly beating heart to calm down.

As they recovered, the figure caught sight of the portrait over the fireplace. The soft glow of the fire illuminated red tresses and laughing blue eyes as the figure stared at it in shock. Rendered speechless by the likeness, the figure read the little brass plaque: 'Lady Marianne Marmis, 1735-1809'. A sudden image came to mind of sitting in a large bright room full of hothouse flowers, talking with an amusing dark-haired man with flashing brown eyes, who carried a red Malacca cane topped with a symbol of a snake eating its own tail, the symbol of eternity…

The figure shook themselves; where on earth had that come from? They couldn't be memories…they hadn't recognised the room or the man…

With one last look at the portrait, which seemed to smile in farewell, the figure opened the door, checking around them with great care they stepped into the blue corridor, then closed the door and walked back to the Great Hall. Pausing by the foot of the stairs and hearing nothing, they entered the dark telephone booth, picked up the receiver and waited for the operator.

There was a long pause before a tired female voice answered. "What number, please?"

The figure replied in a hushed tone. "A Paris number, 2626, and I'll wait. Hurry, please."

"Paris, France?"

"Yes."

While they waited, the shadow wondered just how many places called Paris the operator thought there were in the world. After several interminable minutes had passed, the receiver was picked up and a clipped, male voice appeared on the line, "The Johnson residence."

"May I speak with Mrs Johnson, please?"

"It is very late—"

"This is a matter of extreme importance! Please tell Mrs Johnson that Angellis wishes to speak with her."

There was a pause. "Very well."

There was a clack as the butler put down the receiver, then silence.

After another few minutes had passed, a woman's anxious voice arrived on the line. "Angellis, is everything all right? What has happened?"

"I'm afraid it is as we feared, Mrs Johnson. I am sorry to inform you that there have been two murders here in the last few hours."

The figure heard a swift intake of air. "Who…?"

"One of the victims was on the list you gave me, and I very much fear that the method of murder was as your son reported. It bears all the hallmarks of__" The figure paused, there had been a sound beyond the booth, out in the hall. "Mrs Johnson, I must go. I will contact you again when I have more information."

"Very well, Angellis. Thank you, and please…take care."

The figure smiled. "Always, Mrs Johnson."

Angellis replaced the receiver and looked out of the frosted-glass pane of the booth. They saw no movement. Opening the door slightly, they pushed their head through the gap and looked around the hall. The glass ceiling high above let in the foggy moonlight, casting long shadows that could hide anything within.

Closing the door, they hurried to the stairs, holding their blue robe away from their feet. When they reached their room, they beat out a coded knock, entered, and locked the door before collapsing in a heap on the bed.

As they entered the room their servant, who had been waiting patiently, poured a stiff gin and tonic mixed with elderflower cordial. As Angellis struggled to get out of the robe the servant waited for a few moments then sighed, placed the drink on the table, and hauled the offending material over their employer's head.

Dumping the robe on a chair, the servant handed the drink to the now-uncovered figure who accepted it gratefully, taking a large mouthful before sitting in a cosy wingback chair by the fire, their nightclothes in disarray.

Angellis looked at their servant. "Ye Gods, what an evening! There must be an easier way to earn a living!"

○

02:25am

The midnight train to Penzance chugged and steamed its way through the foggy English countryside, the sweep of tilled fields and genteel orchards becoming more rugged as the train passed through Wiltshire's rolling, moonlit countryside and entered the mountainous county of Westrenshire.

Safely tucked away behind the pulled blinds and blissfully oblivious to the freezing fog that awaited them at Benchester, Detective Sergeant Thorne snored and dreamt of fishing in Windermere with Veronique.

As the steam locomotive swept through the steep valleys that nestled in the heart of the hidden shire, Elliott thumbed his way through the thin file Commissioner Bolton had left for them.

After a particularly loud snore from Thorne, Elliott

hooked his foot around his friend's leg and gave it a tug. Thorne gave a snort and woke as he started to slide off his seat.

"Ah, Thorne, now that you're awake, listen to this. Going on information received, it would appear that Lord Scott-Brewer was not the first victim. That dubious honour went to the butler; quite a lot of effort went into despatching him too. Here, read this and try not to be sick, there's a good chap."

Thorne took the file from Elliott, fixed his galleried monocle over his left eye and read through the list of injuries. An occasional wince marred his elegant features until he came to one paragraph, when incredulity and revulsion took over. Holding out the file and pointing at the offending lines, he said, "I didn't realise people still knew how to do that!"

Elliott nodded grimly. "Yes, that one is a point of interest; we need to be clear which injuries were caused before death and which, if any, were inflicted afterwards."

Thorne pursed his lips, an expression that looked incongruous on his finely drawn face, and handed the file back. "For his sake, I hope that last one was after his death!"

"We'll need a full coroner's report to find that out. The nearest one is in Benchester, but apparently, he's on holiday, so we will have to see about possible substitutes."

Thorne tucked his monocle away and rested his feet on one of the large pigskin cases in front of him. "So who reported it? Who gave us the list of injuries?"

Elliott sighed and handed Thorne another sheet of paper. "Our very own Lord Vyvian Lapotaire."

Thorne's eyebrows nearly disappeared into his hairline. "Is the Commissioner comfortable with us investigating a murder in which an…associate of ours is involved?"

Elliott shrugged and leant back in his seat. "A somewhat

distant and rather invisible associate, Thorne, and actually the Commissioner does not know of our, ah, connection. It is one of the many things that I did not see fit to include in my personal file."

Thorne grimaced. His friend had informed him fully of Commissioner Bolton's theory as to the profession of the aspirant thief, and Thorne was not happy. Indeed, over the many, many years he and Elliott had known each other, working with the British police seemed to be the most dangerous of the roles they had assumed: for his friend, for himself, and for their shared past.

Elliott broke into his ruminations. "Here, this is the injury list on Lord Scott-Brewer," he said, handing Thorne a single sheet of paper.

Thorne skimmed the page. "Is Lord Lapotaire qualified in identifying causes of death, or has he made a few educated guesses?"

Elliott grinned as he settled back into his seat. "Not exactly. One of the guests staying at the hall is the nerve specialist, Mr Weatherly Draycott."

Thorne rolled his green eyes. "One of those modern chaps who relates every nasty event in your adult life to an obsession with your mother's décolleté when you were two years old?"

"Sounds about right. But even to do that he would need a medical background, which he has. He has worked at Guy's and, according to his file, he also spent several years working in army hospitals. Given the mess that appears to have greeted him in the gallery, he did quite a thorough job. So here we are, almost at Benchester, and we already know the names of both the victims and the manner of their deaths. We also have backgrounds on all of the guests and I have to agree with the Commissioner that some of them are very interesting. We know that the butler was the first to die and given the amount of time taken to inflict his injuries, that he was the intended victim. Lord Scott-Brewer seems to have been dispatched in a rather dismissive manner...almost as an afterthought, which suggests to me that he was almost certainly in the wrong place at the wrong time. Perhaps the killer made some mistakes; we shall see. Look lively, Thorne, we're slowing down, I think we've arrived." Elliott leaned over and raised the blinds, and as the thin material flew up it revealed the train's slow, graceful approach to the nearly empty and incredibly foggy platform, which bore the legend 'Benchester'.

Elliott and Thorne hurriedly put the files away and pulled on their Ulsters. Before they had left the capital they had sped to their apartments to pack, change and plead with their landlady to look after Thorne's adored and spoilt Labrador, Veronique...to which pleadings Mrs Hardcourt had only acquiesced to get them out of her private apartments at such an ungodly and scandalous hour. Veronique was duly walked into the good lady's sitting room, ensconced on her very own eiderdown bed with her favourite silk pillow, and instructed to do as Mrs Hardcourt told her. Which, Thorne was honest enough to admit, she would ignore as soon as he had closed the door.

Having changed before leaving London, Thorne was now resplendent in mustard tweed, a difficult colour for those without the panache to carry it off. Elliott was sartorial elegance itself in a deep-russet tweed three-piece that complimented his colouring and also matched his cane.

Squashing his matching flat cap onto his head, Elliott opened the window and pushed his head through. Apart from a sleepy porter propped up on his trolley and a shadowy figure standing by the gateway to the lane, no one else appeared to be on the platform.

Elliott put his arm through the window, opened the

door from the outside and stepped off the train just as a burst of steam gushed from the engine. He grinned and took a deep breath as the warm, damp, coal scented air wrapped around him. Travelling by train never ceased to cheer him, regardless of the circumstances. Turning back to their compartment, he removed his Gladstone bag and the case containing the files from the Commissioner before helping Thorne with the larger, wheeled chests that contained their photographic equipment...amongst other things.

Once they were on the platform, Elliott stopped, and dropping the heavy case he was carrying, put his fingers between his lips and blew a piercing whistle. The porter, almost asleep on his trolley, shot upright and wearily pushed the little cart towards the two men. The night train blew its own whistle, and with a secondary effusion of steam, continued its journey towards the Westrenshire coast and the distant Cornish town of Penzance.

The middle-aged porter walked through the clouds of steam and stopped next to Elliott. "Good mornin', ginnel-men," he said in a soft accent.

Elliott looked at the porter with interest as he loaded their luggage. "You're a long way from home, friend. Where-abouts in New Zealand are you from?"

The wiry little man smiled incredulously; in the six years he had worked at the station, no one had ever recognised his accent. "South Island, sir, Queenstown born and brid. How did you know?"

Elliott returned the man's smile. "I spent a happy few years on the South Island, at a lovely place called Akaroa."

"Ah, it's a beautiful part of the world, sir."

Elliott smiled, somewhat wistfully. "Yes, it is, and I hope to return soon for a much-needed holiday." He looked at the porter. "Though I'm sure you'll agree that whether by boat or airship, the journey there and back is absolutely bloody awful!"

The porter laughed and slapped the handle of his trolley. "That's the one thing stoppin' me from going back right now, sir; the journey home."

Elliott grinned back, and handing his Gladstone bag to the still-chortling porter he turned towards the exit. As he did, the shadowy figure hurriedly detached itself from the wall and walked towards them.

Elliott had never seen such a swaddled shape in all his life. The figure approaching him was almost smothered by a heavy blue serge coat and a thick multi-coloured scarf wound around their neck and face to the point where they must have had a devil of a time breathing.

Recognising the signs of a devoted parent equipped with knitting needles, Elliott smiled and murmured quietly, "Does your mother know where you are, lad?"

The figure tugged at the scarf futilely before pulling the whole thing over their head and taking a deep breath of cold air.

The young man standing before Elliott and Thorne with a now-bare and gently steaming head was about twenty, with cropped reddish hair and a very young face which even the dim light of the station showed to be smothered with freckles.

"Sorry, sir," the young man said cheerfully, wiping a hand over his pink face. "I couldn't really see you through the wool."

Elliott smiled. "I doubt you could breathe either. Are you our official welcome?"

"Sort of, sir. Constable Thom Greyling, sir."

"Detective Chief Inspector Elliott Caine, and this is Detective Sergeant Abernathy Thorne. What do you mean by 'sort of', Constable?"

The young man's cheerful look turned to embarrassment. "Mr Rigsby-Boothe, our High Constable, sir, he's in the Waggonette. He says the night air...well, he says it isn't good for his tubes, sir!"

Elliott's left eye narrowed slightly as he took in this information. Thorne saw the look on his friend's face and swallowed a grin. Oh, Rigsby-Boothe was going to know that the CID had arrived!

In a deceptively calm voice Elliott inquired, "Where is this 'Waggonette', Constable?"

A worried look on his face, Thom pointed over the hedge into the foggy lane. "You can't miss it, sir, it's the only vehicle with a cover. Mr Rigsby-Boothe had it made special so he could travel in any weather."

Elliott could make out a dark horseless carriage and a figure within puffing away on a cigar. Bad for his tubes? Bah!

"Right!" Elliott hissed. He took off at some speed down the little ramp that led into the lane, followed by a worried looking Thom, a grinning Thorne, and a rather amused porter.

Elliott marched towards the dark vehicle, his temper well and truly ignited by this selfish behaviour. High Constable he might be, but that gave him no right to force a young constable out in the freezing fog while he sat cosy in one of those infernal contraptions! Besides, sending a young and inexperienced constable to meet a visiting superior officer was just not on, and he was going to damn well going to let him know!

Elliott passed through the wooden gate, approached the dark little vehicle, and grabbed the door handle. The door swung open and the High Constable, who had smoked himself into a stupor, nearly fell out. Spluttering in surprise, he righted himself and fixed a bloodshot eye on Elliott, an expression of blank politeness on his face. "Detective Chief

Inspector Caine?" he enquired. "Welcome to our little town."

His voice suited his appearance, which was, in a word, oily. Middle-aged and spreading rapidly, Mr Maxwell Rigsby-Boothe, High Constable of Westrenshire, was the most unlikely High Constable that Elliott had ever seen, and he'd seen some odd fish! From his heavily pomaded and suspiciously dark hair, to his flamboyantly tailored puce velvet coat that unduly emphasised his roundness, the man appeared to be an utterly useless poseur who resembled more a toad in a suit than a High Constable of the Hundred. Most holders of that particular title were of a suitable military background...and somewhat less flaccid than Mr Maxwell Rigsby-Boothe. Elliott blew a mental raspberry; obviously this was another ridiculous appointment via the Society Bridge Brigade.

The creature spoke. "I do hope you didn't mind my not coming to greet you, gentlemen," he murmured. "Some people cannot abide the smell of these herbal cigars—"

"Not at all, Mr Rigsby-Boothe." Elliott interjected, the cloud of smoke around the sergeant had a very sweet, rather familiar smell. "Several of our colleagues at Scotland Yard cannot function without such herbal assistance, but we have learned that colleagues who favour a leaf-based mix are preferable to those who use a seven percent solution!"

Rigsby-Boothe's jaw dropped as Elliott's remarks hit home, and a warning light flashed in Elliott's eyes as the two men stared at each other. Rigsby-Boothe was first to look away.

Elliott waved his hand at the automobile. "Get out of the vehicle, please; we need the room for our equipment."

Rigsby-Boothe, his flaccid jowls flapping alarmingly, oozed out of the Waggonette, buttoning his thin velvet coat and wrapping his arms around himself in an effort to stay warm. Elliott watched him with an expression as chilly as the night air while Thom helped Thorne and the now openly grinning porter load their cases into the back of the Waggonette.

Once Elliott had tipped the porter and the three men had settled into the vehicle, the incredulous High Constable bleated, "But you can't leave me here, I'll freeze!"

A scarf was thrown from the snug interior of the automobile, and Elliott's voice rose over the sound of the engine as they rumbled away. "Never mind, old chap, it's excellent weather for clearing the tubes!"

As the little vehicle made its way through the foggy countryside on the outskirts of Benchester, Elliott turned to Thom. "How in the Nine Hells did that hideous old flapjack become High Constable?"

The young constable laughed. "It wasn't by choice, sir. No one really wanted the job, the previous High Constable had been in the position for forty years, and Lord Marmis wasn't keen on bringing in an outsider who didn't know the people. So Benchester Council put out a call for one of their own to stand."

Thorne looked incredulous. "And the powers that be chose Rigsby-Boothe? I dread to think what the other applicants were like!"

Thom shook his head. "Oh no, sir, that's just it. He was the only applicant, so they had no choice."

Elliott frowned. "Is he any good?"

Thom looked sober. "He was, sir, until a few months ago. I get the feeling he's just waiting for them to retire him, he's just going through the motions." He paused. "Is that true, sir, what you said about them cigars?"

"Unfortunately, yes. Hashish has a certain odour that singles it out from other such imports. I think you'll find that's why his work has suffered lately."

"I don't think the High Constable is going to enjoy having you here, sir."

"Everything will be fine as long as he leaves us to our investigation and doesn't try to interfere."

"Oh, I doubt he will, sir. Like I said, he's just going through the motions these days."

Elliott looked at the young man thoughtfully. "What about you, Constable? Will you enjoy having us here?"

Thom's response was enthusiastic. "Oh yes, sir. It will be nice to see a real investigation. I mean, it's not like dealing with the usual scrumping and poaching, is it?"

Elliott caught Thorne's eye, pointed at Thom, and mouthed, "What do you think?" Thorne looked at the young constable and nodded approval.

Elliott cleared his throat and prodded Thom. "Right, Thorne and I need someone who knows the area and the people, and can dig up the information we will need to solve this case. Will you help us?"

The Waggonette slewed suddenly to the left as Thom turned in his seat to look at Elliott. "I would be grateful for the opportunity to prove myself, sir!"

Elliott smiled. "Jolly good! Your first task, then, is to fill us in on the case. We were given the basics back at the Yard, but what other information do you have?"

Thom gestured under Thorne's seat. "Mr Rigsby-Boothe brought the file with him, sir."

"By Jove, that was good of him," Elliott murmured as Thorne handed him the file. He opened the thin folder and scanned the few pieces of paper inside.

"Oh, it's not to do with the murder, sir; we didn't have time to get much information together on that. It's information we already had on one of the victims: Gregory Hardcastle, the Marmis family butler. A bit of a bastard, sir, if you'll pardon my honesty. Several verbal complaints from village girls and a number of maids, but nothing we could charge him with."

Elliott scowled as he flicked through the file. "One of that sort, was he? Why didn't Lord Marmis get rid of him?"

"The servants didn't tell him, sir; they judged it a below-stairs matter. They should have told him, though. This whole mess might never have happened if they had, sir, and that's a fact."

Elliott pulled out one of the pieces of paper and studied it. "It says here that only one of the girls went to the police to make a formal complaint?"

"Yes, sir. Everyone knew what he was like, but none of the girls would press charges because of the shame. But a local girl called Edith Baker, she went to see Mr Rigsby-Boothe." Thom's voice cracked but he cleared his throat and contin-ued. "He may be backsliding now, sir, but back then he did his job and he believed her. The problem was that when Hardcastle found out, he put her in hospital and she clammed up."

Elliott looked at Thom thoughtfully; the anger in the young man's voice showed more than just professional distaste. "Where is Edith Baker now?"

Thom stared ahead. "After Hardcastle attacked her the second time, she tried to kill herself. She was taken to St Brigid's Asylum near Pelloehaven. She came home three weeks ago, she's staying at the Dolphin and Anker Inn, where she works now. She was going to be charged over the suicide attempt, but Mr Rigsby-Boothe had a word and the charges against her were dropped."

Thorne looked at the young man. "You don't look happy, Constable. Why not?"

Thom gripped the steering wheel, his face pale and set. "Not charging Edith meant not charging Hardcastle, sir. Don't get me wrong, keeping it quiet-like has helped Edith no end, but it meant Hardcastle was free to carry on. I honestly don't know what would have been for the best, sir."

Elliott passed the dossier to Thorne, a cold expression on his face. "So the poor girl was abused by a man who had power over her, then sent to an asylum for trying to kill herself. Call me old-fashioned, but it sounds to me as if this killer has done the village maidens a favour."

Thorne looked up from his perusal of the file, his elegant face as cold as Elliott's. "May I retract my previous wish and say now that I hope the certain injury we were talking about on the train was caused *before* death?"

Elliott gave him a grim smile. "Changing the subject entirely, Constable, have any plans been made for our accommodation?"

Thom straightened in his seat. "Well, sir, no official plans were made, so I took it upon myself. I had a word with the landlady at the Dolphin and Anker on my way to the station this morning, and she said that although one gennelman came down yesterday evening, there's still room for both of you with some over, so I asked her to keep three rooms to one side...two as bedrooms and I thought a third could be used as an office."

Elliott grinned. "That sounds excellent, Constable...but is this inn clean? I have spent quite a lot of time in questionable hostelries and I have no wish to do so again. A place with a bath and no insect life would be nice."

Thom laughed, and his face lost the drawn look it had worn during the talk about Edith Baker. "They do good clean rooms, sir, and Mrs Mickle the landlady has already put you down for the two bedrooms next to the bath."

Thorne pricked up his ears. "Do they do food?"

"Marmis Parva is halfway along the main Pelloehaven tour route, sir. Mrs Mickle prides herself on the cleanliness of her rooms and the quality of her food; they get a lot of visitors in high season, families and the like. It's a good place, sir, and I can recommend their cottage pie. Mrs Mickle is one of the best cooks in the area."

Thorne sighed happily, and pulling the brim of his tweed cap down over his eyes, dozed as Thom drove the Waggonette and Elliott continued his perusal of the pile of documents from the Commissioner and the High Constable.

A little over six miles and an hour later, the squeaking vehicle entered the village of Marmis Parva: all four lanes of it. Built on a valuable place of trade to the Romans, Marmis Parva had followed in the usual tradition of the English village and gone from trading-place to quaint day-tripper destination almost overnight. Luckily for Elliott and Thorne, the day-tripper season had ended in August, so they didn't have to elbow their way through ravaging hordes to reach the inn.

Almost absorbed into the Westrenweald, the thick, wild forest that covered the shire from her mountainous borders in the north to her rugged southern coastline, and that was still home to wild boar, wolves, and the famed Huishmoor ponies, the slightly more manicured and definitely more civilised woodlands surrounding Marmis Parva had been given the innocuous name of Cuckoo Woods. The village itself was bisected by a little tributary of the larger Westren-grey River which wrapped around the county like a thick silver ribbon, turning it into a vast island surrounded by mountains to the north, west, and east, and by the English Channel to the south.

Entering the village from the north, along the imaginatively named North Lane, Thom guided the Waggonette past the tiny police house and the post office before passing over the crossroads and the narrow packhorse bridge. He pulled up in front of a large, well-kept Tudor building with a neatly painted sign that bore the legend 'The Dolphin and

Anker Inn', and underneath, in bold gilded letters, 'Coaching Inn'.

Thom applied the brake, settled the little vehicle and indulged in a stretch, which led to a yawn, which in turn infected Elliott, who yawned back and growled good-naturedly, "Don't do that again, Constable."

The young constable laughed. "No, sir. You're in rooms three, and four, with the office in room six. Do you want to go up to your rooms while I deal with Mrs Mickle, sir?"

Elliott shook his head. "I think we should go in together and thank the good lady for jumping into the breach and supplying us with three rooms." He gestured at Thorne. "Besides, I need to make sure it *is* three rooms. I'm not sharing with him, he snores!"

Ignoring Thorne's outraged splutters to the contrary, Elliott climbed out of the Daimler and gave it a distrustful look; he still couldn't quite make out the colour.

Thom saw the expression on Elliott's face. "You don't approve of automobiles, sir?"

"I neither approve nor disapprove, Constable. I simply chose to reserve judgement until I have more knowledge. But I do believe that travelling in a machine that has no brain is rather dangerous. If you blindly approach a hazard on a horse, the animal will usually endeavour to let you know." He gestured at the little motor. "Could this contraption warn you in time?"

Thom smiled. "Well, sir, if it's the safety side of things that worries you, the police in Benchester are thinking about getting a Simulandro driver for__"

Elliott lifted a hand with a pained expression. "Simu-ladro's automatia are a case in point, Constable. If I, as a passenger, have no great desire to travel in a contraption like this which has a human driver, whatever makes people think I would be willing to travel in something that was being driven by an automated equivalent? Designing the driver to resemble a human doesn't fill me with either the desire or the willingness to be conveyed by a creation that cannot think for itself. To be honest, if it were a choice between this vehicle, an airship, or a Simulandro driver, I would choose this vehicle...she is very comfortable, and quite swift, but overall, I think I still prefer trains, horses, and boats!"

Thorne grinned at the young constable's obvious puzzlement. "You'll never get Elliott to admit that any new-fangled invention is useful until after it has proven its worth...many, many times over! He's still not too sure about telephones... and don't get him started on airships!"

Elliott sniffed. "If machines can be proven useful and with no harm caused, then and only then shall I fully accept their worth. I refuse to blindly welcome their immersion into our daily lives without query. If the fact that I'm not a fervent supporter of machines makes me a Luddite, then so be it and I shall bear that medal with fortitude, bravery, and honour!" He lifted his Gladstone bag from the back seat and pointed at the dark front door of the inn with his cane. "Now...will we need a battering ram, do you think?"

Thom hefted one of the bags from the back seat. "I wouldn't have thought so, sir. The door to the kitchens is usually kept unlocked."

Thorne looked curious. "Why?"

"Well, sir. After Mr Mickle closes for the night, he tends to go a-wandering round the village, him being a bad sleeper, sir, so they leave the door unlocked."

Elliott rolled his eyes at Thorne. "Oh Gods, not another one!"

"Oh, no, sir," said Thom. "Mr Mickle really is a bad sleeper; he has trouble sleeping at night so he works then and sleeps during the day. He's nothing like Hardcastle. The only person around these parts whose reputation was nearly as bad as Hardcastle's was Lord Scott-Brewer."

Elliott walked towards the inn, then looked at Thom. "You're sure we can just walk in? I wouldn't want to terrify the good lady into fits."

"Don't worry, sir. When I spoke to her at just after one o'clock this morning', she was already starting on her baking and preparing the stews for lunch. Chances are she's still cooking."

Thorne's eyes lit up. "Superb! We can have a slap-up breakfast before we go on to the hall."

Elliott smiled. "Nothing ever changes; stomach first! Mrs Mickle might not want to feed three starving policemen at nearly four in the morning, Thorne."

Thorne rubbed his hands together and picked up his case. "We'll see. I'm prepared to throw myself at the lady's feet if necessary."

The three men, with Thom in the lead, walked past the inn's closed and shuttered front door to the narrow alley that led towards the back of the old building. As they hurried through the dark, confined space, their surroundings opened up into a delightful well-lit courtyard with large planters full of evergreens. On the far side of the courtyard, three brightly lit windows shone a welcome that was accompanied by mouth-watering smells of baking bread and roasting meat.

Thorne breathed in deeply as Thom headed for the barn door next to one of the windows, pulled the top half open, and called, "Morning, Mrs Mickle, can we come in?"

A muffled but obviously female voice came from the depths of the wonderfully fragrant kitchen. "Is that you, Thom? Come in, lad, come in. Have you brought them with you?"

As the three men stepped into the kitchen, the figure seated at the large table grinned at them over a mound of baking tins. Mrs Ellie Mickle, landlady of the Dolphin and Anker Inn and undoubtedly the best cook in the district, sat in cheerful contemplation of a small mountain of freshly baked bread. The warm, yeasty smell from the loaves wrapped itself around the cosy, well-used room and mingled with the aroma from the massive haunch of meat suspended over the large fire in the corner.

Well-padded, as a good cook should be, and with her greying hair still showing a trace of its original red, Mrs Mickle's dark eyes twinkled impishly as she regarded the three tired and hungry men before her.

Thom returned her cheerful grin. "Mrs Mickle, these are the police officers I told you about earlier. Detective Chief Inspector Caine and Detective Sergeant Thorne of the CID, come down from London to see about what happened up at the hall."

Mrs Mickle nodded at Caine and Thorne. "Gennelmen."

Elliott took off his hat and bowed from the waist, holding his hat in the same hand as his cane, then walked up to Mrs Mickle and gallantly kissed her flour dusted hand with a smile. "Mrs Mickle, Constable Greyling has informed us of your very kind offer of accommodation, which we gratefully accept. May we throw ourselves even deeper into your debt by enquiring whether you could spare any of that delicious smelling bread for three hungry policemen?"

The landlady chuckled. "I've not heard such waffle since Mr Mickle asked for me hand! Help yourselves, gennelmen, there's fresh butter on the table and spreads in the pantry." She waived her hand at a large door set into the wall in the far corner of the room.

Elliott beat Thorne and Thom to it, and the three men stood in happy silence for some time, gazing at the multitudinous jars, bottles and crocks full of nourishing home-made foodstuffs, just made to go on a crusty loaf!

With a happy sigh Elliott pulled out a jar of apricot jam and handed it to Thorne, who stood perusing the shelves until he saw what he wanted. A jar of anchovy butter joined the apricot jam on the table as the two CID men sat down with Mrs Mickle. By the time Thom found what he fancied, a good thick strawberry jam, Elliott and Thorne were deeply involved with a large, warm cottage loaf and freshly churned butter.

Thorne tore a chunk of bread from the large loaf in front of him and spread it liberally with butter. Elliott watched with a grin as his old friend stuffed the appetising morsel into his mouth.

Mrs Mickle got up from her chair at the head of the table and gave Elliott a cheerful nod. "Tea?"

Elliott, silenced by bread and apricot jam, could only nod while he worked through his mouthful. "Thank you for breakfast, Mrs Mickle. We really do appreciate it, especially at this time of the morning."

Ellie Mickle grinned as she looked at the three men. "Don't you worry, lad. I've been up a while getting things ready, and besides, I wasn't about to send you to the hall starving, was I?" She bustled over to a large cast iron kettle hanging next to the roast on the ancient iron range. Picking up the kettle, she poured a stream of hot water into a battered old china teapot, warmed the pot, then took a tea caddy from an open shelf by the pantry and measured out several spoonful's of black tea. Elliott sighed with relief; so many people these days drank that awful green China tea that tasted of hay and made his teeth itch…give him a good strong Assam any day!

As the three men sat in the comfortable kitchen, Elliott had a sudden thought. "I understand that Thom has informed you of the reason for our presence, Mrs Mickle. Would it be possible for us to use your knowledge of the village and gather more information about the two victims?"

Mrs Mickle stirred the tea and placed the lid on with a clang. "Aye, lad, go on with your questions."

Elliott settled back in his chair. "Was Hardcastle known in the village? Did he have any friends or acquaintances that you can think of?"

Mrs Mickle carried the teapot, cups and saucers to the table and set them out. "He had no friends. And he wasn't from round here; I can tell you that. Milk?" At Elliott and Thorne's nods she poured a small quantity of creamy milk into the cups and started to pour out. "Said he was from Kent, but some of my husband's family are from up that way and that's not how they sound."

Elliott looked up at her as she handed him a full cup. "So you think he lied about his origins?"

"If that means where you come from, aye, I do. He was a born liar, that man. He used people, especially girls who weren't old enough to tell the difference between charming and nasty. Young girls like Edith Baker, poor thing."

Elliott put three sugars in his tea, stirred it and took a deep sip. "Do her parents know she is back in the village?"

Mrs Mickle sat down. "Aye. The poor lass tried to go and see her mother, but her father wouldn't let her in; said she was cursed by God for trying to take her own life. After what she's been through the good God would understand, but that old terror Mickey Baker threw her out and told her own mother not to see her! He's almost as bad as that swine Hardcastle. 'Scuse my language, gennlemen, but it's the truth!"

Her voice dropped to a whisper. "Aye, almost, but there was always something different about Hardcastle. He charmed people who were useful to him and he hurt those who weren't, and it was deliberate. It was like he thought he had the right to do it, and no one had the right to say no." She gripped her cup hard. "But I dealt with him and his ways." She looked at Elliott. "Edith is here, Detective Inspector, at the inn, and has been ever since they let her out of St Brigid's. Her mother knows and they can see each other without old Baker knowing. And even if he did, he wouldn't dare come here and cause trouble. The only reason he got upset about any of it was because he lost the money his poor girl brought home from working up at the hall."

Elliott put down his empty cup. "Mrs Mickle, what did you mean by 'I dealt with him and his ways'?"

She looked at Elliott steadily, then leaned forward and picked up his cup. Putting it on the saucer upside down, she turned it three times then picked it up again. She gazed at its contents for a few moments, then placed the cup in front of the young CID man and pointed to a dog-shaped clump of tea leaves on one side of the cup.

"That's old Grimm: he brings violent death to those who see him and those who are shown him. You've met with him before, haven't you?"

○

03:55am

Elliott dumped his Gladstone bag on the homely patchwork cover of the comfortable-looking single bed and sighed contentedly. Across the hall Thorne was not quite so formal, and threw himself face down on the thickly stuffed mattress with a groan of tired approval. After a moment's deep appreciation of the comfortable bed, and the prospect of a good night's sleep beckoning all too seductively, Thorne dragged himself back to his feet, removed his jacket and splashed his face with water from the jug. He applied a touch of Pomade to his hair before pulling his jacket back on and returning to their automobile to retrieve one of their work chests, leaving the far heavier cases that contained their photographic equipment in the Waggonette for later use at Marmis Hall.

Back in his room, Elliott unpacked the clothing he had brought and put it away, then turned back to the bag and released the catch that held the false bottom in place. He reached inside the padded compartment and took out a small square of purple silk, which he draped across the bedside table before removing a small, beautifully carved green jade box which he carefully placed on the silken square. With tender fingers, he gently traced the swirls painstakingly carved into the exquisite stone.

Gazing at the small box that housed his most treasured possessions, Elliott was tormented by memories and thoughts still far too painful to bear. Turning abruptly, he went in search of Thom, who was in the room they had set aside as an office.

As Elliott entered the room and nodded at Thom, they were joined by Thorne who placed the chest on one of the chairs in front of the fireplace and began to unpack the contents; forms and assorted paperwork in triplicate, fountain pens, bottles of ink, rubber stamps, large manilla envelopes and the other necessary items of official police work were placed neatly on the small desk by the window, alongside some rather more unusual curiosities. Thom picked up a small wooden box securely locked with a peculiar looking mechanism. "What's in here, sir?"

Thorne's expression was bland. "Thumbscrews. We have to get our confessions one way or another!"

Thom laughed. "Right, sir!"

Thorne paused and patted his waistcoat pocket. "I left my monocle in my room...I'll be right back."

As Thorne left, Elliott looked at the young constable. "Is Mrs Mickle always like that?"

"Oh yes, sir, she's the village witch. No dancing naked or that sort of thing, but she sees for people, sir. Talks to them that's passed on, heals people if they're sick, the doctors being so expensive and all. She helps people, so Mr Rigsby-Boothe leaves her alone."

Elliott nodded thoughtfully as he gazed into the flickering flames of the little fire that warmed the sitting room.

Thom carefully placed the wooden box back on the table. "Sir, when do you want to go up to the hall?"

Elliott looked at the young constable. "Is there a reason why we have to hurry?"

Thom looked stunned. "Well, sir, the murders!"

Elliott held up his finger. "Lesson number one, Constable Greyling. Leave suspects to stew for a while and they become unsure; leave them a little longer and they start to worry; leave them too long and they become angry. A fine line separates the last two points, and we need to take full advantage of that worrying margin. That is when we will get most of our information, so that is when we will arrive."

Thom looked puzzled. "When will that be, sir?"

Elliott consulted his watch. "Well, it's ten minutes past four now, so the best time to arrive would be..." He turned. "Thorne!"

Thorne appeared in the doorway of the room opposite and raised an enquiring eyebrow.

"Saddle up, old chap; we're off to the hall."

Thorne grinned. "I take it we're at the worrying point, then?"

"We are indeed. Get yourself ready and bring the thumb-screws. This could well be dirty work!"

04:30am

Thom brought the little automobile to a stop at the ornate gatehouse that guarded the entrance to Marmis Hall. The three men sat in silence in the foggy blue light of early morning and looked at the massive iron gates that barred their entry.

Elliott turned to Thom. "Remember that battering ram you said we didn't need?"

Thom got out of the vehicle. "Don't worry, sir, the gate-keeper is my grandfather. He's expecting us."

The young constable walked up to the gates and tugged at the large bell pull on the gate post. An answering bell rang in the distance, as old Morris appeared from his little gatehouse and ambled towards them.

Arriving on the other side of the gate, he nodded. "Morning, Thom, happen they're expecting you up at hall." The old man threw his weight against the counterweight, and as the gate swung open he waved at the two men in the Waggonette. Turning to Thom, he whispered, "Them the London police, lad?"

Thom looked back at the automobile. "Aye, Grandpa, they are."

Morris clipped Thom firmly round the ear. "You know not to call me Grandpa while I'm on duty, lad!"

Thom rubbed his sore ear ruefully. "Sorry, sir."

"And so you should be. Now get up there and sort this bloody mess out so's we can get back to our normal duties!"

Thom walked back to the car and climbed in with an embarrassed look at his superior officers. Elliott looked at him with a smile. "What was all that about, or shouldn't I ask?"

"I made the mistake of calling my grandfather 'grandpa' while he was on duty, sir."

Thorne grinned from his slightly squashed position on the back seat, sandwiched between the door and the two chests that contained everything they needed for their forensic investigation. "An old-fashioned type of gentleman, is he?"

Thom started the engine. "You could say that, sir, if by old-fashioned you mean ancient!"

Elliott and Thorne grinned as they drove slowly past Morris, who stood stiffly to attention by the gate and watched the Daimler make its way towards Marmis Hall. As the little car puttered along the meandering drive, it was swallowed by the wooded belt of land that wrapped around the hall and joined the even thicker swathe of forest two miles to the west.

Elliott turned to Thom. "So, tell us about the current generation of the Marmis family. Are they still local?"

Thom nodded, keeping his eyes on the driveway in front of him. "Yes, sir, the Marmis family have been here for over four hundred years. They have a good reputation for helping their tenants and workers, like my mother, father, and grandfather, sir. Granddad is in the gatehouse and has been for over forty years, and my father is the head footman. Years back, my mother was the cook. When she died, Lord Marmis – it was old Josua Marmis at that time, sir – he could have thrown us all out, but instead he asked my dad if he would leave his position in Benchester and work at the hall. Dad said yes, and Lord Josua took him on as a footman. Now he's head footman, and has been for about ten years. He was a good man, Lord Josua…in spite of…well!"

Elliott looked at the young constable with a searching expression. "In spite of what?"

Thom fidgeted, and tugging his collar, he coughed. "Well,

sir, he didn't have a reputation for being a bastard like Hardcastle or Lord Scott-Brewer..."

Elliott and Thorne exchanged glances, and Elliott looked at Thom. "Go on, Constable."

Thom fidgeted again. "He had more of a reputation for being a proper ladies' man, sir, but Lady Caroline put up with it!"

Thorne spoke from the back seat. "By 'ladies' man', do you mean he didn't take his pleasure by force?"

Thom flushed. "That seems to have been the case, sir."

Elliott settled back in his seat and gazed out of the vehicle as they crested the driveway and the view opened up before them. The section of driveway they were currently on clung to the side of a steep, wooded hill and afforded a perfect, though foggy, view of the stately home. One hundred feet below them, wrapped in the sleepy, soft blue half-light of the moon, Marmis Hall sat in its five-acre dip, surrounded on three sides by woodland, while to the south glimmered a large, man-made lake.

Elliott took in the beautiful, and somewhat familiar view. "Oh, yes," he murmured softly. He turned to Thom. "This is a new approach to the house, isn't it?"

Thom looked surprised as he carefully guided the little motor around a sharp bend in the driveway that enclosed a large, gnarled oak tree whose girth nearly blotted out the view of the hall. "Yes, sir...how did you know? Oh, it must have been in the files. Yes, sir, this driveway was only put in about twenty years ago."

Elliott and Thorne shared a smile; it had certainly been more than twenty years since their last visit to Marmis Hall. The motorcar puttered along the drive as Thom continued. "Lord Josua decided he wanted a new view of the hall when he returned from business, so they dug up the old drive and put in this one. Thing was, the architect wanted to take out old Jack over there," Thom indicated the oak tree, "but Lord Josua wouldn't let him. They came to blows over it; Lord Josua didn't want to lose his tree, and the architect didn't want to give in to a client. So they came to an agreement: Lord Josua kept his tree, and the architect took Lord Josua's wife!"

Thorne looked at Thom incredulously. "Pardon?"

Thom smiled. "The rumour was that that was the real reason for the fight. My dad saw it, and he said it was a real humdinger. Lord Josua was in his fifties at the time, but apparently he gave as good as he got, if not better!"

Elliott looked quizzical. "So what happened to the lady of the house?"

"Lady Caroline obviously decided she'd had enough, she left with the architect."

"Why 'obviously'?"

"Well, Lord Josua's behaviour, sir. With regards to his lady friends. Anyway, Lady Caroline went off and we haven't seen her since. She didn't even come back for Lord Josua's funeral, so she can't have missed him much."

"Indeed. A question, Constable: didn't she return when her youngest son was taken prisoner by the Boers?"

Thom eased the car into the turning circle and pulled to a smooth halt by the steps leading up to the massive front door. He turned to look at Elliott. "No, sir, she hasn't been back at all. We would have known in the village; the staff would have said. If anything, they talked about how she never came, not even to see her eldest boy, Foster, as he was before he got the title."

Elliott nodded thoughtfully. "Hmm, strange indeed. Now unless I am very much mistaken, the preoccupied-looking man coming out of the front door is the master of the house, yes?"

Thom looked up the steps. "Yes, sir, that is Lord Marmis; the gennelman does look a bit unstuck, doesn't he?"

"He does indeed! Let's get out of this contraption quickly, shall we?" The three men climbed out of the Waggonette as Lord Marmis, closely followed by Lord Lapotaire, began to walk down the steps.

As Elliott and Thorne bundled themselves out of the vehicle, Lord Marmis took the opportunity to observe the men Lord Lapotaire had suggested for the job. His friend had described them well, Lord Marmis allowed his gaze to skim over Thorne before resting on the darker of the two men; not too tall, perhaps a little shorter than himself, but with rather shaggy, almost unkempt dark hair that curled upon his collar. He was, however, immaculately dressed in what Lord Marmis recognised as a bespoke tweed travel suit, finished off with a matching cap and a Malacca walking stick topped with an ivory handle, the design of which Lord Marmis couldn't quite make out.

As Elliott approached the steps Lord Marmis noted the sharp, almost patrician nose in the centre of a gentle, expressive face. Well, almost gentle: the brown eyes above that sharp nose were intense, and at that moment all their intensity was centred on Lord Marmis.

Realising the man was aware of his scrutiny, Lord Marmis held out his hand, and in a slightly flustered voice very unlike his own inquired, "Detective Chief Inspector Caine, how do you do? I'd like to say welcome to Marmis Hall, but...well, given the current situation I don't believe I could get away with it."

Elliott shook the lord's hand and turned towards Thorne. "Lord Marmis, allow me to introduce Detective Sergeant Abernathy Thorne. I believe you know your village Constable, who has been seconded to us for this investigation."

Lord Marmis nodded. "Yes of course," He nodded at Thorne. "Detective Sergeant Thorne. Constable Greyling."

Thom touched the brim of his helmet. "Morning, my lord."

Lord Marmis turned to the man standing beside him. "I understand that you and Lord Lapotaire have already met, Detective Chief Inspector Caine."

Lord Lapotaire held out his hand. "I'm sorry the request for your assistance arrived through somewhat...irregular channels, Caine, if we'd had the time it would have arrived by more conventional means, I assure you. But given the circumstances, we urgently needed someone who would understand the importance of discretion. You've dealt with this sort of thing before and you know the protocols, so you were the first person who came to mind."

Elliott's face was inscrutable as he looked at Lord Lapotaire, who appeared slightly embarrassed. He took the offered hand. "I'll have to take your word for it, Lord Lapotaire. As long as you are both willing to accept that this case will be solved, regardless of who the killer turns out to be. Is that acceptable, my lords?"

Lord Marmis nodded. "Perfectly acceptable, Detective Chief Inspector Caine."

Elliott waved his hand. "Please call me Caine, I'm not much of a one for formality, as Lord Lapotaire is quite aware. Now, shall we go in? You can inform us of the occurrences of the last day or so, preferably over a pot of Indian tea."

An explosive sigh came from Lord Marmis. "That sounds like a very pleasant idea. May I suggest my study? I will inform Greyling that we are not to be disturbed."

Elliott pricked up his ears. "Greyling?"

"Our new butler. It may seem a little unsympathetic, Detective –er, Caine, but a house this size needs constant supervision and the loss of a butler can be a catastrophe. Greyling was the head footman. Now he is the butler, and unlike the last incumbent his background is beyond reproach…as is his behaviour towards the female staff." Lord Marmis looked at his watch. "Shall we go inside, gentlemen?"

The four men followed Lord Marmis up the steps into the Great Hall, where the newly ensconced Greyling greeted them and took their coats and hats.

As they proceeded down the corridor to Lord Marmis' study, Greyling winked at his son, then turned smoothly back to Lord Marmis as he took the order for morning tea to be served in the study.

○

04:45am

Lord Marmis opened the door and ushered them into the plush room. Thom took a high-backed chair next to the door and Thorne sat on the settee against the left wall, quietly removing his notebook as Elliott and Lord Lapotaire settled into the two armchairs by the fire. Lord Marmis checked the lock on the French windows and sat heavily behind his desk. Rubbing his face, he turned to Elliott. "Well, gentlemen, where do I begin?"

Elliott arranged himself in the comfortable armchair, and was about to reply when his attention was caught by the painting over the fireplace. Deep red hair and laughing eyes shone down on him as he sat beneath her portrait…Lady Marianne.

Thorne also looked at the large painting, and holding his first reaction in check, stared steadily at Elliott, before turning to Lord Marmis.

"Are you a follower of Giselle Du Lac too, my lord? That is a very lifelike portrait." He indicated the painting.

Lord Marmis looked at the painting and smiled. "I have to agree with you that the likeness is incredible, but that is not Giselle Du Lac. That is my great-great-great-great-grandmother, Lady Marianne Marmis, wife of the eighth Lord Marmis who built this hall, nearly bankrupting the family in the process, I might add!"

Lord Marmis pushed his long, sensitive fingers together into a steeple then looked at Elliott, the smile vanishing from his face. "To business, gentlemen. This has certainly been a most distressing experience."

Elliott nodded calmly and murmured, "I would venture to suggest a bloody inconvenient one too, hmm?"

Lord Marmis' brows knitted and he turned his eyes on Lord Lapotaire, who smiled and settled back in his chair with an expression of wry amusement on his sharply drawn features. "Caine has a great deal of experience in dealing with this particular form of hideousness, Marmis." Lord Lapotaire looked at Elliott and his grin faded slightly. "It is by way of being his speciality."

Lord Marmis turned back to Elliott. "In that case, Caine, I shall be absolutely honest with you; this evening has been in one way wonderful, and in another way an utter bloody shambles! Unfortunately, I mean bloody in the worst possible sense." He turned to the drinks cabinet and poured out five large glasses of single-malt scotch which he handed out. Thom looked as though he couldn't quite believe his luck; unsure what to do with the sizeable crystal tumbler that had suddenly supplanted his pencil, he placed his notebook on his lap and tried to take notes one-handed.

Lord Marmis continued, "I assure you, gentlemen, I do not usually drink at this time of day, but I think this is an exception to the rule." He glared at his drink as though it were an affront to his dignity to be seen with it, threw it back, and sat down abruptly. Placing his hands on his knees, he stared at Elliott. "This is appalling. I have never – my family, to my knowledge, has never been in this ungodly position before, so I am at a loss to know how to deal with it."

Elliott considered his options; he had to see just how honest this young lord would be. He sipped his whisky and placed it on the table next to him, then standing, he approached the fire and leant against the mantelpiece. "Firstly, Lord Marmis, may I offer you our sympathies over the loss of both your butler, and a dear friend."

Lord Marmis gritted his teeth. "I assure you that will not be necessary. I have discovered tonight that not only was my butler a degenerate who habitually abused the maids, but that my guest, who far from being a dear friend was invited solely to make up the numbers, was also so inclined."

Elliott nodded, satisfied with his reaction. "Good, that's that out of the way. I was going to ask if you had any inkling of Hardcastle's behaviour before this evening."

Lord Marmis stared at Elliott, his face pale. "None whatever, and I can assure you that had I known, I would have dealt with him: either privately, or by bringing the full force of the law down upon him! I can tell you one thing, though; there was always something about the man that made my teeth itch, though I could not have said what it was. However, I was only informed of his behaviour this evening, after I had received some rather startling news."

Elliott raised his eyebrows. "Do continue."

Thorne silently discarded his now-blunt pencil and whipped out a spare sharp one. Thom had long since given up trying to juggle his tumbler, notebook and pencil, and was content to watch the speed with which Thorne scribbled his notes.

Lord Marmis paused, his long fingers twisting together on his lap in an unusual display of emotion. "Two years ago, my brother Frederick was arrested by the Boers in Southern Africa. He was gathering information for the British government at the time, and so he was arrested on a charge of spying. Needless to say, he was found guilty and sentenced to death. That was the last we heard of him until this evening, when to our shock and unspeakable happiness Frederick walked into this very room. I cannot begin to explain the joy we felt."

Elliott stared into the fire, taking great pains to avoid looking at the portrait above. "I believe I can understand to a certain extent, Lord Marmis. Allow me to explain. You felt hideous guilt at his suffering because it was you who gave him the orders to travel to Southern Africa. Am I correct?"

Lord Marmis swallowed hard. "Yes, you are quite correct. Frederick was a very promising young diplomat, gifted with a natural charm that cannot be taught. He spoke with various Boer factions over the course of several months but we needed more information. Talking with the people they were willing to send wasn't enough; we had to send someone who could speak the language and blend in. Damn it, Fred was the only man in the diplomatic who could speak Afrikaans! Most of the rest could speak Dutch but they are different languages. Bertie and I agreed that it had to be him, and after a fashion, so did Fred. We convinced him of the necessity in this very room! And I have spent the last two years cursing myself for it." His face cleared. "Then earlier this evening, Frederick returned."

"You had no advanced warning?"

"None whatsoever."

Elliott looked at Lord Marmis. "Do you have a photograph of your brother?"

"Yes, of course." Lord Marmis picked up an ornate gilded

frame that stood near a large marble inkwell on his desk and handed it to Elliott, who gazed with deliberation at the young face captured in sepia. The colour of the young man's eyes could not be discerned through the soft peachy shading of the photographic process, but the dark hair and the set of the jawline, while thicker and broader than his older brother's, was very similar. Elliott passed the photograph to Thorne.

Lord Marmis leant forwards in his chair and an eager expression swept across his face, turning it into that of a much younger man. "Frederick came home, battered and tired but safe. Apparently the much-publicised death sentence of the son of an English peer was just so much humbug; they jailed him and tried to get information out of him." Lord Marmis' jaw clenched. "They tortured him, but he refused to tell them anything. After several months, one of the doctors who treated the prisoners helped Frederick escape, and he made his way home." Lord Marmis gripped the arms of his chair. "But he didn't return empty-handed. The doctor who helped my brother gave him documents with names and details of traitors and Boer agents in England, and one of the names on the list was Gregory Hardcastle!"

Elliott raised a questioning eyebrow. "Your now very dead butler?"

"Indeed! One of the things I could never understand was how the Boers found out about Frederick, and now I know. Hardcastle started working for us shortly before I gave Frederick his orders to travel to Southern Africa; he must have passed that information to his masters. It is the only possible answer."

"Were there any other names of note in the documents, Lord Marmis?"

"Yes, there were three other names: John Rook we now

know was Gregory Hardcastle, and the other three were John Stable, John Wisdom and..." Lord Marmis paused and looked directly at Elliott. "There is a fourth name, but it seems to have been added later, in a different ink."

Elliott smiled slightly. "What is the fourth name?"

"Versipellis."

Thorne looked sharply at Elliott, who ignored his friend and carried on smiling at Lord Marmis. Lord Lapotaire caught Thorne's eye and shook his head slightly as Elliott murmured. "They sound like code names."

"They are; they have not yet been decoded."

"Pardon me for asking, Lord Marmis, but how do we know that your former butler is the man referred to in the documents?"

"Because the young doctor who helped Frederick knew the codes; he deciphered that name to prove himself to Frederick."

Elliott looked thoughtful. "What happened to this paragon of South African virtue?"

Lord Marmis regarded the fire. "He and Frederick made it to the border. Fred managed to cross, but the doctor was killed before he could escape."

Elliott frowned. "I'm sorry, Lord Marmis, but how can we be sure this doctor's statements are to be believed?"

Lord Lapotaire raised his head. "Because he too was one of our men, Caine. A young Englishman of Dutch descent, deep undercover as a Boer sympathiser, who offered his abilities as a doctor and was thrown into a place of utter darkness: a torture camp where his sole purpose was to keep men alive so the Boers could prise information out of them. His name was Wallace Johnson, and he was a damn brave man."

Elliott nodded slowly. "I am sorry; I did not mean to cause offence."

Lord Lapotaire waved his hand. "How were you to know? Ours can be a twisted game at times."

"Did Dr Johnson pass on any information about the other names on the list?"

Lord Marmis nodded. "Yes. Unlike John Rook, or Hardcastle as we knew him, who was actually born in Pretoria, Stable and Wisdom are English by birth. He passed on nothing more of Versipellis' background or origins in the document; we know a little of the agent, but nothing of the man who calls himself by that name." Lord Marmis paused, a troubled look on his face. "The nom de guerre 'Versipellis' has existed in various forms for well over five hundred years. I can't presume to know who or what he is, or how the name is passed down to the next in line for the position. What I do know is that he is an independent operative: an information-gatherer who has worked for the British government and, more recently, the Americans. We use him, sub rosa of course, for espionage, private investigations, and adventuring in the high seas – that sort of thing – but there is no further information about his more recent incarnation in the documents that Frederick brought, or any suggestion as to why he now seems to be working against us. However, Dr Johnson passed on some worrying information about the other two. John Wisdom is a well-placed middleman, passing the information which people like Rook, Stable, and Versipellis gave him to Boer headquarters. Apparently he is, God help us, highly placed in the government."

Elliott's smile widened, his overlong canines flashing. "Our government?"

"Hmm."

"How very fruity. And John Stable, what of him?"

Lord Marmis shot a look at Lord Lapotaire and took a deep breath. "Considering his abilities and his use within the Boer campaign, he is perhaps the more concerning of the four. Not from a political point of view, you understand? John Wisdom is the political worry. Frederick informed me that this man Stable is a master torturer, highly trained and undoubtedly deranged; it was he who tortured my brother." He leant forwards in his chair. "And the worst of this is that Johnson told Frederick of certain injuries he had seen on this man's victims. They bore exactly the same hideous injuries as were inflicted on Hardcastle, in this house, last night!"

○

05:00am

Thorne broke the silence. "Where is your brother now, sir?"

"In his room, asleep. After we found the bodies, it was thought best that he withdrew to his rooms. So, he was escorted there by both my wife..." Lord Marmis paused and passed his hand across his face before continuing. "And his mother."

Elliott fastened his sharp gaze on the young man's tired face. "His mother? Forgive me, but I thought his mother left some years ago."

Lord Marmis sighed, then looked at Elliott with some embarrassment. "I trust this will go no further, gentlemen? *My* mother is currently living in a very ostentatious palazzo in Venice with her second husband, the architect she left my father for...but *Frederick's* mother is still very much present in this house: she is our housekeeper, Mrs Higginson." He held up his hand as though to stall any unpleasant remarks. "I assure you our father was not in any way similar to Hardcastle. He could be a charming man when he wanted, and he had a reputation for being very, very charming. He enjoyed the company of a variety of women, and he was, apparently, extremely attentive. Mrs Higginson personally reassured me many years ago that though their relationship was socially unacceptable, my father's behaviour towards her had been quite gentlemanly. It lasted for one social season before he found another…companion."

Elliott flashed a look at Thom. "Very well. Lord Marmis, we now know where your brother is. Could you tell us the whereabouts of your other guests at this precise moment?"

"Of course. As I said, my brother retired to his rooms almost immediately we discovered the bodies, and his mother, Mrs Higginson, is now in the kitchen overseeing her duties as housekeeper. My old friend Sir Hubert Kingston-Folly is also in his suite; he was terribly shaken by what he saw in the gallery and withdrew almost immediately to his rooms. Lord Coalford also retired after he was informed: he is quite elderly. My wife, Lady Marmis, checked on our children and Nanny, then retired to our rooms shortly after we informed Lady Scott-Brewer of her husband's, er, demise. Mlle Giselle Du Lac was shown to her room upon arrival and hasn't been seen since, although my wife went to see her shortly after she arrived. Mr Weatherly Draycott retired shortly after he examined the bodies." He paused. "I have to say that for a doctor whose practice revolves around nervous ladies, he handled the situation rather well. Lady Scott-Brewer and her rather formidable maid are in their rooms—"

"Excuse me, Lord Marmis, but you said you and your wife informed Lady Scott-Brewer of her husband's passing?"

"Yes, my wife insisted on accompanying me." Lord Marmis explained what had passed between the four of them. "Her maid came down approximately half an hour later and informed me that Lady Scott-Brewer had taken a sleeping cachet and would be right as rain in the morning. Her words, not mine."

"And the other guests, the day guests – where are they?"

"Given the circumstances, I thought it best if they

returned to their homes to await any necessary questioning. I thought it the right thing to do."

Thorne made a quiet harrumphing noise in the back of his throat. Elliott nodded at him, then looking at Lord Marmis, murmured, "We will need the names and addresses of all your day guests, my lord. How many were there?"

"Only eight: four couples. I can give you their addresses now, if that would help?"

Thorne immediately turned to a fresh page in his notebook. Lord Marmis opened a drawer and removed a large address book. Flicking through the pages, he intoned, "Sir Mitchell Cruise-Branford and his wife Lady Felicity. I'll give you their country address as they are out of town: Blickling Hall, Meadowford. The Reverend and Mrs Michael Beardsley, The Vicarage, Benchester. Lord and Lady Pearson-Vault, Jaycalyn Hall, Pelloehaven, and Mr and Mrs Solomon Feldstein, The Lodge House, Pelloehaven." He closed the book and looked at Elliott with a wry smile. "I have to say they were all rather pleased to leave. Our weekend guests were rather put out at having to stay, and I can't say I blame them. They came here for a gentle weekend party and to hear Giselle sing, and now they are in the midst of an appalling murder investigation. I suppose in the interest of good taste, the party must be cancelled."

Elliott studied his neatly manicured fingernails. "Not necessarily."

Lord Marmis raised his eyebrows. "We can't really continue the weekend after two murders, surely?"

"It might be a good way of keeping people here until we have excluded them from our enquiries, Lord Marmis. Sneaky and possibly not in the best of taste, I grant you. But needs must when the devil drives, and all that."

Lord Marmis nodded tiredly. "Very well. What else do you need?"

Elliott threw himself back into his chair and fixed his penetrating gaze on the lord. "Right now, I would like both of you to relate the evening's events in as much detail as you can."

The tired young lord nodded, and with a barely covered yawn he reached for the bell pull. "In that case, as we shall be here for some time, I shall tell Greyling to bring in the tea and perhaps some hot buttered crumpets." He smiled for the first time since Elliott's arrival. "My wife refers to it as comfort food."

Elliott glanced over at Thorne and Thom. "I agree, tea and crumpets sound most refreshing."

Greyling entered quietly. "You rang, my lord?"

"Yes, Greyling. We are ready for the morning tea now, and I think some of Mrs Higginson's crumpets are in order."

"Very good, my lord. The tea is ready but the crumpets will take a little while."

Greyling bowed and left the room. Several minutes passed in polite discussion about the weather and cricket as they waited for Greyling's return with the tea. As the butler reappeared wheeling a laden trolley. Elliott studied him quietly. "Greyling."

The butler turned. "Yes, sir?"

"I should very much like to hear your honest opinion of your predecessor."

Greyling turned to look at Lord Marmis, who nodded. "It's quite all right, Greyling, please answer the detective."

The butler nodded. "Very well, my lord. He was an unmitigated bastard, sir. He looked upon the maids as his property, anything that wasn't nailed down he took, and he tried his hand at a spot of blackmail when he thought he could get away with it."

Elliott's ears pricked up. "Blackmail? What makes you say that?"

"I wouldn't like to say, sir," Greyling murmured, his face wooden.

Lord Marmis raised his hand. "It is quite all right, Greyling; they know about my brother's true parentage." He paused. "Did Hardcastle actually try to blackmail Mrs Higginson?"

Greyling's face tightened. "Yes, my lord. However, Valerie being Valerie, she sent him off with a flea in his ear."

The ghost of a smile appeared on Lord Marmis' face. "I can well believe that she did! Thank you, Greyling, that will be all."

Elliott looked up from his contemplation of a heavily buttered crumpet. "Just one moment, Greyling."

The butler turned. "Sir?"

"Is there anything you wish to tell us, or Lord Marmis, before we begin our investigations?"

Greyling's face became blank. "Nothing that I can think of, sir."

"Very well, you may go."

The butler bowed and left, closing the door behind him.

Elliott looked at Lord Marmis with a knowing expression. "He's lying."

"Why do you think that?"

"Instinct. He's very knowledgeable of, and rather protective towards, your housekeeper."

Lord Marmis smiled. "Perhaps I can help with that. I happen to know that Colin Greyling and Valerie Higginson were married six months ago." He turned to look at Thom, who appeared distinctly worried. "Is that not true, Constable Greyling?"

"Yes, my lord, but how did you find out?"

"I cannot claim any form of higher knowledge; your stepmother informed me last night."

"They won't lose their positions, will they, my lord?"

Lord Marmis shook his head. "No, Constable. The rules against fraternisation were meant to stop people like Hardcastle, and they were no use at all in preventing that. I think Marmis Hall will benefit greatly from having a husband and wife as butler and housekeeper."

A relieved expression appeared on Thom's face. "Thank you, my lord."

Elliott mopped up the copious quantities of butter that had dribbled down his wrist. "Back to the job in hand, then. I will need to interview people to ascertain where they were at the time of the murders." He paused to rifle through the file Thom had given him, leaving buttery smears that Thorne would hold against him later. "However, may I just confirm something with you? It says here that your wife was the last person to see Hardcastle alive, other than the murderer of course, and that she saw him in the cloakroom off the Great Hall at a little after five minutes past nine. Is that correct?"

"Yes, apparently he was pawing through the guests' cloaks. He told my wife some tosh about Draycott slamming the door and knocking the hanging rail down, but that rail is absolutely solid. I dangled from it often as a child, playing hide and seek, and there's absolutely no danger of it coming away from the wall that easily."

"Mr Draycott was on his way out, you say?"

"Yes. He probably went outside for a cigar; my wife doesn't allow smoking indoors."

"Would you happen to know when Lady Scott-Brewer last saw her husband?"

"As a matter of fact, I would. When her maid came to let me know her mistress was sleeping, she said Lady Scott-Brewer last saw her husband at approximately ten minutes past nine. This was confirmed by several of the day guests who witnessed a slight contretemps between husband and wife in the library. Nothing serious – she was just issuing her usual orders because she kept him on a tight rein on account of his behaviour. Apparently, it was the talk of the county, but I wish someone had informed me! I don't tend to listen to county gossip; I'm generally too busy with the international variety."

Elliott stroked his chin thoughtfully, his long slender fingers pulling at his neatly clipped beard. As Elliott moved his hand, Lord Marmis caught sight of a faint pattern on the skin around Elliott's left wrist. Good God, the man actually had a tattoo!

Impervious to this scrutiny, Elliott continued. "So that gives us the starting time for the murders. Both men were last seen alive at no later than ten minutes past nine, and both by at least two witnesses: Hardcastle by both your wife and Mr Draycott, and Lord Scott-Brewer by his wife and several other guests. Excellent. Could you now give an account of the evening from the beginning until the discovery of the remains, giving the approximate time you entered the gallery and what you found there?"

Lord Marmis and Lord Lapotaire informed them of the previous evening's entertainments until the discovery of the bodies, omitting nothing. After a visceral account of the gruesome find, the state of the remains, and the effect it had on various members of the group, Elliott held up his hand. "Have you got all that down, Thorne?"

Thorne looked up from his notebook and nodded.

Elliott settled himself in his chair and fixed his sharp eyes on Lord Marmis. "Please can you tell me again where and when the remains were found, and by whom?"

Lord Marmis sipped his tea. "The remains were discovered in the gallery at approximately twenty-five minutes to ten by Lord Lapotaire, Sir Hubert, Greyling, Jenkins and myself."

"Who is Jenkins?"

"One of our maids."

"You allowed a maid to accompany you into a room where you believed a Boer spy was hiding?"

Lord Marmis held up a hand. "Let me explain. After Fred informed me of Hardcastle's true identity, I left my wife, my brother, and his mother in the study and went to find Lord Lapotaire and Sir Hubert—"

"They were not with you in the study?"

"They were not. When Frederick reappeared, they understood that it was a private family moment and left us. Sir Hubert went to get Mrs Higginson from the kitchen, then went on to the billiard room, and Lord Lapotaire went to the music room. When Frederick informed me of Dr Johnson's accusation against Hardcastle I realised we had to find him. I went in search of Bertie and Lord Lapotaire and informed them of the irrefutable evidence that proved Hardcastle was a spy. But as we left the study to hunt him down, Greyling and Jenkins were already looking for him."

"Why?"

Lord Marmis sighed and rubbed his forehead. "One of the maids had gone missing; she was Hardcastle's most recent victim, so when they couldn't find either Smith, that's the maid's name, or Hardcastle, they were worried. One of the footmen had seen Hardcastle letting himself into the gallery and they thought he might have taken Smith in there against her will. That is why Jenkins accompanied us; she refused to leave in case Smith needed the presence of another woman."

Thorne spoke from the settee. "Did you find the missing maid, my lord?"

Lord Marmis nodded wearily. "Eventually; she had been helping to set up a room for our official meeting with Lord Coalford and Lord Lapotaire." He shuddered. "My God...if Hardcastle had been alive to eavesdrop on that, the effect on our campaign in Southern Africa would have been disastrous!"

"Would it be possible for you to give us a smidgeon of information about your meeting this weekend?" Elliott asked delicately.

Lord Marmis looked amused. "A smidgeon? I might be able to manage a little more than that. Lord Lapotaire here has told me about your, ah, background. Not a great deal," he added, seeing Elliott's face. "Just enough to confirm your trustworthiness."

For a moment the young lord pondered how strange it was that he, with all his training in politics, should seek to placate a man who was only a Detective Chief Inspector. Then again, Lord Lapotaire had mentioned his invaluable assistance to the Crown on more than a few occasions. Perhaps, given the circumstances, it would be best to pander to the man.

He cleared his throat. "As you know, the Boer War was finished with back in 1881. However, since then there have been the usual issues in Southern Africa: arguments over land rights, and so on. Some want us to go to war again; some think we should leave the entire blasted place to its own devices. Certain circumstances brought the situation home to us in a rather vicious manner two years ago, seeming to suggest that quite a few of our politicians and some of the Boer leaders were literally back on the warpath. Ever since then, I have been studying the whole damned mess for any way of making a breakthrough."

He drank some more tea. "There are several Boers who claim to be the leader of one particular faction or another; unfortunately, it tends to change depending on the region you are in. I needed information about the other side; inside information. I contacted Lord Lapotaire with a few tactful enquiries; he proposed a meeting with Lord Coalford to discuss sharing information between parliament and a branch of government that my brother members do not care to admit exists. They think spying rather unsporting and un-English, and perhaps they are right, but sometimes it is the only way to prevent unspeakable horrors; nipping such possibilities in the bud before they occur is far better than having to fix the damage after it is caused. The meeting was set for tonight; the plan was that while Giselle Du Lac entertained our other guests, Lord Coalford, Lord Lapotaire, Sir Hubert and I would disappear to a room on the third floor and discuss what we knew about the current situation, what we were willing to accept or reject, and hopefully agree on any possible future scenarios from which we could glean... er, difficult to come by information, shall we say? It was agreed that the only other person I would inform of my distinguished guests' arrival would be my wife." Lord Marmis smiled. "Unlike so many of the fairer sex, my wife can actually keep a secret."

He put down his cup. "When Lord Coalford and Lord Lapotaire arrived, that would have been the first Hardcastle knew about the meeting. It must have been a surprise to him; many butlers would have given notice for that sort of slight." He grimaced. "Mrs Higginson witnessed the aftermath and apparently it wasn't pretty. Hardcastle ranted about most of us, including Bertie and Mr Draycott, but oddly it was Lady Ellerbeck and her maid who seemed to bear the brunt of his rage."

Elliott cocked his head to one side. "What makes you say that?"

"Because he referred to Lady Ellerbeck as a...well, if you'll pardon me, gentlemen, he called her a bitch and complained about her bringing a 'kaffir' maid with her. Mrs Higginson said that she knew something was wrong earlier this weekend because, unusually for Hardcastle, he wouldn't go near Lady Ellerbeck's maid; he'd walk out of the room if she entered. Mrs Higginson didn't realise what 'kaffir' meant, and only told us about Hardcastle's dislike of the maid after his death." He mused. "I must be honest, Caine, I don't think very many people in England would know what the word 'kaffir' means, much less know someone they could use it against."

Elliott seemed deep in thought, then shook himself. "Well, it certainly confirms that he was a Boer. As you say, very few people here would be aware that it's an offensive term for a black person." He frowned. "Out of interest, did Hardcastle live in?"

"Yes, though not actually in the hall; he had a cottage in the grounds."

"We will need to pay that little cottage a visit, Thorne; pop it in your book." Elliott took a little notebook from his breast pocket and skimmed the contents; his next question was blunt, but it had to be asked. "Were you aware, Lord Marmis, that your butler was also responsible for the attempted suicide of one of the village girls? He assaulted a young woman named Edith Baker on at least two occasions, one of which was here at the hall."

Lord Marmis looked sick. "No, I was not aware of that."

"Edith Baker was the only girl who came forward; it's understandable that the others did not."

Lord Marmis looked at Elliott sharply. "What do you mean, 'understandable'?"

Elliott stood and faced the young lord. "My lord, we judge women by their purity, and if they fall off the high pedestal we put them on, we blame them. Even if they are dragged from that pedestal against their will, the woman is still punished. Village gossip, insults, shame, family estrangement, lack of references, possible institutionalisation, and loneliness. Justice, usually of some moralistic and socially damaging type must be seen to be done. Edith Baker's father has banned her from the family home because he believes she has brought shame on them; her mother can only see her when she goes to the inn where her daughter now works, Mrs Mickle being the only person prepared to offer the young woman a position. Edith has no money of her own because her father took it all, and because of Hardcastle's actions it is now highly unlikely that she will know the joys of a loving sweetheart, marriage, and a family."

There was a soft sob from where Thom was sitting as Elliott continued. "That poor young girl – and she is young, Lord Marmis, barely the same age as the constable here – will never know the feeling of being loved and protected—"

"Stop, sir, please!" Thom leapt to his feet, tears in his eyes. "Please stop," he whispered.

Elliott looked at the young man with a compassionate expression. "I'm sorry, Constable, I had to be sure."

"How did you know?"

"Your reaction to what Hardcastle had done to her. Right-eous anger is one thing, but the expression on your face was blind rage."

Thom straightened; his dark-blue eyes glistened. "I wasn't here, sir, when he…when it happened. I was in Benchester. I had asked for a promotion. We needed the money to get married, sir; we just couldn't afford it on a constable's wages. I was refused the promotion – Mr Rigsby-Boothe said I wasn't ready – and when I came home I found…" He sat down and covered his face with his hands.

Elliott placed his hand on the young constable's shoulder. "I know this is a very insensitive question, Constable, but it is one I have to ask; where were you when Hardcastle and Lord Scott-Brewer were killed?"

Thom looked at Elliott with wide eyes. "I was at home, sir…in the police house in the village."

Elliott looked at him. "Can anyone corroborate that, Constable?"

Thom shook his head. "No, sir. I went to the inn to see Edith…but I left at nine o'clock and went home."

Elliott nodded his head. "And what about Edith?"

Thom leapt to his feet. "You can't believe…Sir, Edith's tiny! She's only five feet tall. She couldn't kill anyone!"

Lord Lapotaire nodded. "I would have to agree with Constable Greyling, Caine…it took a great deal of physical effort to kill Hardcastle, a small woman acting alone would be incapable of the strength required to commit such an act."

Elliott looked at Lord Lapotaire before turning back to Thom. "Yes…but if she had assistance…"

Thom shook his head violently. "I didn't, sir…I swear!"

Elliott paused before replying. "And I believe you, Constable. Now, another question. Are you and Edith still sweethearts?"

Thom sat back in his seat and wiped the back of his hand across his eyes. "Yes, sir, we see each other every day. I let her know as soon as I could that I still loved her and that I would wait, and that however long it took for her to accept me, I would be there." A gentle smile touched Thom's face. "We're still engaged, sir, and I hope that as soon as I have enough money together for a cottage and our future, we'll be wed."

Thom pulled a handkerchief from his pocket; as he blew his nose, Lord Marmis saw a letter T neatly embroidered in green cotton near one corner. He closed his eyes as the tragedy of Thom and Edith's situation struck him. If he had been told, he might have been able to stop Hardcastle; perhaps if he had listened to his own intuition and investigated his butler, things would have been different. There was no way for him to solve the problems of the past, but he could help people deal with the future. He opened a desk drawer and took out a chequebook, wrote a sum and signed the piece of paper with a sharp movement.

Standing up, he walked past Elliott and stopped in front of the young constable. "Nothing I can say will take away any of this terrible tragedy, Constable. I am more sorry than I can possibly express. I can only hope that this will, in some small way, help you both towards the future you seek."

He handed the cheque to Thom, who looked at the piece of paper blankly, then turned pale. "Sir – my lord – two hundred and fifty pounds!"

"I hope that both you and Edith will accept it, and use it as you see fit, but above all things, have a happy life together. Do not let the past, or the ghosts of the past, damage the love you feel for each other; that is all I ask."

Lord Marmis sat back down and leaned forward. "I wish you to do something for me, Constable Greyling. Please seek out the other young women whom Hardcastle harmed; I believe Mrs Higginson will be able to help you with their names. I cannot change the past, but I *can* help with their future." His voice shook, and his face was grey, with two spots of vivid red on his cheeks. "I am sorry, gentlemen, so many things have happened this evening; it is just too much to take in."

Elliott looked at the young lord closely, exchanged glances with Lord Lapotaire, and quietly cleared his throat. "Lord Marmis, you have, as you say had a highly emotional evening. I suggest you take yourself off to bed and try to get some sleep. One last question, before you leave, my lord, I take it the bodies have not been removed?"

Lord Marmis shook his head. "No, Mr Draycott performed a...I believe he called it a visual post-mortem. Bearing in mind the visible damage, it was obvious that both Lord Scott-Brewer and Hardcastle were very dead, but their bodies were still warm. Mr Draycott believed they had both been killed less than twenty minutes before we discovered them."

Thorne looked up from his notes. "The good doctor was able to ascertain the internal injuries without a thorough post-mortem?"

Lord Marmis' face blanched, if it were possible, to an even paler shade of grey. "The instrument used to kill Hardcastle was left inside his body. Gentlemen, murder is appalling at any time, but this—" He swallowed hard. "This was something truly obscene." He stood up, swaying slightly. "Gentlemen, if you will excuse me, I believe I shall take your advice and retire for the evening, or rather what is left of the morning. Lord Lapotaire, I know it is not protocol for a guest to assume the role of master in another's house, but I would be most grateful if you would assist Caine and his men and ensure they have everything they need. I will bid you good morning, gentlemen."

The four men stood as Lord Marmis stumbled from the room. Elliott turned to Thorne and Lord Lapotaire. The three men shared a look before they cast a glance at Thom who was scribbling furiously in his notebook. Elliott addressed Lord Lapotaire in a barely audible voice only the young lord could hear. "We will discuss the fourth name later...when we have some privacy."

Lord Lapotaire flicked his eyes towards Thom and nodded slightly as Elliott settled back in his chair and continued in a normal voice. "He seems to be taking this very badly indeed."

Lord Lapotaire's laugh was distinctly lacking in humour. "Seeing the brother he believed dead return, discovering his own butler was complicit in his arrest and torture, then discovering that butler butchered all makes for strained nerves. You haven't seen the gallery yet, Caine; it's a godawful mess. I respectfully suggest you don't go in there with a full stomach, nor indeed while it's still dark. I have seen many things, as have you, but my stomach was turned by what I saw in that room."

Elliott turned to Thorne. "Perhaps we should wait until the full light of day to go in, Thorne; what do you say?"

Thorne closed the cover of his half-filled notebook and yawned. "Might be a good idea. Perhaps, if we ask nicely, Greyling will put on a pot of coffee while we sneak through the house."

Elliott looked injured. "Sneak? I never sneak. I may snoop occasionally, as the situation dictates, but I never sneak. Right, gentlemen, a suggested plan of campaign; firstly, let us adjourn to the butler's cottage to see what we can find. After we finish there, we can wait in the library until full daylight, it might make the contents of the gallery somewhat easier to deal with. As I recall, the gallery has a south-facing aspect, so we will have a goodly amount of light to work with. What say you?"

Thorne stood and tucked his notebook back into his pocket. "Sounds like a plan to me."

Lord Lapotaire nodded and rang the bell pull; soon afterwards, Greyling appeared. "Yes, my lord?"

"Greyling, we shall be going out to Hardcastle's cottage shortly, when we return we will retire to the library for coffee." He looked at Elliott and raised his eyebrows. "How long shall we need?"

Elliott shrugged. "Shall we say one hour?"

Lord Lapotaire turned back to Greyling. "In one hour please, Greyling."

"Yes, my lord."

Elliott raised his voice. "Greyling?"

"Yes, sir."

"We will also be requiring the key to Hardcastle's cottage."

Greyling nodded. "I shall get that for you now, sir."

He cleared the crockery onto the trolley with swift, economical movements, then wheeled the trolley out and closed the door behind him, he returned a few moments later with a young footman bearing four lit lanterns. Greyling handed a small iron key to Elliott. "The key you requested, sir. The cottage doesn't have gaslights, please take these lanterns to assist you in your search."

Elliott stood up. "Thank you, Greyling. Gentlemen, to the cottage."

Thom smothered a yawn as the four men filed out of the study and down the blue corridor into the Great Hall.

○

05:45am

Lord Lapotaire led Elliott, Thorne and Thom out to the moonlit turning circle and past the well-tended stables that housed eight coddled horses.

Before they went any further, Thorne stopped at the Daimler and removed one of the large wheeled chests he had shared the back seat with. Taking hold of one of the thick leather straps, he proceeded to tow the heavy wheeled chest behind him.

After several minutes of walking along the tree-bordered pathway from the hall to the tied cottages that the senior staff used as dwellings, Elliott spoke. "How far is it to Hardcastle's cottage, Lord Lapotaire?"

"Not that far. Marmis told me it was just beyond the kitchen gardens and I believe that's where we are now."

The tree-lined pathway had indeed opened up; in the blue pre-dawn light, the men could make out a large clearing dedicated to the provision of foodstuffs for the hall. The path weaved gently along thick outer borders planted with elder, hazel and rowan. Regimental rows of recognisable vegetable crops marched across the clearing; carrots and potatoes were the most obvious, while apple trees threw their long shadows across high, netted frames that were home to blackberries. At the far end of the clearing a clump of cottages sat partially hidden behind a massive weeping willow, whose whip-like branches hung some forty feet to the ground.

As they approached the cottages Lord Lapotaire spoke. "Marmis said it was the cottage nearest the garden." He pointed at the group of buildings huddling in the soft light. Built of the same gleaming white stone as the hall, they were well kept on the outside, at least; Elliott would reserve judgement until he had been inside.

There were three cottages; one for the butler, one for the housekeeper and one for the head footman. Hardcastle's cottage was on the end nearest the men. On the outside, it looked just like the other two; beyond the low wooden fence the small front garden was well-tended, tendrils from an ancient wisteria wrapped around the little porch and nearly obscured the small mullioned windows. Elliott opened the wooden gate and they walked down the stone path towards the front door.

As Elliott pushed his way through the thick wisteria, he paused. Turning his head slightly towards Lord Lapotaire, but not taking his eyes off the door, he inquired, "Lord Lapotaire, did you or Lord Marmis come down here at any time?"

Lord Lapotaire frowned. "No, Marmis and I thought it would be best to leave everything until you arrived. Why?"

"It appears that someone couldn't contain their curiosity. This door is open and it hasn't been forced."

Elliott approached the open door and carefully peered around it. The door opened onto a dingy narrow hall with a somewhat rickety set of stairs on his left. On the right, a door led to what Elliott presumed would be the parlour, while the short hall continued past the stairs to the kitchen at the back

He stood quietly on the threshold and listened, alert for any sound, smell or movement. Satisfied that he could sense nothing alive within, Elliott motioned to the others and they all entered the cottage. Thom shut the door and stood next to it with his back to the wall. Elliott and Thorne nodded approval as they and Lord Lapotaire walked further into the cottage.

Lord Lapotaire went into the kitchen while Thorne disappeared upstairs and Elliott entered the front room, which was indeed the parlour: a rather miserable affair in varying shades of brown.

Directly in front of Elliott was a single worn brown armchair placed before a dead fire. A tatty penny dreadful lay on the side table, also brown. The dirty window was curtained with what looked like brown sackcloth, while just behind the door was a small bookcase stuffed with literature that would have seen Hardcastle serve a good few months in gaol under the obscenity laws.

Elliott wrinkled his nose; the more he discovered about this man, the more he wanted to buy his murderer a drink. Without a backward glance Elliott walked back into the hall and through to the kitchen. As a room, it was marginally better than the parlour; the glow from the two lanterns spreading their soft light through a room that had been distempered in a warm yellow.

As Elliott surveyed the little room, Lord Lapotaire, who had been rummaging in the cupboards, looked up and shook his head: nothing here. He left the kitchen, leaving Elliott alone. At the far end of the little kitchen was a stable door. Turning the key, Elliott opened the top half and looked out on a small, rather scruffy and untended back garden with a privy at the far end.

Elliott closed the door, made sure it was locked, and retraced his steps to the parlour, where Lord Lapotaire stood looking faintly disgusted at the literature on display. Elliott was about to speak when a dull thud came from upstairs. He stuck his head around the door. "Are you all right up there, Thorne?"

A distant voice replied, "I'm fine, Elliott, but someone has definitely been here before us. It's a bloody mess up here and no mistake!"

Elliott and Lord Lapotaire hurried upstairs. The top floor of the cottage was one room that had obviously been used as Hardcastle's bedroom; a narrow bed sat under the window on the south facing wall, another bookcase that had contained questionable literature rested next to a chest of drawers and a table…all of which were no longer in their original positions. The room had seemingly been turned over and stampeded through by a herd of elephants; books, papers, bedding, and the dead man's clothing were strewn around the room. Some of the clothing looked as if it had been ripped apart with a knife. Elliott and Thorne looked at each other: Interesting!

Elliott set his lantern down on the rickety table, picked up a handful of torn paper and looked through the shredded mass. "Well, someone was certainly after something. I wonder if they found what they were looking for?" He looked at Thorne, who gazed at him steadily.

"I know what you are going to say, Elliott, and the answer is no! You know how I feel about paperwork."

As Elliott continued to smile at him, Thorne glared back. "This is because I told you to take the Commissioner's telephone call last night, isn't it?"

Elliott raised one immaculate eyebrow and placed his hand on his chest. "Thorne, I ask you, would I be so petty?"

Thorne glared at Elliott through a narrowed left eye. "Yes, damn it, you bloody well would!"

Elliott grinned at his friend. "Then I shall help you gather up all this paperwork and you can go over it after we have dealt with the remains in the gallery. Take heart, old friend, you might crack the case with something that's hidden in here!"

Thorne looked at Lord Lapotaire who was trying not to smile, and scowled. He stomped downstairs, returned with his camera and fingerprinting paraphernalia, and ordered Elliott and Lord Lapotaire out. After fifteen minutes he called them back, and the three men spent another fifteen minutes gathering all the bits of paper. As they sorted through the ransacked room, Elliott decided to check the hiding places where people would not expect a policeman to look. He turned over the cracked mirror and checked inside the mattress, but found nothing.

As Elliott looked out at the kitchen gardens and the wooded belt of land that led beyond his line of sight, a sudden thought came to him. He reached up and felt along the pelmet at the top of the curtain. As he neared the end of the rail he stopped; something was there. He withdrew a package wrapped in brown paper, roughly the same size as a gentleman's hip flask.

Thorne looked up from the large pile of paper in front of him and spotted the package. "What have you found?"

Lord Lapotaire joined the two men by the window as Elliott carefully unwrapped the package. "Something of interest, I think." Elliott folded the paper back to reveal several opened envelopes, addressed not to Hardcastle, but to John Wisdom ℅ John Rook, The Post Office, Pelloehaven, Westrenshire; they had been posted from both London and Constantinople.

Elliott frowned. "Now, what do you think Hardcastle was

doing with letters addressed to John Wisdom?"

Thorne stared at the envelopes. "We know that Wisdom works for the British government, he couldn't afford for these to be found in his possession...it would mean the absolute end for both his career and his life; even the protected and privileged can be hanged for treason. Perhaps Hardcastle also worked as Wisdom's assistant, a picker-upper of unconsidered trifles and treasonous orders to ensure his continued anonymity."

Elliott frowned. "If so, why are the letters still in Hardcastle's possession? How did he pass the information on to Wisdom...did Hardcastle keep the letters and simply contact him? I don't understand why these letters are here, if Hardcastle was found with these letters in his possession, he too would dangle from the end of a hempen rope."

Lord Lapotaire raised his voice. "Remember Greyling said that Hardcastle tried to blackmail the housekeeper? Maybe he thought he could try a spot of blackmail on one of his co-conspirators, for a little of easy money."

Elliott narrowed his eyes in thought. "So he kept the letters and threatened the middleman rather than the torturer? That makes sense. We know John Wisdom is in a position of power in the government, so that would make him a wealthy man and perhaps someone Hardcastle wouldn't feel threatened by, unlike this man Stable. It might be an idea to interview the Post Office clerk in Pelloehaven and see who paid for the service.

Elliott riffled through the letters; most were written in a code that the lads at the office would have fun deciphering. He pulled one out and checked the postmark. "This is the most recent, posted in London less than two weeks ago! We need a list of any government guests who have stayed here in the last two weeks."

He scanned the contents, and his large brown eyes

opened even wider as he read the contents. "They didn't bother to encode this one! Listen to this. 'Important: when ignorance is bliss, the prodigal brother returns. Urgent removal necessary; employ Stable if available. Payment will be arranged via the usual channel: end'."

Lord Lapotaire turned a worried face to Elliott. "They were after Frederick! Oh my God!"

Elliott grasped his arm. "Steady! Is anyone with the boy now?"

Lord Lapotaire grimaced. "No, I didn't think—"

"Can someone be placed on guard outside his door?"

Lord Lapotaire suddenly looked relieved. "Yes! Vanamoinen is with me!"

Elliott frowned. "That damn great Finn you found on one of your Foreign Office expeditions?"

"Yes."

"Is he armed?"

"Heavily. It's one of the many things he refuses to change. It makes it rather difficult to get into the office sometimes, and he ends up in the most godawful arguments with the guards in the Commons!"

Elliott appeared satisfied. "Then young Frederick should be safe until our meeting with him later. How are you doing, Thorne? Got everything?"

"I think so." He was holding a large pile of paperwork in danger of obstructing his vision as it slid around in his arms. Lord Lapotaire insisted on carrying half of the documents to avoid them once again carpeting the floor in paperwork.

Elliott collected Thorne and Lord Lapotaire's lanterns and the three men made their way downstairs. Thom opened the door as they headed back outside. Thorne nodded at the young man. "Bring my case, will you, Constable?"

Elliott paused by the open door, and taking out the key that Greyling had provided he closed and locked it. He pocketed the key and with a swing of his cane set off after Thorne, Lord Lapotaire, and Thom.

So intent were Thorne and Lord Lapotaire on preventing their burdens from shifting, so interested was Thom in what they had found, and so deep in thought was Elliott that none of the men realised they were being watched.

The dark figure hidden in the shadows of an elder thicket watched the four men from their vantage point. As the men approached the path that led through the wooded swathe to the hall, the figure saw what the man with the cane was carrying: a bundle of envelopes! The dark figure snarled in anger. Too late – they had been too late!

06:25am

As Elliott, Lord Lapotaire, Thorne and Thom mounted the steps that led into the Great Hall, Elliott looked at Thorne. "I think it would be best if we left the paperwork somewhere it will not be disturbed until you can study it, old friend."

Thorne gave him an unhappy nod as behind them, Thom struggled to carry the heavy chest full of forensic equipment up the steps to the front door.

Lord Lapotaire spoke. "Perhaps we can put it in the library while we wait for daylight. We shall be there, and that should put off any would-be thieves."

"Sensible idea, Lord Lapotaire," said Elliott. "To the library."

Lord Lapotaire carefully juggled the pile of paperwork in his arms, freeing one hand he pulled the rope that hung by the door, after a few moments Greyling appeared and admitted them.

As they entered the massive, well-appointed hall, Elliott

heard a voice coming from the telephone booth. He stopped and motioned to the others to be silent, and after a few moments they heard the receiver click. The door slowly opened, then a young black woman in pristine maid's uniform appeared and carefully closed the door behind her.

Lord Lapotaire broke the silence. "Alisha, what are you doing?"

The young woman jumped. Turning, she relaxed slightly when she saw Lord Lapotaire, and replied in a soft American accent. "I was placing a call to Lady Ellerbeck's grandfather in New York."

"For what reason?"

The pretty young woman looked nervous. "My lady wanted me to tell him what had happened, my lord. He will be worried, Lady Ellerbeck being his only kin and all."

Elliott smiled at her. "Did you manage to get through?"

Alisha smiled, her cheeks dimpling. "Why yes, sir, I did, and the first time too. He's going to send her butler from the house in Surrey, to give her a little more protection."

"My dear girl, why on earth would your mistress need protection?"

Alisha's warm brown eyes flashed. "Sir, you might be used to dealing with murder, but my lady is not. If it makes her feel safer, then that is the important thing! If you will excuse me, my lord." Alisha curtsied to Lord Lapotaire, glowered at Elliott, ignored Thorne and Thom, and swept upstairs.

Elliott looked at Lord Lapotaire, an amused glint in his eye. "That put us firmly in our place."

Lord Lapotaire smiled at Elliot, handing his burden to Thom, he pointed at the ornate door to the right of the staircase. "That is the door to the library. If you will excuse me, gentlemen, I will go and inform Vanamoinen of his new duties."

As Lord Lapotaire left the hall, Elliott walked over to the

door and flung it open. Entering the large room, with its extensive collections of books and incunabula, he nodded with satisfaction. "Now, this is what I call a library." He paused as he took in the leather clad collections that marched across the crowded bookshelves...quite a few of which he could remember from his last visit. He took a deep breath. "Come along, chaps. I shall call for Greyling and remind him about those refreshments."

As the men entered the room, Thom paused by the open door. With a quick movement he pushed the door shut with his heel, and it closed with a sharp click.

After a few moments had passed, Alisha reappeared at the top of the stairs and glanced down. Looking behind her to make sure she could not be seen, she hurried down the passage to her mistress's room. She knocked and a high voice inside called out. "Who is it?"

"It's me, my lady: Alisha."

Bolts scraped back as Bunny opened the door. Alisha dodged in and the door was swiftly relocked.

Bunny stood by the door and looked at her maid, her young face pale and worried. "Well, what did grandpa say?"

"I placed a call to Fillesby Hall first, as you requested... then I placed a call to your grandfather. He's going to send Clay to watch over you, my lady; he's coming on an air-carriage. He should be here in a few hours."

○

06:35am

The figure carefully closed their door and sat at their dressing table, thoughts tumbling through their mind. Being unable to sleep, and hearing voices downstairs, they had opened their door and witnessed the arrival of someone they had been expecting…but seeing them again after so long had still come as a rather unpleasant surprise. Hopefully, he wouldn't recognise them…but then, how could he? They had taken great pains to make sure they looked rather different from the last time they had met, so very many years ago.

It was far too late for him to interfere with their plans; they had finally managed to discover the whereabouts of the items they had been searching for, and quite by accident, they had also managed to use their position to make a great deal of money trading information to the Boers; two birds with one very well chosen stone.

They smiled, perhaps adding a certain name to the documents had been a little childish…but things were always so much more amusing when one had an appreciative audience.

The figure sighed; they would, however, have to have a quiet chat with John Stable about his somewhat…vigorous treatment of Hardcastle. It was well known in certain circles that Stable enjoyed their work, but when all they had asked for was the simple removal of an unwanted human being, the use of a red-hot poker during a genteel weekend house party could be considered a touch extreme, even by them!

They considered the possibility of John Stable being just a little beyond their control; perhaps that was something that needed to be taken care of…and sooner rather than later.

As they stroked their face thoughtfully, their features began to blur, bones cracking and lengthening as they settled back into their true appearance. They stood and stretched, pulling their now loose dressing gown around them tightly to ward off the chill as they considered how best to deal with the interesting situation they found themselves in.

07:30am

Elliott looked at Thom with an understanding eye. "Constable, I suggest you go and have a sit down in the kitchen."

Thom dragged a shaky hand across his mouth and nodded. He left the gallery on unsteady legs and made his way to the kitchen, where his father and stepmother were talking as cook, the terrifying Mrs Champlin, and her assistants were busy preparing the usual breakfast feast of kedgeree, pheasant hash, bacon, devilled kidneys, and three different types of eggs. As Thom entered the kitchen, his father looked at him with an understanding expression, pulled out a chair and pointed at it. "Sit yourself down, lad. You went in there, didn't you?"

Thom swallowed hard, trying to clear the bitter taste in his mouth. "Yes, Dad, I did."

His stepmother gave him a hug. "I'll put the kettle on; a cup of strong sweet tea and a little brandy will do you the world of good."

As she bustled away Thom looked at his father. "They know about Edith."

His dad sighed. "Aye, lad, they would if she were in the files. Did they tell Lord Marmis?"

"Yes. Dad, look, he gave this to Edith and me."

Thom pulled out the cheque and passed it to his father, who whistled. "Well then, lad, are you and Edith going to get wed?"

Thom blushed. "I hope so, Dad."

Mrs Higginson, looked at the cheque, then eyed him sharply. "And what does Edith have to say about that?"

Thom looked at his stepmother. "When Edith came out of the hospital, we spoke about everything. Edith said that what Hardcastle did to her had nothing to do with us, but she needed time. All I can do is ask her if she's ready to wed. It's up to her...but I'll wait, however long it takes."

Mrs Higginson nodded, satisfied. "Right answer, young man. Here's your brandy."

Thom knocked the little tumbler of spirit back in one and shuddered as the burning sweetness slid down his throat. Looking at his father, he croaked. "God, Dad, he was a mess. I don't know if I could have done that to him even after what he did to Edith. I could have killed him but it would have been clean, not...not what they did, with his hands and the... the poker. It was—"

Colin squeezed his son's shoulder. "Aye, lad, I know; I saw it. But there's something you need to understand; there are a lot of people like Hardcastle in this world and the unfortunate truth is that most people like that are going to be murdered at some point...they're hated too much to die of natural causes. The worse they are, the worse their way out of this world will be, and it has to be said that Hardcastle was an ugly, unlikable bastard!"

Thom gratefully took the steaming mug of tea his stepmother handed to him. "He was even worse than we knew, Dad. He was sent to spy on the family, he was passing information about Lord Marmis and the government to the Boers." Thom looked at his stepmother. "He was responsible for Frederick being taken."

Mrs Higginson nodded, her face pale. "I know, love, Fred told me." She settled back into her chair. "I know what you saw in that room turned your stomach, Thom, but I'm glad he met his end in such a painful way. You can write that down and give it to the Scotland Yard man if you like, I don't mind. I am glad Hardcastle is dead and I hope it hurt!"

○

07:30am

Elliott closed the door behind Thom, then looked at Lord Lapotaire. "Well, the lad did say all he has dealt with round here was poaching and scrumping. Moving from that to torture, murder, and ritual disembowelment is quite a leap!" He looked at Lord Lapotaire with a raised eyebrow. "Well, now we are alone…let's have it."

Lord Lapotaire sighed. "As Lord Marmis said, the name Versipellis was added to the document in a different shade of ink. What also leapt to my eye was that it had been added at the very end of highly detailed information about the three other agents, with no further particulars about Versipellis' possible actions on behalf of the Boers. All that had been added was the name. It is my humble opinion that it was added not by Dr Johnson, but by someone who wanted to smear one of our nation's best agents."

Elliott smiled. "Why, Lord Lapotaire, you haven't spoken so highly of me for years! Well, I'm sure we shall discover who it was who added my name to that list, and why." He paused and looked at Thorne. "Odd they didn't mention your name, old friend."

Lord Lapotaire cleared his throat. "Very few people are aware of the name Shadavarian__"

Thorne nodded quietly. "And that is just how I would like it to stay."

Lord Lapotaire spread his hands. "That is why I thought it best to approach you both via official government channels and not through the Espion Court. Caine, as soon as I saw your nom de guerre on that document I realised you had to be the one to investigate this case. You are, in your current guise, a highly placed police officer of good standing with a long and varied history of dealing with miscreants. That fact alone enabled Marmis to accept your presence here officially and without question. To those of us who are aware of your work as Versipellis, we know that you have detailed experience of dealing with murder, espionage, intrigue, and the distressing aftermath caused by other people's poor choices in response to personal moral dilemmas. You also know how to deal with the mess they leave behind…discreetly! Which is why my department had absolutely no misgivings about my approaching Commissioner Bolton personally to request your presence in this investigation. I hasten to add that neither Marmis nor the Commissioner have been made aware of our connection, they were merely informed that you were the best man for the investigation and that I requested you by name. As long as we keep everything sub rosa, we can keep your nom de guerre out of this mess. Discretion, remember gentlemen?"

Elliott smiled faintly and waved a hand at Hardcastle's hideously displayed remains. "Then let's get back to the matter at hand, shall we?"

The early morning sunshine cast its watery light through the stained glass panels that served as the wall between the gallery and the orangery; the beautiful multi-coloured light serving only to emphasise the shocking ugliness of the obscene object that stood in the centre of the room. Streaks of green and blue light fought with the violent splashes of red on and around the display as the three men studied the posed corpse.

Hardcastle's body had been bound to an easel and eviscerated, his organs left to hang where they chose; some of them hadn't stayed the course and rested in foul-smelling, viscous puddles against the side of the wooden prop.

Elliott walked to the front of the easel and paused, his long fingers plucking lightly at his beard. "From the point of view of a novice to crime it is quite appalling, but to people like us it is also rather interesting; do you see the cutting marks here?" He indicated the wounds around the corpse's neck, "And here too: cleanly cut, not ragged in any way. The killer used an incredibly sharp instrument to inflict these wounds." He muttered under his breath. "Very sharp indeed, but why is this familiar?" He looked from the wounds on the neck to the other damage inflicted on the butler's remains.

Elliott whistled between his teeth as he saw the main instrument of death, which had been left inside the corpse. The classic means of removing an unwanted monarch, the red-hot poker had all but disappeared from modern recorded crime. Elliott could only think of one or two such cases within his memory, and his memory went back a long way.

He looked at Lord Lapotaire. "Was the fire in here lit last night?"

Lord Lapotaire nodded. "Yes. Marmis didn't give an order for it to be lit; it may have been done by Hardcastle when he entered."

Elliott shook his head as he turned back to the body. "More likely to have been the killer if this method of murder were planned, as it appears to have been." He looked at the ugly implement; there was no chance of getting any fingerprints from that length of corroded, bloodied metal.

Elliott focused on the butler's head, which had been separated from its host and rammed onto the wooden spike atop the easel so that it now sat a good twelve inches above his neck. The sight of the raw gaping wound did not unsettle Elliott, who had seen much worse in his lifetime, but the unusual use that the hands had been put to did. Severed with the same level of skill as the head, they had been strapped to the butler's face, fingers interlocked, with the palms covering his eyes. That, too, was very familiar.

Elliott turned to his friend. "Right, Thorne, you've got the bag of tricks. What do you want to do first?"

Thorne looked from the remains on the easel to the crumpled heap of evening wear in the corner. "I need to take some photographs of the scene, but first I think we will have to turn up all the gaslights...the coloured light from the stained glass windows might make it a bit difficult to see some of the finer details."

Elliott and Lord Lapotaire walked around the room and quickly set the lamps to blazing as Thorne fished around inside the wheeled chest and removing his camera, a stand and various other equipment. Thorne took several photographs of the remains 'in situ', the now-dead fire, and the bloody footprints that wandered around the room and out into the orangery.

As the last of the smoke from the flash powder cleared, Thorne looked at Elliott. "I'll finish in here before going out into the orangery. It'll give me a pleasant few hours putting the photographs in the right order back at the Yard."

Elliott flashed him a tight grin. "Very well. You deal with his lordship; I will take the hooded beauty here. We just need the rest of our equipment." He left the gallery, returning a few minutes later with the second of the two chests from the Waggonette.

Elliott opened the wheeled chest. Inside, neatly arranged in a series of tiered pull-out shelves, were bottles and jars of nefarious-looking multi-coloured powders, chemicals, liquids, brushes and much more.

As he removed a pair of fine kid leather gloves, a jar of deep-blue powder, and a large round-headed brush, Lord Lapotaire peered over his shoulder. He saw several ornate knives strapped to the inside of the lid before Elliott swiftly closed the chest. "No peeking, my friend; you would start to think far too much about things that do not concern you."

A faint smile touched Lord Lapotaire's lips. "It is one of the many curses of our working arrangement. I am always concerned about you...Caine."

Elliott stood up and looked straight into Lord Lapotaire's

eyes. "You have no reason to be, all is in order…as it usually is."

Lord Lapotaire watched as Elliott unscrewed the little glass jar, dipped the brush in, and began to sprinkle the vivid powder over the unstained areas of the butler's skin and the easel. Lord Lapotaire again leant over Elliott's shoulder and watched with interest.

Elliott heaved an exasperated sigh and glared at the young lord, who held up his hands and withdrew to watch Thorne treat Lord Scott-Brewer to a similar assault, this time with a bilious-looking green powder. After a few minutes had passed, Lord Lapotaire asked quietly, "What is the powder for?"

Thorne shifted his position. "Galton's Details, or as we call them, fingerprints."

"And the lurid colours, how do they assist you?"

Thorne put his brush back into the pot, placed it by the corpse and picked up his camera, the style and make of which Lord Lapotaire could not tell. "We cover exposed parts with the powder to better see the fingerprints. The vividness of the powder makes it easier for the camera to differentiate between the lightness of the skin and the darkness of the pigment. Therefore, when we develop these particular pictures, we shall see the skin in white and the fingerprints in black, with the swirls and whorls of the prints clearly visible. For darker skin, we simply switch to a very light powder, and develop the photographs as a negative image which gives us the same amount of detail."

Lord Lapotaire frowned. "Why the vivid colours? Why not simply use black or white pigments?"

Thorne carefully set up the camera. "Because the only black pigment that works is a swine to get off your clothes, and the white pigment gets absolutely everywhere!"

He looked hard at the green patches daubed onto the old

lord's wrinkled flesh and set the camera down. Bringing out a large magnifying glass, which he held almost to his nose, he studied the corpse. After several minutes, he rocked back on his heels. "Elliott, have you found anything?"

"Nothing so far, Thorne. I think our killer was wearing gloves when he dispatched the unfortunate butler. What about yours?"

Thorne shook his head. "Nothing: no fingerprints, just smudges. Same with the weapon."

"Have you removed the weapon?"

"Not yet. I'll do that now."

Thorne rummaged in the chest and removed a large, thick brown envelope on which he wrote his name, the time and the date. Flexing his gloved fingers, he carefully separated the silver ice pick from the old lord's neck; the gleaming instrument came free with a damp, sucking noise and Thorne placed it on the floor. Pausing to remove a ruler from the chest, he took two photographs of the weapon, making notes on the length and width of the blade, then two more pictures of the wounds in Lord Scott-Brewer's neck.

Elliott removed his gloves as he approached. "What have you found, old friend?"

Thorne sat back on his heels again and sighed. "Not much, I'm afraid. Silver and crystal ice pick exactly nine inches long, obviously the murder weapon as it was left in the wound and the width of the injuries match the blade. Blood all over the shaft of the blade, very little blood on the handle, and no fingerprints. But the wounds are ragged, as though he were in a hurry to finish and tore with the blade in his haste. How goes it with the butler?"

"The same as your lord, in manner if not in means; no fingerprints on the remains that I can dust, and there is very little evidence of the killer. This is going to be an interesting case, my friend."

Lord Lapotaire knelt by the recumbent corpse and pointed to one of its sleeves. "Lord Marmis noticed something earlier. Lord Scott-Brewer may have been many things, but a slovenly dresser he was not. He wouldn't have dreamed of coming downstairs without finishing off his outfit and yet, as you can see, gentlemen…he isn't wearing cufflinks. Where are they now?"

Elliott looked at the loose cuffs, with their untidy excess material. "Hmm. I wonder if the murderer took anything from the unfortunate butler, other than his life?"

Thorne raised an eyebrow. "Trophies?"

"Possibly. I don't think we can jump to any conclusions, gentlemen. There are some very interesting currents here, but I think we shall just have to see where the fates take us. A most intriguing case indeed!"

Lord Lapotaire looked at the remains on the easel and the corpse on the floor. Turning back he remarked, "Are we all so used to dealing with the debauched that the contents of this room neither sicken nor disturb us, but merely pique our interest and curiosity?"

Elliott flashed him a glance. "Being honest, yes. Thorne and I have been exposed to far worse than this in our lifetimes, and you have an exemplary record within the government, the services, and the Espion Court. We may or may not have seen worse, but we certainly know what we can expect from the human race."

Lord Lapotaire nodded slowly. "There is something you should know about the ice pick that was used to kill Lord Scott-Brewer."

Elliott raised an eyebrow. "Oh yes? Do tell."

"It came from the bar that had been set up in the library; its absence was only noticed after it had been used to kill him."

Thorne looked at the implement. "Who realised it was

missing?"

"One of the footmen, a boy named Jones. He noticed when I asked him to pour Bunny – that is, Lady Ellerbeck – a whisky"

Elliott's lip twitched. "And why were you encouraging a lady to indulge in a stiff drink, Lord Lapotaire?"

Lord Lapotaire looked flustered. "Lady Ellerbeck had just been informed about the deaths and was feeling faint – damn it all, she did faint! She needed a drink, so I asked Jones to get her one and when he went to the bar the ice pick was not there."

Elliott looked at Lord Lapotaire and smiled. His grin broadened until Lord Lapotaire couldn't help himself. "What is so amusing?" he asked sharply.

Elliott's grin spread to his eyes, which twinkled in an outrageous fashion as he nodded at Lord Lapotaire's lapel. "Have you declared your feelings for the young lady, or are you going to wait for a more sensible opportunity?"

The expression on Lord Lapotaire's face flickered between irritation and amusement; amusement won. "Go on, astound me with your reasoning."

Elliott smiled. "You comforted the young lady." He reached out and removed a long blonde hair from Lord Lapotaire's lapel. "Thoroughly! And there is also a smudge of powder on the same lapel."

Lord Lapotaire grinned. "How very simple. I'm really rather disappointed I wasn't given away by a more esoteric clue."

Elliott shrugged. "If you want esoteric reasoning, read Sherlock Holmes. If you want fact and a little more than mere esotericism – maybe even mysticism – come to me and I shall give you your fill!" He spread his arms wide and grinned back at Lord Lapotaire, who looked at him with a mixture of amusement and concern.

"I sometimes forget just how dangerous you can be, Caine." He shook his head ruefully. "Sometimes I wonder at the sense of my being the only human in the Espion Court."

Elliott's grin slowly disappeared. "The position your family hold within the Espion Court is one your ancestors have always excelled in; and you, Lord Lapotaire, are no exception."

Lord Lapotaire acknowledged the praise with a slightly self-conscious nod. "Thank you, Caine. All I shall say is that I am glad you and many of your associates are on our side..."

He faltered as a brilliant green light flashed in Elliott's eyes. It was gone almost at once, but in that one brief moment Lord Lapotaire felt a sudden, acid fear. "I am sorry, I won't mention it again."

Elliott's face was like a mask. "Good. Let's get back to the issue in hand. Thorne, have you finished with his lordship?"

Thorne tucked the pot of green powder back into the chest. "Yes, all done and literally dusted; I'll have lots of photographs to plough through back in London."

"Very well. Finish off with the butler, will you? Then we can get started on the interviews."

Thorne nodded. Picking up his camera, he approached the easel and started to take the close-up shots needed for the file.

Elliott turned to Lord Lapotaire. "There is a door nearly hidden behind the tapestry next to where his lordship was murdered. Where does it lead?"

"To the staff kitchen, I believe."

"Is it usually kept locked?"

Lord Lapotaire nodded. "According to the maid, Jenkins, it hasn't been used for many years. What are you thinking?"

Elliott looked at the wall. "I am trying to establish what Lord Scott-Brewer was doing over here: how he came to be *here*...by this wall. We know the butler was killed first – that

171

was the planned killing – so when Lord Scott-Brewer entered this room, the butler was already murdered and laid out on the easel. Lord Scott-Brewer would have had to walk within a few feet of the body to reach this door…and that doesn't make sense."

Lord Lapotaire looked at the elegantly dressed corpse by the wall. "Is it possible he was killed somewhere else in the room and his remains dragged over here?"

Thorne looked up from his photography. "Unlikely. Aside from his lordship's bloody footprints, which started when he walked through the blood around the easel, and some rather odd footprints leading out to the orangery, there is no blood trail either from his lordship or from the butler. The amount of blood pooled around their bodies indicates that both men were killed where they were found."

Elliott frowned. "So, if the butler was where he is now, something must have prevented his lordship from seeing the body. If he had seen the display on the easel, he would have run out of here as fast as his aged legs could have carried him. So, the question is, why didn't he?"

He looked around the room. All the furniture was pushed against the walls and covered with dust sheets – all except the grand piano by the far wall. "Thorne, have you noticed the lack of a dust sheet on this piano?"

"Yes I have, and no, I haven't found it yet." Thorne carefully placed his camera on the lid of the chest and walked over to the piano.

Elliott gestured at the floor. "The bloody footprints walk all around this area, crossing and doubling back on themselves, and then continue this amusing little solo waltz into the orangery. Have we looked out there for the missing dust sheet?"

Thorne looked injured. "Elliott, I've only just finished in here."

The three men looked towards the large, heavily orna-mented stained glass wall and the arched entrance that led through to the orangery. Elliott glanced at Thorne and Lord Lapotaire, neither of whom showed any inclination to enter the large, jungle-like room.

Elliott also felt trepidation, but not for the same reasons as his colleagues. His memories of the last time he had visited Marmis Hall were concentrated in that glowing, gem-like room with its waterfall and lily-strewn pond.

But needs must.

Suppressing a sigh, Elliott brought his hands together in a sharp clap which echoed in the empty gallery like the knell of doom. Both Thorne and Lord Lapotaire jumped and glared at him.

"Well, gentlemen, shall we?" Elliott gestured at the room, and after a brief pause Thorne and Lord Lapotaire passed through the green doorway ahead of him.

The room beyond was immense. Twice the width of the gallery, it ran the full length of the south side of Marmis Hall and rose up to the roof, affording the bedrooms above a beautiful view of the tropical plants, the thirty foot high waterfall, and the lily-covered pond at its foot.

Thorne was staring at the ground, and held out a warning hand. "There are more footprints out here, Elliott. They lead to the pond, then disappear. Look, there's a bloody palm print on the raised edge of the pond."

Elliott stood next to Thorne, looking at the bloody smudge. "Can we get a print from that, do you think?"

Thorne shook his head. "I doubt it. Palm prints do differ from person to person but I doubt we could get much from this. There's far too much blood and not enough definition."

Lord Lapotaire, who had wandered further into the room, saw a flash of white tucked behind a flamboyant flow-ering cactus near one of the shuttered French doors leading to the terrace. "Caine, over here." He pointed to the patch of white. "Could this be our missing dust sheet?"

Elliott walked over and leant down, tugging at the thick white material which unravelled from behind the large terracotta pot. As the stream of cloth emerged the men could make out several liberal smears of bloody matter, which had soaked into the material and dried to a sticky, jam-like consistency. Elliott held out the sheet. "Now we know why Lord Scott-Brewer didn't vacate the gallery screaming. The killer must have covered the butler's body with this sheet when they heard him approaching."

Lord Lapotaire gestured towards the gallery. "What's your theory, Caine? The killer came out here to hide the sheet and wash their hands, then returned to mingle with the other guests?"

Elliott shook his head. "I think the killer brought the sheet out here for another purpose. There's far too much blood; with the injuries inflicted on the butler, the killer would have been drenched in gore and worse."

Thorne stared at the pond. "Perhaps the killer hid a set of clean clothing in the orangery, washed themselves, and changed."

"If so, where are the clothes they wore during the attack?" said Elliott. "Take another look at the footprints nearest the corpse, my friend, and tell me what you see."

Thorne walked into the gallery and looked down at the nearest prints. He called back, "There's far too much blood to get a clear shoe print, Elliott."

Elliott continued to stare at the floor in the orangery. "Now come back into the orangery, following the footprints, and tell me what you see."

Thorne reappeared in the doorway and walked past Lord Lapotaire; his gaze fixed on the ground as he slowly made his way back to Elliott. Elliott looked at him. "Well?"

"The blood on the shoes gets lighter the further the killer walks from the scene."

Elliott nodded. "And?"

Thorne looked at him, but Lord Lapotaire spoke first. "And what, Caine?"

Elliott gestured at the marks on the floor. "Come now, think. How many styles of shoe are you aware of that show the imprint of a toe?"

Realisation dawned on the men's faces as they stared at the bloody footprints. As they approached the pond, the prints became better defined and the outline of an arch and individual toes were indeed visible.

Thorne shook his head in disbelief. "I can't believe I missed that."

Elliott waved his hand in the air. "You see it now, old friend, you see it now."

Lord Lapotaire cleared his throat. "Caine, are you saying someone did this barefoot?"

Elliott looked at him and grinned, his sharp canines flashing white in the bright daylight. "No, Lord Lapotaire, I'm suggesting someone did this naked!"

Lord Lapotaire's jaw dropped as Elliott sat on the raised edge of the pond.

"It may sound bizarre but it makes sense. This is what I think happened. The killer lured Hardcastle here, by means as yet undiscovered. They staged the scene; setting up the easel as a prop, lighting a fire the master hadn't ordered, setting the poker in the flames, and waiting for the butler to arrive. Once he was here they subdued him somehow, possibly with a blow to the head, and then killed him, taking their time. Suddenly the sound of someone in the hall beyond reaches them and they have to hide. They take the dust sheet from the piano and throw it over the easel, and I conjecture that they turned the lights down. Not off, or Lord

Scott-Brewer wouldn't have been able to see where he was going. The silly old fool entered and made his way to the far end of the gallery__"

"But what of the ice pick?" asked Lord Lapotaire. "Why did the killer bring it from the library? It wasn't used on the butler, so how could they have known they would need it for Lord Scott-Brewer?"

Elliott smiled. "I don't think the killer did bring it. Follow me." He led the two men back into the gallery and headed towards the door next to the huddled husk that had once been a lord of the realm. He pointed at the large lock on the door. "Can you see the scratches here and here? I think his lordship brought the ice pick from the library, probably on the spur of the moment. He used it to try and force this door, and for his pains the very tool he had brought to facilitate entry to the servants' quarters was used against him. I can't say I have very much sympathy." Elliott stared down at the lock. "Take some photographs of this lock please, Thorne, and we will also need some of the dust sheet, the bloody palm print, the pond, and the footprints."

Thorne, picking up his camera, returned to the task at hand as Elliott and Lord Lapotaire walked back to Hardcastle's body. Elliott spoke first. "Who is going to do the post-mortem: the local coroner or a government chap?"

"All things considered, I think it will have to be a government man. Probably Sir Isadore Shard, as he's the top man in London. Why do you ask?"

Elliott mused. "Here is what is causing me difficulty: look at the size and shape of these footprints. Slender, and not too long, which would suggest that the killer is of a slight build, how could the killer physically restrain someone of Hardcastle's size? He was a big man, and would have had military training. Here we have a man trained to kill with his bare hands, who was overcome and tortured to death by someone much smaller and without a single sound to disrupt the evening. Strange, don't you think?"

Lord Lapotaire rubbed his hand across his forehead. "I was listening to the phonograph in the music room just across the hallway Perhaps the sound from that..."

Elliott shook his head. "No, Lord Lapotaire. No person on this earth could tolerate that level of pain without their screams penetrating the very walls of the building. Someone would have heard."

Lord Lapotaire stared at Elliott, then cast a brief glance at the butler's remains and suppressed a shudder. "You're right, of course; it's impossible. Someone must have heard something."

Elliott held up his hand. "Unless…"

Lord Lapotaire raised his eyebrows. "Unless?"

"Unless Hardcastle had been given something before-hand, in a drink or food or possibly even an injection. A local coroner might miss something a bit unusual, but someone like Sir Isadore Shard has all the resources at his disposal to investigate stomach contents and possible injection sites."

"Yes, of course. I'll place a call to the office and suggest Sir Isadore Shard take the case." Lord Lapotaire walked past the butler's remains, but as he opened the door Elliott stopped him.

"Lord Lapotaire?"

Lord Lapotaire turned, a wary look on his face. "Yes?"

Elliott looked at his watch. "As it is now very nearly half past eight, may I request breakfast for Thorne and myself, somewhere out of the way of any guests who might be awake at this ungodly hour? Then we can get down to the marvel-lous job of interviewing a large number of people who will be adamant that they saw and heard nothing. What do you say?"

Lord Lapotaire smiled; his handsome face painted by the

dazzling array of colours cast from the sunlight streaming through the stained-glass windows. "I shall see about breakfast in the morning room. It should be empty at this time, and if it isn't— Well, I can make sure it will be." He nodded at Elliott and Thorne and closed the door behind him.

Thorne glanced at Elliott. "He is a nice young man, in spite of his interest in our past...but I think I preferred dealing with his grandfather."

Elliott wagged his finger. "Now don't you start."

Thorne grinned and started to pack his camera and fingerprinting equipment away. After several minutes of companionable silence he looked over at Elliott, who was standing by Hardcastle's corpse. "What do you think, Elliott?"

"About Lapotaire?"

Thorne rolled his eyes. "No, not Lapotaire. About the case."

"Ah."

Elliott moved away from the butler and pushing a dust sheet off the nearest settee, he sat down on the pristine upholstery and looked up at the stained glass panels that covered the far wall like a vibrantly hued waterfall. The panels had been designed by the widow of the eighth Lord Marmis as a memorial for her husband. Made in twelve huge panels, each section showed the gradual transmutation of the soul to the light of God. Elliott sighed. Lady Marianna had always been a highly spiritual woman. It had been quite a while since his last visit to Marmis Hall, and under very different circumstances. He shook his head gently and returned to the present. Thorne was looking at him with an understanding expression. "Old memories?"

Elliott smiled bitterly. "Old ghosts," he said quietly. He took a deep breath. "You asked about the case, didn't you? There's an awful lot to be going on with. A spy, a torturer, a traitor; a top-level government meeting the Boers would literally kill to be in on; the murder of the spy and a lecherous lord who found himself in the wrong place at the wrong time; abused maids and angry sweethearts; a younger brother just returned from imprisonment; an older brother suffering from understandable anger and justifiable self-recrimination." Elliott settled into the couch. "Then, along with the aliases of three Boer spies, the name Versipellis turns up, added to the files *after* Frederick returned home. I wonder why that was thrown into the whole seething mess, hmm? Was it done, as Lord Lapotaire suggested, to besmirch us? Or is there something else afoot?"

Thorne perched on the edge of the chest and leant forward. "Elliott, you don't think they—" He stopped; Elliott had raised his hand, his head turned to one side.

The door opened and Lord Lapotaire entered the room. "I've ordered our breakfast to be served in the morning room. I have also spoken with the office and they agreed that Sir Isadore Shard is the perfect man to do the post-mortem. I placed a telephone call to the good gentleman himself and was assured that he will arrive in Benchester on the quarter to one train from London."

Elliott took out his pocket watch and noted the time. "It will be past three o'clock by the time he arrives at Benchester, but that will give us enough time to organise the removal of the, er, remains."

Lord Lapotaire nodded. "He couldn't come any earlier; he needs time to organise his Harley Street practice and placate several rather upset patients."

"What does he specialise in?"

Lord Lapotaire pulled the rest of the dust sheet from the settee and sat down with a groan. Leaning back into a plump cushion he replied, "Nerves."

"Like Mr Draycott?"

Lord Lapotaire smiled. "Ah, no, not like Mr Draycott at all."

Elliott's eyebrows rose slightly. "Your words or the good Sir Isadore's?"

"Oh, the good Sir Isadore's, of course. I mentioned that Mr Draycott was here and Sir Isadore directed some rather unflattering and really quite slanderous invective at our tame specialist."

Elliott looked at him with interest. "Do tell, I'm always open to a good bit of gossip."

Lord Lapotaire gazed at him with a pained expression, and Elliott grinned. "Shall we use the official line of 'it may have some bearing on the case', if it makes you more open to sharing?" He widened his eyes and gave Lord Lapotaire a hopeful look.

Lord Lapotaire rubbed the bridge of his nose and smiled ruefully. "Very well. He made several derogatory remarks about the colourful Mr Draycott's qualifications and abilities as a specialist. Sir Isadore also mentioned that he had dealt with more than one of Mr Draycott's former patients who had gone to him with one problem, and after undertaking the treatment Mr Draycott suggested, ended up with another, more serious difficulty. He was also quite scathing about the fact that Mr Draycott has been named as a beneficiary in the wills of several elderly ladies, including one of Sir Isadore's oldest bridge friends, Lady Carstairs."

Elliott looked at Lord Lapotaire. "Lady Emily Carstairs?" he asked sharply.

"Yes. You know the name?"

"We investigated the case. It was a simple unexplained death that came under the jurisdiction of the police, so the Espion Court wasn't involved in our inquiry. Her nephew, a Mr Valentine Carstairs, was adamant that there was no possibility of his aunt killing herself, but we couldn't find anything to support his theories. We closed the case with a finding of death by suicide; the poor chap was very upset about the whole thing."

Lord Lapotaire nodded. "He certainly seems to have made it his mission in life to upset Mr Draycott."

Elliott raised his eyebrows. "Why Mr Draycott?"

Lord Lapotaire smiled. "According to Sir Isadore, Lady Carstairs' nephew decided that there was only one person who could have harmed his aunt and that was Mr Weatherly Draycott, the specialist she was seeing at the time of her death. He won't give up without a fight, he's even followed him here; Valentine Carstairs is staying at the Dolphin and Anker Inn, and has been since Mr Draycott arrived on Friday."

Elliott sat back with a thump. "How very interesting. None of that came out in our investigation…it would appear Carstairs was playing his cards very close to his chest. If we see him during the course of our investigation, it might be an idea to have a polite chat about any further information that he would like to share." Elliott shook his head. "However, at present we are rather busy investigating two murders, so let us turn back to our current situation. As we are sharing a spot of relatively harmless gossip, and you are the inside man, as it were, you know some of the people in this house on a close if not personal basis…and some in a rather more in-depth manner considering the necessary government checks. May I be so bold as to ask for your personal opinions and knowledge of the people here this weekend?"

Lord Lapotaire pursed his lips. After a few moments he murmured, "I can't say I approve of this, Caine; these people have invited me into their lives and their homes."

Elliott shook his head. "It is not your approval I seek, Lord Lapotaire. Someone in this house has committed at least two murders, and that same person could very well be a torturer. My Gods, I hope it is the same person. Having to find one madman is one thing, but having to find two could very well finish me!"

Lord Lapotaire sighed. "Very well, but not here; let us withdraw to the morning room." He stood up and the three men walked out of the gallery. Lord Lapotaire locked the door and handed the large key to Elliott as they walked down the white corridor to the morning room.

The door was already open and the sounds and smells of breakfast greeted them as they entered the bright, well-appointed room, a world away from the stench and death of the gallery next door. Greyling and the maid Jenkins were setting out chafing dishes piled high with eggs, bacon, and kedgeree on a table by the French doors that led out onto the side terrace, as a large pot of coffee steamed quietly on a table laid for four.

Greyling finished his task. "Breakfast is ready, gentlemen. Will you require anything else?"

"Yes, Greyling," Elliot replied. "Would you find our young constable and inform him that we are starting breakfast, and that if he desires a morning meal, he should get here before Thorne eats everything!"

Greyling smiled over Thorne's outraged splutters. "He's already on his way, sir."

The door behind them opened as the young man in question came in. Thom halted as the four men turned to look at him, and flushed under the sudden scrutiny. "I'm sorry about earlier, sir."

Elliott shook his head. "No need to apologise. You have gone from investigating small local crimes to walking into a room touched by horror. You have nothing to apologise for. Now, if your stomach is up to it, I suggest you have a spot of breakfast while we discuss our findings. Thank you, Greyling."

The butler and Jenkins left the room, closing the door firmly behind them.

The four men helped themselves to the hearty breakfast, with even Thom returning for seconds. As they ate, Elliott filled the young constable in on what they had deduced from their time in the gallery.

Thorne put down his fork and dabbed at his lips with a napkin. "The person I feel most sorry for in this affair is Frederick Marmis: he went through two years of Hell in Southern Africa, returned home to a place that should have been safe, and instead his nightmare continued." He shook his head.

Elliott drank deeply from his coffee cup and placed it back on the saucer. "Constable, did you garner anything interesting from your time in the servant's kitchen?"

Thom swallowed a mouthful of kedgeree and nodded. "Everything so far reinforces Hardcastle's reputation, sir. Apparently young Florence Smith was Hardcastle's latest victim – William Case, her sweetheart, had threatened to kill Hardcastle on more than one occasion."

Elliott shook his head. "Too easy. Besides, if it does turn out to be a sweetheart protecting his lady, then regardless of the viciousness involved I'll do everything within my not inconsiderable power to ensure it doesn't get to court. Anything else?"

"Yes, sir. You remember Lady Ellerbeck asked her maid to call her grandfather in America? Well, I found out his name, sir."

Elliott held up a hand. "Hold onto that name for the time being, Constable, while Lord Lapotaire gives us some background information on the Marmis family and this week-end's guests."

Lord Lapotaire squirmed slightly in his seat. "I still don't like this, Caine. It just isn't—"

"Cricket," finished Elliot. "I know, but some things won't ever be sporting. Now, gossip!"

Lord Lapotaire sighed. "Very well, Lord Foster Marmis, first-class politician and Member of Parliament, dedicated husband to Lady Rebecca Marmis and father to Evie, Roman, and Norman."

"A very clean-living young man, this Lord Marmis, so far," mused Elliott. "Anything in his past that could be used against him?"

Lord Lapotaire shook his head. "None that we could find. You know we check the background of every minister to make sure that if there *is* scope for blackmail or intrigue, we know about it."

Elliott's brown eyes twinkled at Lord Lapotaire, who had the good grace to cough before he continued. "Lord Marmis' background is beyond reproach; no mistresses, no gambling, and no other damaging habits. However, if you want me to give you a fuller picture, I will. Lord Marmis is the eldest son of Lord Josua Marmis. Now there was a man with an…interesting background."

Elliott nodded. "We know about his enjoyment of charming company."

Lord Lapotaire took a deep breath. "Jolly good. Foster Marmis went to the usual schools. No embarrassing political adventures, fairly staid and proper. He met his future wife at a debutantes' ball and they were engaged and married within the year, which is unusually fast but not unheard of. Their twin sons arrived two years later. It's a Marmis family tradition that at least one son should go into politics and Marmis wanted to make his own way in the world, so while Frederick was still at school and his father was still alive, he entered the Foreign Office. His first posting was in India, so he and Rebecca, as she was then, left England, taking Roman and Norman with them. They stayed in India until Lord

Josua's death, after which they returned and Marmis took over the running of the estate. He stood for parliament in his father's seat and won. Their daughter, Evie, was born five years ago."

"What about his wife?"

Lord Lapotaire started. "Lady Marmis? Caine, I really must protest: her reputation is above question. She is devoted to her family; there is nothing for you to see there."

"No dalliances?"

"Nothing."

Elliott raised his eyebrows.

Lord Lapotaire gritted his teeth. "We checked her background as well as her husband's. The only daughter of Lord and Lady Holbry, good upbringing, finished in Kent rather than on the continent, no unfortunate attachments, and nothing in her life but her family!" He paused. "One thing of interest was that she went to finishing school with a girl named Penelope Lake, who is here this weekend under her stage name, 'Giselle Du Lac'."

Elliott choked on his coffee; Lord Lapotaire looked at him with a raised eyebrow as he spluttered into his napkin. "I understand that Giselle Du Lac is one of your favourite singers, Caine. But do either of those names mean something else to you?"

Elliot regained his composure. "Nothing I didn't already know, Lord Lapotaire. We will come to her later. Now, what about Sir Hubert Kingston-Folly?"

Lord Lapotaire looked surprised. "Bertie? He has been a friend of Lord Marmis since school. Again, the standard political background: his father was in the Foreign Office so it was obvious that Bertie, with his brilliant tactical brain, would follow in his footsteps. His background is also beyond reproach. One failed engagement; a mutual lessening of affection, shortly after he returned from a two-year posting to the Ottoman Empire about six years ago. He and Lord Marmis have always been close; even while Bertie and I were stationed in Constantinople and Lord Marmis was on attachment to the Viceroy, they still kept in touch."

Lord Lapotaire paused, a look of amusement on his face. "I remember we had a bit of an issue when Bertie was first posted out and the fool got lost." He laughed. "On his first full day, Bertie went into the Grand Bazaar and couldn't escape the traders. It took me hours of wandering through the streets before I could find him, the two of us had a good laugh about it later, but it was a bit worrying at the time. Those fellows would have your head on a plate soon as look at you."

Elliott sipped his coffee. "Frederick Marmis?"

The smile disappeared from Lord Lapotaire's face as though it had been wiped away with a cloth. "A damn good man who has proved his mettle many times over. A good sportsman, played rugger and cricket at Oxford. A highly gifted orator and linguist...he can pick up languages seemingly without effort. Frederick was always interested in adventure. He didn't have to join the Foreign Office, Caine, he could have been the quintessential wastrel younger brother, but instead he chose to join us. In the end he was posted to the Southern Rhodesia Office, but the paperwork and boredom that are an unfortunate part of a diplomat's daily life weighed him down. He wanted to get out in the field, to travel, and I suppose he wanted to see the Empire." Lord Lapotaire's eyes held a faraway expression. "See the pink bits, as my old tutor would say, before we have to hand them all back or other nations take them from us." He looked at Elliott. "I don't know just how damaged Frederick is from this experience, but I hope he will return to the diplomatic. We need young men like Frederick; we cannot afford to lose him."

Elliott consulted his notebook. "That covers the immediate family and close friends, except one." He looked up with a smile. "What about you, Lord Lapotaire, where do you come in?"

Lord Lapotaire stared at Elliott, then smiled. "I suppose I deserved that. Yes, where do I come into all this?"

He settled back in his chair and flicked a sharp glance at Thom; there were certain things the young constable, amongst others, need not wot of. He cleared his throat. "Constable, please understand that certain things must stay in this room, they cannot be written in your notebook. Do you understand?"

Thom looked at Lord Lapotaire, before turning to Elliott who nodded. "Best to just listen…and then forget, Thom."

Thom nodded. "Yes, sir." He closed his notebook and placed it on his knee as Lord Lapotaire continued.

"Marmis Hall was suggested as a neutral meeting place for the purpose of finally agreeing a mutually acceptable arrangement between the government, represented by Lord Coalford, and our somewhat esoteric agency, the Espion Court, represented by my good self. We were hoping they would consider accepting our offer of assistance in gathering information about the South African situation, amongst other things." He sighed. "In spite of our excellent results, and even though we are a part of the Foreign Office…albeit rather an opaque part, they still aren't too keen on the idea of our more rarefied work. I think the fact that most government ministers are unaware of our existence is rather a sticking point for the few who do know. Lord Coalford in particular is a major stumbling block to our official admittance into the fold, he considers the idea of information gathering about our friends and enemies to be a form of ungentlemanly theft, and finds the very thought of using spies a personal affront. Because of his personal distaste for the term, and because we need his support, 'spying' is a word we no longer use before him, instead we mention operatives, agents, machinists, in the hope that he, and the government, may find their worth more palatable. All cogs and pieces in a game of strategy and mutual sophistry with our own government. It is a very strange situation." He looked at both Elliott and Thorne with a faint smile. "One I am sure you both understand."

Elliott studied his fingers, a distant expression on his face. "Yes, of course. Was Hardcastle aware of the meeting?"

Lord Lapotaire shook his head. "No, thank God! Marmis took great pains to make sure that only he and Bertie knew the real reason for our coming here. He didn't inform Hardcastle of our coming at all, which must have grated somewhat when we arrived."

"He didn't inform his wife?"

"Oh yes, but not the real reason; Lady Marmis thought it was yet another dull government briefing."

Elliott returned Lord Lapotaire's smile. "'And is your background all it should be?"

Lord Lapotaire stared at Elliott before replying quietly, "You should know."

"Indeed I should and indeed I do: spotless, in fact. Now, the other guests...Giselle Du Lac. What do we know of this songbird?"

Thorne looked up from his notes and hid a smile; Elliott's obsession, and it was an obsession, with the beautiful young opera singer was quite well known, but the truth behind it was not.

The fact that several pieces of artwork from operas she had performed in were displayed on their office walls had not gone unnoticed, but it had gone unmentioned. Luckily no one at the Yard had visited his and Elliott's lodgings just off St Michael Mews where more pictures and objects from

Giselle's performances littered Elliott's large suite of rooms. Some rather more…unusual items had been collected through the years and placed in the sitting room he shared with Thorne and Veronique; an original Roman fresco, an Egyptian papyrus, and a fine portrait in sanguine and black by Da Vinci that all showed the same image: a beautiful, vivid face with sparkling blue eyes and tumbling auburn curls.

Lord Lapotaire took a sip of orange juice. "Again, we checked her background as soon as we found her in Lady Marmis' history. Standard procedure, as you know."

Elliott shrugged noncommittally and Lord Lapotaire continued. "Giselle Du Lac, real name Penelope Lake. Born in England to an English father and French mother and orphaned at a young age. Her father was murdered, her mother was injured in the same attack and died shortly afterwards. After the death of her mother she was raised by her maternal grandfather, a highly successful opera singer by the name of Emile Cotillard. Giselle is twenty-nine years of age, young for a celebrated opera singer. No suitors that we could find: her background seems remarkably untainted, given her travels and the occasional unfortunate associations. You know the sort of thing, performing Mozart for a despot in New York or Paris." He took another sip from his drink and mused. "Apropos of nothing, there does appear to be a surfeit of such people these days; it would appear that all one needs to become a despotic monocrat is money, a brattish demand to have everything you want, and sycophants who are willing to do your bidding regardless the consequences." He paused thoughtfully. "A few terms in an average British boarding school at a suitable age, the application of the word 'no', and the firm but fair use of the birch may have lessened their tendencies towards such behaviour, but I digress. Back to Mlle Du Lac. One odd thing we did find was a tendency towards being in places where crimes have or were about to occur. Nothing that could be linked to her, of course; perhaps a case of being in the wrong place at the wrong time. She has known Lady Marmis since they attended the same finishing school in Kent, and they have a similar relationship to Marmis and Bertie: friends since childhood who stayed in touch."

Elliott nodded as he made notes, then, studiously ignoring Thorne's twinkling scrutiny over the coffee pot, Elliott cleared his throat. "What do you know about the deaths of her parents?"

"One night twenty years ago, several men broke into their home in Paris and attacked them. Her father was a manager at the Great National Bank. The belief was that he and his wife were deliberately targeted, possibly by someone trying to get information about the bank, but he refused to cooperate and they killed him, his wife was struck trying to protect her husband and she died from her injuries. Shortly afterwards another manager was kidnapped, a young chap by the name of Gerard Tournay. They obviously had more success with him, because the same day he was taken the bank was robbed of several millions in bearer bonds. Tournay's body was found inside the vault; he had been stabbed. No one was ever caught or tried."

Elliott stared down at his notepad. After a few moments of silence, Thorne inquired. "What about the new widow, Lady Scott-Brewer?"

The young lord frowned. "Rather a sad case: an arranged marriage of sorts which suited both families, but poisoned Lady Scott-Brewer. She had been engaged to another man, but her family forced her to break the engagement. Lord Scott-Brewer was massively rich and a good fifteen years older than his wife, but he had the same unpleasant reputation as a younger man. It's one of the many reasons why he was rejected as unsuitable for the diplomatic service; his background checks showed him to be entirely open to blackmail and bribery. His family thought that marriage to a much younger woman would put a stop to his behaviour and it did, in a fashion. Lady Scott-Brewer has run herself almost ragged trying to keep him under control. She has spent her entire married life as…well, a wardress would be the best description for what she became, because it was her only way of dealing with the life that was forced upon her."

Elliott shook his head. "A powerful counter argument for those who support arranged marriages. Perhaps now she can reclaim her life; she is not too old for happiness."

"I believe she is forty-seven years of age; she was forced to marry very young," Lord Lapotaire replied.

"Still not too old to enjoy the life she has left. Tell us a little bit more about the good Mr Draycott."

Lord Lapotaire set his empty glass down on the table. "Mr Weatherly Draycott is, in spite of the opinions of both Valentine Carstairs and the good Sir Isadore Shard, a highly successful nerve specialist. His parents owned a tobacconist shop in Bayswater. He worked hard and got a scholarship to St Georges in London, went on to train at Guy's, and served in the field hospitals during the Boer War. When he returned to England, he chose to specialise in the effect of brain storms and nervous distress on the human psyche. He has a practice on Harley Street, many highly placed, influential patients, and a Riviera lifestyle that made us check his background with rather more interest than usual – and before you ask, his background appears to be fairly damage free."

"What do you mean by 'appears to be'?"

"Well, aside from the allegations of Valentine Carstairs, the alacrity with which elderly ladies leave him bequests in their wills, his frequent overseas journeys to give talks on nervous distress, and the fact that he is a fussy, oily little man, his background seems fine."

Elliott grinned, as did Thorne, who murmured, "Took an instant liking to the gentleman, did you?"

Lord Lapotaire smiled; he hadn't forgotten Draycott's heavy hand with the alcohol the previous evening. He took a savage bite from his piece of toast.

Elliott looked at his notes again. "Lady Barbara Ellerbeck, also known as Bunny?"

Lord Lapotaire coughed and took a hurried sip of coffee. "Lady Barbara Ellerbeck's background was checked because she was on the guest list: English, though her mother was American. Both parents were killed in a yachting incident on the Riviera when she was twenty. She is now twenty-five years old and has lived in England all her life. Her only travels abroad have been to her grandfather's residence in New York."

Elliott nodded at the young constable. "You said you had found the name of Lady Ellerbeck's grandfather."

"Yes, sir." Thom opened his notebook and flicked though the pages. "He is a Mr Quincy Cater of New York City."

Thom was not the only man to jump as Elliott slammed his hand down on the table, making the cutlery bounce. "Of course, Thorne! The Carrie Lynn Cater case! That's where I've seen the peculiarity with the hands!"

Lord Lapotaire looked at Elliott, eyebrows raised. "Carrie Lynn Cater?"

Elliott sat back in his chair and closed his eyes. "It must have been about nine or ten years ago. Carrie Lynn Cater was a young New York socialite found murdered in appalling circumstances very similar to this case. According to the family butler who discovered her body, she had given the servants the night off and made preparations for a friend's visit. The friend never came forward after her death, which led us to believe that the person in question may well have been her murderer."

Lord Lapotaire looked Elliott in mild astonishment. "You can clearly remember a case from several years ago that you were not involved in? You astonish me."

Elliott met his eyes. "In ten years, will you not remember the horrors of this case? And besides, what makes you think I was not involved?"

Lord Lapotaire paled slightly.

Elliott said softly, "I was involved, but not in the way you are thinking, nor was I involved in any official capacity on behalf of either the British Government or the Espion Court." He stood up and refilled his plate with more bacon and eggs. "I was called in by her grandfather, Quincy Cater. I owed him a personal favour; my actions were not questionable in any way."

Elliott sat back down and took a deep draught of coffee. Setting the cup down, he looked at the three men. "I think we need to take the Carrie Lynn Cater case into consideration, gentlemen. The similarity between the injuries and the use the hands were put to would suggest that the killer is either the same person or someone with inside knowledge of the original case."

He turned to Lord Lapotaire. "And if that is so, then we must protect Lady Ellerbeck as well as young Frederick; Carrie Lynn Cater was her aunt, the sister of Lady Ellerbeck's mother."

Lord Lapotaire stiffened in his chair. "You think Lady Ellerbeck is in danger?"

Elliott stretched out a restraining hand. "Calm yourself; you won't do yourself or your suit any good by having a fit of the vapours."

Lord Lapotaire's eyebrows lowered as he stared at Elliott. "What?"

Elliott lifted his coffee cup, his warm brown eyes twinkling at the young lord. "Oh, come now, Lord Lapotaire…it is rather obvious. I hope for your sake you are intending to court the young lady in question. Working yourself into a tizzy for no good reason is merely foolish and a waste of energy."

Lord Lapotaire took a deep breath, the air shuddering as it travelled down his throat, then swallowed hard and looked at Elliott and Thorne. Thorne had a small smile on his lips as he looked at the young lord opposite. It got everyone in the end, and usually when it was least expected. Thorne hoped it would treat Lord Lapotaire well, he was a nice chap...for a politician.

Thom looked up from his notes. "Excuse me, sir."

Elliott turned from Lord Lapotaire. "Yes, Constable?"

"We know that Lady Ellerbeck's maid Alisha telephoned her mistress's grandfather in New York, because we heard her make the call and she told us who she had spoken to."

"Yes, why do you ask?"

"Well, sir, before I came in to breakfast I called the operator on the telephone. She said that before the call to America two other calls were made; one at half past one, placed to a number in Paris. The second, at a quarter past five, was placed to..." Thom studied his notes. "Fillesby Hall in Surrey, sir. The call lasted several minutes."

Elliott saluted Thom with a raised coffee cup. "Well done, Constable. After breakfast we must fingerprint the telephone booth. Paris, hmm...did your friend happen to hear a name?"

Thom shook his head. "No, sir, but she did get the number." He passed a piece of paper to Elliott, who took it with a smile.

"At this moment in time," he said, "there is only one way I can think of to find out the identity of this number's owner."

Lord Lapotaire stared at him. "You can't telephone someone at this hour of the morning!"

"Can't I? Even though someone in this house clearly

called them at a far earlier time." Elliott walked briskly out of the room and headed for the telephone booth. Sitting down, he pulled out a handkerchief to lift the receiver, and as he did so a scent tickled his nose. He sniffed at his handkerchief – no it definitely wasn't him – then brought the receiver to his face and the scent grew stronger. Elliott closed his eyes and breathed in the familiar fragrance as the soft scent of attar of roses wrapped around him in the cramped booth.

Smiling at the familiar scent, Elliott rang the operator. "Operator? Yes, a Paris number, please."

Elliott gave the number, hung up, and waited for several minutes before the telephone rang shrilly in his ear. Grasping the receiver he heard the tinny voice of the operator. "I have your number, sir."

Her words were almost cut off as the telephone began to ring. Once, twice...then a breathless young female voice answered the phone. "The Johnson residence."

Elliott's eyes focused on the wall just above the telephone as his brain recalled something he had heard earlier that morning.

The young woman spoke again, her voice more urgent. "Is anyone there? Who is calling, please? Who is this? Frederick...Frederick, is that you?"

Elliott gently hung up the receiver and left the booth. He walked back into the morning room, sat down, and drained his coffee cup. Looking at Lord Lapotaire as he poured himself another, he murmured, "Out of interest, Lord Lapotaire...Wallace Johnson, the young man who died helping Frederick escape, did he have any family?"

"He did; both his parents are still alive and living in Paris. His father is in the diplomatic, and he also has a younger sister, Clarice. Again, why?"

Elliott waved his piece of paper at the lord. "This is the number for the Johnson family residence in Paris, and when

I didn't speak, the young female who answered asked if I was Frederick. It is possible that Frederick called the house, but if that call was not placed by him, then someone else in the house probably knows what we do." Elliott sighed and rubbed his temples. "To continue with Thom's discoveries, does anyone know where Fillesby Hall comes in?"

"According to my files, Fillesby Hall is the country house where Lady Ellerbeck lives," Lord Lapotaire replied. "It was her father's family estate." He frowned. "Why would anyone telephone the estate when Lady Ellerbeck is here?"

Elliott leaned forward. "It could have been for any number of reasons; perhaps someone sending word to the house of what has occurred here. Does Lady Ellerbeck have any servants with her, besides her maid?"

Lord Lapotaire shook his head. "The only servant Lady Ellerbeck brought with her was her maid, Alisha Clay."

Lord Lapotaire jumped back in his seat as Elliott's finger nearly jabbed into his nose. "Alisha...Clay?" Elliott choked out.

Lord Lapotaire nodded, bemused. "That's right." He paused. "You know the name?"

Elliott opened his mouth to reply, then closed it as Greyling entered.

"Excuse me, my lord, but there is a servant at the door. He's just arrived by private air-carriage. He claims that he has been sent to attend one of the guests. I can't find Lord Marmis at the moment, so I didn't know if I had permission to admit him."

Lord Lapotaire stood. "You have, Greyling; Lady Ellerbeck's maid informed us of his arrival earlier this morning. Please show him in."

Greyling bowed. "Yes, my lord."

As he turned to leave, Elliott said, "Greyling?"

The butler turned. "Yes, sir?"

"Is this butler a tall, black man of between forty and forty-five years, and with an American accent?"

Greyling looked surprised. "Yes, sir: exactly so."

Elliott smiled. "Very good indeed. Oh, before you take him to see his mistress, will you bring him in here, please?"

As Greyling nodded and made to leave, Elliott spoke again. "And Greyling?"

"Yes, sir?"

"Would you make sure that the telephone booth is locked and the key given to Thorne, please?"

An expression of un-butler-like curiosity crossed Greyling's face. "Yes, sir."

The butler walked out of the room, closing the door quietly behind him. Elliott looked at Thorne with an expression of extreme satisfaction. "Warrick Clay, Quincy Cater's butler. I do so enjoy being right!"

Thorne smiled. "Do you think he will recognise us, being in different skins, as it were?"

Elliott's eyes flashed as Lord Lapotaire darted a quick look at Thom. "That term should not be used where any can overhear—"

Lord Lapotaire stopped as Greyling entered the room with a tall, well-built man of middle years. Warrick Clay's appearance had changed little over the ten years since Elliott and Thorne had last seen him; a touch of grey at his temples was the only visible sign of his advancing age.

Lord Lapotaire stepped forward. "Mr Warrick Clay?"

The butler nodded, his gaze drawn to the breakfast table as Elliott stood up and approached him.

"Hello, Clay, it's been a long time."

09:30am

The large horse-drawn wagon from Benchester hospital pulled into the turning circle. Three morgue attendants; two men of experience and one young novice, climbed down and shivered in the chill autumn sunshine as Greyling greeted them on the steps.

The four men stood before the entrance of Marmis Hall, seemingly deep in discussion, before two of the men went back to the wagon and retrieved several sheets of waxed canvas before following Greyling around the hall to the outer door of the orangery. Here the men stopped, as Greyling again explained what awaited them in the room beyond. The men moved through the orangery and into the gallery, moments later the youngest attendant ran out and was violently sick in the garden. Greyling took the young man through the staff entrance to the kitchen, where he was left in the capable hands of Mrs Higginson.

The two remaining attendants tied rags soaked in a strong mix of pine and camphor around their faces to deaden the smell, and got to work. Mercifully for them, the poker had been removed by Thorne and wrapped in a thick piece of canvas, ready for transportation to the morgue. Unfortunately, the only piece of canvas both suitably clean and big enough to cover the hateful object was from the nursery; a large sheet that young Evie Marmis had used for painting, her childish artwork still visible on the outside of the unwieldy package. The carefully wrapped parcel had been placed by the door that led from the gallery into the orangery, ready for collection.

While the attendants set about their revolting work, Thorne sat not fifty feet away in the morning room. The thick pile of paperwork they had rescued from Hardcastle's cottage was now spread out on the table in front of him, jostling for room with a nearly empty pot of coffee. He sighed; their current placement was interesting, but the paperwork was a nightmare.

How were they to know, though? When they had been offered the positions, no one had mentioned the bloody paperwork! When they had first started out so very many years ago, paperwork had never been necessary as long as they got the job done. No one had ever asked for pieces of paper…pieces of people, occasionally, but at least the paperwork was non-existent. Here they asked for sheaves and sheaves of it, and worse – signatures in triplicate!

Signing his name to something he had done was still rather new for Thorne, and he would be the first to admit it was a little worrying to do something that could be traced back to him. Never mind: this particular line of work would only continue until Yule, and then…freedom!

Thorne drummed his fingers on the table as he scanned the piece of paper in front of him, one of many pieces of paper that were causing him trouble at the moment. It was a summary of names, times, opportunities and alleged alibis which had taken him over an hour to compile. He had been tempted several times to throw it through the window overlooking the sunny orangery.

Thorne bit into a still warm oatmeal biscuit as he glared at the offending list. Elliott, the devious little swine, was down the hall in the music room where he planned to conduct his leisurely interviews with Lady Marmis, Lady Scott-Brewer, Lady Ellerbeck, and of course, a little later when he had more free time, Giselle Du Lac.

Thorne grinned good-naturedly; he and Elliott had been together far too many years to allow little things such as a sunny autumn day, the company of lovely ladies, a long-awaited reunion that may or may not go as Elliott hoped, and a huge pile of paper to damage their friendship. He sighed, and throwing the piece of paper onto the pile in front of him, his mind returned to the events that had occurred just after breakfast.

Warrick Clay had been stunned to see both Elliott and Thorne at the hall. Thorne had sensed unease in the man before him, but behind that, determination. Clay's responses had been monosyllabic to the point of rudeness; Elliott had seen the futility of interviewing him just then and had asked Greyling to show the butler to Lady Ellerbeck's room. Elliott believed the best course of action was to do nothing and wait for Clay to approach them, which freed up the morning for a spot of gentle questioning in the music room.

Thorne picked up his cup and took a deep draught of lukewarm coffee. Grimacing, he put the cup down and frowned at several pieces of paper that Thom had given him. The young constable had spent the earlier part of the morning in the servants' kitchen continuing his own line of questioning. He had finished with the house staff and had returned to the main kitchen in order to discover the where-abouts of Lord Lapotaire's valet, Vanamoinen, who was at that time still seated outside Frederick's room. Thom had also yet to speak with Giselle's maid, Lilith, and Lady Ellerbeck's maid, Alisha, who seemed as relieved as Lady Ellerbeck at the arrival of her father, Clay.

Contrary to Thorne's belief, Elliott was not having a good time of it with his attempts to question the ladies. Lady Marmis had acquiesced to his request for an interview, but had stipulated their discussion be carried out in her boudoir, rather than the music room. She had been honest in her answers. She had last seen Hardcastle at five past nine or thereabouts, when she had come downstairs from visiting her good friend Giselle in her rooms. She had been with her husband and her brother-in-law in the study at the time of the killings, and no, she had heard nothing. After the bodies had been discovered, her husband had sent her to their rooms with her maid and the only detour she had made was to visit the nursery to inform Nanny Parker of what had happened and to check on the children.

Elliott thanked Lady Marmis and left to interview the new widow, Lady Scott-Brewer. He was not looking forward to this; dealing with upset ladies was, in his opinion, one of the worst aspects of his particular line of work. He smoothed his Ascot and knocked on the door to Lady Scott-Brewer's suite. The door was flung open by an elderly maid who looked at him suspiciously before snapping in a voice like a corncrake. "Are you a police officer? You don't look like no police officer I ever seen!"

Elliott raised his eyebrows, reached into his inside breast pocket, and held out his warrant card. The grey-haired maid looked at it with even more suspicion, then nodded grudgingly.

"You might well be, I'll give you that. I'll let my mistress know you're here." Whereupon, she shut the door in his face. Returning a few moments later she held the door open with a sniff. Elliott entered the well-appointed suite and took in the decor. The cool blue walls were made vibrant by the autumnal sunshine flooding through the high windows, which fell in turn upon a solitary figure seated before a bureau.

Elliott's first observation of the lady before him was that although a trace of bitterness remained in the thinness of her lips, the rest of her face was relaxed; he recognised the signs of a woman who no longer had to pretend. She wore a peach day dress, and her dark blonde hair, touched with grey, fell loose to her shoulders.

Lady Scott-Brewer was writing a letter, and Elliot could

see that it was several pages long. Her face was pale but determined; the face of a woman who had made up her mind. She finished the letter with a voluptuous signature before folding the thick sheaf of paper and tucking it into an envelope which she sealed carefully with purple wax. Putting this to one side, she took another sheet of writing paper, wrote a few words, and folded it in half. "Philips, will you see that this letter is posted as soon as possible, please, and that this telegram is sent at the same time."

Philips bobbed and took the envelope and paper. "Of course, my lady, I'll see to it myself." She indicated Elliott grudgingly. "This is Detective Chief Inspector Caine, my lady."

Lady Scott-Brewer nodded. "Yes, of course. I've been expecting you, Detective Chief Inspector. Thank you, Philips, that will be all."

The elderly maid disappeared into a small room, returned with a thick shawl, and left, closing the door with a final sharp look at Elliott. He turned to look at the lady before him and was in turn studied; sharp blue eyes conducted a polite appraisal.

"Please allow me to be honest, Detective Chief Inspector Caine, I did not love my husband. You might find that shocking – do you?" The words were evenly spoken, without hesitation; Elliott suspected they were words she had wanted to say for many years.

"No, Lady Scott-Brewer, I do not find it shocking, under the circumstances."

A faint smile appeared on her lips. "Do you think I am suffering an attack of nervous exhaustion?"

"No, my lady. I think you have realised that you are finally free from someone you never wished to marry in the first place."

She sat back in her chair, a look of mild relief on her face, and waved her hand towards the chaise opposite. "Please sit. You seem to understand my feelings on this hideous matter almost as well as I."

Elliott walked through the sunshine that dappled the room and softened the blues on the walls and floor, settled himself on the royal-blue chaise and looked at the stately woman before him. The lines that had cut remorselessly into the skin around her eyes and mouth were softened; he knew they had once existed, the evidence still lingered, but the strain and anger that had once caused them to bite deeply were no longer there.

Elliott opened his notebook. "Lady Scott-Brewer, I'm afraid I must ask you some questions about yesterday. Would you please tell me when you last saw your husband?"

She settled in her chair and arranged her gown before replying. "I last saw my husband just before I retired for the evening, a little after a quarter past nine. My husband and I had just played a game of Bridge against Lady Ellerbeck and Mr Draycott, in which we had been firmly beaten. I had had enough of my husband's...wandering attention during the game, and decided that I would retire for the evening. Dinner was to be a buffet, so our hostess would not have any difficulty dealing with one fewer guest."

"You mention your husband's wandering attention, Lady Scott-Brewer; what exactly do you mean by that phrase?"

She sighed. "Whenever a young maid came in to tidy around the guests, he would stare at her. He did the same thing with young Lady Ellerbeck. He simply couldn't help himself. I found his behaviour humiliating and embarrassing...as always"

Elliott closed his notebook. "Lady Scott-Brewer, if you will pardon my imposition, why did you put up with his behaviour all these years? A marriage may be ended if a good enough reason is given, and I am sure that any judge would have granted you a divorce."

Lady Rowan shook her head. "You don't understand, Detective Chief Inspector Caine. When Bartholomew and I were married it was not an arranged marriage – it was a forced one! Neither of us wished to marry. Barty's family thought that marrying him off to a much younger woman with a threat to accept the marriage or be disinherited from his family's vast wealth would keep his behaviour under control. In some ways they were right, but in many ways they were wrong…so very wrong." Her lips set. "They offered my family a good deal of money for me. My father and grandfather both had a great many debts, so they forced me to break my engagement to the man I loved in order to save the family name and estates." Her expression hardened, and Elliott realised the strength that had carried her for so long.

"Both families thought we had accepted our fate, and that we would do what we had been told, but unbeknownst to them, Barty and I came to an agreement. He would not demand his husbandly rights to my person, if I would turn a blind eye to his willing partners. You will please note my use of the word 'willing' there, Detective Chief Inspector; whenever Barty went after someone and the answer was no, I did all I could to uphold that answer."

She heaved a sigh. "As far as Barty's father was concerned, I had kept my side of the bargain. He paid off all my family's debts. But my father thought he had created the perfect golden goose, a daughter married to the scion of a wealthy family, and with access to that family's not inconsiderable fortune…he thought he could merely snap his fingers and I would use my husband's connections to provide for his every whim. It gave me great pleasure after my father-in-law died to inform my father that neither my husband's money, nor indeed my father-in-law's connections, would ever be available to him again. He died two weeks later from brain fever, and I am glad my mother never lived to see what he had done to his life and mine!"

She smiled suddenly, the expression lighting her face from within. "In spite of my father's demands, I refused to give up the man I loved; I have been faithful to him and he to me for the last twenty-nine years. I have sent him a telegram informing him of the events of this weekend, and asking him to come for me."

A gentle smile touched Elliott's face. "He has waited for you all this time, my lady?"

Lady Rowan Scott-Brewer's smile deepened in response; a smile that removed all trace of sadness and bitterness from her face. "What is time to those who truly love, Detective Chief Inspector Caine?"

○

10:20am

On his way to the music room, Elliott directed Greyling to request separate audiences with Lady Ellerbeck, and Giselle Du Lac, then dropped in on Thorne in the morning room to deliver his notes and be informed that all the fingerprints in the telephone booth were smudged and unusable.

Elliott smiled through Thorne's good-natured stream of invective, then continued to the music room to await Lady Ellerbeck, and heart of hearts, Giselle.

Shortly after he had settled himself in a comfortable armchair, Giselle's maid, Lilith, arrived with a message that the unseasonable sunshine had caused a severe migraine and that her mistress had taken to her bed until it had passed.

A few moments later, Warrick arrived with a message from Lady Ellerbeck, also pleading a sick headache. Elliott paused in the reading of Lady Ellerbeck's note and wondered at the seemingly sickly nature of the modern woman. He nodded at Warrick and gave him the same response he had given Lilith. "Very well, Clay, but please inform your mistress that I must speak to her before this evening."

Warrick bowed slightly, his strong features impassive as he left and returned to the servant's hall, passing the locked doors that led into the gallery as the morgue attendants continued their unpleasant work within.

Elliott sat in the music room and plucked at his beard with a thoughtful expression. If there were to be no further interviews at that time, he might as well make himself useful to Thorne. Shaking his head with a sigh, he headed to the morning room.

Entering the bright room, Elliott made his way the table, where Thorne regarded the heaped mass of paperwork which sat, fell, and slid in equal measure across the shiny wooden surface. Elliott picked up the list of names and times. "Any luck so far?"

Thorne sat back with a sigh. "It's the same as usual, Elliott; some could have, most couldn't, and the alibis for those who could are a nightmare. Anyone could have, but no one did. Look, I'll show you."

He took the piece of paper from Elliott and laid it down on the table. "We know that both Hardcastle and Lord Scott-Brewer were murdered between 9:15 and 9:35. Hardcastle was last seen just before 9:10 by Lady Marmis, and Lord Scott-Brewer was last seen at 9:15 by his wife and the day guests. The bodies were discovered at approximately 9:35 by Lord Marmis, Lord Lapotaire and Sir Hubert, with the help of Greyling and Jenkins. As far as I can see the only people who couldn't have done it are Mrs Higginson, Frederick, and Lord and Lady Marmis...purely because they were all together in the study, they are each other's alibis. So…this is what I have come up with so far."

The List

Higginson, Valerie.
Housekeeper.
Motive: Hardcastle's abuse of the maids and the later discovery of Hardcastle's involvement in her son's disappearance and torture. Also, he knew about her marriage and had threaten blackmail.

No known motive for killing Scott-Brewer.

Alibi: she was in the study with her son Frederick, and Lord and Lady Marmis.

Opportunity: none known.

As with most of the female staff in the house, I rather doubt she could have lifted Hardcastle's torso onto the easel.

Greyling, Colin.
Head Footman, now butler.
Motive: revenge – for his wife, his son's sweetheart, or for his step-son, possibly for the abuse of the maids…or to take Hardcastle's position as butler.

No known motive for killing Scott-Brewer

Alibi: Seen by several members of staff in the kitchen and the dining room laying out the buffet.

Opportunity: none known.

Smith, Florence.
Maid.

Motive: repeatedly attacked by Hardcastle.

No known motive for killing Scott-Brewer.

Alibi: helping footmen set up the nursery for Lord Marmis.

Opportunity: none known.

Case, William.

Head groom.

Motive: the oldest – anger at the wrong done to his sweetheart Florence Smith.

No known motive for killing Scott-Brewer.

Alibi: putting the carriages away and tending to the horses with three other stable lads who swear he never left.

Opportunity: none known.

Spence, David and Harry.

Footmen.

Motive: none known for either murder.

Alibi: they claim they were both with Florence in the nursery.

Opportunity: None that I can see…the nursery needed quite a bit of tidying and it was done as ordered.

Vanamoinen, Kimi

Lord Lapotaire's valet.

Motive: not yet interviewed.

Alibi: not yet interviewed, but believed to have been on his own in Lord Lapotaire's suite.

Opportunity: not yet interviewed.

. . .

Clay, Alisha.
　　Lady Ellerbeck's maid.
　　Motive: none yet interviewed.
　　Alibi: not yet interviewed, but believed to have been in the staff kitchen with Lady Marmis' maid, Mary Parker.
　　Opportunity: not yet interviewed.

Jenkins, Millie.
　　Maid.
　　Motive: hated Hardcastle.
　　No known motive for killing Scott-Brewer.
　　Alibi: was in the kitchen helping with the buffet.
　　Opportunity: none known.

Lady Ellerbeck, Barbara (Bunny).
　　Motive: not yet interviewed.
　　Alibi: not yet interviewed, but known to have been alone in the saloon from 9:05. She was next seen by Lord Lapotaire in the library at around 9:45, shortly after the remains were discovered.
　　Opportunity: none known…she was on her own while the murders took place.
　　Again, I don't think she could have lifted Hardcastle onto the easel…not without assistance.

Mr Draycott, Weatherly.
　　Motive: Not yet interviewed.
　　Alibi: Not yet interviewed but known to have left Lady Ellerbeck in the saloon at 9:05 to go outside for a cigar, and was not seen again until after the bodies were found.
　　Opportunity: he was on his own in the turning circle,

and was not seen coming back into the house until after the bodies were found.

Kingston-Folly, Sir Hubert (Bertie).

Motive: not yet interviewed.

Alibi: not yet interviewed, but known to have left the study at approximately 9:10 for the billiard room, where he stayed until he was called back to the study to hear Frederick's statement about Hardcastle.

Opportunity: was on his own in the billiard room.

Lord Lapotaire, Vyvian.

Motive: none for either murder.

Alibi: none. Went from the study to the music room and was there from 9:10 until he was sent for by Lord Marmis.

Opportunity: was on his own in the music room.

Lord Coalford, Titus.

Motive: not yet interviewed.

Alibi: not yet interviewed. But he was in his suite unattended from 9:10.

Opportunity: yes, but the idea of that stuffy old windbag creeping around the house like an evil uncle in a penny dreadful is both ridiculous and rather delicious.

Lord Marmis, Foster.

Motive: none, until the return of his brother and the discovery of Hardcastle's true identity.

No known motive for killing Scott-Brewer.

Alibi: was in the study with his wife and brother from before 9:15, and was in the party that discovered the bodies.
Opportunity: none.

Lady Marmis, Rebecca.
 Motive: as husband.
 Alibi: as husband.
 Opportunity: none.

Parker, Mary
 Lady Marmis' maid.
 Motive: none known for either murder.
 Alibi: in the staff kitchen with Alisha Clay.
 Opportunity: none.

Parker, Jane, aka Nanny.
 The Marmis family nanny. Aunt to Lady Marmis' maid, Mary Parker.
 Motive: none known for either murder.
 Alibi: in the nursery with the children, but they were asleep.
 Opportunity: possible, but unlikely.

Marmis, Frederick.
 Motive: Hardcastle was the spy allegedly responsible for his incarceration and torture in Southern Africa.
 No known motive for killing Scott-Brewer.
 Alibi: was in the study with his brother and sister-in-law from 9:15.
 Opportunity: none.

. . .

Lady Scott-Brewer, Rowan.
    Motive for killing Hardcastle: none known.
    Motive for killing her husband: possibly, but as she had lived with his behaviour for many years it is unlikely.
    Alibi: was in her room with her maid from 9:15 and day guests saw her leave the library.
    Opportunity: none known.

Philips, Amy.
    Lady Scott-Brewer's maid.
    Motive for killing Hardcastle: none known.
    Motive for killing Lord Scott-Brewer: she hated him for what he had done to her mistress.
    Alibi: was in her mistress's suite when Lady Scott-Brewer returned at a little after 9:15.
    Opportunity: none.

Du Lac, Giselle, real name Lake, Penelope.
    Motive: not yet interviewed.
    Alibi: not yet interviewed, but believed to have been in her suite of rooms since her arrival.
    Opportunity: none known.

Tournay, Lilith
    Giselle Du Lac's maid.
    Motive: not yet interviewed.
    Alibi: not yet interviewed, but believed to have been with her mistress at the time.
    Opportunity: not yet interviewed.

. . .

Thorne rubbed his eyes and groaned. "And then there are the rest of the assorted maids, boot boys, stable lads, and tweenies no one ever sees who Thom and I need to talk with...I think more people work in this house than in the entirety of Scotland Yard!" He sighed and fixed Elliott with a glare. "And yes, I know I haven't added Thom or Edith Baker to the list; even though they both have good reasons for wanting Hardcastle dead. Like you I just don't think__"

Elliott nodded. "I understand your reasoning, Thorne. But put them on the list anyway." Thorne shot him a look. Elliott raised a placating hand. "Just...smooth over their possible motives and make sure we have their alibis."

Thorne nodded. "Understood." He paused before he prodded a manicured finger in Elliott's direction. "Just promise me that you will talk with Giselle today...that's all I ask."

The two men looked at each other, Elliott's face held a sheepish expression. "Yes, Thorne, I will get around to interviewing the lady of the lake before the evening is over. For my own sake, if not hers." He paused and touched one of the names. "Lilith Tournay... I have heard that name recently, but where? Yes! Thorne, do you remember Lord Lapotaire told us Giselle's father was murdered by attackers who were after information about the bank he worked for?"

Thorne nodded, and Elliott continued. "They failed to get what they needed, so they kidnapped another manager whose name was Tournay. I wonder if Giselle's maid Lilith is a relation?" He looked at Thorne. "It probably has no bearing on this case, but it is interesting. Now, I think I will go and find Mr Draycott and have a quiet word. After the remarks from Sir Isidore I'm rather looking forward to finally meeting him." He rang the bell by the door, and a few moments later Greyling arrived.

"Yes, sir?"

"Greyling, I need to speak with Mr Draycott. Which suite was assigned to him?"

"The gentleman was given the Sage Suite, sir."

"How very apt. Whereabouts is it?"

"If you will excuse me, sir, if you are looking to speak with Mr Draycott, you will not find him in his rooms."

Elliott looked at the butler sharply. "Do you know where he is?"

Greyling smiled. "You will find the gentleman on the turning circle, sir, in the company of his cigar case."

"Thank you, Greyling."

Elliott checked his pockets for his notebook, and walked back to the table where Thorne slumped, surrounded by crumpled balls of paper. He took a swig from Thorne's now-cold coffee cup and squeezed his friend's shoulder. "If you haven't found anything in twenty minutes, dump the lot and have some elevenses!"

Thorne gave him a tired grin and continued to flick through the pieces of information gleaned from Hardcastle's cottage.

○

10:40am

Elliott left the comfort of the morning room and walked towards the Great Hall. As he entered the massive galleried atrium he heard someone call his name. Turning, he saw a man he had not yet been introduced to, but based on earlier descriptions he took this windswept and rather worried looking man to be Sir Hubert Kingston-Folly.

Elliott stopped as the young tactician hurried towards him. "Detective Chief Inspector Caine? Yes, of course it is. Please allow me to introduce myself, Sir Hubert Kingston-Folly." He grasped Elliott's hand, his own hand firm, if a little tremulous. "I understand that we have to be interviewed. I was in no fit state to talk to anyone earlier – the...mess, you understand – but if there is time now, I am entirely at your disposal."

Elliott thought quickly. He wanted to speak with Draycott before the morning was over, but as Sir Hubert was here. He smiled politely. "That is very good of you, and I quite understand the cause of your distress."

Sir Hubert gestured to the library door. "Will you join me in a cup of coffee?"

They entered the library. The morning sunshine could not penetrate the north-facing windows; only indirect light reached the dark room, whose first editions and incunabula marched along the heavy mahogany shelves, and nestled in glass-topped display cases dotted throughout the room.

The temporary bar and the card tables used the evening before had been removed earlier by Greyling and Jones and replaced with the usual discreet drinks table, Lord Marmis correctly deducing that most of their guests would prefer to spend their time in the comparative safety of their own rooms, behind lockable doors.

Sir Hubert sat down with a thump in a large green leather chair by the fire. Elliott sat down opposite him and studied Lord Marmis' oldest friend. Plump, with a pale face and baby-fine blond hair, his large blue eyes were disarmingly vague. Yes, Elliott could well believe that some people took this young lord at face value and were sorely put out later.

Sir Hubert picked up a cup of black coffee from the table beside his chair, took a gulp, and shuddered. He looked at Elliott with an expression like that of a young boy caught scrumping in the farmer's orchard. "I'm afraid I drank a little too much last night, Detective Chief Inspector. It was the only way I could sleep, under the circumstances. Oh, and please call me Sir Hubert...the full title is a bit of a mouthful!"

Elliott took out his notebook and looked at the man, whose expression became apprehensive. Sir Hubert put his coffee cup down on its saucer, where it rattled slightly, then placed his hands in his lap and fiddled with his signet ring, spinning it round his little finger.

He looked at Elliott, and his eyes seemed almost twice their natural size. Elliott recognised the symptoms; he had been there himself a few times. "Sir Hubert, before we start, how many cups of coffee have you had this morning?"

"Um, two full pots of coffee, I don't quite know how many cups..."

"About five in each pot, Sir Hubert! If I were you, I wouldn't drink any more coffee today, and I suggest you drink only water and wine this evening."

Sir Hubert nodded and pushed the coffee pot away from him.

"Now, Sir Hubert, we have spoken with both Lord and Lady Marmis about last night's events, and I will be speaking with young Frederick Marmis later this afternoon—"

"Yes, young Fred! Foster told you of his return to the family; absolutely marvellous news!"

"Yes, Lord Marmis informed me of the circumstances of his brother's return, as did Lady Marmis. Now, Sir Hubert, I have an idea of your whereabouts during the evening, but could you clarify for me exactly where you were between a quarter past nine and twenty-five minutes to ten yesterday evening?"

Sir Hubert sat forward. "Yes, yes, of course. Now let me see: I was in the study with Foss for most of the evening, setting up the meeting with Lord Coalford and Lord Lapotaire." He hesitated and looked at Elliott. "Should I have said that?"

Elliott smiled. "It's quite all right, Sir Hubert; Lord Lapotaire has divulged the basics of why he and Lord Coalford were here."

Sir Hubert looked relieved. "I thought I had made an error there. Right, shortly after half past eight, Frederick arrived. He was just standing there…literally out of the blue, as it were—"

"Standing where?"

"Well, on the other side of the French doors in the study. Foster nearly collapsed and so did Fred; the shock of getting home and seeing his brother, I think. Anyway, we opened the door and got him inside. The poor chap was shivering, in a shabby old coat that he said he'd picked up at the Salvation Army hostel he had stayed at when he arrived in London."

"Why didn't he try to get word to his brother before coming?"

"He said the money he'd been given in Southern Rhodesia wasn't enough for the airship to London, so he used it to get passage on a ship to Marseille instead, and then travelled by bus to Calais. He had nothing left for a telegram."

Elliott frowned. "Why didn't the British authorities send a wire informing the Foreign Office of his escape?"

Sir Hubert looked at Elliott and tapped his nose. "I believe Fred didn't tell them who he was; if they had sent such a telegram and the Boers had intercepted it they would have gone all out to get Fred back. The escape of the younger brother of a minister in the British government from under the very noses of his captors? He would have been stalked every step of the way."

"But when he landed in England, why not inform his brother of his return?"

Sir Hubert shook his head sadly. "Fear, I imagine, Detective Chief Inspector Caine, and with good reason. When Fred and Dr Johnson escaped, they brought documents detailing four men of interest to our government: John Stable, John Rook, John Wisdom, and Versipellis."

Elliott nodded with a faint smile. "Please, continue, Sir Hubert."

"John Rook, we now know, was—"

"Gregory Hardcastle, a Boer spy and a very dead butler."

Sir Hubert looked slightly put out. "Oh, Foster told you."

"Indeed he did. Interesting, don't you think, that Versipellis was included with foreign spies and traitors, bearing in mind that he has always worked for Britain and the Empire?"

Sir Hubert shrugged. "people change; perhaps we were not paying him enough." He looked at Elliott sharply. "Tell me, how exactly does a Detective Chief Inspector from Scotland Yard know of this particular...er, occasional government employee?"

Again, that faint smile crossed Elliott's face as he looked at his plump interrogator.

Sir Hubert held up his hand. "No, don't tell me, I've changed my mind. I really don't want to know!"

"Very wise, Sir Hubert. Now, you were telling me of the time you can account for during the evening."

"Yes...Fred arrived and I thought it best to leave them to it so that Fred could renew his acquaintance with his brother, his sister-in-law, and his mother." He paused and looked at Elliott apprehensively. "I take it that you *have* been informed about Fred's parentage?"

Elliott nodded and Sir Hubert, looking relieved, continued. "At that point I felt rather superfluous, and making my excuses I went to the billiard room and played a game of Patience until approximately half past nine, when Foster and Lord Lapotaire came to find me. That was when I was informed about the documents Fred had brought. We returned to the study and decided that it was time to hunt out Hardcastle and confront him with the evidence against him. Lady Marmis and Mrs Higginson took Fred up to his room, while, the three of us, Foster, Lord Lapotaire and I, made our way towards the gallery where we met the head footman and a maid. We said we were looking for Hardcastle, and they explained why they were looking for him and one of the maids. They thought he might be in the gallery with her, so we entered…and there he was." Sir Hubert shuddered. "I have seen photographs from battlefields, Detective Chief Inspector, but those were nothing compared to what waited for us. My God!" Sir Hubert's face was deathly pale and sweat appeared on his upper lip.

Elliott strode to the drinks table at the far end of the room, and poured a generous glass of brandy which he placed in Sir Hubert's hand. He swallowed the contents in one go, then spluttered and coughed as the burning liquid sent warmth flooding through his veins.

"Keep breathing, now, deep breaths; that's it." Elliott took the now empty glass and sat down opposite. "Have you eaten anything this morning, Sir Hubert?"

Sir Hubert closed his eyes and shuddered. "God, no, I couldn't face food after…that."

"Ten cups of black coffee on an empty stomach is never a good idea Sir Hubert. I suggest we continue this later, when you are feeling more capable."

Elliott stood and gave the bell pull a tug, and when the young footman entered Elliott gestured at the wan politician. "Will you please see to it that Sir Hubert has something to eat?"

As the footman bowed and left the room, a faint voice

from the depths of the wingback chair murmured, "Thank you, Detective Chief Inspector."

"Not at all, Sir Hubert. Oh, there was one last thing."

"Yes?"

"Were you aware of any letters for John Wisdom being delivered to the hall?"

There was a pause. "I certainly wouldn't have seen anything. I'm afraid I don't check the post. Why do you ask – what have you discovered?"

"We found a bundle of letters in Hardcastle's cottage; all were addressed to John Wisdom, care of John Rook."

A tuft of blond hair appeared above the armchair's high back as Sir Hubert looked at Elliott, wide-eyed. "But surely that proves Hardcastle *was* John Rook!"

"Indeed, but it also proves that he and John Wisdom were in almost constant contact. Why else would John Wisdom have his letters delivered to Hardcastle? Good morning, Sir Hubert; and remember, no more black coffee today."

Elliott left the library, closing the door quietly behind him, then looked at his notebook and closed it with a snap. Now he only had three more men to interview: Mr Draycott, young Frederick Marmis, and Lord Coalford. Elliott shuddered. He had no desire to interview Lord Titus Coalford: there was far too much history there!

He straightened his shoulders and marched towards the front door. Hopefully the good doctor would still be at the turning circle, and then, when their headaches had passed, he could focus on his interviews with Lady Ellerbeck...and Giselle.

Parva Steps

PART III

11:00am

Crossing the hall, Elliott paused to admire the white marble Corinthian columns supporting the glass dome; the carvings matched the frolicking nymphs on the gates at the entrance to the estate. He nodded at the footman who opened the front door as he walked through to the turning circle beyond, strolling around it until he saw the thin plumes of purple smoke that led him to Mr Weatherly Draycott.

The specialist was leaning against the back wall of the stables, watching one of the stable boys brush a dappled grey mare who shied and snorted a great deal, swishing her tail in her enjoyment of the game of brush evasion. Elliott took the opportunity to study Weatherly Draycott. From what he could see of the man, he seemed to go for the more dapper and colourful style of day dress rather than the more professional and subdued fashions of a respected medical man.

Outfitted in a heavy winter three-piece suit in a rather splendid shade of heather, his dark hair smoothed with a pomade Elliott could smell from where he stood, the doctor cut a figure that certain impressionable women of any age would describe as charming, and which would automatically be dismissed by men as rather too charming. Elliott understood Lord Lapotaire's obvious dislike; he had a sudden overwhelming desire to kick the little man in his impeccably tailored posterior.

Elliott's mind turned to the discussion earlier with Lord Lapotaire about the presence of Valentine Carstairs at the village inn; he frowned, the important thing was discovering what Draycott knew, if anything, about the two murders at Marmis Hall. Perhaps now was not quite the right time to bring up the name of Valentine Carstairs.

The object of his sudden and inexplicable dislike turned, somehow aware that he was being watched. Draycott's smooth, relaxed face broke into a polite smile that crinkled his pale eyes at the corners as he observed the man standing behind him; rather short for a policeman was his first thought. Luckily, Elliott didn't have mind-reading on his list of abilities, or that would have irritated him tenfold. As Draycott studied the sharp-eyed man, his second thought was that this was a man of whom criminals ought to be afraid. A man to be reckoned with, indeed!

"Detective Chief Inspector Caine, I believe? Lord Marmis informed me of your arrival earlier this morning. A most unfortunate turn of affairs for Marmis; I hope it doesn't harm his future prospects in the House." The man had a languid way of speaking, as though it were too much effort to raise his voice.

Elliott smiled, his prominent canines flashing. "I doubt it will damage anyone's prospects other than the killer's, Mr Draycott."

"I hope you are right, Detective Chief Inspector. I understand you wish to question me regarding my whereabouts last night?"

Elliott was about to reply when a sudden movement from the house caught his attention. Frederick Marmis had emerged from the hall and was standing at the top of the steps, staring at Cuckoo Woods with an expression of utter joy. He walked down the steps and headed towards the path that led to the village, his thick green riding coat flapping around his boots as he strode. He hadn't noticed either man as they stood in the shadow of the stables.

Mr Draycott pulled on his cigar and turned to Elliott. "Who is that young gentleman? I don't recall seeing him yesterday."

"That is Frederick Marmis, Lord Marmis' younger brother."

Draycott's eyes opened wide and his thin-lipped mouth described an O. "The young man who was captured in Southern Africa! He escaped? How marvellous! But what an appalling homecoming for the poor young man. Oh, dear me."

Elliott took out his notebook, and flicking through it, found the page he had already started on the doctor. "I need to ask you some questions, Mr Draycott."

Draycott nodded benevolently. "As you wish."

"Would you please confirm your whereabouts last night?"

Draycott paused, and knocking ash from the end of his cigar, he gazed up at the roof of the stables. "Let me see; for most of the early evening I was involved in a rather one-sided game of Bridge in the library. My partner was Lady Ellerbeck and we were playing Lord and Lady Scott-Brewer…ah, the other unfortunate gentleman. Yes, I decided that I had had my fill of the game, so when I was dummy, I made my excuses and left the library—"

"At what time?"

Draycott waved his cigar. "I believe it was nearly a quarter to nine when I left. I went straight to the saloon, where I poured myself a very large Scotch. Believe me, after that length of time with the Scott-Brewers, I needed it." He paused. "I know one shouldn't speak ill of the dead, Detective

Chief Inspector Caine, but Lord Scott-Brewer was an intolerable man!"

"What did you do then?"

"Lady Ellerbeck also managed to escape their tender ministrations and joined me in the saloon at a few minutes past nine. I made her a drink – non-alcoholic, I hasten to add, I had already blotted my copybook in that regard with the lady, so I poured her a refreshing elderflower cordial instead."

Elliott scrutinised Draycott, noting the thin dark eyebrows plucked into sharpness over a pair of incredibly pale eyes. Their colour was hard to tell, even at that small distance.

"You blotted your copybook? In what way?"

Draycott lifted his cigar to his thin lips, and the thin plume of smoke vanished, reappearing from the specialist's nostrils. "I made Lady Ellerbeck a cocktail earlier in the evening, and I was unaware that the lady had a low tolerance for alcohol. I may have made the cocktail a touch too strong. I apologised in the saloon, and all was forgiven."

"How long were you in the saloon?"

"After Lady Ellerbeck arrived, not that long. I mixed her cordial and then came out here for a cigar. Lady Marmis is rather a dragon on the subject of smoking indoors."

Elliott nodded. "Lord Marmis doesn't smoke."

"No, he doesn't. Rather unusual for a man in his position, don't you think?"

Draycott again drew on the cigar and exhaled through his nose, his enjoyment evident. Elliott, who also didn't smoke, thought it quite a revolting sight. He ignored the question.

"Did you happen to see the butler on your repeated trips through the Great Hall?"

Draycott raised his manicured eyebrows. "As a matter of fact, I did. He was in the hall when I went out, I asked him when the buffet would start, and whether he could come and give me an early warning, as it were."

"What was his response?"

"He didn't seem that keen. Insisted he had to stay inside and oversee the finer details, so I decided to use my pocket watch instead."

Elliott nearly laughed, but managed to check himself. "At what time did you re-enter the house?"

Draycott paused, a faint frown furrowing his forehead. "Do you know, I am not sure. I do remember seeing Sir Hubert Kingston-Folly going back into the house from the stables. I entered shortly after, but they had already discovered the bodies by the time I went in, if that's any help?"

Elliott looked at the little man, and in a quiet voice said, "You say you saw Sir Hubert Kingston-Folly outside the hall. Are you sure it was Sir Hubert?"

"Oh yes, but he didn't see me; I was over there on the other side of the house. I'm sorry, I'm not sure of the time."

Elliott closed his notebook. "Thank you, Mr Draycott, thank you very much." He turned, then hesitated and turned back. "Mr Draycott, you have seen the bodies and you are a specialist in nervous disorders. Do you have any idea what would make someone do that to another human?"

Draycott again raised his eyebrows. "To another human? My dear chap, you make it sound as though you are of a race apart. But I take it you are referring to the injuries inflicted on the butler." He smoothed one immaculate eyebrow. "It is my professional opinion that his killer may well be suffering from Dementia Praecox or, quite possibly, plain, old-fashioned, and rather tedious homicidal insanity. There are such people, who are quite wearisome and rather catholic in their peculiarities. Now, give me someone with a mania for his mother's pearl necklace and his father's riding boots, and I can show you someone of real interest to a specialist!"

Draycott held out his hand, and after a moment Elliott took it. "Thank you, Mr Draycott."

"You're very welcome, Detective Chief Inspector, very welcome indeed."

Elliott left the specialist standing by the stables as a calm bay mare was brought out for her daily check and brush. As Elliott walked towards the hall, he thought it rather strange that Draycott hadn't mentioned the possibility of simple sadism.

Elliott headed back into the hall, making straight for the library, but Sir Hubert was not there. He pulled the bell and waited. As the door opened behind him, Elliott turned. "Ah, Greyling, have you seen Sir Hubert?"

Greyling nodded. "Yes, sir. Sir Hubert went out a few minutes ago."

Elliott paused. "I didn't see him leave by the front entrance."

"No, sir, he left by the morning-room door. He said that he believed a good walk would make him feel better."

Elliott pursed his lips, giving the rather unfortunate impression of wanting to kiss the butler. "Thank you, Greyling, that will be all."

"Yes, sir." Greyling left the room.

Elliott walked briskly towards the morning room. Thorne was still deep in thought over the now slightly less-ened pile of paper, though the torn, crumpled papers in the waste-paper basket beneath the desk were a testament as to how he was dealing with the task at hand.

He looked up from the remains of a plate of buttered crumpets as Elliott appeared, and frowned as he saw his friend's expression. "What's wrong?"

"Did Sir Hubert come through here a few minutes ago?"

Thorne wiped his buttery hands on the damp cloth that Jenkins had thoughtfully provided with the crumpets. "Yes, he did; he asked if it would be acceptable for him to take a walk along the lake, and then go to the village to have lunch at the inn. I said it would be fine as long as he returned before the end of the afternoon." Thorne took a sip of his tea. "I'm not sure that was the only place he was going, though."

Elliott's voice was sharp. "Why do you say that?"

"Well, he wasn't carrying a rod, but he *was* carrying a fisherman's bag...the lake here doesn't have any fish. The only other place to fish near here is the sea and that's a good four miles away." Thorne paused as he dabbed at his lips with his napkin. "A good walk might do him some good, he did look a little green about the gills. What's happened?"

"Sir Hubert wasn't quite honest with me this morning. When I questioned him he said he left Lord and Lady Marmis and Frederick in the study, went straight to the billiard room and stayed there until Lord Marmis and Lord Lapotaire came for him. However, he didn't tell me about his little jaunt to the stables."

Thorne raised his eyebrows. "I take it someone saw him?"

Elliott nodded. "Draycott."

Thorne's response was just as terse. "Is he an honest witness?"

"Possibly. He's also vain, languid and prone to hubris. That's why I wanted to speak with Sir Hubert again, to get his version of his whereabouts." Elliott paused and rolled his eyes. "Whereabouts...Gods, I am really beginning to dislike that bloody word!"

○

11:20am

On the far side of the estate, Frederick Marmis walked quietly along the pathway that led through a deep thicket of hazel and dead bracken towards the tiny village lane. The bright sunshine had yet to burn off the heavy early-morning dew, and the trees and ground were still saturated with moisture. Frederick rejoiced and breathed in deeply; after two years in a place with no rain, just constant, crippling heat, the damp scent of the woodlands reinforcing his happiness at finally being home.

So deep in thought was he that it took a moment for him to realise he was sharing the pathway with another traveller...one who was heading towards Marmis Hall.

Frederick looked at the man before him; mid-twenties, and very slim, his collar-length blond hair made several shades darker by the dampness of the woods. His face was furnished with an Imperial Van Dyke trimmed to within an inch of oblivion. He wore a purple velvet suit desperately unsuitable for walking in the country, as the state of his trousers and black patent leather shoes showed, and he was also without a decent winter coat.

Frederick looked at the lavish, damp young man and realised he was talking. "I am sorry, sir, I didn't hear you."

"I asked whether you were from Marmis Hall."

Frederick nodded, his dark-brown hair falling against his forehead. "Yes, I am from the hall. I live there."

"Do I have the honour of addressing Lord Marmis?"

"No, Lord Marmis is my elder brother. I am Frederick Marmis."

The young man held out his hand. "My apologies, sir, Please allow me to introduce myself. My name is Valentine Carstairs, at your service."

Frederick shook the man's cold hand. The firm grip belied the man's foppish appearance, as did the determined expression that had appeared on the shivering young man's face.

"Please may I walk with you awhile? I must bring something to your attention; I regret to say that it involves one of your brother's guests."

○

11:35am

The figure pushed their way through the thicket. The overgrown understory of dead bracken, young trees, and trailing ivy slapped damply at the walker's legs as they hurriedly made their way along the shortcut to the village lane; they didn't have much time!

○

11:35am

Valentine Carstairs made his way down the steep steps at the foot of a massive oak tree and walked doggedly along the wet path that led him back towards the village. His shoes were nearing the very end of their existence and he could feel the creeping dampness in his socks. As he walked, Valentine's mind sped through his conversation with Frederick Marmis. It had been very productive; the young man had been completely unaware of the questionable background of one of his brother's guests, and had been grateful for the information. He had promised to take the issue up with his older brother as soon as he returned to the hall.

Valentine smiled grimly. If he couldn't get the authorities to deal with The Man, as he thought of him, then he would just have to wear The Man down until he voluntarily informed the police of his crimes, and if Valentine was correct in his supposition, The Man's crimes were many.

Valentine struck the palm of his left hand with his fist.

Dear Aunt Emily could not have killed herself! It was against everything she had stood for in life. Taking the Grand Tour without a chaperone, staying with the Bedouin in North Africa, travelling the length of the Silk Route in order to prove to her dressmaker that Chinese silk was superior to Indian. She had grasped her life with both hands and she had lived it, to the extent that even her more questionable exploits were talked of by ladies at dinner parties, and in the company of the opposite sex! His aunt had merrily and firmly brought down barriers as she blazed a trail for other women who were willing to follow in her mighty footsteps, and there were many women who were prepared to do so.

Valentine felt a sudden wave of affection for the woman who had taken him in and raised him after the death of his parents. She had taken him on many of her travels, repeatedly scorning any suggestion of boarding school with the reply that the world would be his school and that he would learn of life as he lived it. That was how it should be learned – not from a stuffy, proselytising professor in an equally stuffy schoolroom, using books several years if not decades out of date. No, for such a woman as she, suicide was not an option his aunt would ever have considered, even if, as the coroner had stated, she had left a note explaining the reasons. Presumed ill-health – bah! Valentine gritted his teeth and kicked out at a stone as he walked. He had to prove it, and he would!

He carried on down the little track that would bring him to the edge of the village. As he passed another huge old oak, he heard a muffled sound behind him and turned. The path disappeared back into the damp gloom of the hazel coppice he had just trudged through. Valentine stared into the dark, bracken-filled thicket beyond, but could see nothing.

He listened as he gazed into the dark, his damp blond head cocked to one side as he focused on the rustling of dead

leaves in the breeze and the snuffling sound of small crea-
tures as they made their way through the dell. Obviously that
had been the cause of the sound he had heard.

Valentine turned and continued along the path. He had
chosen the most direct route back to the village, one which
would drop him almost in the very ample lap of his landlady,
Mrs Mickle. It was a different path from the one he had
taken to Marmis Hall, which he had picked up as it crossed
the main lane half a mile from the village. Parts of the path
were slippery in wet weather, so Lord Marmis, as the
landowner, had ordered that they be made safer with steps
made from large stone flags and logs.

Making his way awkwardly along one such section,
Valentine entered a large clearing with a babbling stream. It
was rather picturesque, and if he'd had more time he could
have composed something rather lovely about it, but there
was nothing remotely lovely about the steep steps before
him. Nearly fifty feet in height, providing a manageable but
painful shortcut over the steep crest of the hill to the village,
the Parva Steps were avoided by the locals in all but the
driest of summer months.

Valentine looked at the steps with some trepidation.
Bordered by the stream on the right and a dense thicket of
trees and bracken on the left, there was no other way around
unless he chose to go back and climb up to the lane. He
remonstrated with himself. Aunt Emily had travelled to far
more dangerous places than this. Had she not scaled a mountain in the Himalayas to consult with a yogi? Ha! He should
be able to manage a little climb that wouldn't wind a child.

Valentine removed a little charm on a gold chain from his
waistcoat pocket. The small golden disc gleamed in the
winter light; he kissed the oriental dragon charm and tucked
it back into its padded compartment.

In truth, the climb was far more dangerous than he had

admitted to himself. The stone flags were slippery, and the light flashing off the mica trapped within the stone made it hard to see where to put his feet.

As Valentine focused on the climb, he ceased to pay attention to the sounds around him. If he had been listening, the sudden lack of birdsong would have drawn his attention to the fact that he was no longer alone. A silent figure stood just a few feet behind him.

Valentine's foot slipped, but as he slid down the stones, he managed to jam his other foot on a different step and arrest his descent. Breathing a sigh of relief, he steadied himself to continue the short climb; he knew that from the top of the steps it was only a brief walk to the village and the inn. He silently thanked the young man from the hall for his generosity; the gift of his riding coat had definitely made his journey easier, and certainly somewhat drier.

There was a sudden sharp crack, as of a twig snapping. Before Valentine could look down, he felt strong hands grasp his ankle and pull. Valentine gave a strangled cry and slid violently down the rough steps to the ground; as the young man tried desperately to get to his feet, the thick green riding coat Frederick Marmis had lent him covered his face. As Valentine struggled with his attacker and tried in vain to stand, his assailant pulled a knife from their belt and brutally stabbed the young man in the neck and chest.

After several minutes of frenzied, bloody work, the attacker paused. Breathing heavily, they climbed off the still figure and pulled the bloodstained coat away. Valentine's shocked blue eyes stared blankly at his killer; his pale, dead face flecked with blood from his hideous wounds.

The killer snarled. Still kneeling, they grasped the coat and glared at it. Then a flash of gold caught their attention; the little dragon charm that had been a gift from Lady Carstairs to her nephew. Covetous eyes widened. With a sharp tug the figure snapped the chain and wiped the blood from the charm before tucking it inside their boot.

They looked down at the young man they had just killed, as without a word, the knife came down again and again to sever Valentine Carstairs' head.

○

11:40am

Elliott left the morning room just as Thom was walking out of the servants' kitchen. "Ah, Constable, I need your help. Come with me, please."

Thom hurried to keep up as Elliott stalked out of the house and into the turning circle. Elliott surveyed the grounds, then turning to Thom, said quietly, "We need to find Sir Hubert. He said he was going to the village by way of the lake. We walked to the ice house that affords a good view of the lake and we can't see him, so; which is the quickest route to the village from here?"

Before Thom could answer, Thorne appeared in the doorway, pulling a coat over his broad shoulders. He was carrying Elliott's coat, which he threw at his friend with a smile. "You didn't think you could leave me in there with all that paperwork while you got on with the interesting things, did you?"

Elliott took the coat with little grace and pulled it on. He looked at Thom who, resplendent in his serge uniform, didn't seem to feel the damp or the chill. "Well, which way?"

"Oh, yes, sir. Um, I would go this way." Thom pointed to a narrow path on the far side of the turning circle.

"We're going that way, then. Lead on."

The three men crossed the turning circle and walked down the path. After several minutes, the pathway dropped into a heavily wooded walk surrounded by beech trees; gnarled and twisted into incredible forms, their leaves already beginning to turn orange and bronze.

They passed the beech trees and walked through a hazel coppice to a fork in the path. "Where now?"

Thom pointed to the left fork. "That one is longer, but it will take you to the main lane into the village…it cuts across the driveway." He gestured to the path on the right. "That one will get you to the village quicker, sir, but you'd have to climb the Parva Steps and they're bloody steep, begging your pardon, sir. I wouldn't try it at this time of year, it's far too damp!"

"I see. Thorne, you come with me, and we will go along the main lane. Constable, follow the path to the steps. If you find anything, use your whistle."

Thom nodded, pressing his hand against his pocket.

"Don't try anything brave, Constable! I don't want to have to explain any unfortunate happenstance to your step-mother; she would probably get the cook to turn me into a curry!"

Thom smiled faintly. "Just so you know, sir, there is a bit of a climb at the end. The path is a little bit lower than the lane so you'll need to climb up the bank a bit." He walked down the right-hand path, his uniform disappearing behind a thick mound of bracken.

Elliott and Thorne looked at each other. "We'll need to climb up the bank 'a bit'," Thorne murmured. "How much is a bit around here, do you think?"

Elliott shrugged. "We'll find out soon enough. Let's get up there."

The two men started along the path, which seemed to be in rather better condition than the one Thom had taken. After several minutes, they realised the path was on a gradual incline; their calf muscles complained volubly as they stomped along the wet, slippery path.

After a few minutes spent in mutually painful exercise, they came at last to the point where the pathway met the drive; they paused and looked at each other with pained sighs before crossing the well-tended driveway and continuing along the narrow track that cut through the damp undergrowth beyond.

As they made their way around a thick clump of hazel trees, they stopped dead on the path and stared. The weaving track came to an abrupt end at the foot of a massive embankment that reared up before them; wickedly steep and cluttered with bracken, tree stumps, and spring lines, it resembled an artistic nightmare in mud.

Thorne looked resignedly at Elliott. "I suppose it's too late to say I need to catch up with my paperwork, isn't it?"

Elliott nodded silently and pointed upwards.

With a sigh, Thorne chose what he hoped was the path of least resistance, Elliott followed him, a little further to the left in case Thorne should fall. Thorne might well be his friend, but he wasn't going to be used as a soft landing.

After several minutes of grunting, swearing, and prayers to the patron saint of stain removal, Thorne reached the road and staggered to a halt. Bending over, he drew in a deep breath then looked up and recoiled. A man's head, neatly placed in the middle of the lane, stared back at him, an expression of shock still visible on his once-handsome face.

Elliott made it to the top and saw the bloody lump in front of Thorne, who was angrily trying to keep his breakfast and various elevenses down.

Thorne straightened up and looked at Elliott. "The head isn't the problem, it's the shock of not expecting it; that's the problem."

Elliott looked down at the severed head, which bore the

face of a man he recognised. He frowned at the puddle of gore that had gathered under it. "Where do you suppose the rest of him is, Thorne? I seem to remember that this gentleman was, in life, somewhat taller."

Thorne was about to reply when the piercing sound of a police whistle piped from the woods below. Elliott ran to the edge of the embankment, sat down, tucked his coat tails underneath him, and slid all the way to the ground. He stood up, checked the back of his coat, and with a grimace waved at Thorne.

"Come on, Thorne," he called. "Officer in need of assistance."

Thorne nodded and sat gingerly on the edge of the bank, the hideous squelching noises not helping in the slightest. He pulled his coat around him, and pushed off.

The tree root had been the problem, he later complained to his tailor. He hadn't seen it in the mud and other indescribable filth, so when he struck the offending item with his posterior it spun him round to continue his journey backwards. That in turn robbed him of the opportunity to either see or avoid his landing area, which, though soft, was far too wet and squashy to be healthy.

Thorne pulled himself to his feet with a groan and limped damply through the undergrowth as he followed Elliott back across the driveway and down the path. As the two men reached the fork in the path that led to Thom and the Parva Steps, they started to run.

After several minutes of lopsided running that he was sure resembled Quasimodo on a bad day, Thorne finally came abreast of Elliott as they loped down a wider part of the path. The two men looked at each other. "Police life has made us soft, old friend," Elliott panted. "We need to get back to the old ways and the old job. What say you?"

Thorne grinned, a twinkle in his eye. "Oh Gods, yes, I could do with less paperwork!"

They continued down the path, which bent round and brought them to the clearing which was the home of the Parva Steps. As they entered the large glade they became aware of the stillness, even the stream seemed subdued as it wound its way along the edge of the treeline.

Thom sat at the foot of the steps, his pallor throwing his freckles into stark relief and making his face appear waxen. Elliott and Thorne were relieved to see he was unharmed. The same thing could not be said for the corpse at his feet, however: the headless figure of a man in a green riding coat.

Elliott breathed in sharply; he recognised that coat! Carefully lifting the bloody material, he looked at the headless body in its dashing purple suit. He turned to Thorne. "My friend, I think we have found the body to go with our head."

Thom swallowed. "There's a head?"

Thorne patted Thom on the shoulder. "Most people come with one, Constable."

Thorne knelt by the corpse and looked at the broken chain dangling from the waistcoat. "Something's been taken, Elliott; there was something on the end of this chain." He lifted the torn, bloodied coat away from the body. "He was stabbed repeatedly through his coat. Look: the material is almost shredded." Pushing the coat to one side, he lifted one of the dead man's hands. "His hands are soft and manicured, but the nails are torn and there are abrasions on his palms." He examined the suit. "Two of the buttons have been torn off. I think he was climbing up the steps and he either fell, or—"

"Or someone pulled him down. Keep going, Thorne."

Carefully peeling one side of the blood stained purple jacket away, Thorne checked the inside pocket and pulled out a leather wallet He looked inside, then sat back on his heels and looked at Elliott, his face set. "It's Valentine Carstairs. What the hell is going on here?"

He handed the pocketbook to Elliott. "My question is this," Elliott said slowly. "What is Valentine Carstairs doing wearing Frederick Marmis' riding coat, which I saw him in less than an hour ago? We must get back to the house; if we are quick, the morgue attendants can gather another corpse before they head off to Benchester." He turned to Thom. "I'm afraid I must ask you to stay with the body, Constable; we will send the attendants as soon as possible."

As Elliott moved away from the corpse, something caught his eye. "Thorne, look at this."

Thorne and Thom turned to look where Elliott was pointing. Lying halfway between the body and the stream was a tack knife, sharp and covered in blood.

Elliott looked at Thorne. "Sir Hubert can wait. We need to find Frederick!"

○

12:20pm

On their return, they found and hurriedly informed Lord Lapotaire of their concerns. He looked worried.

"I had no idea he had left his room...I shall tell Vanamoinen to find him immediately and stay by his side."

Elliott and Thorne left Lord Lapotaire and discovered the morgue attendants just finishing their foul task. The attendants had not been happy to hear of another corpse, nor of its cleaved state in two separate parts of the woods, but the sum of five shillings each had changed hands and three suddenly much happier men had left with Thorne, his camera, and a bag of equipment.

Elliott had been taken in charge by Greyling, who had

escorted him to an unoccupied suite, handed him a generous hot toddy, and introduced him to the large copper bath that steamed in the middle of the bathroom. After utilising a sizeable quantity of lavender soap, and soaking for a decent amount of time, Elliott left the tub to find that one of the boot-boys had been sent to the village to fetch him a clean set of clothing from the inn.

Clean, warm and dry in a chocolate tweed three-piece, Elliott thanked Greyling and gave the young boot-boy a shilling. As the boy was about to leave, the door opened and Thorne came in, covered with mud and muck. He shivered as he passed two large beige packets to Elliott. "The larger is the coat; the other is the knife."

"If you will come with me, sir," said Greyling, "I will draw you a hot bath. Ned, go back to the inn and collect some clean clothes for the gentleman." Elliott dug out another shilling, and the grinning young boy fairly ran out of the room.

Elliott left Thorne in Greyling's capable hands and went in search of Lord Marmis. Tracking him down to his study, he knocked and entered the room, intent on informing the young lord of the events of the morning and what they had discovered in the woods.

As Elliott entered the room, he found Lord Marmis looking deeply disturbed. Without speaking he handed Elliott a piece of paper. It was covered with childish drawings, somewhat similar to the artwork on the piece of canvas they had used to wrap up the poker. The stick figure on the paper was a classic image of childish art...the copious quantities of red paint that doused its form, however, were not.

Elliott looked sharply at Foster. "Where did you get this?"

"Nanny Parker found it in Evie's bedroom. Nanny asked why she had painted such a thing, and Evie said...Evie said it was something she had seen the night before. Caine, I cannot allow you to question my daughter, but I can tell you what she told me."

Elliott sat by the fire and leant forward, his face intent. "Please do."

Lord Marmis took a deep breath. "I am grateful to say that my daughter did not witness the figure commit the outrage that was perpetrated here...but she did see them enter the orangery from the gallery, and wash themselves in the pond. She saw them redress, and return to the gallery."

Elliott nodded. "I need to speak with your brother, Lord Marmis. Lord Lapotaire doesn't know where he is, do you know where he might be?"

Lord Marmis looked worried. "Why do you wish to speak to my brother? He has an alibi for the murders."

Elliott held up the large package which he had brought to the study. Opening it carefully, he pulled out the torn and bloodstained riding coat. "I'm afraid there has been another murder. Lord Marmis, is this your brother's coat?"

Lord Marmis' face showed shock and fear. "Oh my God, yes, it's Fred's coat! What – not Fred...!"

The door opened and Lady Marmis entered, smiling. Her smile vanished as she looked at her husband, and hurrying to his side, she grasped his arm. "Foster, what's wrong?" She looked at Elliott, who had stood at her arrival, and seeing the bloody mass of green material he was holding, she blanched. "What is that? Is it from the gallery? Foster, please answer me—"

Elliott addressed her. "Lady Marmis, perhaps you can help us. Have you seen either your brother-in-law or Sir Hubert in the last hour?"

Lady Marmis looked at her husband. "I haven't seen Bertie at all this morning, but Frederick is in the kitchen with his mother—"

Lord Marmis leapt from his chair and ran from the room.

Lady Marmis and Elliott looked at each other, then Lady Marmis hitched up her skirts and ran after her husband, with Elliott following close behind.

They ran along the corridor and followed Lord Marmis into the kitchen. Frederick was standing by the range, a cup of tea in one hand and a large iced bun in the other. He turned as the door crashed open, and stared in surprise as his brother ran in, followed by his sister-in-law and a man whom he did not recognise but took to be the police officer his mother had told him of.

Lord Marmis took one look at his brother and collapsed. Lady Marmis cried out his name and ran to his side, Frederick's bun and teacup fell to the floor as he ran to help Elliott manhandle his brother to the settee by the stove.

Elliott examined the young lord's head; a lump had already started to swell. "He took a good crack to the skull." He turned to Lady Marmis. "We need a doctor."

She turned a stricken face to Elliott. "Dr Marchant is Foster's doctor, but he's in London!"

Elliott turned to the butler. "Greyling, go and find Mr Draycott; inform him of what has happened, and ask him to come to Lord Marmis' suite immediately."

The butler nodded sharply as he ran out of the kitchen.

Elliott turned to Mrs Higginson. "What is the quickest way to get Lord Marmis to his room?"

Mrs Higginson, clutching the front of her apron covered dress with a white-knuckled hand, blinked rapidly. "The servants' staircase, straight through that curtain there. But it's a spiral staircase. It would be quicker to use the main stairs in the Great Hall."

Elliott looked at Frederick, crouched next to his brother, his face white. "Help me carry your brother, quickly."

Led by Lady Marmis, the two men carried Lord Marmis through to the Great Hall and up the stairs to the suite of rooms he shared with his wife. Placing him gently on the bed, Elliott turned to Frederick as Lady Marmis undid her husband's necktie. "Answer me this. You went for a walk, you met a young man, and you gave him your coat. Why?"

Frederick looked bemused. "He was wet and cold. I told him he could return it later."

"Your act of kindness saved your life, but ended his. I need to speak to you about many things; however, for your own safety, I want you to go to your room and lock the door behind you. I don't know where Vanamoinen is, so I'm afraid we'll have to rely on a locked door." Elliott grasped Frederick's wrist. "Do not let anyone in until I arrive. Go!"

The young man stared at Elliott with a confused expression.

Elliott hissed under his breath, "It concerns John Stable!"

The effect on Frederick was immediate; his broad face paled beneath its tan. He swallowed, and nodding jerkily, left the room.

Elliott closed the door and turned back to Lord Marmis, who was draped across the bed, Lady Marmis was gently placing a pillow under his head. The young lord's skin was pale and clammy, with the start of a large bruise evident on his temple.

Lord Marmis moaned, and tried to sit up, but Elliott put a firm hand against his chest. "Steady, my lord; you've taken a nasty crack to your skull. You shouldn't be moving, you know." Elliott helped Lady Marmis ease her husband back down onto the well plumped pillow. As Lady Marmis hurried into the bathroom for a damp cloth for her husband's head, Elliott sat in a green velvet armchair next to the bed, and leaning back, he crossed his ankles and gazed with interest at Lord Marmis, who was now coming round fully and feeling quite the worse for wear.

The first thing Foster Marmis saw was the face of Elliott

next to his bed. He looked at Elliott through half closed eyes. "Damn you, Caine, why in God's name did you make me think that Fred was…" He swallowed hard then whispered. "I'm sorry."

"Don't apologise, my lord. The apology is mine to make and I make it now. I should have thought how the coat would have appeared to you. How's your head?"

Lord Marmis touched his temple and winced. "Bloody painful, now that you ask." He looked at Elliott. "Seeing Fred's coat, after everything that has happened, I thought…" He closed his eyes. Lady Marmis reappeared with a damp cloth that she gently pressed against her husband's forehead; Lord Marmis squeezed her hand gratefully before turning back to Elliott. "Who now has been murdered?"

"A young man by the name of Valentine Carstairs. His mistake was accepting your brother's offer of help; he borrowed Frederick's coat, and I believe the killer murdered him in the mistaken belief that he *was* Frederick."

Elliott stood. Moving to the door, he opened it and looked down the corridor. Satisfied that no one was there, he closed it and sat down again. "Now, if your head is up to it, please let us return to what young Evie saw…and in particular, if she saw their face."

Lord Marmis blinked. "But she wouldn't have recognised them as a guest, she was already in bed when most of them arrived."

Elliott nodded. "But she could tell us their sex, hair colour, and physical build. I understand that you don't want us to frighten her, Lord Marmis…but we desperately need that information."

1:15pm

Weatherly Draycott closed the door of the master suite behind him, leaving Lady Marmis at her sleeping husband's bedside.

Elliott looked up from the chair that had been placed by the door. "Well, Mr Draycott?"

Draycott sighed and passed a weary hand across his temples. "He should be fine. He's received a nasty blow to his head, there's no denying that, but luckily it is nothing serious. A mild concussion and rather a bad headache is the worst-case diagnosis."

"Is there anything he can take for the headache?"

The dapper man nodded, his oiled hair gleaming in the sunlight. "I have given him an injection of a muscle relaxant to help with the pain. I have also given Lady Marmis a box of cachets that he can take as needed after he wakes."

"Thank you, Mr Draycott."

"Not at all; though one is now a specialist, one is always a doctor. Good afternoon, Detective Chief Inspector."

As he walked away, Elliott consulted his watch. "Sir Isadore Shard should be on his way by now," he muttered. Tucking the watch back into his pocket he walked the short distance to Frederick's bedroom, and knocked.

There was a pause, then a low voice inquired, "Who is it?"

"It is I, Detective Chief Inspector Caine; open the door."

A bolt slid back, then the door opened slightly and Frederick peeked around the edge. Elliott entered and Frederick once again shot the bolt.

Elliott looked around the cosy bed-sitting room which on the plan was known as the Silver Suite. A large fireplace surmounted by a heavy grey marble mantlepiece covered most of the left side of the room, while the wall on the right was filled with overflowing bookcases. A large silver-framed photograph of a very young Frederick clutching a spaniel sat in pride of place on the kneehole desk, while in the corner, a door led to what had once been the valet's room and that was now a very modern bathroom. Opposite the main door was a comfortable bed under a large picture window with views of Cuckoo Woods; in the distance Elliott could see smoke rising from the chimneys in the village.

Frederick studied the man in front of him. Dark hair and eyes, and with a gentle manner, but the hand that had gripped his wrist earlier had an unexpected power and strength. Frederick spoke, and to his disgust, his voice trembled. "You mentioned John Stable; where does he come into this?"

"I will come to that, Mr Marmis." Elliott continued. "Earlier this morning, you left the house and took the path to the village." Elliott fixed his large dark eyes on Lord Marmis' younger brother. "Tell me what happened on your walk."

Frederick sat down on the edge of the bed, his thick fingers fiddling with the silver-blue tassels on the coverlet. "I wanted to get out of the house. I wanted – no, I needed some air. Just to walk and walk under an open sky. A gentle sky, you understand; an English sky without that damned burning sun...I just needed to get out." He took a deep breath. "I headed for the pathway that would take me up to the lane. The path crosses it and continues on the other side, but before I got to the fork in the path, I met rather an odd chap."

Elliott sat in a pale-grey armchair next to the fireplace. "Go on."

"He introduced himself as Valentine Carstairs, and said that he was staying at the Dolphin and Anker. He said there was something I should know about one of the guests in the house."

Elliott smiled. "Mr Draycott, by any chance?"

Frederick looked surprised. "Yes. He said…well, he came out with an incredible story about Draycott murdering his aunt for the sake of an inheritance. He seemed quite sincere, and asked me to inform my brother of his suspicions as soon as I returned home."

Elliott leaned forward. "What did you do then?"

Frederick smiled, the expression softening his face. "He was perfectly dressed for a night at a bohemian club in London, but not for an autumnal walk in the country. The poor chap's feet were soaked through, and he didn't have a coat, so I – I gave him my riding coat and said he could return it later."

"What happened then?"

"Under the circumstances, I thought it would be best if I came home and had a word with Foss. Mr Carstairs said that he would return to the inn to await my brother's thoughts on the matter of Mr Draycott. I suggested he accompany me to the hall, but he refused. So, I walked up to the driveway and returned to the hall; you can ask Greyling…he let me in. Anyway, when I got home Foss was in his study going through some documents and I didn't want to interrupt, so I thought I'd leave it until later."

"Returning by the driveway probably saved your life. Did you see which way Mr Carstairs went?"

Frederick looked at Elliott sharply. "What do you mean, 'saved my life'? And earlier, you said I 'saved my life, but ended his'. What has happened?"

"I will explain, but first, did you see where Mr Carstairs went?"

"No. He said he had some thinking to do, so I left him by the stream."

"Did you tell him about the Parva Steps?"

Frederick looked worried. "No, I didn't. Look here, has something happened to the chap? He didn't fall down the steps, surely?"

Elliott looked at the worried young man before him. There really was no way to soften such a blow. "No, Mr Marmis, Valentine Carstairs did not fall down the steps. He was attacked at the foot of the steps, stabbed repeatedly, and then decapitated."

A riot of expressions flooded the young man's face. Shock, fear, despair, and nausea jostled for position; nausea won hands-down and he bolted for the bathroom. When Frederick had finished, Elliott heard the sound of running water.

Elliott entered the little room, passed him a clean towel from the rail and stood in the doorway. "I need to know the truth, as painful as that may be. Come back into the other room, please."

The two men sat down by the fire, and Elliott looked at the young man. Boy might be a better word, since at close quarters he looked barely into his twenties, though the tremor in his hands and his ashen face had suddenly added years to his appearance. He decided that attack was probably the best way of getting a straight answer. "Mr Marmis, when was the last time you had any contact with Dr Wallace Johnson's family?"

Frederick started. "How did you— Oh, of course, government and all that. It was just before I arrived back in England. I returned home via France."

"Why?"

"When Wally was dying, he asked me to tell his mother what had happened to him, and I gave my word that I would. When I arrived at the British garrison in Southern Rhodesia, I didn't tell them who I was or what I was really doing there;

they'd have thought me a fool out for adventure who found more than he bargained for." He paused with a wry expression. "They would have been quite correct! They gave me enough money to get to France by ship, so I travelled into Kenya and managed to arrange passage. I arrived in Marseille and begged a few francs to send a telegram to Wally's mother, who wired me enough funds to get to Paris. When I arrived, Wally's father was away on business, but his mother and his sister – Clarice – well, they wanted me to explain what had happened. I felt they ought to be told everything, so…so I showed them the documents Wally had taken from the camp files."

Elliott had noticed how Frederick's voice softened when he mentioned the sister's name. "Did you show them the names of the spies?"

Frederick nodded, and his young face assumed a stubborn expression. "Yes, I did. They had every right to see the names of the men who bore the ultimate responsibility for Wally's death."

Elliott sat back. He too had been young and idealistic… once. Perhaps it was best for Frederick's future prospects if he left the diplomatic service and found another source of income to keep young Clarice happy as his wife.

"Please be honest with me, Frederick. Did you place a telephone call to the Johnson family residence in Paris at half past one this morning?"

Frederick looked at him, incredulous. "Before the events of the last two years, I had barely any experience of that time in the morning, Detective Chief Inspector Caine. No, I haven't spoken to Mrs Johnson, or…or to Clarice since they gave me the means to return home."

Elliott nodded slowly. "Tell me everything you know about these men, starting with John Rook."

Frederick took a deep breath. "He was a spy. His job was

to gain employment in the home of a well-connected member of the aristocracy or a highly placed Member of Parliament, and pass on anything that could be used to either further their cause or be used for blackmail purposes. He was sent here several years ago and furnished with excellent and utterly false references to assist him. He used those references well, gaining employment with several well-placed and trusted families who could provide him with both real references, and the information he sought."

"Put simply, a gossip-monger and a passer-on of unconsidered and long-forgotten trifles, hmm?"

Frederick managed a small smile. "Exactly that."

"Tell me what you can about John Stable."

The smile disappeared and Frederick's face became, if anything, more ashen. Elliott went into the bathroom and filled a tooth glass with water. Handing it to Frederick, he sat back down and waited.

"John Stable was…is…a sadist. He was the torturer at the camp." Frederick swallowed. "He hurt me. But I was one of the lucky ones: I survived. When they decided they had no further use for you and Stable was there, he would kill you, slowly—" Frederick closed his eyes and tears ran down his face. "I'm sorry, I can't…I can't say what he did."

Elliott leaned forward. "It's quite all right, Mr Marmis, you're doing very well. You said, 'when Stable was there'. So, he wasn't a permanent fixture at the camp?"

Frederick wiped his nose and blinked rapidly as he looked at Elliott. "No, he wasn't always there. Sometimes he would be gone for several months, return for a few weeks, then leave again."

Elliott smiled grimly. "As though he had other things to attend to. Tell me about John Wisdom; what do you know about him?"

A touch of colour returned to Frederick's pale face and he

set his jaw. "He's a traitor! He's British, and a member of the government, but he's been selling information to the Boers for at least eight or nine years."

"Is he selling secrets for money, or for position within Southern Africa?"

"Purely money. I am sure. Some of the paperwork Wally found detailed large payments made in gold sovereigns."

"Do you have any idea how the money was changing hands?"

"I do; the money was wired to an office in Calais, then sent on to a village on the coast of Brittany. The money was left in a lobster pot with a buoy of a different colour, and a boat would come across from England to collect it."

Elliott sat back, a look of amusement on his face. "Remarkable! Someone had fun dreaming that one up, didn't they? Now, an important question, did you at any time see John Stable's face?"

Frederick swallowed hard and nodded.

"Good. I will ask Thorne to come up here with his sketchbook: he's a very good artist. In the meantime, I want you to stay in this room and lock the door and windows."

Frederick looked worried. "Why?"

Elliott sighed. "Because I believe that John Stable is here, and that he is responsible for the murders committed this weekend. Steady, now!"

Frederick's face paled to a colour beyond ashes, his hazel eyes rolled back in his head as he slumped in his chair.

Elliott swore and leapt to his feet as the half full tooth glass fell to the floor. Propping Frederick's head between his knees, he headed to the bathroom, soaked his handkerchief under the tap and returned, pressing the damp cloth to the back of Frederick's neck.

The young man groaned slightly. Elliott gently moved

him into an upright position and poured him a fresh glass of water.

Frederick took the water and sipped, then looking at Elliott with a desperate expression, he whispered, "You could be wrong. Please God, I hope you're wrong."

Elliott squeezed the young man's shoulder and stood up. "I'm very much afraid that I am right, Mr Marmis, and it is vital that you stay in your room. There are only two people in this house who have seen the killer's face, and I plan on keeping you both safe. When I leave this room, lock and bolt the door behind me. Do not let anyone in except me, Thorne, your mother, brother or your sister-in-law."

Elliott walked to the door, then halted. "Just to confirm, Mr Marmis. When you received the documents from young Dr Johnson, how many spies did they name?"

Frederick frowned, then looked up at Elliott with a confused expression. "Three: John Rook, John Wisdom and John Stable."

"You are sure? No other names?"

Frederick shook his head. "No other names. Those documents were all I had to read on the journey home; believe me, Detective Chief Inspector Caine, they contained three names, no more." He stared at Elliott, and pushed himself up in his chair. "Why do you ask?"

Elliott gave the bemused young man a grin. "Because someone is playing a game with me, Mr Marmis: a game I intend to win. Now, lock this door and get some rest." He closed the door behind him, and listened as Frederick shot the bolt and turned the key in the lock.

Walking towards the staircase, Elliott didn't notice that one of the doors on the corridor was slightly ajar, as the silent figure within watched him walk downstairs.

1:35pm

Elliott found Thorne in the billiard room, playing a quiet game of Patience in an attempt to garner enough of that very virtue to enable his willing return to the paperwork that awaited him in the morning room; so far, it was failing.

"Thorne, I want you to fetch your sketching things and go up to Frederick's room. He knows what John Stable looks like; see if it matches the description young Evie gave us."

Thorne placed the deck of cards back in its box and stood up with a yawn. "You are aware that Evie didn't see the killer's face? All the poor child saw was the murderer washing and dressing themselves. She could only confirm that they were male and they were wearing evening dress."

"I am aware of that. Perhaps it is as well that our killer didn't finish Hardcastle off in full view of the nursery, but it does narrow our search somewhat." Elliott sat down. "Still no sign of Sir Hubert?"

Thorne shook his head. "Nothing since he left the hall."

Elliott stared into the distance. "Hmm. Strange that Frederick didn't admit to seeing him on the path…but then he could have travelled by the lane, I suppose." Elliott tapped his chin. "Did you happen to notice whether he was carrying anything other than his fishing bag?"

Thorne considered the question. "Yes, he had a white envelope, about so big." Thorne measured a distance between his hands of some twelve inches by eight. "The fishing bag looked quite full too."

Elliott nodded, his face brooding in the gaslight. "I wonder. Go quickly, Thorne. Things are moving at a faster pace now, and the killer may also be aware of that."

Thorne pawed through the larger of the two chests they

had brought, and taking out his sketching equipment, made his way to Frederick's room. It took some time to convince the wary young man, but at last the door opened and Frederick let him in.

A little after four o'clock, Thorne left the young man safely locked in his suite and returned in triumph to the billiard room.

○

4:10pm

Frederick sat alone on his bed. Thorne had been and gone with his sketching pad and charcoal pencils. It had taken many false starts and quite a lot of paper before Frederick saw the face that had poisoned his dreams appear on the cream-coloured sheet. When, after more than two and a half hours of scribbling and shading, Thorne had held up a detailed portrait, Frederick felt his stomach churn with nausea. Gritting his teeth, he nodded. That was him; that was John Stable.

Frederick hadn't understood the look of triumph on Thorne's face as he thanked him and all but flew out of the door, the sketch held like a trophy before him. Thorne only paused to make sure Frederick bolted the door behind him.

Frederick's gaze wandered around the little room that had been his from the age of twelve. The soft silver-grey of the walls was dim now as the sun began to sink; only a few months to go before the winter solstice. He walked over to the fire, now the only real source of light in the room. Reaching towards the fire-irons, he hesitated before removing the poker and prodding the fire. He placed some coal and another log on the burning embers and gazed at the dancing flames in the grate.

As he stood by the crackling fire, Frederick's thoughts veered away from John Stable and the current, hideous events, and returned to the few days he had spent in Paris with Wally's mother, and his sister, Clarice. He closed his eyes. Beautiful Clarice, with her golden-brown hair and gentle deep-blue eyes. She had been so concerned for him and his safety that she had begged him to send a message to let her know he was safely home. He realised to his shame that he hadn't as yet sent one.

A sudden movement under the door caught Frederick's eye. In the corridor outside, the gas lamps sent their soft yellow light flickering under his door – except for a shadow about a person's width. There was a pause, then the door handle slowly began to turn…

The breath caught in Frederick's throat. Suddenly he was back in the camp. The stench from a pack of men in close confinement rose around him, and panic threatened to engulf him. He dropped to his knees and crawled behind his bed as the shadow beyond the door moved. There was a pause, followed by a sudden violent rattle of the handle as the person on the other side realised the door was locked. Another strange flicker of light, then the figure was gone and the light shone unbroken under the door.

Frederick whimpered softly. He stayed put until he was sure the figure had gone, then on his knees he moved slowly towards the door. He looked down at an envelope that had been pushed under his door; his name written in a flowing, ornate hand. He pressed his face against the grey carpet and looked under the gap to the hallway beyond, but could see no movement.

Stretching out a tremulous hand he picked up the envelope and opened it; within, a single piece of paper with a ragged edge was covered with writing: a harsh scrawl in thick black ink. Some words were underlined, while others had been violently scratched out; some passages made no sense at all, while others were so vile in their implications that they left Frederick in no doubt as to their meaning. Detective Chief Inspector Caine was right: John Stable was in the house, and he knew Frederick was, too.

○

4:12pm

Bunny sat in front of her dressing table mirror and brushed her long blonde hair. The gentle, rhythmic movement helped to calm her nerves; it reminded her of when her mother had performed the task, usually just before bedtime.

There was a soft tapping at the door. Bunny listened carefully; hearing another tap and then silence, she put down her brush and turned. Half-pushed under the door was a little envelope.

She walked to the door and hesitated, then with a sudden movement pulled the door open and looked outside. The gas lamps burned brightly, but no one was there.

Bunny closed the door and picked up the envelope. Opening it, she found a single piece of folded paper, torn along one edge and covered with a few flamboyantly written words.

She read the contents of the short note; her look of curiosity was followed by incredulity, then determination. She rang the bell, and after a few minutes, Alisha entered.

"Alisha, I have decided to go for a walk before dinner. Please lay out my tweed walking dress and my boots."

Alisha looked curious, but nodded. "Yes, my lady."

Bunny placed the note on her bed and went into the bathroom. As she closed the door behind her, Alisha hurried to the bed and unfolded the piece of paper; as she read the note, an expression of extreme concern appeared on her face. Placing the note back on the coverlet, she went to the wardrobe, trying to think of a way of getting her mistress to invite her on the walk without letting her know she had just broken her trust by reading a private message. Favouring an almost honest approach, she called out. "Would you like me to come with you, my lady? It is beginning to grow dark outside."

Bunny left the bathroom, dressed only in her corset and voluminous undergarments. She shook her head as Alisha helped her climb into the stiff tweed dress. "No, Alisha, I want to be on my own for a little while. Don't worry so, I'll be fine. Just help me with these blessed boots!"

As Alisha buttoned her into the boots, Bunny pulled on her warmest coat and paused at her mirror, taking the opportunity to pinch her cheeks before she left Alisha alone and worried in the pale-yellow room.

○

4:20pm

The early afternoon had passed without serious incident. Although two of the guests had caused a commotion when they found the American butler Warrick Clay ostensibly tidying their rooms. The matter was cleared up when Greyling informed Lord Coalford and Mr Draycott that Clay was assisting him by ensuring all the guests' rooms were tidy. Considering the possibility of a murderer running around the estate, he and the housekeeper had decided to keep the maids safe by restricting them to kitchen and dining duties, while the male servants carried out the rest of their responsibilities...he was sure the gentlemen would understand.

They did, but with rather bad grace. Lord Coalford had

snatched his hand-sewn spectacle case from Greyling and slammed the door in his face, Weatherly Draycott wasn't much better, going so far as to check his box of cigars, his embroidered cigar case, and his Gladstone bag, to make sure everything was still in order, before leaving Grayling and Clay and making his way to the library to choose a book for the evening.

Greyling and Clay finished their duties and made their way back to the kitchen. The English butler stood by the range and cast a glance at his American peer who sat in silent thought gazing into the fire.

For his part, Warrick's mind was not in the cosy kitchen, but was instead dwelling on a foggy and evil night a decade earlier; something had piqued his attention…but, what was it?

The door opened and Alisha entered. When she saw her father she smiled a greeting, but it faded as she saw the look of worry on his face. "Pa, what's wrong?"

Warrick's rich baritone rolled out. "Where is Lady Ellerbeck, child?"

"That's what I was coming to tell you, Pa. She went out for a walk. I tried to go with her, but—"

Warrick's jet black eyebrows snapped down over his nose. "You let her go alone?"

Alisha looked at her father, wide-eyed. "I had no choice; she told me not to accompany her. I—"

Warrick shot to his feet and grabbed her arm. "Did she say where she was going? Think, Alisha!"

Alsiha shook her head. "She didn't say, but I saw."

Warrick stared at her. "What do you mean?"

"She'd received a note. She didn't show me, but when she went into the bathroom, I read it."

"Go on."

"It said that the person who had sent it knew who had

killed Miss Carrie Lynn, and Lady Ellerbeck was to meet them at the lake."

As Warrick looked at his daughter, he was suddenly struck by a bolt of horrified realisation. He looked at Greyling, who was standing by the range, an expression of concern on his face. "Greyling, I need to go back to one of the guest's rooms. I now realise what it was I saw. We have to find Versipellis and Shadavarian and tell them what has happened. We must find Lady Ellerbeck!"

Greyling frowned as they headed towards the spiral stair-case. "Who are Versipellis and Shadavarian?"

Warrick took the stairs two at a time. "They currently call themselves Detective Chief Inspector Caine and Detective Sergeant Thorne!"

○

4:20pm

Carrying his sheet of paper carefully, Thorne found Elliott in the billiard room, playing Patience at the same table and with the same deck of cards that he had used earlier. Elliott looked up, his face questioning. "Anything usable?"

Thorne grinned tightly. "Only the face of John Stable."

Elliott flung the deck of cards down, and a green light flashed deep in his eyes. "Show me!"

Thorne presented the parchment with a flourish. Elliott stared at the portrait for some time before remarking, in a controlled voice, "That is a damned remarkable likeness!"

Thorne smiled proudly. "Isn't it, though?"

The two men spun round as the door to the billiard room was flung open and Lord Lapotaire ran in, his usually smooth hair dishevelled and his attire following the same trend. "Lady Ellerbeck is missing!"

"Missing?" Elliott snapped. "How do you mean, missing? Define missing?"

Lord Lapotaire caught his breath. "Her maid said she went out for a walk near the lake."

Elliott waived his hand. "There you are, then. Lady Ellerbeck went for a walk by the lake, ergo, she is walking by the lake, she is not missing. You know what she is doing and where she is doing it." Elliott paused. "Although I have to say that given the current state of affairs, and the hour of the day, it isn't a very sensible idea!"

"No, no, please, Caine, listen. Clay and his daughter are looking for you, I met them both in the hall. Alisha says her mistress was given a note that she wouldn't let Alisha see, but the maid managed to get a glimpse of it."

"Go on."

Lord Lapotaire took a deep breath and looked at Elliott and Thorne. "It spoke of the sender having information about the killer of Lady Ellerbeck's aunt, Carrie Lynn Cater, and asked her to meet them at the lake. Caine, I believe she's gone to meet the murderer!"

Elliott pointed at the portrait Thorne was still holding. "Put that somewhere safe," he barked.

In the Great Hall they met Clay, Alisha, and Greyling. Lord Lapotaire looked at the American butler. "I've just informed Caine of your concerns for Lady Ellerbeck.

Greyling looked worried. "Detective Chief Inspector Caine, there's something else." Greyling looked at Warrick with an apologetic expression as he explained. "Mrs Higginson and I were concerned about the maids going into the rooms to tidy, so Clay and I along with some of the footmen took it upon ourselves to take over that particular duty. While I was tidying, Clay found some odd things. I think he should tell you, as you're investigating these murders."

Elliott looked at the silent butler with such sharp intent that the manservant had some idea of how a butterfly felt as it was pinned to a display board. Warrick stared back, his stubborn expression matching Elliott's.

The two men were in the middle of the Great Hall, in front of the stairs. A group of onlookers, mostly male staff who had followed Greyling and Clay, along with one or two guests were watching. The staff observed with innocent enjoyment, the guests with polite reserve and hidden relish; one didn't often get to see a human dogfight.

Elliott's took a deep breath. "We know that Lady Ellerbeck is missing, Clay, and we are about to begin the search for her. But please understand that withholding information pertinent to an investigation is a criminal offence...not to mention utterly bloody foolhardy, given the current circumstances! If you don't inform me of what you have discovered, I will have you charged with tampering with police evidence, and if it has to do with something you discovered in a guest's room and removed, the charge of theft will also be added. Do not misunderestimate me, Clay...you know what I am capable of! Now, what exactly did you find?"

Thorne's eyebrows were in a position they had not managed to achieve for several years: almost on a par with his hairline. He had never heard Elliott use so many official police terms, or such long words in one sentence before; he usually relied on swearing when dealing with civilians who tried his patience.

Warrick spoke, his face as angry as Elliott's. "I promised Mr Cater that I would look after his little girl back in New York and I failed! When Alisha placed that call to Mr Cater and told him what had happened, he was worried. He telephoned me at Fillesby Hall and sent me here to protect his granddaughter. When I arrived, and Greyling confirmed what the killer had done with Hardcastle's body...and his hands, I realised Mr Cater was right to be worried. He knew the injuries that bastard had inflicted on his child, and it almost killed him when Alisha told him the same thing had happened here."

Elliott held up a hand. "Alisha, how did you know of the injuries inflicted on Hardcastle?"

The young American maid looked worried. "When we were told about the murders, Jenkins told me what she had seen. Are Jenkins and I in trouble, sir?"

Elliott shook his head slowly. "No Alisha, you are not in trouble." He turned back to Warrick. "Go on, Clay."

Warrick looked at him. "It's the same killer, Caine, it has to be! I lied to Greyling about wanting to help with the tidying…it gave me the opportunity to search the rooms. I found some paperwork that you might find interesting…but in one of the rooms I also found this."

Warrick held out a small, stiff pouch made of silk, covered with minute stitches depicting a William Morris twisting vine pattern of extreme intricacy. Elliott took the pouch and looked at the manservant.

"You remember, I told you Miss Carrie Lynn was working on a piece of embroidery for her niece's coming-out ball in London. After she was killed, I looked for it in the house, but it was gone. You told me it could have been taken by the killer…"

Elliott didn't move, and his voice was quiet. "As a trophy. Yes, I did."

Warrick's eyes shone with unshed tears. "I only realised what it was that I'd seen after Alisha told me about the note. I went back to the guest's suite to find this pouch. I wanted to confront them…but they weren't there. He's gone after her… he's gone after Lady Ellerbeck. Please, please help me find her." Warrick closed his eyes and bowed his head. Elliott turned to Thorne, and was about to speak when he noticed

Frederick making his way warily down the stairs. "I thought I told you to stay in your room with the door bolted," he snapped.

Frederick, looking nervous, gave a piece of paper to Elliott. "I think you should see this; it was pushed under my door a few minutes after Thorne left."

Elliott read the note in silence. "Good Gods!" He passed the note to Thorne, who read the literary vitriol, his face blanching as he worked his way through the scrawled words that covered the page.

Frederick turned to Lord Lapotaire. "This probably isn't the right time, Lord Lapotaire, but I wish to give you fair warning. Please expect my resignation from the diplomatic within the week."

Lord Marmis, grey-faced and trembling, suddenly appeared at the door to his study. "Caine, there you are...I must tell you something— Oh God, what's happened now?"

Elliott briefly informed the lord of the reason for their assembly, and Lord Marmis looked even more worried. "This is terrible. I don't mean to play down this fear for Lady Ellerbeck, but I must tell you: the documents Fred brought home...they've vanished!"

Frederick sat down with a thump on the bottom stair and closed his eyes in despair. Lord Coalford looked at Lord Marmis in rheumatic outrage. "Sir, I must protest! We are in public! Have you no understanding of the serious and secret nature of the information of which you speak?" His thin, reedy voice rose to bat-like heights and his watery, goose-berry-coloured eyes bulged at Lord Marmis in abject disapproval.

Lord Marmis turned to face the irate old lord, whose face had also turned an alarming shade of puce. He spoke calmly, his very formality an insult. "Lord Coalford, when we are in the House you may address me as sir. However, in the ances-

tral home of my family you will address me by my title –
from respect for that title, if nothing more. Perhaps you have
forgotten, my lord, that I sent my brother to a place where he
was captured, imprisoned and tortured for two years, and
that another man died bringing him and that information to
safety. So yes, my lord, I have complete understanding of the
seriousness of the situation!" His voice became louder and
more forceful as he spoke, while Lord Coalford was reduced
to wheezing at him in disbelief.

The hall was silent as the civilian occupants took in the
deepening danger of the situation; not only Lady Ellerbeck's
disappearance, but also the awful thought of yet another war.

Elliott ignored the elderly lord and addressed Lord
Marmis. "When did you realise the documents were
missing?"

"Not five minutes ago. I woke feeling better, with only a
slight headache, and decided to go over the documents again
to see if we had missed anything."

"Go on."

"I entered the study, which was just as usual, tidied
some inconsequential documents away, put the combina-
tion into the safe and removed the packet." He clutched at
his head. "Oh God, Caine, the horror – I opened the envelope and inside was a sheaf of folded writing paper, all
utterly blank! I swear to you, just hours earlier that envelope was full of information that could have prevented
many deaths. We had details on the traitor: not his real
name, but enough to prevent him from selling any more
secrets."

Elliott looked at the exhausted young man, his pale face
flickering in the dim light of the gas lamps. He sighed and
rubbed his forehead; it had indeed been a tiring day for
everyone. "Lord Marmis, have you seen or heard from Sir
Hubert since breakfast?"

Lord Marmis looked confused. "Bertie? No...why? Do you think something has happened to him as well?"

Elliott held up his hand. "Calm yourself, and answer me this. Sir Hubert was last seen walking along the terrace path by the morning room; can you tell me where that leads?"

Lord Marmis nodded. "Yes, of course. It's the south path, it goes past the ice house and the lake and descends to a natural harbour in the estuary about four miles away, Bertie visits with us so often he likes to keep his yacht anchored there. There's rather a beautiful beach with views of the English Channel and the island of Cove some thirty miles down the coast."

Elliott immediately turned to Thorne, and in a voice that brooked no arguments he snapped, "Get to the telephone. Don't call Commissioner Bolton, call the private line; you know who to ask for. Tell them everything that has happened. Whitehall will not be happy!"

Lord Marmis looked at Elliott in disbelief as Thorne produced the key and unlocked the telephone booth. "Caine, you cannot possibly believe that Bertie— I'd have known...I would have known!"

Elliott looked at the shocked young man and found there was very little he could say. He laid a hand on Lord Marmis' shoulder instead. "We can't always tell, my lord. Please, what is the name of Sir Hubert's boat?"

Lord Marmis, utterly stunned, whispered, "The Phoenix."

As Lord Marmis turned away, distraught, Elliott continued. "Ladies and gentlemen, we must conduct a search for Lady Ellerbeck; she is somewhere in the grounds and in dire peril. Gentlemen, the person we are dealing with is extremely dangerous, I suggest you arm yourselves accordingly. I also suggest that all the ladies retire to the library and bolt the shutters and doors until we return. Gentlemen, shall we begin?"

The men in the party swiftly disappeared upstairs to relieve their travel and gun cases of various firearms and Greyling and Clay went to inform the ladies of the need to retire to the library.

Thorne relocked the telephone booth door and nodded at Elliott. Moving closer, he murmured, "I've spoken to the chief; he has the information and he will see to it. He also said not to inform the local police as our men will watch the ports. Oh, and Elliott, they found out who tried to steal our files."

Elliott had pulled out his revolver and was checking the mechanism; he looked up. "Do you know, in the midst of all this I had forgotten. Do tell; who was it?"

Thorne looked grim. "It was the clerk!"

"The one who was injured 'fighting off the intruder'? Did they find out why?"

Thorne placed his arms on the ornate newel post at the foot of the stairs and rested his chin on top. "He said he was approached by a government man who told him that we were spies for a foreign power. He tried to get the files to hand them over, but the man he shared the office with became worried about the length of time he had been gone and called him. Startled, he fell down the stairs and injured himself. Useless twit!"

Elliott looked at his watch. "Did he say who asked him to go through our files?"

Thorne nodded. "He did."

"Who?"

"I will give you two guesses!"

"Ah. Well, he shall be dealt with. Who would be foolish enough to accept the idea of us as spies against the Empire? Can you imagine us as spies for a foreign power, Thorne?"

Thorne grinned. "We've got enough problems with the work given us by the authority we work for, without having to deal with work offered by a foreign government. Can you imagine, Elliott? No Assam, no Times, no perambulations around Hyde Park, no cocktails...perish the thought! And the paperwork – good Gods, man, the paperwork!"

As the two men turned towards the huge double doors, the ladies made their way into the library. Lady Marmis, Lady Scott-Brewer and their maids, Parker, and Philips, who had refused to leave their mistresses, settled themselves into various armchairs. As he turned, Elliott caught a flash of red hair and a yellow silk dress. Brilliant blue eyes gazed into his, as with an expression of shocked recognition, Giselle walked past him to join the other ladies in the library, her maid Lilith following closely behind.

Elliott stood transfixed, an equally stunned expression on his face, as the library door closed behind them and the bolt slid across.

4:45pm

Bunny stood by the lake and shivered. Perhaps this had been a mistake; perhaps it wasn't too late to return to the hall and ask Clay to accompany her. She looked at her little pocket watch. Drat! Far too late now; the note had instructed her to be at the lakeside no later than ten minutes to five. So here she was, extremely early, extremely cold, extremely damp, and rather nervous.

A few hundred feet away, hidden in a dip behind a thick green curtain of firs and pines, and quite some distance from the manicured grounds where Lady Ellerbeck stood, old Mickey Baker, poacher of the parish, sat in a deerskin hide and cleaned his traps.

Wiry, with sharp little eyes and a backswing that packed a

power belying his small size, as both his wife and daughter could testify, the grubby little man sat in his self-made den smoking an equally grubby pipe. He would put his pipe out before he left. Couldn't have the prey getting a whiff and straying away from his traps; that wouldn't do.

Old Peters in the next village had promised to stand him ten pints of ale and ten shillings for a deer and a few rabbits. Never mind that the meat would end up in a good fifty stews and bring in many more times that; free ale was free ale, and ten shillings was ten shillings. It might shut that blasted wife of his up with her whinging about their damned daughter – and damned she was for trying to take her life, that was in the good book, that was! And she had to be punished for what she'd done; going off to bedlam and taking the money she'd earned from the big house. That was his ale money, the stupid bitch! He looked down at the trip wire he was tying. Not too tight; if he wasn't careful, he'd take his own fingers off!

He grinned; his few remaining teeth black stained stumps in his foul-smelling mouth. There would be blood tonight, but not his! The lake was always a good provider of meat, especially deer; they came down of an evening to drink in the shallows. Aye, the lake it would be. He jumped as a twig snapped; he listened as the sound of something snuffling around the den grew louder. He picked up his shotgun and slowly pushed his head out of the flap. Seeing nothing, he unravelled his stubby body from the dank hide and stood in the dimly lit dell.

There was a sudden movement to his right. He spun round; his shotgun pointing dead straight at a rapidly retreating deer.

He lowered his gun with an oath. Missed one! Hopefully there would be more later. He turned back to the hide, and knocking out his pipe, he shoved it, still warm, into a ragged canvas bag which he swung onto his back. Picking up the traps and snares he had fixed, he started for the lake.

After some minutes of trekking through the thick, dead undergrowth he made out the lake in the distance, its outline hazy and indistinct in the mist that had started to form. Ducking through the low hanging branches, he paused; a figure stood on the nearside bank. Baker swore; of all the luck! He tucked himself well within the tree line and stared at the slender female figure gazing at the lake.

Another thought came to the old poacher's filthy mind. With a vicious grin, he quietly removed his bag and leant the gun against a tree.

He was creeping towards the figure some fifty yards ahead when a twig snapped behind him. Turning quickly, Baker caught sight of a flash of colour as something moved behind the gnarled trunk of a beech tree to his left. It could be someone from the big house, in which case he needed to scarper, and quick! On the other hand, he had caught young Jimmy Fletcher trying his hand at a spot of poaching on his patch a few nights ago; he had taught the boy a lesson he wouldn't forget in a hurry and no mistake! Maybe the young brat needed another telling!

The added possibility of a little fun by the lake also weighed heavily in the old poacher's mind. If the young tart had come down to the lake to meet with a sweetheart, she couldn't blame him if she met with trouble.

Deciding the sounds had to be Jimmy Fletcher, and that he should flush him out to make sure he had no witnesses to his planned entertainments, Baker crept silently to the tree and peered around the huge old trunk. As he did, he heard the soft, papery sound of someone moving across the dead leaves on the other side.

He moved around the tree. No one was there, but he knew he had heard something. He saw a heaped pile of leaves and bent to touch them; they were still warm, as though someone had been sitting there. His sharp eyes scanned the area; no one was there except the distant figure of the young woman by the lake. Someone had been watching her, and for some time.

Baker turned back to the pile of leaves, and so he didn't see the bare legs that slowly descended from the thick branch overhead. Nor did he see the grinning figure that landed silently and moved towards him, until there was another sharp snap as a twig broke under their tread. The old poacher turned and stared in stupefied shock at the rapidly approaching figure; desperately stumbling backwards to try and escape, he had no time to scream before the blade came down.

○

4:55pm

Giselle sat in the library with Lady Marmis and the others, her mind spinning as she bit at an immaculately polished fingernail. She recognised him, of course; those warm brown eyes and the red Malacca cane were the same. He was the man she had seen when she had looked at the portrait in the study. And he had recognised her too; she was sure.

She caught her maid's eye, and guiltily removed the bitten nail from her mouth. She knew his name and his position, but who or what was he to her? And why was he so familiar?

4:55pm

Bunny turned and scanned the area behind her. She thought she had heard — but no, there was nothing, not even a sign of someone approaching from the house. She looked at her fob watch and bit her lip; they were going to be late for their appointment.

Across the lake the late-afternoon sun was sinking behind the thick spread of trees that lay beyond the still body of water. The dim light that remained was rendered opaque by the soft mist that seemed to float on the surface of the lake, turning the weeping willows that jostled with evergreen pines into dark islands in a soft white sea.

Bunny stood by the lake and shivered, wrapped in the clinging white mist. There really was no point in staying here and giving herself pneumonia if the person who sent the note wasn't going to appear. She sighed and made her way to the little path that rambled along the lake and back towards the hall. It followed a natural tree line which the garden designer had chosen to keep intact. Majestic pines and a most unusual monkey puzzle tree marked the boundary between the manicured lakeside walk, with its established rhododendrons, and the thick, deep hazel coppices and pine plantations that marked the boundaries of the estate's farmland.

As she walked towards the hall, Bunny pondered the note and the thoughts it had stirred. Her aunt's death had affected her severely; she had only been a few years younger than Carrie Lynn, and they had had a great deal in common. Bunny had found it easy to talk with her aunt, and Carrie Lynn had confided in her young niece, writing to her several times a month.

And then she was gone and no one would tell her what had happened; just that her beloved aunt was dead and there would be no more letters. The family had even concealed the cause of her aunt's death, choosing instead to tell her that Carrie Lynn had died from a sudden illness.

When her parents had died aboard their boat on the Riviera in the summer of 1893, Bunny had found out the truth by accident. In the process of organising their paperwork, she had found a scrapbook with the newspaper reports amongst her mother's possessions. The shock of her discovery brought back the pain she had felt when her aunt had died, made much worse by the knowledge of her appalling death, and increased further by the sudden deaths of her beloved parents.

Her grandfather had travelled from New York and taken her from the London house to the family estate at Fillesby. She had all but thrown the scrapbook in his face, demanding the truth, and he, ashen and trembling, had told her what she insisted she needed to hear.

He had hidden nothing, and when he had finished, Bunny locked herself away from society. The hideous nature of her aunt's demise was unbearable. It had taken her grandfather more than three years to break down her resolve and convince her to return to the world.

Bunny could never bring herself to tell him of her fears. The person responsible for her aunt's murder had never been caught; they had left no clues, nothing that pointed to a face or a name. What distressed her most was that it could have been anyone; a stranger, a servant, or far worse…a friend.

As she walked, Bunny rubbed her cold hands together inside the ermine-trimmed fur muff that had belonged to her aunt. She sighed and looked up at the darkening sky. The light was fading rapidly now and stars had begun to appear in the chill autumn sky above the low-lying mist; faint silver pinpricks twinkling in the firmament.

She was still quite a distance from the house; putting an extra spring in her stride, she walked up the wooded hill that would bring her to the ice house. From there, it was only a few hundred yards to the hall.

As she walked beside the thick rhododendron hedge, Bunny became aware of a faint sound just on the upper edge of her hearing, it sounded like…mewling. She was country-bred, and did not recognise the sound as that of any animal she knew. A shiver ran down Bunny's spine; she walked faster, her eyes focused on the path, while behind her the noise grew louder, a sibilant hiss that became softly spoken words. "Lady Ellerbeck, you remind me so much of your aunt. You have her eyes…Ah, but I forgot – I took those from her!"

Bunny stumbled in shock and turned…there was no one there. Terrified, she turned back to the path and hurried along the hedge line. Inside the fur muff, her right hand gripped the ornate end of her sturdiest hat pin.

With a sob building in her throat, she managed to climb to the top of the path as the vile words behind her continued. The hall was visible in the distance, as were the torches of several people making their way across the lawn. Bunny tried to call out but the constriction in her throat wouldn't let her.

Throwing her dignity to the wind, she hitched up her skirts and ran. The path was fairly straight now, with only one or two artfully placed trees blocking her view of the hall. As she ran, Bunny heard laughter behind her. Sobbing, she ran towards the ice house, slid on a muddy patch, and came to a sudden halt by the strange, dome-shaped building. Terrified, she looked behind her, but could see nothing.

Her eyes flicked to the solid door of the ice house; built

more than a hundred years earlier to provide Marmis Hall with a year-round supply of ice, the ice house was a peculiar building; built of stone and brick, and domed like a beehive, it was set deeply into the ground to keep the large room at the bottom of the steep steps cold enough to preserve ice brought from the lake.

Reaching out a trembling hand, she drew the steel bolt and opened the heavy counterweighted door. The room inside was small, dark, and impossibly cold with an almost vertical flight of stairs leading to the ice storeroom below.

Bunny rapidly changed her mind about hiding in the freezing room at the foot of those steps and backed away from the door; but as she did so, soft, high-pitched giggling came from the path that led to the lake. Bunny ran out of the ice house in a panic; too frightened to do more than push the door to, she found a hiding place on the other side of the dome and crouched shivering in the cold evening air.

As she trembled against the side of the little building, the voice floated towards her. "Lady Ellerbeck...dear Lady Barbara...may I call you Bunny? Your aunt wrote you a letter, you know. Oh yes, she mentioned me by name. A good thing I arrived when I did. She did have such lovely hands...I put them to a suitable use. I never could stand to have them look at me, you understand?"

Bunny closed her eyes as the unseen figure giggled its way up the path. It paused at the ice house and tutted primly. "My dear young lady, if you are going to hide yourself, let this be a lesson for you: always ensure the door is locked and bolted."

The figure entered the ice house, and Bunny, almost paralysed with fear, heard faint sounds of movement as they began to walk down the steps. A sudden sense of certainty flooded her mind; she ran to the door, slammed it shut and rammed the steel bolt home. She stepped back unsteadily then turned and ran as the trapped figure within the locked room screamed and hammered at the door; the sounds of their rage echoing within the brick and stone dome...but beyond the bolted door, the serenity of the misty lakeside remained unsullied as their screams were dulled to silence by the thick walls and lead-lined door of the ice house.

As she ran onto the croquet lawn at the back of the house, one of the distant figures spotted her and shouted towards the hall.

Lord Lapotaire threw down his torch to catch Bunny as she collapsed. Lifting the now-unconscious young woman in his arms, he carried her back to the safety of the hall.

5:30pm

Elliott ran up the stairs to Lady Ellerbeck's suite of rooms in the south wing of the hall. Lord Lapotaire was just leaving, his face pale but relieved. Elliott raised his eyebrows. "How is she?"

Lord Lapotaire gave him a tired smile. "Frightened but safe. Alisha has given her a sedative. She's asleep now."

Elliott frowned. "That should not have been allowed, Lord Lapotaire. The killer is still out there, and only she can tell us what happened. I need to talk with her."

He reached for the doorknob and Lord Lapotaire grabbed his hand. "Caine, do you have any idea what she has just gone through? How can you be so inhumane?"

Elliott put his other hand over Lord Lapotaire's and looked into his eyes. "Years of practice!"

Lord Lapotaire removed his hand as though he had been burned.

Elliott sighed. "I don't mean to be unkind, but I am trying

to make sure this person never inflicts such savagery on anyone else. I know you care for Lady Ellerbeck, Lord Lapotaire, but surely you understand?"

Lord Lapotaire glared at Elliott. "If it were Giselle, would you insist on interrogating her in this condition?"

Elliott's dark face flushed at the phrasing of the plea, but it had hit its mark. "I promise I will be kind."

Lord Lapotaire moved away and sat in a chair by the door. Elliott's face was expressionless as he entered the suite and closed the door. He sighed; his job was certainly interesting, but it had its moments! Best to focus on the job in hand, as Thorne had said a while ago, because while Commissioner Bolton believed that they would be taking a month's holiday once they had solved the case, Commissioner Bolton would never actually see them again. With the discovery of the traitor attempting to determine their true identity, it would appear their time with the Metropolitan Police had come to a natural conclusion.

Squaring his shoulders as he walked through to the bedroom, the first thing Elliott saw was the manservant, Clay, standing by the window; Lady Ellerbeck's suite overlooked the orangery but Clay's gaze was not focussed on that room, instead he stared through the orangery's massive windows, down towards the lake. Alisha sat in silence by her mistress's bed.

Elliott walked towards the bed. Lady Ellerbeck was sleeping, the soft yellow coverlet pulled up to her neck, her blonde hair loose around her shoulders. She looked terribly young. Elliott felt like an ogre as he sat down opposite Alisha. "How is she?"

Warrick answered from the window. "She is safe; she knows that now."

Elliott looked at him. "And what of the killer?"

Warrick turned and looked at his daughter, Alisha

nodded and walked out of the room. As the door closed quietly behind her, Warrick looked directly at Elliott. "My lady needs her rest, Caine. Lady Ellerbeck told me much of what happened to her this evening. What do you want to know?"

"The most important thing; did she see the face of her attacker?"

Warrick shook his head. "She never saw their face. She heard their voice, but it was too soft, and she was too terrified to recognise it."

Elliott sighed and looked again at the face of the sleeping woman. "She looks very much like her aunt, but she is fair where Carrie Lynn was dark. What did she tell you about this evening, Clay? Did she say anything about the note, or what happened after she reached the lake?"

Warrick looked towards the lake again, and Elliott's attention was caught by the movement. The look on Warrick's face was intense, and he gazed at something Elliott could not see as he answered Elliott's questions.

"She received a note in the same fashion as Frederick Marmis; it was pushed under her door shortly after young Marmis received his. She didn't tell anyone what was in the note, but after we brought her back to her room, she gave it to me."

Warrick held out the folded piece of blue paper. Elliott took it, and with some difficulty read the flowery, ornate handwriting.

Dear Lady Ellerbeck,

I have information pertinent to the death of your aunt, Carrie Lynn Cater.

I was in New York City when she died.

After the events of yesterday evening, I realised what I

277

had witnessed all those years ago in New York, and it finally made sense to me.

Please meet me at the lake at exactly 4:55pm and I will tell you everything I know.

Please come alone as a sign of good faith.

A Friend

Elliott looked from the note to the manservant, still staring out of the window. "Thorne and the servants are searching the grounds, Clay; we will find him. Now, you said earlier that you found some things I might find interesting...I ask you now to share with me; what else did you discover in your search of the guests' rooms?"

"Perhaps it would be easier if I showed you." Warrick opened the door and walked into the sitting room, where Alisha sat beside the window. He nodded at his daughter. "Child, sit with your mistress."

Alisha nodded and returned to Bunny's room. Warrick opened the outer door and looked at Lord Lapotaire who was still sitting outside.

"Would you care to sit with Lady Ellerbeck, my lord?"

The pale young man blinked rapidly. "I would be honoured."

Lord Lapotaire entered as they left, and Elliott heard the bolt slide across as Warrick led him down the plushly carpeted hallway. Pausing at one of the many closed doors, Warrick looked at him silently, and not bothering to knock, entered the room.

The suite was between Frederick's and the door to the servants' staircase. As Elliott looked around the neat sitting room, he noted an elevated level of tidiness almost oppressive in its fussiness. Had it not been for the large leather bag on a table under the window, he would have doubted the room had been occupied at all.

He walked over to a travelling writing-desk and opened it; inside was a selection of pale blue writing paper and matching envelopes, monogrammed in gold. Elliott held up Lady Ellerbeck's note. The paper looked identical; a strip had been torn off the sheet to remove the monogram.

"Versipellis?" Warrick was standing by the wardrobe; he opened the doors and lifted out a small wooden chest. "There are some things in this box that you might be interested in. The diary that covers 1889 in particular, look at the month of August." Warrick handed the box to Elliott who looked at him with a faint smile.

"I think it would perhaps be better for both of us if you forgot that name, Clay." The American butler nodded without question as Elliott opened the box and ran an eye across the contents; a collection of small journals, a British passport, and several small items that any investigating officer worth his salt would refer to as 'trophies' were tucked within. One of the items was a golden coin, stamped with the image of a Chinese dragon.

Elliott paused and studied the lining of the wooden chest itself before suddenly emptying the contents onto the bed. Tilting the box, he pressed his thumb against an almost invisible mark and with a soft click, a secret drawer shot open. Hidden within was a book bound in dull brown leather; it was an unpleasant looking affair, the leather had not been properly cured, and there was something else…a familiar and none too pleasant smell. With an exclamation of disgust, Elliott flung the little book on the bed and looked at Warrick, who looked sickened. He too had recognised the material used to bind the book: human skin.

With a grimace, Elliott picked up a fountain pen and used it to flick the book open. Inside were neatly made notes on torture methods tried and tested, anatomical drawings of the damage those methods could inflict on the human body, and the pièce de resistance…several sepia photographs that bore witness to the effects of John Stable's work on his victims, all showing the proud, smiling face of their creator standing beside the fruits of his revolting labour.

Elliott closed the book, sat on the edge of the pale-green bed, and turned his attention to the journals; they were diaries of sorts…filled with flamboyant writing in thick black ink: detailing accounts of travelling, holidays, appointments, hotels booked, and monies paid for special works.

Elliott pored over the entries until he found the date he was looking for. On the 29th of August 1889, shortly before Carrie Lynn Cater had been murdered, the owner of the journal had travelled to New York. On a sudden whim Elliott flicked through the other journals, several dates caught his attention. 11th February 1891, arrived Constantinople. 16th February 1891, arrived Calais. 17th February 1891, arrived Dover. The previous journal had shown Clay that its owner had been in New York at the time of Carrie Lynn's death, but the other diary showed something quite different to Elliott. He shot to his feet. "Take me to Sir Hubert's room, quickly."

Warrick led Elliott down the corridor and past the massive windows overlooking the central courtyard. Entering the Peach Suite, Elliott opened the bureau and pulled out what few papers he could find. He rifled through them, then flung them down. "Damn and blast! He's taken it with him!"

Warrick stared at him. "What are you looking for?"

Elliott dragged his hand through his hair. "Sir Hubert's passport. I need to check those dates."

Warrick reached into his breast pocket and pulled out a bundle of folded papers covered with dates and notes written in a neat, small hand. "Would these help?"

Elliott fairly snatched them from the butler, eagerly scanning the dates that Warrick had copied from every passport he had found in the house, including that of Lord Marmis… and Giselle. Elliott's brow furrowed; there were some rather interesting dates and equally interesting destinations in Giselle's passport. Frowning, he tucked that particular sheet of paper into his breast pocket, and brandishing Sir Hubert's passport dates, he held up the passport from their suspect's room.

With a tight grin Elliott turned to Warrick. "February 1891: Constantinople. The dates match. Sir Hubert was in Constantinople at the same time as John Stable! Now I know who and why, you will tell me what you know about the whereabouts of the killer. And you will also tell me why you keep looking out of Lady Ellerbeck's bedroom window."

Warrick's face set, he nodded. "I will show you in the morning. I promise you, Detective Chief Inspector Caine… they aren't going anywhere." He frowned; he thought he had seen a green light flash in Elliott's eyes, but that was not possible. It must have been a trick of the light in the room.

Elliott faced the butler. He was a few inches shorter than the manservant, but of the two, Elliott was the more threatening. "Clay, why are you behaving like this? We need to find this man before he—"

He stopped as something caught his eye. Walking round the silent butler, Elliott lifted an empty shoulder holster from the back of the chair. "In the course of your 'tidying', Clay, did either you or Greyling find a gun?" Elliott's voice was quiet but there was a note of authority that left Warrick in no doubt as to who was in charge.

"No, we found no guns in this room. Plenty in the other rooms…I understand there was to be a shoot on Sunday." He paused as shouting came from the Great Hall.

Warrick looked at Elliott, who was staring at the holster with a faraway expression. "We have not yet finished."

The murmured words sounded to Warrick as though more than one voice had spoken. He shivered as Elliott hurried away, leaving Warrick standing alone in the room.

○

5:50pm

In the Great Hall, Thorne and Thom were standing next to one of the biggest men Warrick had ever seen. Built like an oak tree, Lord Lapotaire's valet, Vanamoinen, stood ramrod-straight next to Thorne, who seemed rather irritated by the young man's muscular form. As soon as he saw Elliott coming downstairs, he prodded the young tree and nodded towards him. The young man all but saluted, a canvas bag and shotgun gripped in his left hand.

Lord Marmis entered from outside. Taking off his thick coat, he nodded at Elliott and Thorne, then saw Elliott's expression. "What's wrong, have you found something?"

Elliott nodded. "I'm sorry to say that when Sir Hubert left, he took a gun with him."

Lord Marmis' eyes widened. "Why? Do you think he is going to..."

He couldn't bring himself to finish the sentence, so Elliott did it for him. "Do I think Sir Hubert is going to kill himself? Possibly. Do I think he is going to kill someone else? Maybe. We will just have to see what happens over the next few hours."

Lord Marmis' face was shocked and pale. He looked at Lord Lapotaire's man, and in a low, unsteady voice inquired, "Have you found anything, Vanamoinen?"

The young man nodded and replied in his accented

English. "I followed the directions in the note given to the lady. I was searching by the lake when I found a body."

Lord Marmis rubbed a hand over his tired face. "Oh God, not another one. Do we have any idea who it is, or rather, was?"

Vanamoinen held up the shotgun and canvas bag. Placing the gun carefully against a chair, he reached into the bag and pulled out a handful of tightly wound snares. "I found these near his body. He was old, short, and he smelled very bad!"

Lord Marmis frowned. "Did he have a gold hoop earring and dark eyes?"

The valet shrugged; his rugged face unperturbed. "There was no earring, and his eyes had been taken so I could not tell."

Elliott's face hardened. "His eyes?" He turned to Lord Marmis. "Do you recognise the description?"

Lord Marmis nodded, his face pale but composed. "It sounds like old Baker. I have caught him poaching on the estate several times; he went to gaol for it on more than one occasion."

Elliott looked at Thom, whose expression was shocked… as he hoped it would be. So, Edith Baker's father was now dead; it would be a shock to Edith, but a shock that would lead to happiness for the young couple…and for Edith's long-suffering mother.

Elliott smiled grimly. The case was accelerating nicely and the loose ends were tying themselves up; it was always nice when things moved themselves forward without any urging or excessive work. Yes, murder was murder, but some people went out of their way to deserve death.

He looked up the stairs to where Warrick was standing. "In the morning, Clay…six o'clock sharp!" He turned to Thorne. "I think it would be a good idea if we dealt with Baker's body now, we will need photographs of his remains for the files, but in this light we might not get much detail. It's not ideal, I'll grant you...but the weather is too damp to leave him outside overnight, we could lose valuable evidence."

Thorne shook his head. "I have the necessary Blitzlicht flash powder for night photography. It will be fine."

Elliott nodded. "Very well. Shall we go and observe what we can of the most recent corpse, and add it to our ever-growing collection?"

○

Sunday
05:50am

Elliott sat in the morning room with a strong cup of coffee, and alternated between yawning and sipping as he flicked through Sir Isadore Shard's preliminary post-mortem report, preferring to focus on anything other than the flash of recognition when he and Giselle had finally met the night before; thinking on it afforded him hope...and that frightened him. He flipped over a page, glared at the reams of words and descriptive terms and tried to concentrate on the matter at hand.

Thorne had made his way to the lakeside the previous afternoon to observe the quality of light and had decided it was acceptable. His use of Blitzlicht powder had enabled several photographs to be taken of the poacher, whose corpse had since been collected and removed to the morgue for Sir Isadore's consideration.

The eminent specialist had spent Saturday night and early Sunday morning investigating the bodies. The time of death was given as between 9:20pm and 9:30pm for both Hardcastle and the elderly lord. The cause of Lord Scott-Brewer's death was judged to be the severing of the jugular by repeated stabbing with a long thin blade such as an ice pick. The cause of Hardcastle's death was the appalling injury caused by the insertion of a red-hot poker, most of his other injuries being inflicted post mortem.

Nothing strange there, but the good Sir Isadore had also found a needle mark just below the severance point on the butler's neck, suggesting the use of a hypodermic to administer an injection. He was awaiting the report on the type of substance used, but it was his belief that whatever had been in the needle had rendered the butler incapable of movement and sound during his last few minutes on earth.

The post-mortems for the last two victims had also been finalised. Valentine Carstairs had been killed by repeated stab wounds to the throat and chest, as had Baker. Again, the worst of the injuries, Valentine's decapitation and the removal of Baker's eyes, had occurred after death.

Elliott sighed and placed his cup down on the table. He consulted his watch and stood up. The light coming through the south windows was dim, but clear enough to see by; it would have brightened considerably by the time they left the house. He promised himself that he would talk with Giselle before the end of the case. He would have to: for his own sanity he must know how much, if anything, she remembered of their past.

Elliott made his way to the Great Hall, where after a few minutes he was joined by Thorne and Thom. Shortly afterwards, Warrick appeared at the head of the stairs. He came down and nodded to Elliott.

"Clay." Elliott took out his revolver and checked the bullets.

Warrick shook his head. "You won't need that, Caine."

Elliott smiled at Warrick. "This old thing? Just for show, you know. Makes me feel better. And with Sir Hubert running around with a gun, I for one am not taking any chances!"

The sound of a door closing upstairs caught their attention. Lord Marmis appeared and joined them. He looked at Warrick. "How is Lady Ellerbeck?"

"Lady Ellerbeck is…managing; Alisha is still with her, and Lord Lapotaire has placed himself in her sitting room."

Lord Marmis frowned. "Is that entirely necessary?"

Elliott smiled gently. "Lord Lapotaire seems to think so."

Lord Marmis raised his eyebrows in understanding, the black and purple bruise on his temple peeked over the bandage. "Ah!"

Elliott looked at Warrick, the gentle smile fading. "Shall we?"

Warrick nodded, ducked inside the cloakroom door, and returned with three lit candle lanterns. Handing one to Lord Marmis, another to Thorne, and keeping one for himself, he led them outside and down the path that led onto the lawn at the back of the hall.

As they walked, a voice called out from the house, and turning, Elliott saw young Frederick approaching at a run, his face pale but determined. "I want to come with you…I need to see him."

Lord Marmis looked at Elliott, who nodded. "That's a very sensible idea."

Frederick walked alongside his brother, who placed a companiable arm around his shoulders as they walked past the dew-covered croquet hoops that glimmered in the chill blue light. Their lanterns glimmered dimly as they walked down the path towards the lake, the cold autumnal air casting its icy fingers across the lawn and through the artfully arranged borders as they continued the game of follow-my-leader behind the American butler until they finally arrived at the ice house. Elliott looked at Warrick with a raised eyebrow.

"Lady Ellerbeck was chased here." Warrick explained. "She opened the door thinking it would be a suitable hiding place, but when she looked inside, she changed her mind."

"I'm not in the least surprised!" Exclaimed Lord Marmis. "The ice house gets damn cold even at the height of summer; God knows what it's like in there now!" He exhaled, his breath appearing as a thick mist as he wrapped his arms around his chest and stamped his feet to keep warm.

Elliott drew his revolver and nudged Thorne, who grasped the bolt and carefully withdrew the metal spike. He looked at Elliott. "One...two...three!"

Thorne swung the door open. Elliott and the others braced themselves, but no one came out. Then Thorne noticed something on the door itself. "Elliott, look."

The heavy door was made of two layers of oak with lead between them to keep in the cold. The inner wood was splintered and covered with trailing paths of blood where someone had torn at the door with their fingernails.

Elliott saw something small on the top step, bent down to see, and recoiled. He looked at Thorne with an expression of disgust. "Pass me a spare envelope, would you, Thorne? I think I've just found old Baker's eyes."

Thorne passed the necessary container to Elliott, who used his handkerchief to scoop up the offending items and drop them into the envelope, creating a revolting little package which he handed to Thorne, who handed it with a grimace to Thom, who turned and realising he was last in the line, resignedly put it in his pocket.

Elliott stood at the top of the stairs with a decidedly put-out expression; he would never be able to hum Gilbert and Sullivan's sublime 'Take a Pair of Sparkling Eyes' again!

Warrick opened his lantern fully, the soft yellow flame

dancing in the chill breeze. Thorne nudged Thom. "You stay here and make sure we're not locked in, eh?" Thom, relieved at not having to enter, nodded and stood next to the open door as the other men slowly made their way down the steep stairs into the bitterly cold and dark chamber below.

Elliott went first, followed by Thorne, Lord Marmis, Frederick and Warrick. They passed through a brick arch into the freezing room beyond. The light from the lanterns giving off scant warmth that the ice filled room seemed to suck away. Their breath hovered around them like a thick mist, and the flickering light made the dark-red brick walls dance in a bloody, barbaric display. It rather set the scene, Elliott thought.

Frederick, staring intently around the room, was the first to see it; the others turned at his hoarse cry.

"That's him! That's Stable!"

As Elliott and the others turned to see, the lanterns threw their dancing light over a figure in the corner. On its knees, mouth stretched wide, as though screaming at the men standing between him and his freedom, was the naked, frozen corpse of Mr Weatherly Draycott.

09:30am

The morgue attendants had visited again, and had left, taking the earthly remains of Weatherly Draycott with them. It had been a rather unpleasant task to remove the body of the noted specialist from the ice house; his unclothed corpse had frozen to the ground in such a way as to necessitate the breaking of both his legs to remove him from his icy tomb.

It was shortly after breakfast, and all the guests had gathered in the morning room, as Elliott had requested, for what

Lady Marmis smilingly referred to as a dénouement; she was an avid reader of Poe.

The guests entered the room singly or in pairs. Lord and Lady Marmis sat together, and Frederick sat next to his brother, an expression of deep relief bringing calm to his face; Stable was dead and the fear of seeing him again would no longer haunt his dreams. He had also telephoned Clarice and her mother in Paris to inform them of recent events and to promise that he would be visiting them as soon as he could.

Opposite them sat Lady Scott-Brewer, her previously rigid carriage much relaxed; the gentle-faced man who had arrived that morning, and who was currently sitting in the library, seemed to be the cause of her contentment. Next to her was a rather preoccupied-looking Giselle, stunning in an emerald-green day dress. Her gaze never left Elliott's face.

Lord Coalford sat in the most uncomfortable high-backed chair in the room, his wizened black-clad body ramrod-stiff, and his watery eyes glaring straight ahead as though the other people in the room were there on his sufferance. Opposite him, Lady Ellerbeck sat alongside Lord Lapotaire. Her face was faintly pink and very happy, while Lord Lapotaire's face, though happy, also bore an expression of mild shock; he blinked rapidly and often.

All of their maids had been persuaded to join the other servants in the kitchen, where Elliott was quite sure that Greyling, Clay, Alisha and Vanamoinen would happily inform them of the happenings of the last two days, not least because he had told them they could. Nanny Parker had opted to stay in the nursery with the children. She had no wish, she had announced, to hear any nastiness! Besides, the children needed a bath.

Elliott looked around the room. One last piece of information had been confirmed for him that morning; a boat which the harbour master had sworn was the Phoenix had berthed in Pelloehaven Harbour the day before. Sir Hubert had gone ashore to buy supplies and had last been seen taking his yacht into the English Channel.

Elliott shuffled through his notes, trying very hard not to stare at Giselle. She, on the other hand, was not trying very hard at all, her wide blue eyes gazing at him as he walked around the room, waiting for everyone to settle.

Giselle was greatly perturbed; her sleep had been disturbed by dreams too real, too worrying to release her. Memories of this man, as that was obviously what they were, what they had to be; memories that crowded in on her of this house and other places, far distant places, and of being different people, but still with him...always with him. She suddenly realised that he had started to speak, and she smiled; even his voice was familiar.

"My lords, ladies and gentlemen, thank you for your patience. As you know, over the course of the last two days four men have been murdered, a young woman and a young man have been terrorised, and an attempt to spy on a government meeting has been foiled."

Elliott stood in the middle of the floor, the soft autumnal sunshine flooding through the windows as he wandered back and forth. "This case began not with the murders of Lord Scott-Brewer and the Marmis family butler, Gregory Hardcastle, but with the murder of a young woman in New York, ten years ago this very month. Carrie Lynn Cater was the youngest daughter of Mr Quincy Cater, the American arms manufacturer. Unbeknownst to his customers and even his most senior employees, Mr Cater kept information on every order that passed through his company. Anything of interest to the American government, or indeed the British government, he passed on as a matter of professional courtesy. One such contract that caught his eye was for a large shipment of arms that were to be delivered to what was described as a private garrison outside Johannesburg in Southern Africa. Mr Cater personally questioned the order, and found it to be an attempt by the Boers to purchase a large quantity of arms. Mr Cater went to his club to meet with a British diplomat and pass on this worrying turn of events. While he was there, his youngest daughter Carrie Lynn Cater was quite brutally murdered in their home in New York City.

There was utter silence in the room; even the little fire in the grate seemed to snap and flicker in an apologetic manner as everyone focused on the man before them.

Elliott settled himself into an armchair and turned towards Bunny. In a gentle voice, he said, "Carrie Lynn Cater was your aunt, Lady Ellerbeck, was she not?"

Bunny fought back tears as she nodded and whispered, "She was so nice. She was much younger than my mother, not that much older than me, so we had much in common." She swallowed painfully, and Lord Lapotaire took her hand, giving it a gentle squeeze. Bunny smiled at him and pressed her handkerchief to her eyes, but she didn't remove her hand.

"I was never told that Aunt Carrie was murdered, only that she had died suddenly. Grandpa only told me after my parents passed. I made him tell me everything…and then I wished I hadn't! I couldn't…I just couldn't believe what had happened to her." Bunny looked up at Elliott, her eyes brimming with tears. "I've spent the last few years thinking awful, terrible thoughts, because no one would tell me, even Grandpa, whether Aunt Carrie had died before…before what was done to her!" Bunny burst into tears and wept into her lacy handkerchief.

Lord Lapotaire now not only flew his colours, but nailed them to the mast as he gently put his arm around Bunny's shoulder and looked at Elliott. "Could you…? Please?"

Elliott looked at the young lord and the upset young lady next to him, and in his mind ran through what he remembered from the case. His mind lingered, much against his will, on the level of mutilation inflicted on the young woman's body after death. She had been dismembered, much like Hardcastle, and several parts of her body had been placed in the kitchen range after her death. Her hands, like Hardcastle's, had been strapped over her empty eye sockets. At least it had been after death, thank the Gods; it wasn't much, but it might help.

He chose his words carefully. "From the evidence at the scene, we deduced that your aunt was struck on the head. That injury was the coup de grâce, her death was almost immediate. I can confirm that your aunt was dead before the rest of her injuries were inflicted."

Bunny covered her face with her free hand and started to sob in earnest.

Elliott looked at Lord Lapotaire, who had a death grip on her hand. "Look after her, my lord."

Lord Lapotaire nodded; his attention fixed on the weeping young woman next to him.

Elliott turned back to the other occupants in the room; even Lord Coalford, much against his will had leant forward in his chair. "There were many things in the murders here at Marmis Hall that were reminiscent of the Carrie Lynn Cater case. In the Cater house, the two men who discovered her body, Officer O'Malley and the family butler, Warrick Clay, also found bloody footprints leading upstairs. They followed the footprints into the bathroom, where the killer had left a rather peculiar clue; the bloody footprints led from the kitchen, up the stairs and into the bathroom…but no further. We believe that after they crept upstairs the killer washed themselves, then ransacked Quincy Cater's study, searching for information on how much he knew about the attempts to ship arms to Southern Africa."

Elliott looked at Bunny, whose sobbing had calmed to the occasional hiccough. "I shall be honest, Lady Ellerbeck, and speak of all that I remember of the investigation. It may not be very pleasant, but it will be the truth. Will you accept that?"

Bunny looked up and gave a tremulous nod.

Elliott straightened. "Carrie Lynn was alone in the house. Her father was at his meeting, it was the staff's night off, and Carrie Lynn also gave Clay the evening off. It's very unusual to leave a house without any servants...we came to the conclusion that she was making sure she would be alone: why?"

Giselle looked at Elliott and raised her rich contralto voice in a remark that was more a statement than a suggestion. "She was expecting someone."

Elliott gaped at her. She smiled back at him as he gazed into her blue eyes and mustered the ability to nod. "Exactly, she was expecting a visitor she didn't want others to know about. But who, at that time of the evening, would visit a young lady alone at home, and without a chaperone?"

He turned to Bunny, who had composed herself and was now listening as eagerly as the others. "Lady Ellerbeck, your aunt wrote to you regularly. Did she mention anything about any health problems she was experiencing?"

Bunny nodded, twisting her little handkerchief. "Aunt Carrie said...she said she was having strange attacks where she couldn't breathe properly, and that she was seeing someone about them: a specialist she had met at a lecture. Aunt Carrie was very interested in medicine."

"Did she mention a name, Lady Ellerbeck?"

She shook her head. "No. She said that she had seen him several times but her attacks were getting worse."

Elliott nodded. "As soon as Carrie Lynn knew her father would be out for the evening, she sent word to her visitor. She invited him to visit her at home, and he leapt at the chance to enter Quincy Cater's home unchecked."

Bunny looked at Elliott, her eyes were wide. "You mean he...he knew who grandpa was...and that's why...?" Her voice trailed off.

"Certainly. Lady Ellerbeck, I would hazard a guess that your aunt's attacks probably started after she met him at the lecture. A man of his abilities would be able to use auto-suggestion or hypnosis to encourage your aunt's attacks, so that he could finally inveigle entry to your grandfather's home, and indeed, anywhere else he wished to go." Elliott paused. "We know he entered the house without Carrie Lynn's knowledge because of the evidence of the cabby who dropped him off. He commented on the oddness of his smartly dressed fare walking down the side alley to the servants' entrance. The killer entered the kitchen, lured Carrie Lynn there by some means, and murdered her." Elliott paused, deciding to gloss over the list of injuries that had been inflicted on Carrie Lynn after her death. "Leaving her body in the kitchen, he went upstairs and washed in the bath-room. Returning downstairs, he proceeded to ransack Quincy Cater's study. Finding little to help his cause, he returned to the kitchen to take one last look at his handiwork and heard the butler, Warrick Clay, and Officer O'Malley at the front of the house. Here, something even more odd occurs. The killer screams. We are not sure why; perhaps he hadn't finished admiring his work. For whatever reason, he screams and escapes through the open back door, as the policeman and the butler enter the house via the front door"

Elliott looked at the silent room. "I mentioned a cabby who dropped a fare just outside the Cater house shortly before ten past seven. He said his fare wore a black felt hat that obscured his face, that he was dressed in an oversized black Ulster that covered him from neck to ankle, and that he was carrying a large Gladstone bag. We found a second cabby who swore he picked up the same man in the same clothes just two city blocks away and dropped him at Grand Central Station. That fare was the murderer of Carrie Lynn Cater, and he was a guest here this weekend."

In the ensuing silence Elliott took a sip from a tall glass of elderflower cordial that Greyling had furnished him with earlier and turned back to the room. "So now we spring forward ten years to the events of this weekend." He looked at Lord Marmis, who gave an almost imperceptible nod. "This weekend was in actual fact a facade, a perfectly harmless party involving bridge, opera and feasting that would cover the real purpose of the weekend: a secret meeting between the government and certain others to discuss the possibility of another war in Southern Africa."

There was an outraged exclamation from Lord Coalford which was ignored as Elliott continued. "The guests were carefully chosen to create a safe environment in which the parliamentarians could mingle without hindrance to their true purpose. However, there was a problem; at the last minute one couple had to make their excuses and Lord and Lady Scott-Brewer were invited to replace them. All the guests had been checked and passed as suitable for the occasion except for Lord Scott-Brewer due to his, ah, predilections, but he would simply have to do as a replacement. All the other guests were very carefully chosen: people with interesting lives; lords and ladies and business men who could quite literally talk or indeed sing for their country, with one notable exception. Tell me, Lord Marmis, why did you invite Lady Ellerbeck, a young woman who, though attractive and quite charming, would be utterly out of her depth in such a gathering?"

Lord Lapotaire frowned. "I say, Caine!"

Bunny touched his arm. "No, Vyvian, I would like to know. As Detective Chief Inspector Caine said, I was out of my depth, and I knew it. I would like to know why I was invited, too."

Elliott gave Lord Marmis a questioning look.

Lord Marmis' face was pale but composed. "Because... because Bertie asked me to."

"Sir Hubert?"

"Yes."

"Did he give any reason?"

Lord Marmis looked uncomfortable. "He didn't say, but I...I thought he was fond of Lady Ellerbeck. I thought that was why he wanted her here, so I didn't ask."

Elliott smiled, and a faint green light flashed in his brown eyes.

"On the Friday evening the house party started and Giselle arrived." Elliott nodded at the beautiful young woman, who smiled back, and he had sudden difficulty breathing. That smile he knew so well...He stumbled on. "But there was another guest, one who though not invited was very welcome. Young Frederick Marmis had escaped his captors and returned home, and he had also fulfilled his mission by bringing with him valuable information on the state of affairs in Southern Africa." He ignored another outraged harrumph from Lord Coalford. "Frederick brought with him evidence to prove there were three men in England in the pay of the Boers. They went by codenames. The first, John Wisdom, was a member of our own government, a traitor who sold secrets to the Boers and passed on orders to the other two. The second, John Rook, we now know to have been the Marmis family butler, Gregory Hardcastle, it was he who was ultimately responsible for the capture of Frederick Marmis. And the third, John Stable, the most worrying of the three, was a sadistic killer in their employ…"

Lord Marmis frowned. "But there was a fourth name on the list__"

Elliott politely cut Lord Marmis off while studiously avoiding Lord Lapotaire's eyes. "Yes, there was, and that threw me off course. You see, Lord Marmis, I recognised the name Versipellis. I know the man and I know his motives. Damaging this country is not something he would do unless the government needed removing, and believe me, if the government needed removing, Versipellis would do so himself. He would not snivel in the dark with traitors and sadists! But then, I was informed that the name Versipellis had been scrawled in different ink and at the end of the document; was it possible that this name had been added after Frederick had returned home? When I interviewed Frederick, he confirmed the documents had contained three names, not four. It looked to me to be nothing more than a deliberate attempt to smear a genuine operative by throwing his name in with the others."

Lord Marmis stared at Elliott, while next to Bunny, Lord Lapotaire regarded Elliott with a curious mix of intrigue, curiosity, and deep concern.

Elliott coughed and gave the group a somewhat embarrassed look. "But I digress. To continue, these three names were of immense importance. Only one of the codenames had been broken, that of the spy 'John Rook', who we now know as Gregory Hardcastle—"

"Rook meaning castle, as in Hardcastle?" asked Bunny.

"Exactly, Lady Ellerbeck. If that were the case, would the other names be as easy to break? How easy would it be to discover Wisdom and Stable's true names? However, they were not important at that precise moment. What was important was finding Hardcastle and placing him under arrest. The other two could wait, but Hardcastle had to be removed to limit the damage he could cause if he carried word to his masters that Frederick Marmis had managed to return home with evidence of the traitor within. Frederick was escorted to his room while his brother Lord Marmis, together with Lord Lapotaire and Sir Hubert, set out to search for Hardcastle. Just outside the study they met Greyling and the maid, Jenkins, who were also looking for the butler. They believed him to be in the gallery and so the two groups proceeded to that room."

He paused; his face grim. "I shall not go into detail about what they discovered, other than to say that Hardcastle was indeed there and he was dead. So too was Lord Scott-Brewer, whose body was found some distance from the butler's. The evidence discovered in that room seemed familiar, but at the time, I could not quite understand why. Only later did I realise, when constable Greyling informed me of a telephone call Lady Ellerbeck's maid placed to her mistress's grandfather in New York. Then I remembered the original case. The murder in New York and the killings here were committed by the same man: a sadistic killer who committed his unspeakable acts whilst naked!"

Lord Coalford sat up in his chair. "I say, sir, there are ladies present!"

Elliott shook his head at the elderly lord. "Honesty will prevail, my lord, even in the face of propriety. The murderer had to be naked, since for his chosen method of murder he could not wear clothing. Pardon my bluntness, my lord, but he would be covered in blood, and people would certainly notice! Both here and at Carrie Lynn's house the killer had water at his disposal; in New York an empty house and a bathroom, and here at Marmis Hall, the pond in the orangery."

Lord Marmis leaned forward, one hand clasping his wife's as he stared at Elliott. "That explains what Evie saw that night...what she painted!"

"Exactly, my lord. Unbeknownst to the killer he had a witness; a little girl who couldn't sleep and who heard him prowling in the orangery. Young Evie saw the killer wash themselves in the pond, climb out and dress, and walk back into the gallery."

Elliott looked at the small group gathered in the morning room, and smiled. "So how much do we know now? We know that Frederick returned with evidence that proved Hardcastle was a Boer spy; that there is a traitor within our government; that a third man in their employ is a professional killer. We also know that the murders of Carrie Lynn Cater, Hardcastle and Lord Scott-Brewer were committed by that same killer, and that both he and the traitor were guests in this house this weekend!"

Elliott took another sip of his drink and continued. "Early the following morning, Thorne and I arrived to begin our investigation, Lord Marmis informed us of the real purpose of the weekend, and we set out keen to uncover the truth." He ignored the slight snort from the far corner, where Thorne sat with his ever-present notebook.

"Lord Marmis suggested we leave the gallery until dawn, a suggestion that we were grateful for. Instead, we ventured out to Hardcastle's cottage. When we arrived, we discovered that we were not the first visitors, as the front door was open and the bedroom in complete disarray. However, the searcher missed something vital which was probably what they were searching for."

Elliott waved the stack of envelopes they had discovered hidden on the window pelmet. "These letters are addressed to 'John Wisdom' and were delivered to a post office in Pelloehaven. Most are in a form of code; however, the most recent one, posted only two weeks ago in London, is not. It reads: 'Important; when ignorance is bliss, the prodigal brother returns. Urgent removal necessary; employ Stable if available. Payment will be arranged along the usual Channel; end'."

Everyone turned to Frederick, their faces aghast. Elliott continued. "This letter tells us many things. It gives us the name of the contact and the name of the intended victim. 'The prodigal brother' had to be Frederick. It tells us that the contact knew about Stable's work as a killer – 'employ Stable if available' – and that they would be paid 'along the usual Channel'." Elliott held up the letter. "Note the use of the capital letter at the beginning of the word and the use of the singular; the usual Channel, not the usual channels, which I believe is the correct terminology."

"Why do you say it gives the name of the contact?" Lord Lapotaire asked. "The only name in the letter is that of Stable."

Elliott held up a finger. "Have you never heard the old saying, Lord Lapotaire: 'when ignorance is bliss'?"

Lady Scott-Brewer spoke, her voice calm and steady. "'Tis folly to be wise."

Elliott nodded. "Exactly, 'when ignorance is bliss 'tis folly to be wise'. Therefore, wisdom is folly, which leaves us with Sir Hubert Kingston-Folly!"

There was a stunned silence in the room.

"Sir Hubert was in the pocket of the Boers, and from what we can see, purely for financial reasons. He was being paid in gold, and thanks to Frederick and a young man by the name of Dr Wallace Johnson, who between them smuggled the information out of Africa, we know how. The money was wired to Calais, then transported to a coastal village and left in a lobster pot in the bay for collection. This letter to Wisdom confirms it; 'payment will be made along the usual Channel' means the English Channel. Our belief that Sir Hubert was the traitor was verified by information we received this morning. Yesterday afternoon, Sir Hubert left Marmis Hall ostensibly to take a walk…he instead escaped to his yacht, the Phoenix, and the subsequent last sighting of him and his vessel was of them heading across the Channel in the direction of France."

Elliott nodded at Thorne, who continued to make notes. "After we discovered the letters, we walked back to the hall and found Lady Ellerbeck's maid, Alisha Clay, placing a telephone call to New York. Once we entered the gallery and began our investigation of the scene of the crime, I realised the posed tableau was familiar to me. When Constable Greyling informed us of the name Alisha had requested in New York, I understood why. Discovering that familial link between the two cases helped tremendously in our investigation."

Elliott sat back in his chair and gazed at the paintings opposite him. "It was always a source of deep irritation to me that we couldn't do more to solve the Carrie Lynn Cater case. We knew it was the visitor, but he had literally vanished off the face of the earth. Little did we realise that he was an intelligent man, well placed within high society and with the funds to carry him from London to the Ottoman Empire to America to Southern Africa and back again without the risk of suspicion. He could travel halfway around the world in his private capacity while continuing his work as torturer and murderer for the Boers, the highest bidder, or on a personal whim and never be discovered." Elliott sighed. "When Constable Greyling asked about the call placed to New York, he was also given information on a number dialled a few hours earlier: a number in Paris. I rang that number and was answered by a young woman who declared the house to be the Johnson residence, and who asked me if my name was Frederick."

He turned to Frederick, who stared at him in some consternation. "Dr Wallace Johnson was the gentleman who helped you to escape Southern Africa, was he not?"

"I swear to you, Caine, I did not call Clarice Johnson that morning, and certainly not at that time!"

Giselle glanced at Frederick; his large tanned face looked determined as he glared at Elliott.

Elliott looked thoughtful. "If you didn't place that call to Paris, then__"

"I did."

Elliott stared at Giselle, who gazed back at him with a faint smile. "I telephoned Mrs Johnson in Paris and informed her that one of the three men responsible for her son's death had been murdered."

Giselle smoothed her auburn hair. "I trust that I can speak freely here Gentlemen?" At the brief nod from Elliott, she continued. "Versipellis isn't the only private operative, Detective Chief Inspector Caine. Mrs Johnson hired me to discover whatever I could about the death of her son. She believed everything Frederick Marmis told her, and wanted to know more about the men named in the file." She paused. "You are quite correct, by the way. The name Versipellis did not feature in any of my correspondence with Mrs Johnson."

Elliott looked at the demure young woman who sat opposite him, and when he spoke his voice was rather unsteady. "What...If you can tell me, what is your alias?"

Giselle looked unsure, then she lifted her chin and in a firm voice said, "Angellis."

Elliott closed his eyes and smiled. She knew; she had to! She remembered, even before he had found her this time... she knew her true name! He opened his eyes and gazed at her. "Attar of roses in the telephone booth?"

She smiled, and her blue eyes twinkled as she replied. "Guilty, I'm afraid."

Over in the corner, Thorne coughed. Elliott looked over and continued hurriedly. "So now we know why the various calls were placed. Alisha telephoned Lady Ellerbeck's grandfather to tell him about the murders, and Giselle contacted Mrs Johnson to inform her of the same. Alisha told us that during the call to New York Mr Cater said he would send his granddaughter's butler to stay with her." Elliott paused. "There was also a call placed shortly before the one to New York...that call was to Fillesby Hall." Elliott looked at Bunny. "I take it that was also Alisha?"

Bunny nodded shamefacedly. "I asked Alisha to tell her father what had happened before letting grandpa know. I hoped grandpa would agree to send Clay here...I didn't know the killer was the same person who killed Aunt Carrie Lynn, I was frightened and I just knew that Clay would know what to do."

Elliott paused, wondering how Clay and the others were getting on in the kitchen. He didn't know about anyone else, but he could have cheerfully disposed of a bacon sandwich.

"Thank you for your honesty, Lady Ellerbeck." He took another sip from his glass. "Later that morning, I tried and failed to interview both Lady Ellerbeck and Giselle Du Lac." He smiled at Giselle. "Thankfully, however, Lady Marmis and Lady Scott-Brewer's information was more than helpful. They hadn't witnessed anything odd, but they had both seen the decedents shortly before their bodies were discovered. I also interviewed Sir Hubert, who declared that after Frederick's return he had been in the billiard room until Lord Marmis came for him. He claimed he had neither seen nor heard anything that could be of assistance in the case, so I left the library and went in search of Mr Weatherly Draycott, whom I discovered by the stables."

Elliott paused. "Mr Draycott was voluble; he explained that after he left the saloon he spoke with Hardcastle on his way to the turning circle, where he spent some time smoking a cigar. He insisted the only thing of note that he witnessed was Sir Hubert walking from the stables to the house. Mr Draycott was sure he had seen nothing else. As I continued in my questioning, Frederick Marmis walked out of the hall in his green riding coat. I recognised him from a photograph on his brother's desk. Mr Draycott asked who the young man was and I told him. Frederick wandered off towards the village, and I went back into the house to have another little talk with Sir Hubert about this new witness to his whereabouts."

Elliott scanned his audience. "When I reached the library, I discovered that Sir Hubert had ostensibly gone for a walk to the lake. Meanwhile, Frederick continued on his walk, and on the path, he met a young man named Valentine Carstairs. He was the nephew of Lady Emily Carstairs, an elderly lady whose death Carstairs firmly blamed on Mr Draycott. Carstairs informed Frederick of this and Frederick returned to the hall to inform his brother, but found Lord Marmis busy in his study and decided not to bother him until later. Back in the woods, Carstairs decided to return to the village by the Parva Steps instead of the main lane. The steps are difficult in any weather but were particularly so in the damp, muddy conditions of yesterday morning. He made it part-way up the steps before the killer pulled him back down the steps and brutally murdered him."

Elliott paused again. "Thorne, Constable Greyling, and I were meanwhile continuing our search for Sir Hubert. At a fork in the path Thorne and I took the route up to the lane, while Constable Greyling took the path leading to the Parva Steps. When Thorne and I succeeded in reaching the lane, we discovered something so foul I will not mention it here, but as we studied it, we heard the blasts of a police whistle. Constable Greyling was calling for assistance, so we headed in what we hoped was the correct direction. After several rather muddy incidents we reached the steps and discovered Constable Greyling beside the body of Valentine Carstairs. Not far from the corpse we found a tack knife covered in blood, but that wasn't the only interesting detail, for young Carstairs was also wearing Frederick's green riding coat. The material had covered Carstairs rather bohemian velvet suit. Was Carstairs the intended victim, or had he been mistaken for Frederick?"

Elliott continued. "Things then began to move quite quickly. We returned to the hall, where I made the unfortunate mistake of not explaining myself clearly to a man who had already suffered several severe shocks. I showed Frederick's bloodstained coat to Lord Marmis, who became rather upset, to put it mildly. When Lady Marmis mentioned seeing young Frederick in the kitchen, Lord Marmis ran to that room and on seeing his brother alive and well, promptly collapsed. I apologise for my callous disregard for your nerves, my lord."

Lord Marmis looked a trifle pink as he nodded his acceptance of Elliott's apology.

Elliott walked to the far end of the room and fetched a small easel. Positioning it where the entire room could see it clearly, Elliott placed a piece of paper back to front on the ledge.

"To continue, after sending Mr Draycott to tend to Lord Marmis' slight injury, I interviewed Frederick and gathered some rather interesting information. Amongst other things, I discovered that we were correct about the inclusion of Versipellis' name on the documents. Frederick assured me that the name was nowhere to be seen while the documents were travelling through Africa, and this is now also backed by both Angellis and her employer, Mrs Johnson. Furthermore, Frederick informed me that he had seen John Stable several times in the internment camp, and could describe him in detail. After I had finished our interview, I sent Thorne to Frederick's room with his drawing equipment, and between the two of them they came up with this little beauty. My lords, ladies, and gentlemen, I give you John Stable!"

With a flourish Elliott flipped over the sheet of paper. The portrait was a perfect likeness, capturing the innate fussiness as well as the smug cruelty in Weatherly Draycott's face.

Gasps were heard as the guests who had not been involved realised whose portrait was on the easel. Elliott's voice, though pitched at a calm level, rose to calm the chatter.

"Shortly after Thorne left Frederick in his room, Frederick received this note." Elliott held up a small piece of paper covered with writing. "I shall not tell you the contents: they are quite revolting. Needless to say, John Stable or Weatherly Draycott as we now know him, on seeing Frederick standing in front of the hall, recognised and followed him, but without even realising it Frederick circumvented the killer's plans. In an act of charity, Frederick lent his coat to Valentine Carstairs; the coat that Draycott had last seen *him* wearing. After their meeting on the path, Frederick decided to return home by the driveway, not the path. Carstairs continued along the path to the steps, where the killer caught up with him—"

"But Weatherly Draycott and Valentine Carstairs knew each other," said Lord Lapotaire. "They both went to Lady Carstairs' inquest. How could Draycott possibly mistake Carstairs for Frederick, whom he knew from Fred's internment in Southern Africa?"

Elliott smiled, and his moustache twitched slightly. "Of course Draycott knew what Carstairs looked like, but he didn't expect to see him here, and certainly not in Frederick Marmis' riding coat! Failing to recognise him from behind, with the thick folds of the coat hiding Carstairs face and clothes, and with the damp weather turning his blond hair dark, the killer struck at the figure he believed to be Frederick Marmis, the man he had been ordered to kill. Draycott knew what Frederick looks like; how could he not? His question to me when we both saw Frederick leaving the house was purely to cover himself from what he was planning later. Remember the letters addressed to John Wisdom? Sir Hubert passed on those orders even though he knew it meant his best friend's brother would be murdered."

Lord Marmis looked shaken and sick as he realised the depths to which his friend had sunk. "But why?" he whispered.

Elliott's face was grave as he looked at the young lord. "The only genuine motive I could find for Sir Hubert's treason was that he had been rendered nearly bankrupt by the death duties he had to pay after the death of his father. He needed money, and his position within the government just couldn't provide him with enough. His desperation for money was discovered by the Boers; he would give them any information they asked for, as long as they paid him well. It is my belief he was first approached in Constantinople. Lord Lapotaire, do you recall that Sir Hubert went missing in the Grand Bazaar for an entire day? It was probably then that he met with them and agreed to give them the information they sought. I am so very sorry."

Elliott looked at his notes. "Draycott thought he had killed Frederick; it must have been quite a shock when he realised he had actually killed Valentine Carstairs. In a fit of pique he returned to the hall to finish what he had started, but discovered the young man was not alone. Frederick was in the kitchen with…the housekeeper, and other members of staff."

Elliott cleared his throat; they had agreed not to mention anything about Frederick's slightly questionable parentage. "Shortly after we discovered Carstairs body we returned to the house, and again Draycott was blocked from approaching his target. He had to settle for a hastily scrawled note threatening unspeakable agonies for Frederick and his brother's family. Draycott also pushed a note under Lady Ellerbeck's door, having been informed by Sir Hubert of her connection to his earlier victim, Carrie Lynn Cater."

At the sharp gasp from Bunny, he raised a hand. "You are quite safe now, Lady Ellerbeck, but I must tell you that is our belief that Sir Hubert, knowing the link between your family and the killer, had in fact asked for you to be invited to the hall to be offered up to Weatherly Draycott as payment for his services!"

Bunny's face paled to the colour of chalk. Lord Lapotaire looked sick as he silently clutched her hand and squeezed it.

"In 1889, when Thorne and I assisted with the Carrie Lynn Cater investigation, we spent several days studying the contents of her home. It was during this time that the butler, Clay, brought something to my attention. Carrie Lynn was accomplished in the art of embroidery, and she had started to make a silk purse for her niece, who would have been approaching her coming-out ball at the time of her aunt's death."

Elliott turned a sympathetic eye on Bunny. "Some murderers, usually those of a particularly sadistic type, will take something from their victim so that they can relive their crime over and over again. Sometimes that kind of theft can be their downfall, and in this case the little square of embroidered silk that Carrie Lynn Carter was working on for her niece was Draycott's mistake. He took it because he wanted it; he didn't think it would be noticed. But Warrick Clay noticed; he realised it was missing from his master's home in New York, and when next he saw it, it was in a guest's suite here in Marmis Hall. You also recognised it, didn't you, Lady Ellerbeck?"

Bunny nodded shakily. "Not at first. I never expected to see it again, and certainly not here." She looked up at the company. "I found a beautiful William Morris design, Aunt Carrie and I spent ages choosing the silk colours."

Elliott nodded. "When did you see it here?"

"When I was in the saloon with Mr Draycott. I knew I had seen something familiar but I just couldn't place it. I realise now that it was his cigar case, it was the same design that Aunt Carrie had sewn for me."

"Not just the same design, Lady Ellerbeck, but the same piece of material. It was the trophy he took from your aunt's house." Elliott reached into his breast pocket and handed the small embroidered cigar case to her.

Reaching into his other pockets, Elliott removed other items they had discovered in the box in Draycott's room, and placed them on the small table beside him: the little Chinese dragon coin snapped off Valentine Carstairs's watchchain; amethyst cufflinks from Lord Scott-Brewer; Hardcastle's silver Saint Christopher pendant; and a single gold hoop earring ripped from old Baker's ear.

"These are some of the other trophies we discovered in Draycott's room. We found many others, but we may never find their owners." Elliott shook his head. "We now know that Hardcastle was John Rook, Sir Hubert is John Wisdom and, therefore, Draycott was John Stable."

Lord Lapotaire frowned slightly. "I don't doubt you, but the names were meant to have some kind of connection. I don't see…"

"Hardcastle was John Rook; castle and rook, as in the chess piece; Kingston-Folly was John Wisdom, "tis folly to be wise': and Dray as in horse, so Draycott was John Stable."

Lord Marmis looked at Elliott with a pained expression. "I also don't quite understand. You say that Bertie asked me to invite Lady Ellerbeck as – forgive me – as a gift for Draycott, but I don't understand why, surely the man would prefer to be paid with money?"

"It is our belief that Sir Hubert was being blackmailed by Hardcastle," said Elliott. "Because of that he had decided, without any input from his Boer masters, to wind down the spying operation. He decided to call John Stable in for one last job before trying to salvage his position. What we believe is this: Hardcastle, being a devious, sly creature, discovered the true identity of his handler Sir Hubert and decided to try a spot of blackmail. Sir Hubert decided he'd had enough and informed Draycott, falsely of course, that Hardcastle was a British double agent feeding their masters false information, for which perfidy he had to be removed. As Draycott's handler, he knew about Carrie Lynn's murder, though perhaps not the finer details, and decided to use Lady Ellerbeck's family connection to his benefit. He asked you, Lord Marmis, to invite Lady Ellerbeck in order to get Draycott out into the open." Elliott paused and looked at Lord Marmis. "Did he not also ask you to invite Draycott?"

Lord Marmis stared at Elliott in silence before he slowly nodded his head. "Yes…yes he did."

Elliott continued. "I rather believe that Sir Hubert thought Draycott would remove Hardcastle and then he, Sir Hubert, would kill Draycott heroically, possibly with the gun he had brought with him. With regards to the payment method, let us not forget the simple fact that Draycott was a sadist…the offer of a new victim related to a previous victim would be too great an offer to turn down."

Elliott surveyed his audience. "Then came the discovery of the bodies in the gallery and Sir Hubert saw exactly what his charge was capable of. I believe he was genuinely horrified by the sight of Draycott's handiwork. Remember, all Stable's previous murders were committed without the need for Sir Hubert's input, beyond giving the order. Seeing the horror in the flesh, as it were, shocked Sir Hubert into flight. He gathered all the documents that detailed his treason and headed to his boat. His only thought now is to escape the rope."

A thick silence filled the room.

Thom suddenly spoke up. "But sir, what about Baker?"

"I think Baker was in the wrong place at the wrong time, Constable. Poaching by the lakeside, maybe he saw something he shouldn't, and that was the end of him. I doubt his family will mind too much!"

Lord Marmis looked at Elliott. "So, what happens now? With Bertie, I mean."

Elliott shrugged. "The authorities believe he is heading for France; beyond that I couldn't say."

Lord Marmis shook his head. "I can't believe it! Bertie…" He paused. "You truly believe the Boers got to him when he was in Constantinople?"

Elliott nodded. "Lord Lapotaire mentioned that Sir Hubert went missing in one of the quarters and when he finally appeared, he claimed to have been lost in the marketplace? We believe that was when he was approached and turned."

Lord Lapotaire raised his voice. "He was missing for nearly a full day. We searched for hours. When he finally arrived back at the embassy he seemed distant…almost cold, as though he didn't recognise me. Later that evening, he seemed to wake up and become Bertie again."

Lord Marmis looked at Lord Lapotaire and shook his

head sadly, his eyes distant. "We spoke of that day. He said he had enjoyed getting lost because he found a tiny shop in one of the back streets and made a purchase…it was the ugliest, most hideously ornate wooden chest I had ever seen in my life, bound with iron and covered with the most peculiar carvings; green and purple serpents eating their own tails…I believe they are called ouroboros; you bear one on your cane."

Thorne's notebook fell to the floor as he gripped the arms of his chair, choking out a vile swearword as he turned to look at his friend; faint purple lights flickering in his eyes. Elliott's expression became almost waxen as he turned to face Lord Marmis, who flinched from the expression of utter, snarling hatred in Elliott's eyes.

In a voice that was distant and far calmer than he felt, Elliott enquired, "What happened to this chest, my lord?"

Lord Marmis cleared his throat. "Bertie brought it back to England. I believe it's still in his house in London."

Forcing himself to stay calm, Elliott handed his notebook and pencil to the young lord. "We need that address, my lord."

"Yes, of course." Lord Marmis quickly wrote the address and handed the book back to Elliott, who glanced at it before tucking the notebook away in his inside pocket. He shared a hard look with Thorne before turning to the rest of the room.

"Ladies and gentlemen…I believe that concludes our investigations here at Marmis Hall. We have discovered the identity of a murderer, uncovered their previous nefarious deeds, and can quite categorically state that they will never be able to harm another soul again. We have also unmasked the traitor at the heart of the government; but now we need to catch him. Lord Lapotaire, we shall need your services to convey the evidence to the correct authorities. But first, Thorne, we need to pay Sir Hubert's home a visit."

Thorne nodded; a coldness had appeared on Elliott's face that was almost worse than his previous expression. The two men left the room, and Lord Marmis let out a long shuddering breath before turning to Lord Lapotaire. "What in the name of God is going on here?"

Lord Lapotaire opened his mouth, then closed it again. "I truly cannot say, Marmis."

Giselle stood up and approached Lord Marmis. "I need that address too, my lord."

Lord Marmis stared at her in silence, then Lady Marmis spoke. "234, St Augustine's Square, Piccadilly. Take care, Penny!"

Giselle embraced her friend and left the room. Closing the door behind her, she ran to her room and rang for her maid.

By the time Lilith arrived, Giselle had already dragged out her travelling outfit and was struggling out of her day dress. The young maid started swearing in French, slapped her mistress's hands away and fastened her into the outfit with minimal fuss while Giselle hurriedly explained what had happened. Ringing the bell, Lilith told the maid who answered it to pack her mistress's luggage and send it on to her London address.

As they hurried downstairs, Giselle heard the sound of an automobile in the driveway. Heading outside, she saw Thorne drive the Waggonette past the front door, gritting her teeth she ran after the moving car, waiving her hands. As Thorne brought the motor to a sharp halt in a spray of white gravel, she leant through the open cover and grasped Elliott's arm. "Don't you dare leave me again!"

Elliott turned his head and Giselle found herself staring into eyes that were two shimmering pools of molten green light as he gazed back at her. She gasped but held onto his arm. "I can't say that I understand anything about why I feel I know you, Mr Caine...but I will not lose you again! Let us in."

Silently, Elliott moved across and Giselle sat next to him as Lilith settled herself into the front passenger seat next to Thorne. Elliott turned to face Giselle, his eyes settling back to their usual warm brown. "We will stop at the inn to collect some items, then drive to Sir Hubert's London address. It will take us several hours."

"Good!" Giselle exclaimed. "We need to talk about a great many things, and this journey will be a good start."

In the front, Thorne and Lilith smiled.

At the inn, Elliott and Thorne gathered what few things they needed. For Elliott, it was the little jade box, nothing more.

○

7:30pm

The now-dusty motorcar and its tired but determined inhabitants drew to a halt in front of Sir Hubert's London residence. Thorne applied the brake and turned to look at Giselle, who was now leaning against Elliott's right shoulder.

Thorne smiled. "All things considered; you took it quite well."

Giselle smiled back. "It answers a great many questions. I'm surprised that Lilith didn't have more concerns."

Lilith produced a Gallic shrug. "Life should never be boring. Things have suddenly become even more interesting than usual, that is all."

Elliott kissed Giselle's hand and looked towards the large

white stone house. "It's time to see what secrets this place holds."

The four of them alighted from the vehicle and approached the building. As Elliott raised his hand to the bell, the front door was opened by an elderly but upright butler, who cast an eye over them before intoning, "Detective Chief Inspector Caine?"

Elliott nodded, hiding his surprise as the butler continued. "Lord Lapotaire telephoned to announce your visit, sir; please come in. As instructed, I have searched the house, but have been unable to find the chest Lord Lapotaire described." The butler paused as he shut the door. "But my master had keys to the cellars and it might be down there. No one else was allowed to enter those rooms."

The butler led them into the brightly lit hall, he paused and turned to Elliott, a look of uncertainty on his face. "Shortly before Lord Lapotaire called, a telegram was delivered addressed to a name I did not recognise. As my master is not here, and Lord Lapotaire has vouched for you, and as you *are* the police..." He removed the telegram from a silver salver that was on a massive mahogany sideboard and handed it to Elliott who ripped it open and read the sparse few words within.

Elliott's face twisted in rage as he flung the telegram onto the floor. He turned his back so the butler couldn't bear witness to the wave-like ripples that moved under his skin and the blazing green light that filled his eyes. Thorne hurriedly picked up the piece of paper and read the message.

VERSIPELLIS STOP I ADDED YOUR NAME TO THE DOCUMENT STOP IT WAS EASY TO DO WHILE MARMIS WAS BUSY WITH FRED STOP I KNEW LAPOTAIRE WOULD SEND FOR YOU STOP THE THOUGHT OF YOU AND ANGELLIS UNITED UNDER

ONE ROOF WAS TOO TEMPTING TO RESIST STOP WE
SHALL MEET AGAIN BROTHER STOP PHOENIXUS

Thorne stared at the note, his face deathly pale. Two high spots of colour appeared in his cheeks as he too turned away from the butler; swirling lavender-coloured lights appearing in his eyes as his rage mounted. Elliott gritted his teeth, bringing his Otherness back under control he gripped Thorne's arm before turning to the butler. "You say your master allowed no one to enter the cellars?"

The butler nodded. "Yes, sir."

"Then the cellars are where we shall start."

The butler shook his head. "I have no keys, gentlemen, I cannot—"

Giselle reached into her reticule and produced a small pouch. "That shouldn't be a problem. Take us to the cellar door, please."

The butler's eyebrows shot up, and the disapproval in his voice was evident. "Very well, madam, if you will follow me." He led them to a small door underneath the huge wooden staircase. "This is the door to the cellars."

Giselle removed the two little pieces of metal from her pouch and inserted one into the lock. Elliott turned his attention to the butler. "How long have you been with Sir Hubert Kingston-Folly?"

The butler became even more ramrod-straight, and his voice could have frozen the Thames. "I have been with my master for six years."

Elliott nodded. "He employed you on his return from Istanbul?"

"Yes, sir."

Elliott smiled. "Did he refresh all his staff at the same time?"

The butler paused, then continued with a faint note of

curiosity now evident in his voice. "Yes sir, he did. Butler, cook, maids and manservants."

Giselle inserted the second length of wire into the lock and began to hum slightly; there was a sharp click. Smiling, she put the picks away in her bag, turned the knob and pushed the door open.

The door opened into absolute blackness as the butler, murmuring about finding candles, swept off towards the kitchen. Giselle looked at the almost vertical drop of the stairs and glanced at her heeled boots. "Well, this could be amusing!"

The butler reappeared with three lanterns and handed two of them to Elliott and Thorne. Giselle and Lilith smiled at each other as the five of them, led by Elliott, entered the abyss. The scent of dry, dusty brickwork, and their unease of what might lurk in the bowels of the building grew as they descended the stairs and found themselves in a dark passage that ended at another door.

Thorne gently turned the handle and the door swung open easily; the hinges had been greased, and recently. Elliott took a deep breath, passed inside, and looked at the wall on his left. He reached out and caught one of the two short brass chains by the door; with a faint click, golden light and the soft hissing of gas lamps threw the room into sharp relief.

Running the full length of the building, the room was lined on three sides with floor-to-ceiling bookcases packed to bursting. The fourth wall, on their right, was the backdrop to a huge array of scientific instruments.

But what caught their attention was to the immediate left of the door. A large wooden chest, five feet long and three feet wide, bound with iron and covered with intricately carved and painted purple and green snakes. Elliott placed his lantern on the floor next to the chest and moved his hand towards the lock. "Giselle, Lilith…this could be unpleasant."

Giselle shook her head. "We're staying, Elliott. We have both witnessed unpleasantness. Is it locked?"

Elliot nodded. "Yes. Another one for you, I think."

As Giselle turned her attentions to the chest, Elliott turned his to the butler, who was staring at the room with an expression of total shock. "I never realised," he murmured. "I knew this room was here, of course, but I didn't realise it was anything like this."

"Did Sir Hubert come down here often?"

The butler nodded. "Every evening, sir, after dinner. I thought...well, I don't know what I thought. It wasn't really my place to wonder."

There was a sudden clicking sound, followed by a sibilant hiss from the chest. Giselle stood up and stepped aside as Elliott carefully lifted the lid of the chest.

The butler choked out an oath and backed away from the chest crossing himself, as Elliott, Giselle, Thorne, and Lilith gazed down at the pitiful, long-dead, mummified remains of Sir Hubert Kingston-Folly.

THE END

Death in the Sound
Book 2 of the The Versipellis Mysteries

PREVIEW

Milford Sound, New Zealand
9:30am
15th January 1891

Thomas Nibbs hurriedly tucked the item he had just stolen into his deepest pocket, as shouldering his knapsack he ran for his life through the lush undergrowth of Sinbad Gully, sending up a fervent prayer that the little rowing boat which had carried him to this verdant and deadly place would still be where he had left it.

A few short hours ago, when he had landed to start his

first day surveying the fertile but narrow valley, he truly hadn't expected the terrifying turn his day would take. He had to return to the safety of the hotel: once Coll had been informed of what had taken place and had seen the item, he would become a powerful ally.

Breathing heavily, Thomas ran alongside the stream that threaded its way down the gully, the eye-wateringly green tree ferns slapping at his face and hands as he headed for the little beach where his boat was waiting.

With a sudden gasp he pulled up and looked behind him…he could hear dogs!

Redoubling his efforts, he shot along the sunlight dappled path, past a huge clump of silver beech and onto the shingle strewn shoreline as though fired from a cannon. Yes, he could see his boat!

But alongside the little boat was a much larger tender, one more than capable of carrying the sizeable number of men and dogs now running him down.

Thundering along the sunny beach, Thomas made it to his boat and threw his pack on board. He paused to catch his breath, before pulling a small axe from the pack. Feeling a pair of eyes on him, he slowly turned to look into the bright, button-like eyes of a small green bird; the rock wren was sitting on the edge of one of his oars, judging him quietly. He realised he had only just missed squashing it with his pack.

Thomas nodded at the small bird. Scanning the heavily wooded shoreline, he gripped his climbing axe and rushed to the other boat, then began to hack at the waterline of the craft. After what seemed an eternity, a crack appeared in the woodwork and water began to seep in.

Thomas ran back to his boat and with a desperate effort flung the little craft into the water. As he pulled himself aboard, the small rock wren hopped out, sat on a rocky outcrop, and watched as he began to row steadily away from the shoreline and into the still waters of the Sound.

No other boats were visible. That meant his pursuers would have to patch up their boat to follow him. As Milford City could not be reached on foot from Sinbad Gully, that would take them much longer than the few hours he needed to reach the safety of the little settlement.

Shouting erupted from the beach. Thomas looked up from his oars and saw people crowding onto the shoreline: at least fifteen men with guns, pickaxes, and dogs. They saw Thomas in the water and immediately headed towards their vessel. There was a silence as they took in the damage Thomas had inflicted, then the sudden, sharp crack of gunfire echoed across the water.

One of the men, somewhat larger than the others, grabbed two of the gunmen and banged their heads together. Thomas grinned through gritted teeth as he pulled on the oars. Oh yes, the sound of gunfire carries, especially across water. Can't have the people in Milford City hearing that!

The large man waved his arms at the others, and pushed several of them towards the slowly sinking remains of their boat. As Thomas settled into a rhythm, he saw several men start to bail water, while others began to patch up the hole he had inflicted on their vessel.

The large man, meanwhile, stood on the beach and watched in seething silence as Thomas doggedly rowed his way towards freedom.

The young man threw himself into his work, and after a few tiring hours, he pulled into the little jetty at Milford City. As he climbed out, Thomas cast a look back towards the gully. In the distance, a boat was slowly but steadily making its way towards the settlement. He quickly tied the boat up, grabbed his pack, and hurried to the hotel in search of Coll.

Milford City sounded somewhat larger than it actually

was, consisting of a functional jetty, a few small cottages, and a small but clean hotel. A large number of international walkers were milling around outside the hotel, checking their packs, rolls, and food supplies for their return tramp to Te Anau.

Thomas headed for the front door as Manu, one of the guides from the local Iwi, nodded at him. "Kia ora, Thomas." He paused, taking in Thomas's pallor. "Are you all right, man? You look ill!"

Thomas shook his head. "You'd look ill if you'd just been through what I have, Manu! Have you seen Coll?"

"Yes: he went on ahead to check the track. He'll meet with us and then return tomorrow."

Thomas blenched. "Christ!"

Manu flinched and Thomas held up an apologetic hand. "Sorry, Manu."

It wasn't safe for him to take the item to Coll; the men following him knew who he was and where he was staying. He had to get the item and the information to safety – and then get himself out of the Sound.

He looked at the wiry young Maori. "Manu, if I give you a package, would you give it to Coll when you meet him?"

Manu nodded. "Yes, of course." He looked at Thomas. "What's going on?"

Thomas squeezed his friend's shoulder. "I can't say right now, Manu. I'll be right back."

Heading into the hotel, he paused at the little reception. Looking around to check no one was watching, he walked into the office area, reached into his pocket and carefully placed the item on the counter.

He looked at the object that had caused him so much fear, and with a sudden movement swept it up. He was about to stuff it into his pack when he saw a small figurine of a tui on the counter. Grabbing it in his left hand, he held the object he had taken in his right and judged the weight, shape, and size. They were almost the same.

He placed both on the table before rummaging through various drawers, producing brown paper, string and a pencil. Thomas swiftly wrote a short letter for Coll explaining what had happened, what he had seen, and what he had done. Then he carefully wrapped the tui into a tight parcel and hurriedly tied it with string.

Taking another piece of paper, Thomas wrote a note to his sister Ngaio, explaining the route he would be taking, but not why. Licking the gummed envelope with a grimace, he dropped it, along with a penny, into the postal tray that Coll and his wife Rose left for their guests to use.

Walking back outside, he handed the package to a curious Manu who tucked it into his pack. "I'll see Coll gets it; we should be meeting up tonight at the first hut."

"Thanks, Manu. Take care on the track."

Manu grinned. "Always." His grin faltered slightly. "Kia kaha, Thomas."

Thomas held out his hand and Manu clasped it firmly. Then he headed to the front of the group and called them to order. The twenty or so people, who had travelled from as far afield as England, the United States of America, and France to take in the untouched natural beauty of Milford Sound, quickly shouldered their packs and began their slow and steady hike behind the young Maori.

Thomas headed to his room; the late-morning sunshine boded well for him to cover a good distance before the end of the day. Taking only what he would need for a rapid journey, which consisted of his thickest, warmest clothes and his climbing equipment, Thomas carried his pack down to the kitchens. Putting an ear to the door to check that Rose and her helpers were not there, he entered and took enough provisions to sustain him to Queenstown, placing money on the breadboard to cover the cost.

His pursuers would head to Te Anau via the Milford track, but he knew he had to get further away, and quickly. He couldn't run the risk of the men finding him and the item. The mock package was heading south west, so he would head south east and try to reach Queenstown via Gertrude Saddle, a steep hill that was a suitable obstacle to those who hadn't prepared for such an ascent. The rest of his journey would be a long but fairly manageable valley tramp to Lake Wakatipu, and then he could either continue walking around the edge of the lake, or take one of the station supply boats direct to Queenstown.

Shouldering his pack, the determined young man left the hotel and made for the short track that led to the south east of the settlement.

Pushing through the underbrush, he could still just see the group led by Manu heading up the Milford track. Turning, he looked back towards Milford City. There, tying up their listing vessel, a number of men with dogs stood on the jetty before the largest man led them down into Milford City.

Thomas walked away swiftly, his heart pounding. He now had only half an hour's head start on them; he needed to make it count.

He followed the Cleddau River that wound its way deeply into the mountains. The songs of a bellbird and a tui fought for possession of his ears as he headed up the worn track; he knew to take the left-hand path where the river split, and follow the route up to the Saddle. He filled his lungs with the clean, sweet air. In spite of the frightening events of the last few hours, the mountains always gave him a sense of peace.

After several hours of walking, Thomas looked up at the slope before him. The light was still bright enough to guarantee him a few hours' safe climbing time. If he could reach the top, he should be able to stop for the night and continue his journey at daybreak.

He was almost at the end of his ascent as the light began to fail. Looking back down the slope, he saw smoke; his pursuers had set up camp for the night in the valley at the foot of the mountain. Breathing a sigh of relief, Thomas continued until he crested Gertrude Saddle, and the route he had hurriedly planned opened up before him.

Even in the half-light of the evening, the view was stunning. The soft purples and golds of the setting sun to his right bathed the mountainous, white-capped landscape with a burning light that never failed to take his breath away.

As he stood, his mind focused on the view, a sudden noise made him turn sharply. A large, shadowy figure clambered over the ledge behind him and lashed out violently, cuffing Thomas on his right ear. The blow knocked the young surveyor to the ground. The figure rushed at Thomas, sat astride him, and slapped down his pockets.

Not finding what they sought, the figure glared at Thomas. "Where is it? Where?"

Thomas clamped his mouth shut and shook his head. The figure leapt up, grabbed him by the throat, and with a bellow of anger lifted Thomas off his feet and flung him into the air.

Thomas screamed and flailed desperately for a handhold as he soared over the cliff edge, then plummeted six hundred feet to the dark valley below.

His killer looked down the sheer cliff, listening to make sure there were no sounds from an injured man, then turned their attention to Thomas' pack. Flinging the contents on the ground they pawed through the few meagre belongings before finding what they were looking for inside one of the carefully darned socks.

Pocketing the item, they stuffed the remaining contents back into the pack and threw it after its owner.

Turning, they climbed back down to their comrades sitting around the campfire in the valley below.

○

Find *Death in the Sound* and other great reads from Rhen Garland at www.rhengarland.com

ABOUT THE AUTHOR

Rhen Garland lives in Somerset, England with her folk-singing, artist husband, 4000 books, an equal number of 1980's action movies, and a growing collection of passive-aggressive Tomtes.

"I thought when I finally started writing that my books would be genteel "cosy" type murder mysteries set in the Golden Era (I love the 1920's and 30's for the style, music, and automobiles), with someone being politely bumped off at the Vicar's tea party and the corpse then apologising for disrupting proceedings. But no, the late Victorian era came thundering over my horizon and planted itself in my story, my characters, and my life and would not budge."

I enjoy the countryside, peace, Prosecco, and the works of Dame Ngaio Marsh, Dame Glady Mitchell, John Dickson Carr/Carter Dickson, Dame Agatha Christie, Simon R Green, and Sir Terry Pratchett. I watch far too many old school murder mystery films, TV series, and 1980's action movies for it to be considered healthy.